Next To Impossible

by
Scott White

Dedication

This book is dedicated to my parents, June and Pete White. They never gave up on me, even during my darkest hours. They form the nucleus of a select group of family and friends, who have loved me, supported me and, from time-to-time, picked me up, brushed me off and motivated me to relentlessly pursue my dreams.

Acknowledgments

I would like to thank the following people for helping me create this novel. Without their patience and willingness to help an aspiring author, this book would have never been published. I am eternally grateful to these people for their thoughts, ideas, recommendations, and motivation and, when it was needed (often), for their sincere and constructive criticism of this body of work. I am forever in their debt and pledge to help any other aspiring authors in any way I can, in the same spirit that was demonstrated to me by these people.

Inspiration: James Altucher. I've never met you. I hope I have a chance to thank you in person someday. Until then, I want you to know that your book, *Choose Yourself*, inspired me to sit down and get to work on pursuing my dream. The result of that effort is this book. Please accept my most sincere thanks for writing a book that spoke to me so personally. It's changed my life and motivated countless others to choose themselves. Thank you, James!

Referrals: Theresa Ragan: I've never met you either but am so grateful to you for the referrals that you shared so openly on your website. I was introduced to you and inspired by your story when I read an article about you by James Altucher at: (www.jamesaltucher.com). Once I read about you, I found your website (www.theresaragan.com). I've used the self-publishing tips that you so graciously provided to make contact with, and establish business relationships with Faith Williams and Angel Martinez (via Dara England). Thank you for helping me start my journey.

Copy Editor: Faith Williams. Your quick response to my email request for advice and willingness to help an aspiring author was most appreciated. Your assistance with the editing of this book is sincerely appreciated. With your help, I know I will learn how to be a better writer. Thanks so much for your patience and attention to detail. Your skills will help make this work a product that I will be proud of for years to come.

Cover Art: Angel Martinez. Like Faith, your willingness to take the time to explain the process for developing a cover for this book is sincerely appreciated. You taught me so much and you did it patiently and professionally. Your artwork on the cover will undoubtedly catch the attention of many readers. Thanks so much for your help!

Chapter One

Hope Crosby tilted her head back and looked at the tip of the boom on the gigantic crane that towered above her. An orange windsock, fixed at the tip of the boom, strained against its tether in the gusty winds. She saw it was fully extended, an indication that the winds blew at more than twenty miles per hour. As she craned her neck to look at the boom, she felt her hard hat shift back on her head. The combination of gravity, the high winds, and her long, brunette hair tucked up underneath it made it hard for her to keep it in place. "Damn hard hats," she muttered. "What a pain in the ass." She knew she had to wear it on the construction site but it annoyed her.

Right now, the hard hat was the least of her worries. Her crane operator maneuvered the boom on his crane to position a sling over a huge rooftop air-conditioning unit on the ground in front of her. The wind blew the sling around and the ground crew struggled to catch the flailing sling pendants and attach them to the lifting lugs on the unit.

She raised her gloved hands up to hold her hard hat on her head and shield her eyes from the sun. Then she checked the wind sock again. Now it was fully extended in the opposite direction. Variable and gusty winds. She knew the only thing more challenging for crane operators than strong winds were variable and gusty winds. Based on her observation of the winds, Hope knew she and her crew were going to have a rough day.

She looked over at Buddy Johnson, her foreman. "Winds are right on the edge of limits, Buddy. What do you think the old man will want to do?"

Buddy looked at her and laughed. "You know damn well what

he's gonna do, Hope. He's gonna go for it." He hesitated for a minute and looked up on the roof. "He's your father, though. If anyone can talk him out of it, it would be you!"

Buddy had a twinkle in his eye and smiled while he spoke. Hope knew he was right. A more conservative crew could probably find a hundred valid reasons to scrap the lift today. But Hope's father, and this construction company, did not become successful by backing away from risk. This was an easy decision. She knew her dad would go for it. And she would too.

She smiled and then laughed at her foreman. "Well, I suppose you're right about that, Buddy. What do you think? Can we do it safely? The last thing we need to do today is get somebody hurt."

Buddy looked up at the roof of the building and then looked over at the fifteen-thousand pound air-conditioning unit that sat on the ground in front of them. "I think I'm gonna get to work. It ain't gonna get done with both of us looking at it." He winked at her as he pulled on his gloves and then jogged over to supervise the ground crew.

Hope nodded and then said to herself, "True enough. Let's go."

Aside from the winds, Hope also paid close attention to the operator at the controls of the crane. This was the day she had picked to put Carlos, her brand-new crane operator, on the controls of the company's biggest crane, a hundred-ton jib crane with a two hundred fifty-foot boom. It should have been a pretty straightforward lift, if only the damn winds would behave themselves. She and her father had done hundreds of lifts like these before. But today was going to be a little tricky.

She wished she was sitting in the cab of the crane. She always found it harder to supervise lifts than actually do them herself. But she and her father had trained Carlos well. She knew he was up to the task. Now, like a mother watching her child take his first bike ride without training wheels, she had to step back and let him perform the task himself.

She shifted her gaze to the task at hand and watched as the

ground crew attached the pendants to the lifting lugs. It was too loud to communicate by voice but she was pleased with the way Carlos deftly maneuvered the sling over the a/c unit for the men to complete the hook-up.

She flashed a grin and gave him a thumbs-up.

Carlos saw her and nodded his appreciation. At this point in the lift, his hands and feet were too occupied to otherwise acknowledge her compliment. He was keenly aware of the gusty winds and he could feel the tension in his arms and legs as he toggled the controls on the crane to keep the sling pendants under control while the ground crew did their work. He knew this was the easy part. Once he lifted the air-conditioning unit and swung it up over the roof, he would no longer be able to see the load. At that point, the roof crew would become his eyes. They would be responsible for stabilizing the load over the roof pads and then use their walkie-talkies to signal Carlos to lower it to the attach points on the roof.

A blind lift on a windy day was the toughest lift in the business and he was now one of three people in the company who were now qualified to perform the task. The other two were Hope and her father. Hope monitored the operation from the ground and her father led the topside crew on the roof. Carlos looked up and saw the grizzled old man peering down at him from the roof. He was undoubtedly anxious and well past ready to get the job done but you would never know it from looking at him. It was obvious to him that the winds were wreaking havoc with the crew on the ground, so he was trying to be patient. Carlos smiled. The old man was as cool as a cucumber. That helped Carlos relax too. The last thing he wanted to do was disappoint the boss.

Carlos was one of the best heavy equipment operators in Washington, DC. He had been trained by Hope and her father, who were also widely recognized as two of the more proficient operators in the local area.

He was a completely trustworthy and dependable worker—a rare combination these days. Hope and her father knew he was ready to take on the additional responsibilities of a primary crane operator. They trained him and rode with him during the preceding lifts for the other air-conditioning units for this building. Carlos knew he was ready for the challenge and glad Hope and her father had confidence in him, but with the winds picking up, he had to admit he would be glad when this lift was over.

As the ground crew attached the last pendant to the lugs on the air conditioner, Buddy Johnson inspected the attachments. He visually checked each of the attach points and gave them a tug. When he finished, Buddy gave Hope a thumbs-up and a wind-up signal to indicate to her that it was safe to start the lift. Hope took another look at the wind sock. It still blew around erratically.

She took a deep breath and keyed the radio. "We're hooked up down here, Dad. Are you guys ready up there?"

Her father looked down over the edge of the roof, along with the rest of the topside crew. She heard him key the microphone and bark, "We're ready. Let's go."

She could tell from the tone of his voice that he was getting impatient. She keyed the mic on her walkie-talkie. "All unnecessary personnel, clear the site! Let's tighten up, Carlos."

Carlos nodded and obeyed her command. He eased back on the winch control lever and took all the slack out of the pendants on the sling. He felt the crane shift as the boom started to bear the load. He looked over at Hope and gave her a nod.

"Ground crew clear!"

The ground crew moved back away from the a/c unit and positioned themselves on the tether lines to help control oscillations of the unit as it made its initial ascent to the roof.

"Cleared to lift, Carlos," Hope said. "Topside crew, load is coming up!"

Carlos acknowledged the radio command by putting even more tension on the cables. He gently eased back on the winch control lever and felt the crane shudder as it took on the full load of the air-conditioning unit. He watched the unit break free of the ground and felt the full weight of the load now on the crane.

As the ground crew used their tethers to stabilize the giant air conditioner, he checked his gauges on the dashboard in the cab. All good crane operators kept one eye on their gauges and one eye on their load. Exceeding the load limits or losing sight of the load could lead to disaster.

Stabilization—good. Winch load—within limits. Load—stable.

He knew the margin for error on this lift was small but felt confident he could get it to the roof safely.

Carlos keyed his microphone. "Load is green/green. Ready to take her upstairs."

Hope looked up at the roof one more time and responded, "Roger. You're cleared to lift."

Carlos nodded and began the lift. He heard the cables groan and felt the clutch shudder as the unit made its way skyward. As the load went up, the ground crew released their hold on the tether lines. Now the load was unrestrained. It was up to him to dampen its oscillations until he could get it up to the roof, where the topside crew would regain control of the tethers.

He saw the wind push the unit closer to the building than he wanted it to be. He countered that movement by swinging the boom away from the building. Just as he made his move, the wind shifted and he saw that he had over-corrected.

Instantly, he heard Hope's father on the radio. "Easy with it, Carlos. Don't overcompensate for the wind. Work with it and take your time."

Carlos smiled. He knew the old man was trying to help him and he appreciated it.

Hope's father, Thomas "T.C." Crosby, was a great boss. He was tough as nails but you always knew where you stood with him. T.C. had been in the construction business for more than forty years and he still led crews every day on the job site. All of the day laborers and skilled tradesmen loved to work for Mr. T.C. He worked his men hard but paid them well and had a reputation for taking care of

his people. He had been a young Green Beret at the end of the Vietnam War and ran his construction company like a special operations unit. He didn't ask any of his folks to do anything he couldn't, or wouldn't, do. He had very high expectations for the work they did and he would routinely surprise them by putting in more hours than they did and out-hustling them on the job.

While T.C. was a no-nonsense kind of leader, he also had a compassionate side to him that Carlos and many other Crosby Construction workers had experienced firsthand. When Carlos first joined the company, he helped him and his wife find a place to live, and Mrs. Crosby helped Carlos's wife find a good school and a doctor for their kids. They gave Carlos and his wife a no-interest loan to pay the security deposit on their apartment and gave Carlos time off to help get his family settled. Carlos paid back every penny of the loan he owed to Mr. and Mrs. Crosby and he never forgot the kindness of his boss and his wife.

As the air conditioner cleared the roof line, he heard the boss on the radio once again. "Unit is clear up here. Stop the lift and start the translation, Carlos."

The translation he referred to was the most delicate part of the operation. This was the part of the lift where Carlos had to swing the boom over the roof and complete the lift solely under the voice commands of the topside crew.

He moved the winch control lever to neutral and began to swing the boom to move the a/c unit over the roof. Just as he started the translation, he heard a thump that was followed by a loud bang. The crane shuddered and the boom stopped abruptly. He wasn't sure what happened but he quickly realized that his controls were no longer having any effect on moving the boom. He would find out later that one of the gears that drove the horizontal movement of the boom had failed. It was a very unusual failure and one that he was not prepared for, especially in this wind. He frantically tried to actuate the boom controls but all he heard was a loud grinding noise. The load was stuck and he was helpless.

He keyed his mic. "I've lost translation control!"

The sudden stop of the boom, coupled with the high winds, caused the a/c unit to oscillate. As the winds continued to gust, the crane rocked violently.

Carlos looked down at his gauges. Both the stabilization limits and the load limits gauges indicated that they were outside of limits. The topside crew had not captured the tethers yet. They now flailed in the wind, out of their reach. If the load kept moving this way, the crane would roll over.

Carlos wasn't really sure what to do at this point and he started to panic.

If he released the load, it would crash through the roof of the building. If he didn't drop the load, he might lose the crane. He keyed the mic and shouted into the radio, "I'm exceeding load and stabilization limits! Not sure how to stop it! Should I drop it?"

Hope's father heard the noise from below and saw the a/c unit swinging. He knew instinctively what had happened and assumed that Carlos's crane was out of action.

He keyed the radio. "Hold on, Carlos. Don't drop it. Use the winch control to stabilize the oscillations." Then, without any tension or hesitation in his voice, he said, "Hope, I need the backup crane online, now!"

T.C. couldn't see Hope from his position on the roof. If he could have seen her, he would have seen that she was already running across the construction site to another crane that was a carbon copy of Carlos's stricken machine.

When Hope heard the noise and saw the boom stop moving on Carlos's crane, she started running, with Buddy Johnson in hot pursuit. They both knew they were in trouble and they had to move fast.

As she climbed up on the giant treads of the standby crane, she tried to figure out how she was going to maneuver her crane's hook to intercept a wildly swinging fifteen-thousand pound air-conditioning unit that was ten stories up in the air.

She looked over her shoulder at Carlos's crane and saw it teetered on its outriggers. As Carlos attempted to damp out the swinging unit's oscillations with the winch, she could hear the clutch grind and saw smoke come out of the winch drum. She knew it was only a matter of time before the winch drum seized and the whole crane flipped over.

She jumped into the cab of the backup crane and jammed her gloved thumb into the engine start button. The engine coughed and spit, and then thankfully, came to life.

As the engine caught, she keyed her mic. "I'm on it, Dad! On the way now."

She turned the crane on its treads, pointed it toward Carlos's crane, and firewalled the throttle to get it into place quickly. While she maneuvered the crane into position, she simultaneously held down the outrigger switches to extend them. Once she was in position, she stopped the crane and ran down the jacks on the end of each outrigger.

Buddy and his ground crew anticipated her moves. They placed huge wooden blocks under the jack pads to speed up the leveling process and give her extra stability during the impending lift. All this work was done without a word spoken between them. Everyone knew what they needed to do and they didn't waste any time with words.

Hope nodded her appreciation to Buddy. He met her gaze with a look of concern and then got back to work directing his men. Once the jacks were in contact with the wood blocks, she alternately toggled the jack switches to level the crane. She looked over to see the look on Carlos's face in the cab of his crippled crane and worried that she might already be too late.

Hope keyed her mic. "No worries, Carlos. I'm in place now."

Then she turned her attention to the roof and keyed the mic again. "Boom is coming up!" She grabbed the boom control lever and pulled it back into her lap.

Hope's father watched the deteriorating situation on Carlos's crane. He knew there wasn't much time to save this load before it crashed down on the roof. He could only think of one way to capture the oscillating load. He had to find a way to snag the swivel on the stricken load's sling with Hope's crane hook. That was going to be a real challenge on a load that currently seemed to have a mind of its own.

He keyed his mic. "Roger that. Put your boom as close to Carlos's as you can and drop the hook down to the roof. I'm going to try to catch the sling swivel on the load with your hook."

"Okay." Hope paused and said, "And just how in the hell are you planning to do that?"

From the top of the roof, her father smiled. "Not quite sure yet. Working on that plan right now."

The headache ball was a large iron ball that was fixed directly over the hook on the winch cable of all big cranes. It was designed to limit movement of the hook when there was no load on the crane. It clearly wasn't designed for riders, but T.C. Crosby decided he was going to have to ride it today. It was the only way he could think of to use Hope's hook to snag the winch cable on the swinging load.

As Hope's boom, with its headache ball and hook dangling below it, approached the tip of Carlos's boom, Hope's father shouted into the mic, "That's good, Hope. Stop the boom right there. Hook down five."

Hope had done hundreds of lifts with her father. She knew the nuanced meaning of his commands. He needed her to stop her boom and move the hook down five feet.

Without looking at the winch and boom controls, her hands jockeyed the levers and obeyed his commands perfectly. She had operated cranes, under her father's watchful eye, since she was big enough to reach the controls. She was probably the only woman in the world who was as comfortable on the fashion runways in Milan as she was in the cab of this gigantic crane. She was, without doubt, one of the best crane operators in the country. As a former model, she was also one of the best-looking. The combination was always very well received on any construction site.

As Hope's hook dropped into place over the roof, her father climbed onto it and snapped his safety belt to the winch cable above the headache ball.

"Okay, Hope. I'm on the headache ball," he said. "Bring me up ten and give me five right."

She muttered a curse but admired her dad's courage and started the translation per his direction. It was probably good that she could not see her father hanging off the headache ball. Only the topside crew could see him at this point and they were all pretty well convinced the old man had finally lost his mind.

The a/c unit still swung erratically back and forth over the roof. Now Hope's hook and ball, with her father attached to it, sat directly in the path of the huge gray metal box that had taken on a life of its own.

Hope's father could see the impending collision coming and realized that if he didn't get out of the way, he was going to get creamed.

He shouted, "Up ten now!!" into the radio.

Hope sucked the wind through her teeth and quickly pulled back on the winch control lever. She couldn't tell what was going on above her head but she could tell by his voice that her father needed her to move quickly. If she had been able to see him, she would have seen the a/c unit miss him by less than a foot.

The topside crew watched the load narrowly miss Hope's father and let out a cheer. To them, Mr. T.C. looked like a Spanish matador in a bullfight with the twirling air conditioner. His hard hat had fallen off and his long white ponytail streamed behind him in the wind. His topside crew wasn't sure whether he was the craziest or the bravest man on the roof right then but they knew they could not take their eyes off the spectacle of their boss dueling with this unruly load. They showed him their support by cheering him on.

Just as the load whistled past Hope's father, he keyed his radio again. "Okay, Hope. I think I can get it this time. I need you to give me right two and, on my call, drop me ten."

"Okay, Dad. You got it. For God's sake, be careful!"

She moved the boom two feet right and waited for her father's next command.

As the a/c unit swung away from him, her father shouted, "NOW!!"

She moved the winch control lever forward and dropped her hook ten feet. Her actions placed her father, and the hook he rode on, directly in the path of the swivel on the spinning a/c unit.

Hope placed her crane's controls in neutral and waited for the next command from her father. She knew that was all she could do at this point.

As the load approached him, Hope's father pulled hard against the winch cable at the top of the headache ball and pushed the hook out with his feet to try to snag the swivel on the load. He could see the swivel come toward him and held his breath.

The hook on the good crane snagged the swivel on the sling.

He keyed the mic and triumphantly shouted, "Got it!!"

T.C. was somewhat amazed at his good fortune. But his victory was short-lived as the sudden acceleration of the hook catching the sling jarred him loose from his perch on the headache ball. He lost his grip on the winch cable and slipped off the ball.

Fortunately, he had snapped his safety harness to the winch cable when he first climbed aboard the headache ball. When he slipped, he dropped about five feet below the headache ball and was now suspended between the hook and the air-conditioning unit by his safety harness and lanyard.

Despite the fact that he was hanging at the end of the safety lanyard, he was otherwise okay. He held his finger to his lips as a non-verbal signal to the topside crew to stay off the radios. He didn't want Hope and Carlos to know that he was suspended between the headache ball and the a/c unit at this point in the lift.

Hope felt her crane shudder when it took up the load from the swinging a/c unit. Even though she couldn't see it, she knew she had caught it.

She was glad that she caught the load, but she still had no idea whether her father was safe or not.

She called up to her father on the radio. "Are you okay, Dad?!"

There was no answer as T.C. was currently a bit indisposed. However, the only people who knew it, besides him, were the topside crew.

He slowly collected his wits, repositioned his walkie-talkie and called back. "I'm fine, Hope. Nice work with the hook, kiddo!"

Then he was right back to business.

"Hope, take the load and help me stop the damn oscillations. Break. Break. Carlos, as Hope picks up the load, release tension on your winch to give her some slack."

Both Carlos and Hope followed his commands.

Hope could now use both her winch and her boom to slow the oscillations of the a/c unit. She could feel the load being taken up in her boom and heard Carlos's machine spool down.

"Okay," Hope's father said through his mic. "We've got it now. Let's get this thing on the pad as quickly as we can. Drop it down ten, Hope. That should let the crew get on the tethers."

Hope followed her father's commands and the topside crew captured the tether lines. Once they regained control of the tethers, the oscillations of the unit stopped.

Within five minutes of regaining control of the unit, Hope, her father, and the topside crew had lowered the air conditioner down to the load pads on the roof.

As the unit was bolted down, the members of the topside crew let out a loud cheer that could be heard by the ground crew down below. They knew they had dodged a bullet. But they also knew their team had done something not many other crews could. They were proud of their work and proud to be part of the Crosby team.

Carlos and Hope didn't hear the celebration on the roof. They were still ensconced in the cabs of their cranes, going through their shutdown procedures.

They also didn't see how the topside crew scrambled to get Mr. Crosby unstrapped from his safety harness as he dangled from Hope's winch cable. Later, she and Carlos would find out what he had done up on the roof that day and how close he came to being crushed by the mammoth air-conditioning unit.

His crews would never forget his actions and his daughter would never forgive him for scaring her to death.

During the debrief, in the firm's construction trailer on the site, they all pledged that Mrs. Crosby and the firm's "friends" who represented the government's Occupational, Safety and Health Administration (OSHA) would never get wind of his high-wire act during the lift. If T.C.'s wife or the government ever found out about his acrobatics, he would be out of business forever and none of them were ready for that!

Chapter Two

Mac Callaghan daydreamed as he sat at the conference table in his office on Park Avenue. He studied the New York City skyline through the massive glass windows of the conference room as he listened to a briefing by his risk management team. It was a beautiful day. Clear skies but very windy. He could see the flags on top of the high-rise buildings strain against the ropes that held them to their flagpoles. In the distance, he made out the reflections from the fuselages of the commercial airliners as they took off and landed at La Guardia Airport.

He knew he should be paying attention to the briefing. His team was telling him the pros and cons of committing twenty million dollars to fund the start-up of a software development company. His chief financial officer was worried about the impact on the company's financial ratios and his attorney was worried about potential legal liabilities. It was the usual hand-wringing of the staff prior to committing a truckload of money to a new investment. He knew what they were telling him was important, and he respected their opinions, but today he had trouble keeping his mind focused on the task at hand.

It was the Friday morning before the Memorial Day weekend. Like almost everyone else in New York City, Mac had plans to head out of town for the long weekend. His destination was a three hundred-acre farm on the Eastern Shore in Maryland. After buying the farm, he gutted the old farmhouse and completely renovated it. The outbuildings and the barn got a makeover too. The old tractor shed was now a workshop and garage for his vehicles and the barn had been converted to a state-of-the-art indoor shooting range. After months of construction, the house was ready for occupancy and this was the weekend he had picked to move in. He loved the peaceful seclusion of the farm and couldn't wait to get away and get settled into his new place.

An aviator's expression popped into his head: *wheels in the well.* The expression described the landing gear retracting inside the plane as it took off. He couldn't wait for the meeting to be over so he could be wheels in the well.

Suddenly, he realized his office had become completely quiet.

"Did you hear the question, Mac?" his partner asked.

Mac turned his gaze from the window and looked over at Will Jackson, his partner, and said, "Damn. I'm sorry, you guys. I wasn't listening. What was the question?"

He was a little embarrassed but when Will and the rest of the staff looked back at him and laughed, he laughed at himself. They all knew he was excited about his move this weekend and they had known him long enough to cut him some slack. Normally, he was an engaged and curious listener. Today, his mind was obviously in another place.

Will said, "No problem there, Mr. Deep Thinker. We could all see that you were a thousand miles away. Suspect you were already halfway home when we interrupted you."

He looked at Mac and raised an eyebrow. "Or, perhaps some sweet young thing has captured your heart, my friend?"

Mac laughed. "Not likely! Who the hell would want to date an old, broken-down geezer like me?"

Mac knew he was far from old and broken-down. He was in great shape and prided himself on staying that way. But he liked to pretend, at forty-five years old, that he was over the hill. He felt like his self-deprecating act helped him keep an edge on some of the younger guys.

He smiled at the group and decided he needed to get the meeting back on track. "Okay. That's enough about my love life or the complete lack thereof. Let's try this again. What was the question?"

As Mac reengaged with the group, he knew there was truth to his words. Will, his wife, and Mac's other friends always tried to fix him up with their single lady friends. But, after too many failed relationships, Mac had decided he was not the marrying type. Even dating was hard for him. He had surrendered to the realization that he was going to end up living his life on his own. It wasn't that he didn't want to have a woman to share his life with. It was his other job that always seemed to get in the way of any kind of serious relationship.

Mac's other job was something he couldn't talk about. He was a contractor with the Central Intelligence Agency. His job with the CIA required Mac, and his team, to leave the country for extended periods of time on very short notice. His team was referred to as a Kinetic Risk Management Team at the Agency. That was the politically-correct term for a Special Operations Assault Team. Their job was to covertly infiltrate areas of interest, provide surveillance and take direct action, when necessary, to eliminate risks to the security of the United States.

Normally, they performed their missions and came back home without anyone knowing they had ever been there. In some cases, their work became a little more high profile when they were directed to capture or kill a target who presented an exceptional risk to the government.

In those cases, the enemy knew Mac and his team had been there when one of their colleagues disappeared or experienced a sudden and violent death, but no one had ever been able to directly trace Mac's team, or their actions, back to the United States.

For obvious reasons, Mac and the other members of his team were not permitted to talk about where they went or what they did when they went away. Consequently, none of them had found any women who appreciated having their lovers jump out of bed in the middle of the night and disappear for weeks on end without ever explaining where they were going, when they would come back, or what they did when they went away. Mac was pretty sure he would remain single for a long time, at least as long as he continued to work for the Agency.

Mac's partner, Will, was partly briefed-in on Mac's secret. He had met with Mac's supervisors at the Agency and understood that Mac's job with the government required Mac to make no-notice trips abroad. Mac never explained what he did when he went away and Will never asked him any questions. Between the two of them, they had created one of the most successful venture capital firms in the United States. As far as Will was concerned, he had a terrific partner who just happened to travel frequently and remain out of touch for short periods of time. It was a good partnership and Will was not interested in doing anything that could screw it up.

Will smiled at Mac. "Relax, my brother. You know we were just pulling your leg." He pointed to Mac's attorney, who was seated at the end of the conference table. "John asked you a question about terms of our contract with Soft-Science. He wants to negotiate with them to get us a seat on their board of directors. Once we get that contingency ironed out, we can ink the deal."

He looked back at Mac. "What do you think?"

Mac smiled at Will. He had already made up his mind. He wanted to do this deal. He knew Will wanted to do it too, but still had some reservations about it. Will knew, from his past experience, that anything involving software development was risky. Fortunately, in this case, Mac and Will both knew the chief executive officer of Soft-Science. He was a charismatic, hard-charging, no-nonsense leader who started his career as a programmer. The CEO had hired a new top-level management team for the company and Mac's gut told him this project was a winner. If anyone could do the job, Mac felt like this was the guy.

Mac leaned back in his chair and looked at Will and the rest of the staff. "I think this is a good investment. I agree with you guys and think we should ask them to give us a seat on the board. If they agree with that, I think we should move forward on the contract."

He paused and looked at Will. "What do you think, Will?"

Will smiled. "I'm with you, partner."

With his partner's concurrence, Mac knew the rest of the team could execute the deal. He figured the meeting was pretty much over now, so he pushed back his chair and stood up. "And now ladies and gentlemen, I'm off to the Eastern Shore of Maryland. I hope you guys have a great weekend!"

He said goodbye to the rest of the staff and then turned and looked at the back of the conference room. A large black Labrador retriever sat patiently by the door. The dog's eyes were firmly fixed on Mac's every move. He wagged his tail as his master approached him.

Mac rubbed the big dog's head. "C'mon, Moses. Let's go, boy!"

Mac and his dog Moses walked out the door of the conference room and down the hall toward Mac's office. Moses walked closely by Mac's side, never more than a few steps away. He was a big dog but he moved quietly down the hallway with a spring in his step. His brown eyes sparkled and he had a big, happy-go-lucky Lab grin on his face. Moses was ready to go to the farm too. The Eastern Shore was Doggie Disneyland for him and he was ready.

Mac and Moses were the epitome of a man and his dog. Moses had been a working dog, and part of Mac's team, at the Agency. Unfortunately, Moses had been wounded on a mission with Mac and was medically retired after he recovered from his wounds. Mac couldn't take Moses with him on his missions anymore. With that one exception, pretty much everywhere Mac went, Moses went. When Mac did have to leave him at home, his chief of staff, Sean, took care of Moses while he was away.

Sean had been with Mac for a long time. Mac initially hired him as an assistant but over time, he and Will came to realize that Sean was an extraordinarily talented financier. Over the years, along with becoming Mac's chief of staff, Sean had also become one of Mac's most trusted and valued friends. Besides Will, Sean was the only other person outside the Agency who knew about Mac's ties to the CIA.

When Sean first came to work for Mac, a lot of people asked Mac why he hired a man to work as his assistant. Mac always laughed at that question and curtly replied, "Because he's the best person for the job." And, with a raised eyebrow, he would fire a question back at his inquisitor and say, "Why? Is there some other reason to hire an assistant?"

Their questions always made Mac bristle. He guessed that everyone assumed he would hire some blonde bombshell to decorate his outer office and entertain him like many of his counterparts on Wall Street. The people who asked Mac the question obviously did not know Mac well. Nor did they know Sean. After seeing Sean in action, they usually asked Mac where they could find someone else like him.

Mac also placed great value in the fact that Sean was not a "yes-man." He wasn't afraid to express his opinions. He did it diplomatically and, more importantly, had a way of providing an explanation for his recommended course of action that was logical and usually irrefutable. Mac had learned over time to listen carefully to Sean's advice. It had gotten him out of a couple of jams and prevented him from getting into countless other ones. Sean had a great head for business and was also a terrific cook and estate manager. He and his partner lived in the carriage house at Mac's place on Long Island and managed the property there. Hiring Sean was one of the smartest decisions Mac ever made.

Sean saw Mac and Moses heading down the hall toward Mac's office and quickly moved to the door as Mac tossed his suit on the desk and removed his tie. As Mac stripped off his clothes, he opened the wardrobe behind his desk and smiled. When he came into work this morning, he had hung up his clothes and changed into his suit. He fully expected to fly home in the clothes he had worn to work. But Sean had another plan. While Mac was in his meeting, Sean had replaced his clothes with a fresh shirt, a clean pair of jeans and a pair of Mac's favorite work boots. It was all hung up perfectly. All Mac had to do was strip off his suit, put on his farm clothes, and head out the door.

Mac looked over his shoulder at Sean. "Thanks, Sean. I see you've taken care of me yet again."

Sean chuckled. "Well, boss, I knew you and Moses were heading out today. I wanted to make sure you were dressed properly for your trip down to the farm. I also loaded your travel bag and put it downstairs in the truck. There's some lunch in there for you, along with a treat for Moses. You guys should be all set."

While Mac and Sean talked, Moses ambled over to Sean and nuzzled his pants pocket. Sean reached into his pocket, pulled out a mini-dog treat for the big Lab, and offered it to his friend. As he patted the dog's huge head, and scratched him behind the ears, he fed the dog a treat. "Here you go, Moses."

The big black dog gently took the treat from Sean's hand and wagged his tail. Next to Mac, Sean was Moses's best buddy. The dog knew Sean always had a treat for him. While Moses inhaled his treat, Sean gave him the usual mock-scolding.

"Moses, I'm going to have to stop feeding you these treats. If you get any bigger, you're not going to be able to drag your big ass up into your master's airplane."

Sean turned his attention away from the big dog and looked at Mac."By the way, speaking of planes, I called the hangar and told them you would be there in about an hour. The G-5 is already out of the hangar. By the time you get there, it should be fueled and ready to go."

Mac sat down in his chair to tie his boots. "Roger that. Thanks, Sean. That's perfect." He knew the G-5 would get them down to the Eastern Shore in about thirty minutes. That would give him plenty of time to drive from the airport to the farm. He should get there easily by lunchtime.

Mac looked up at Sean. "We should be back here late on Monday night. I think I'll fly back up sometime after dinner. If anything changes with that, I'll give you a call."

He looked back down at his boots. While he was tying the laces, he said, "Are you guys going to be around this weekend?"

Sean nodded. "Yep. Ben and I have a couple of parties that we're going to go to this weekend but, other than that, we should be around. Is there anything you need me to do to help you down at the farm?"

Mac shook his head. "No. I think the movers should have everything unloaded by the time we get there. I should be able to get everything unpacked over the weekend."

Mac gave his shoelace a final tug. He looked up and winked at Sean. "You and Ben can come down next weekend and help me put it all in the right place!"

Sean laughed. "That's probably a good idea. I suspect the shooting range and the study will be unpacked and set up perfectly. In your mind, I know you will be fine as frog's hair as long as you can bust a few caps and shoot pool. I suspect everything else will be scattered to hell and back for sure. We will definitely fly down there with you guys next weekend and help you get everything else unpacked."

Mac stood and reached out to shake Sean's hand. "Thanks so much for all your help. I don't know what I would do without you, my friend."

Sean laughed and with a wink said, "No problem, boss. I don't know what you would do without me either!"

He patted Moses on the head one last time. "You two need to get going now."

And with that, Mac and Moses headed to the airport.

Chapter Three

The captain of the *Mirrabooka* was nervous. His two hundred foot mega-yacht was behind schedule. He was supposed to be meeting the owner and his guests in forty-eight hours but he still had a thousand miles to go before he was pier-side in Port Blair.

The owner planned to use the yacht for a weekend of diving in the crystal-clear waters of the Andaman Sea. They were flying into the airport at Port Blair, which was located on South Andaman Island in the Bay of Bengal. It was a perfect place for a diving getaway. The captain and his crew had already made arrangements on the island to pick up the owner and his guests at the airport. Once they were safely onboard the yacht, they would proceed to Havelock Island to enjoy some of the best diving in the world.

The owner was a great guy but the captain knew he would not be pleased if his yacht was not sitting in Port Blair harbor when his plane touched down at the airport. The captain should have been able to make it to Port Blair with no problem, except he and his crew had been delayed for ten hours as they tried to clear customs in Singapore, their last port.

The delay in customs had cost the captain precious time. He only had two choices. He could call the owner and tell him they would be arriving late in Port Blair or he could change his voyage plan, leave Singapore at sunset, and proceed to Port Blair at a higher than planned speed.

Calling the owner with bad news would be a significant threat to the captain's job security. Leaving Singapore at sunset and navigating the hazardous Strait of Malacca at high speed, in darkness, would risk the safety of the *Mirrabooka* and his crew. The

Strait was challenging to navigate, but more importantly, it was a well-known haven for smugglers and pirates.

Over the years, the governments of India, Indonesia, Malaysia, and Singapore had dramatically increased efforts to patrol the Strait and prevent piracy. Their efforts had significantly reduced the probability of being attacked. Unfortunately, even with those safeguards in place, there were still sporadic reports of encounters with pirates and smugglers along the entire six hundred mile length of the Strait.

The captain weighed the odds and made a decision to leave Singapore as soon as he cleared customs. He felt the risk of being fired for not making his scheduled arrival time in Port Blair far outweighed the risk of running into pirates in the Strait. The *Mirrabooka* was big and she was fast. He knew he could easily make twenty-five knots and outrun or run over all but the most well-armed pirate ships. When he factored in the speed and size of the *Mirrabooka*, he figured the odds of running into pirates, who also happened to have an extremely fast boat, were next to impossible.

Now, from the blacked-out bridge of the big yacht, he and his crew worked their way toward the Andaman Islands through the Strait of Malacca. It was dark and unfortunately, there was no moon. He pushed the yacht hard, at twenty-five knots. He still had nine hundred miles to go to reach Port Blair. At this speed, he thought he could make it just in time to pull into port, refuel the yacht, take on fresh provisions and then meet the owner and his guests at the airport. It was going to be close but, with a little luck, he thought he could pull it off.

The captain was intensely focused on the flickering screen of his surface-search radar. The Strait was narrow. In some places it was only twenty miles wide. The small islands, oil rigs, and vessel traffic in the Strait looked like hundreds of bright lights on the dark surface of the radar screen.

The captain knew better than to solely rely on his radar to thread his way through the Strait at night. He posted two members of his crew as lookouts, one on the bow and one on the stern.

On the bow, Amanda Anderson, a deckhand and the yacht's assistant chef, peered out into the darkness. As the ship plowed through the cresting seas, the winds whipped her long blonde hair and brought tears to her eyes. She wrapped her hair up into a bun and continued to look out into the moonless night to look for any small boats ahead of the yacht that the captain might not see on the radar. It was a beautiful night. The air was moist and warm and the moonless sky revealed millions of stars.

She didn't complain at all when the captain assigned her to the bow watch. It was a beautiful night and Amanda loved to sit on the bow of the *Mirrabooka* as the enormous yacht moved through the water. She felt so lucky to have finally found a place where she felt safe and immune from the conflicts in her life back in the States.

After high school, she had struggled in college. She made a lot of friends and did a lot of partying but she didn't find much to get excited about in her studies. After spending two years at school and burning through a significant chunk of her parents' money, they all decided that maybe college was not for her.

Amanda's problem with school was compounded by the fact that she lived her life in a fishbowl. Her father was the secretary of state of the United States of America. His job brought constant attention to him and to his family. Although her parents had done their best to shield Amanda from the media, her partying habits and failure to meet the academic requirements at school made news in the tabloids. She really needed some time to figure out what she wanted to do with her life but she knew she needed to do it on her own, without the ever-present gaze of the media. For a while, she thought about enlisting in the Navy. She had always loved sailing and being around the water. The problem with enlisting was that she would never be able to truly escape from her father's shadow or the media's attention, no matter where she was stationed.

An enlistment in the Navy would never give her the space she needed to pause and reflect on what she wanted to do with her life.

One day, while leafing through a boating magazine, she saw an advertisement about a job opportunity as a crewmember on a mega-yacht. She thought the job sounded like fun and assumed a job at sea would help to shield her from the press. She applied for the job and, after her interview, was offered a position as a deckhand and assistant to the chef onboard the *Mirrabooka*. She accepted the offer and began an around-the-world odyssey that gave her exactly what she needed: relative anonymity and an opportunity to see the world while she trained for a new career as a chef. She loved working on the enormous yacht and enjoyed seeing the world from the decks of this floating palace.

On the stern, Chris Foster, the first mate on the *Mirrabooka*, peered intently into the night. His job was to act as lookout on the port and starboard sides of the ship, as well as over the stern. The boat moved along at twenty-five knots, so he wasn't too worried about the stern; he spent most of his time checking the forward quarter on the port and starboard sides of the yacht. Chris was an adventurer. He loved to travel and he loved the sea. He was in his mid-thirties and had worked on many yachts over the years. So far, this gig had been the best, by far. The boat was brand-new, it had a great captain, the owner and his family were chill, and he had the best quarters of any yacht he had ever served on. Sometimes he felt as if it were his own private yacht that took him around the world. There was also an added attraction on the *Mirrabooka* for Chris: Amanda Anderson. He was completely smitten with the assistant chef and they had covertly flirted with each other for the past couple of months.

During their last port visit in Singapore, they had been left alone on the yacht while the rest of the crew enjoyed some much-deserved liberty ashore. While they were alone, Amanda and Chris had whipped up a batch of margaritas and taken them up to the flying bridge of the massive yacht. After the second pitcher, they had their first kiss and not long after that, they decided to go skinny-dipping in the owner's hot tub. Not surprisingly, shortly after their clothes came off, they found themselves engaged in an intense lovemaking session in the hot tub. After a short rest, they moved to the sun lounge on the flying bridge and made love again under the stars. They fell asleep in each other's arms on the flying bridge and, as dawn broke over the harbor the next morning, Chris awoke to feel Amanda's soft hands gently caressing him again. Her fingers quickly worked their magic and, before he knew it, he was consumed with the single-minded need of pressing himself deep into Amanda's velvet core. He would never forget looking up at her seductive silhouette as she climbed on top of him, and rode him to a glorious climax, while the sunrise bathed her body in the soft morning light. It was a night, and following morning, that Chris would never forget. Amanda was an awesome lover. She seemed to be able to anticipate his every need and her stamina left him gasping for breath while his body simultaneously yearned for more of her.

Before she became his lover, she had become his friend. During the past few months at sea, Chris had really gotten to know her. He loved talking with her about their lives, their families, and their friends. They talked about their hopes and dreams and found they had a lot in common. He was beginning to think Amanda was someone who he might be able to settle down with and she seemed to feel the same way.

When they found out the *Mirrabooka* would be staying at Port Blair for a few days after the owner and his guests disembarked, they made plans to go ashore together to spend the night at a local hotel. Chris made a reservation at the Sea Princess Port Blair, one of the most romantic hotels on the island. Amanda was excited about spending an entire day and night with Chris. She looked forward to getting dressed up, going out to dinner, and then spending a night honing the sharp edge of her budding relationship with Chris.

Chris couldn't wait to get close to Amanda again. It drove him a little crazy to hide his feelings about her from the rest of the crew, but he knew if the captain found out, they would both be asked to leave the yacht.

He could see Amanda moving around up on the bow of the yacht. Her long frame was dimly bathed in the reflection of the yacht's green running light on the starboard side. He could see the curve of her hips and the silhouette of her beautiful hair, tied up in a bun. He smiled at the memory of her body grinding hard against him and silently counted down the days until they would be together again.

Chris turned to make his way back aft down the starboard side of the yacht. As he made his way across the stern to the port side, he thought he saw a shadow cross the yacht's wake. He stopped for a moment, looked again, and didn't see anything. He assumed it was just the light reflecting from the foamy froth churned up by the massive propellers as the yacht surged through the sea. Chris didn't give the shadow much more thought. He turned and moved up the port side of the yacht and resumed his observation of Amanda as she stood her watch up on the bow.

Chapter Four

It had been a long week for Hope. After the near-disaster with the air-conditioning unit and her father's subsequent trapeze act at the construction site, she headed back to her house in Georgetown. The Memorial Day weekend traffic was heavy as she inched her black BMW M5 across the Key Bridge.

Despite the traffic, she loved her home in Georgetown. The US Capitol was less than five miles from her house but she felt like Georgetown was in a completely different city than Washington, DC. She loved the unique buzz of this city within the city. The bars and restaurants and the shopping were some of the best in the world, but there was another part of Georgetown that only a few people knew about.

Once you left the hustle and bustle of M Street, the neighborhoods were remarkably peaceful and quiet. Hope's neighborhood was her oasis in the midst of the chaos of the city. She worked hard on her house and gardens, enjoyed her neighbors, and felt comfortable and safe in her neighborhood. She could easily walk to dinner and join her friends for a night out on the town and then safely return to her home in the middle of downtown Washington, all without ever touching the keys to her car.

As she turned up 33rd Street NW, she passed a long line of people waiting to be served at Georgetown Cupcakes. She smiled as she saw the faces of the children, with their parents standing with them on the sidewalk, who waited patiently for their sweet treasures. Seeing the kids with their parents reminded her of her mother, so she toggled the phone on the steering wheel of her car and dialed up her mom.

Catherine Crosby answered her daughter's call quickly. She always kept her cell phone close, just in case one of her children needed to reach her. When Hope called, her mom was always there. Hope couldn't imagine it any other way. Her mother was her anchor.

She answered her phone the way she always did when Hope called. "What's going on, baby girl?" Then she said, "Are you on your way?"

Hope smiled. It always amazed her how just the sound of her mother's voice made her feel completely at ease. "Hi, Mom. No. Not yet. I'm just getting back home from work and I wanted to touch base with you before I hit the road."

Hope's mother said, "It's good to hear your voice. But, I was hoping you were already on your way. I'm trying to get some dinner ready for your father but he's tied up in traffic on the Bay Bridge. What were you guys doing over there today that was so important that you couldn't get off the site a little early?"

If you knew what Dad was doing, you would have a heart attack. Instead of telling her mother the truth, she said, "Oh Mom, you know how it is on the day before a holiday weekend. There are always so many loose ends to tie up. I tried to get him out of there early, but you know how stubborn he can be!"

Hope's mother laughed. "Yes, I know. But you know how he hates to sit in traffic. He's gonna be all wound up when he finally gets home!"

"I know, Mom. I'm sorry I couldn't convince him to get out of there earlier. I'm sure a glass of wine and dinner on the back porch will calm him down."

Hope knew it wouldn't take too much to calm her father down when he finally made it back home. He was always at his best on the farm. The only thing he loved more in life than his farm was his wife and his family. Hope loved to watch her mom and dad when they were together. They had a storybook romance and, after more than forty years of marriage, were still visibly and deeply in love.

Hope's mom laughed. "I know. I doubt you and the rest of the crew together could push him off the site until he was ready to go anyway." She added, "He can still be kind of a pain in the ass at times, you know?"

Hope chuckled. "That's an understatement. But I worry about him, Mom. He pushes himself so hard."

"I know, darling. But it's in his DNA. He wouldn't know any other way. He loves his work and he loves his crew, and I know you know how much he loves working with his little girl."

Hope knew her mom was right. But in time, she hoped her dad would back off a little bit and let her pick up the day-to-day operations of the firm. She knew she was ready to take on more responsibility and she knew he trusted her, but he just couldn't let go.

Hope's mom asked, "So, when are you heading over tonight? Should I save some dinner for you?"

Hope thought for a minute. "I think I will head over later this evening, after the traffic dies down a bit. Don't worry about dinner. I'll be a little late."

"Okay, sweetie. Be careful driving and I will see you tomorrow morning."

"Is there anything I can bring down for Sunday?" Hope asked.

Her mom said, "No. I think we're pretty well covered. I would like you to pick up some crabs for us at Manchester's tomorrow, if that's okay? Dad picked up your new boat. It's on the lift and ready to go."

Then she said, "I've invited a couple of neighbors to join us for a picnic on Sunday. The weather is supposed to be nice, a little windy, but nice so it should be fun."

Hope wondered whether her mother had invited over another potential suitor for her. "You're not going to try to fix me up with someone again, are you, Mom?"

Her mom laughed. "No, not this time. I promise I won't do that again." She hesitated for a moment and added, "Unless someone really spectacular comes along!"

"That's good to hear, Mom. That last one was a doozy. I didn't think I was ever going to be able to shake him!"

"I know. I'm sorry, Hope. His mother is such a wonderful lady, and I thought you might like her son. I promise. I won't do that again."

Hope's mother was constantly trying to find a partner and soul mate for her daughter. Unfortunately, her mother's idea of the perfect partner for Hope seemed to be one hundred eighty degrees out from what Hope was looking for.

Her mother wanted Hope to settle down, grow some roots and have babies. Hope had pretty much given up on having kids at this point in her life. For all intents and purposes, she felt like her baby-making clock had already stopped ticking.

What Hope really wanted was a man who shared her interests, challenged her intellect, and made her laugh. She wanted someone to love her and share her life with her. But she really needed more than that. She needed someone who could regularly blow her mind in the bedroom and match her skills in the boardroom. Hope found men like that to be in extremely short supply.

As she pulled into the driveway of her home on N Street NW, she said goodbye to her mom and headed up to her house to pack.

Normally, after a long week at work, she would have driven home, taken a nap, and then headed out for dinner and a few drinks with her friends in Georgetown. She knew every bar, and more importantly, just about every bouncer on M Street.

She had lived in Georgetown for almost twenty years now. She went to Georgetown University as an undergraduate and graduate student. While she went to school, she applied to a local modeling agency to make some extra spending money. With her looks, her moonlighting gig quickly turned into a full-time job. After she received her master's degree, she went on to become a well-known and very successful model.

Hope was a striking woman. She was a tall, leggy brunette with olive skin, high cheekbones and a dazzling smile. Her face had graced the covers of *Glamour, Vogue*, and a host of other fashion magazines. She was a woman who was perfectly at home on the runway of a haute couture fashion show but just as comfortable in blue jeans and a flannel shirt in the massive cab of a D-9 Caterpillar bulldozer.

In addition to having looks that stopped most men dead in their tracks, she was also a hard-partying siren who could dance all night and drink until dawn. A long list of men had accepted the challenge of keeping up with her, but very few still stood when the sun rose in the morning. She had taken a few lovers off and on but only ever really fell in love with one man. He had broken her heart and the pain she felt during their breakup had kept her from ever getting too serious with anyone else, ever again. She couldn't seem to find a man she could trust who could keep her interest piqued and her passion stoked. As she got older, she realized that maybe she never would find someone to settle down with.

After she finished packing, she watered her plants, set the code on her home security system and headed out the door to start her weekend.

It took about two hours for her to make it to her parents' farm on the Eastern Shore. As she left the city on Route 50 headed east, she opened the windows and sunroof of her M5. She stepped on the gas and felt the instant response of the big V-10 motor in the BMW. She settled back and relaxed as she enjoyed the crisp steering and precise handling of the car as she sped down the highway toward the Eastern Shore.

She could see the stars as she crossed the Chesapeake Bay Bridge. The cool night air flowed through the car as the sounds and smells of the city were replaced by the smell of fresh cut grass and the sound of crickets chirping. At this time of night, the traffic wasn't too bad and the long drive itself was therapeutic. Right before she came to Easton, she turned off the highway and made her way down the country roads that led to her parents' farm.

She listened to country music on her iPod and relived memories of her young adult life as she passed the many familiar landmarks along the road home. It was easy to discard the pressures and worries of her job in Washington and make plans for how she would spend her weekend at home.

As she turned down the gravel lane to her parents' house, she smiled. She could tell from the glow in the distance that her dad had turned on the giant gas lamps at the front entrance of the house. As the gravel on the driveway crunched beneath the tires of her car, her physical journey and mental decompression were complete. She was home. She couldn't wait to get out on the bay again and looked forward to spending some quality time alone, with her mom and dad.

Chapter Five

It was still dark outside when Mac opened his eyes. Through the open window in his bedroom, he could hear the murmur of the geese as they communicated with one another at their overnight resting place on the river. They were awake too and announced the impending arrival of the sun as it made its fiery approach across the eastern sky.

The geese were plentiful at Mac's farm. Although hunted to near extinction in the 1960s, their population had rebounded and now grew at an exponential rate. They certainly thrived on Mac's farm. They were noisy and messy animals but Mac accepted them as part of the fabric of life on the Eastern Shore. Geese were territorial and gregarious. Regardless of whether they were in one of his fields or out on the river, the geese instinctively knew to post a lookout over the flock. Whenever something unusual was going on around them, the lookout was quick to warn the rest of the flock and, if Mac was within earshot, the owner of the farm.

He looked down at the luminous hands on his wristwatch. It was five a.m., time to get moving. He rarely had to set his alarm. Unless he was extremely tired, he seemed to wake up naturally at about the same time every day. His body just seemed to know when it was time to get up. On most days, he would roll out of bed, put on his workout gear and head outside for a run. He was a self-professed fitness nut who loved to work out and rarely missed a day. He didn't care much for indoor treadmills. Rain or snow, his first choice was always to run outside. Today was different, though. Today he planned to go fishing. The run could wait until later in the day.

He rolled out of bed and walked across the smooth surface of his wide plank floors in his bare feet. He could vaguely make out the shapes of the boxes that were still scattered across the floor in his bedroom. He made a lot of progress unpacking last night. There was still much more to be done but, most importantly, he found the box with his fishing gear in it. He had unpacked his gear and loaded it on his boat last night. His favorite shorts, shoes, T-shirt, and visor were on the foot of his bed. He stretched his long frame and dressed in the dark. There was no need to turn on any lights. He wanted to save his night vision for his trip down the river.

He heard Moses get up and stretch too. He chuckled as he listened to the big dog shake his head. The staccato report of his floppy ears and big jowls slapping against his massive head announced to Mac, and the rest of the world, that Moses was awake and ready to go. Mac felt the dog rub against his thigh and instinctively reached down and scratched him behind the ears.

Although he already knew the answer, he said, "Are you ready to go for a ride in the boat, my friend?"

The big dog answered Mac's question by bounding down the hallway. Mac knew he would be waiting for him in the kitchen. He loved to go out on the boat with Mac, or anywhere else for that matter, but Moses had other priorities too. His first priority was eating. After that, he would be happy to help Mac catch some rockfish for tonight's dinner.

After he served Moses his breakfast, Mac grabbed an apple for himself. His normal routine included a banana for breakfast but the local watermen had taught him a long time ago that bananas on boats were bad luck for fishermen. Mac wasn't particularly superstitious, but when it came to fishing, he wasn't about to take any chances. He stuffed the apple in the cargo pocket of his shorts and headed for the back door with Moses. Moses let himself out via the custom dog door that Mac had installed in the kitchen during the renovation. The big dog had quickly learned to actuate the door with his nose. Mac chuckled as the electric motor hummed and the door slid open. *Boys and their toys.* Moses met him on the back porch and they headed down the path that led to the boathouse.

As he opened the door to the boat house, he switched on a bank of green lights that illuminated his forty-five-foot custom fishing boat. Mac had designed it, with one of the local watermen, shortly after he signed the contract for his farm. The boat had been delivered a few weeks before he moved in. He had taken it out for a quick shakedown cruise on a previous visit, but today was the first day he had an opportunity to take it fishing. He flipped the switches to "Down" on the boatlift controls and the electric motors hummed as the winches gently lowered his baby into the water.

The lights in the boathouse bathed the boat in an eerie green halo of light. Mac stood on the dock and admired the lines of the new boat. The workmanship of the local craftsmen was clearly evident as the hull floated off its cradle. She was beautiful to look at and also very fast. The builder had convinced Mac to install twin Cummins commercial grade diesel engines in the boat when she was built. With over one-thousand horsepower available to the skipper, the boat could make thirty-five knots effortlessly. He couldn't wait to get out on the bay to see the sunrise and he knew the *Kestrel*, the name of a small, very fast bird of prey, was the perfect boat to get him there.

Mac and Moses climbed aboard the boat. He turned the keys and fired up the motors. Their initial roar on start-up quickly transitioned to a throaty rumble as they warmed up at idle. Once the motors were ready, Mac smoothly pulled the transmission control levers back. The boat slipped into reverse and backed away from the boathouse. As he backed into the creek, he shifted the port motor to forward. The boat slowed and then spun to the right. As the bow swung around, he brought the starboard motor out of reverse and then shifted it to match its twin on the port side. Now that he was pointed down the creek, he and Moses could make their way out to the Eastern Bay. The air was cool and damp. The water on the river was pitch black and slick calm. His running lights pierced the darkness and illuminated the reflective markers on the buoys that marked the channel. He turned and looked over the stern and studied his wake as luminescent jellyfish shot from his props, like miniature torpedoes, glowing with their phosphorescence.

He loved to go fishing. His father had taken him when he was a little boy and he was hooked forever after that. As he entered the channel, he used his right hand to gently advance the throttles on the giant diesels under his feet. He heard the turbo-chargers whine as they gulped in the air and, with a pleasing rumble, he felt the boat quickly rise up on plane. Within minutes, he was doing thirty knots. At that speed, it was a short ride to the bay.

As the sun crept up over the horizon, it illuminated the bright red roof and white walls of the Thomas Point Lighthouse in the distance. The lighthouse was one of the few remaining operational screw-pile lighthouses left on the bay. The design of the lighthouse got its name from its foundation of iron pilings that were literally screwed into the muddy bottom of the bay. Once the pilings were set, the lighthouse itself was built on top of the pilings. It was an amazing design, a perfect example of the ingenuity of the early engineers who designed and built these structures along the shores of the bay. As Mac's boat drew closer to the lighthouse, he slowed down to trolling speed, set out his lines and waited for his first fish to strike.

Mac spent the next couple of hours fishing near the lighthouse. Much to his delight, he managed to catch a few nice fish. He released all but one. That one went into his icebox. It would make a nice dinner for him and Moses tonight.

He watched the sun climb higher in the sky and decided to head for home before the weekend crowd showed up. He enjoyed leaving the dock early in the morning and returning before the go-fast crowds in their Jet Skis and cigarette boats made it out of their beds and onto the water. They always made him laugh as they roared around, going as fast as they could, seemingly oblivious of the natural beauty of the bay.

Speed and noise. That seemed to be what the go-fast crowd was after. They were mostly middle-aged men with more money than brains. Usually, the go-fast captains were accompanied by their trophy wives or girlfriends who, it appeared to Mac, used their money to make their own investments in silicone and Botox. It was a comically transparent attempt to maintain their grip on youth. All kind of sad, really. Go-fast boats with heavyset, Viagra enhanced, balding men and their women with plastic tits. It seemed to Mac that you couldn't see one without seeing the other. There they were, racing around at the speed of heat while they converted fuel to noise. He never quite understood what they got out of it but then a lot of people didn't understand why he liked to fish either.

He knew it was time to get back to his house and continue unpacking his boxes. He looked over at Moses. "Well, my friend, I think we're done for the day. Are you about ready to head home?"

Moses looked up from his perch on the port settee and wagged his tail. Mac figured that was a good enough answer, so he reeled in his lines and set a course for home.

As he throttled up, he noticed the wind picked up. There was now a slight chop on the surface of the bay as he pointed the bow of his boat back up the Eastern Bay. The choppy water didn't bother him too much. His boat was built to handle the weather and he was comfortable at the helm of the new boat. Almost forty years of steering boats, from small sailing dinghies to big power boats, had given him a sixth sense, a sense of how to ride with the swells instead of fighting against them. He instinctively shifted the wheel to smooth out the ride and slice through the mid-morning chop.

He felt comfortable and at home on the bay. He set his course on the autopilot, engaged the system, and smiled as he watched "George," his nickname for the autopilot, steer the boat along a course toward home.

Chapter Six

The pirates pushed away from their mother ship in a blacked-out rigid hull inflatable (RHIB) speedboat with a full load of marijuana and opium. Their mission was to deliver their last load, for this trip, of drugs from the mother ship to a distributor on a remote beach located southwest of the city of Malacca. Malacca was in Indonesia, on the northern side of the Strait of Malacca. It was located in a perfect spot to facilitate further distribution of drugs across the southern peninsula of Malaysia. The stakes were high for the pirates. They faced the death penalty if they were captured. But the profits in this illegal business were huge so there was no shortage of pirates who were willing to take the risk.

The pirates made their deliveries along the entire length of the coastline from India to Singapore. They had been at sea for over a week now. This was the last load to deliver during this at-sea period. The distributors who received the drugs from the pirates were part of a multi-billion dollar consortium who sold drugs to customers across India, Myanmar, Thailand, Malaysia, and Singapore. The pirates were a small, but critical, part of a huge network that managed their business with sophisticated production and distribution operations controls. It was a massive business that was run with ruthless efficiency.

Although the RHIB was capable of very high speeds, the pirates normally made their deliveries at low speeds, with their running lights extinguished, to help them avoid detection by the local authorities. The RHIB's low profile, coupled with their rubber and canvas construction, made them extremely difficult to see and almost impossible to detect on radar. As long as they kept their wake down, they were nearly undetectable at night.

After they completed their transaction on the beach and received the watertight suitcases of cash from their customers, they made their way back to the mother ship. Right before they checked in, via satellite cell phone, a huge white yacht barreling along in the dark caught their attention. It was highly unusual to see a mega-yacht at night in this remote area of the Strait.

The yacht the pirates stumbled upon was the *Mirrabooka*. Although it was a beautiful yacht, it was much more than just a pretty boat to the pirate skipper of the RHIB. It was a target of opportunity for him, a defenseless vessel that might be easily plundered. He used his night-vision binoculars to scan the yacht. He could see a lookout on the bow. It appeared to be a young woman. Seeing a woman onboard upped the ante. If he could capture her alive, he and his boss could sell her to one of the prostitution or surrogacy markets in Thailand. There was huge demand for young, white surrogate mothers and prostitutes in Asia. He was sure he could get a good price for a young white woman, in good condition, if he delivered her to the right people.

The skipper could see another lookout on the stern of the yacht. It was a man. He could see him move back and forth across the stern of the yacht. He seemed to spend more time looking forward than looking aft, though. A lookout on the stern might keep them from making their approach to the big yacht, but this particular lookout didn't seem to be paying much attention to the wake. That oversight on his part might provide the skipper and his men with an opportunity to make an approach up the stern of the mega-yacht without being detected. None of the lookouts appeared to be armed and none of them had binoculars. That would make his approach to board the yacht that much easier.

After a quick conference with his men, he grabbed his satellite phone and called the captain of the mother ship.

The captain of the mother ship answered the call tersely. "Yes."

"I'm trailing a large private yacht moving at high speed. The crew appears to be unarmed and there is a young white woman on board."

The captain said, "Roger. You want to try to board them?"

"Yes."

"Let me make a call and I will get back to you."

While the skipper of the RHIB waited for permission to attack, he continued to scan the *Mirrabooka* with his binoculars. He could see someone on the bridge. He assumed it was the captain at the helm, although it could be the owner. If it was the captain, the owner and his guests would most likely be down below in their cabins. At this time of night, it was a safe bet that they were fast asleep. He couldn't see anyone else. He wondered whether there might be more crew down below deck. If that turned out to be the case, he would quickly disengage and let the big yacht go on its way. While he studied the yacht, his satellite cell phone chirped.

The skipper answered the call and listened through his earpiece. The captain said, "You have permission to attack the target. Take anything of value that you can find. Bring the girl to me. Don't damage her in any way. Leave no witnesses and set fire to the boat."

The captain knew it was highly likely that the yacht would send out a distress call when they realized they were under attack. He also knew the authorities would be slow to respond at this time of night, so he and his men would have plenty of time to pilfer the ship and shake down the passengers and crew. He also knew that if he or his men beat up or raped the girl on the yacht, her market value would vanish before his eyes.

The skipper said, "Roger."

He turned off the satellite phone and turned the RHIB to intercept the *Mirrabooka*. As he picked up speed and fell in behind the yacht, he and his crew discussed their plan of attack. They assigned responsibilities for boarding the ship from the stern. They knew the frothy wake of the huge yacht would delay their detection and they hoped to surprise the lookout on the stern. If they could kill him before he sounded an alarm, there was a chance they might be able to take out the rest of the crew before they had time to transmit a distress call.

He pushed up the throttles on the three outboard motors on the RHIB. The engines surged and the rigid hull quickly brought the inflatable boat up on plane. He was doing forty knots in a matter of seconds and rapidly closed on the yacht. As he lined the small craft up in the wake, he could see the lookout on the stern of the yacht. He still looked up at the bow. He hoped he could get a little closer before the lookout spotted them.

Chris still watched Amanda from his post on the stern when he heard a noise from behind him. As he turned and looked toward the sound, he was perplexed to see a small boat rocket up the wake of the yacht.

At first he thought, *what the hell are a bunch of kids doing out here wake hopping in the middle of the night?*

He quickly realized these were no kids as he saw one of them raise an assault rifle and fire it at him. The muzzle flashes registered in his mind but his body was too slow to react. The bullets tore through his chest and shattered the sliding door behind him. As he fell to the deck, he felt numb but remarkably aware of his surroundings. He looked up into the beautiful night sky and marveled at how clear the stars sparkled. He thought about his parents and then thought about Amanda. The bright stars soon faded to gray and Chris took his last breath on the blood-stained teak deck of the *Mirrabooka*.

The captain heard the sound of the sliding glass door shattering from his position at the helm on the flying bridge. He toggled the yachts intercom system. "What's going on down there?"

His question was answered with silence. He saw Amanda turn from her post on the bow and hold her hands up in the air as if to say, *I don't know.* He wondered why Chris didn't answer the intercom. He checked the instrument panel on the yacht. All indicators were green and the engines were operating properly. Just to be safe, he pulled the throttles back on the engines to slow the yacht down and left his seat at the helm to see what was going on down below. That decision proved to be a mistake that would cost him and Amanda dearly.

The skipper of the RHIB had almost caught up to the stern of the mega-yacht when the captain reduced speed. The skipper could not react fast enough to the big yacht slowing down so abruptly. He pulled back on the throttles but his momentum caused the RHIB to crash into the stern of the yacht and bounce up on the swim platform. His crew was not prepared for the impact. One of them was thrown from the RHIB, up onto the swim platform of the yacht. His impact with the deck dislocated his shoulder and he writhed in pain as the skipper fought to regain control of the RHIB, which was now propped up on the stern of the enormous yacht.

He shouted at his two other crewmen to board the yacht while he fought to keep the RHIB from capsizing. As they jumped onto the fantail of the mega-yacht, he jockeyed his throttles to use the engines to pull the RHIB back off the swim platform.

Once they were safely aboard the yacht, the pirate crew made their way up to the main deck, where they stepped over Chris's lifeless body and entered the salon.

As they entered the salon, they saw the captain of the yacht come down the stairs from the bridge. As soon as he saw the pirates, he knew his worse fears had been realized. His ship was under attack. His only weapon, a twelve-gauge riot shotgun, was in a locker in his stateroom. He knew he would never get to it before the pirates got to him, so he did what he could do to save his crew. He turned and ran back to the bridge with the crew of the RHIB in hot pursuit. As he reached the helm, he toggled the ship's emergency distress locating system, pressed the key on the microphone of the satellite radio and said, "Mayday, mayday—" His call was cut short by a hail of automatic weapons fire that tore through his upper body and instantly silenced him, forever.

Amanda wondered what was going on back aft. She heard a popping sound and a loud bang but she was so far forward on the yacht's bow that she couldn't see what was happening on the stern. Then she felt the yacht slow down and walked back aft to see what was going on.

She looked up at the bridge and saw the captain return to the helm and start to talk to someone on the radio. Just then, the windows of the bridge shattered as a hail of bullets passed through the captain and exploded through the thick Plexiglas.

Amanda's mind could not accept what her eyes were seeing. She stood there, transfixed by the horror that confronted her. As she watched the captain crumple below the windows of the bridge, she saw two men with machine guns step up and look through the shattered glass. They saw her on the deck below and immediately turned away and left the bridge. She assumed they were coming for her. Then her thoughts turned to Chris, and she realized that he, most certainly, had been on the stern when the pirates came aboard. After seeing the fate of the captain, she realized the popping sound she heard earlier must have been associated with the death of her lover. She sobbed as she realized he must be dead too and then turned and ran forward to the bow of the yacht to try to hide. She bent down over the forward hatch and frantically tried to pry it open. It was dogged down tight and locked from the inside of the yacht. With that escape route denied to her, there was nowhere else for her to run. Amanda looked up and saw the two men with their weapons walk up the deck toward her. They split up and moved closer. They talked to each other in a language she could not understand. Then one of them spoke English and said, "We not hurt you, girl."

The chef on the *Mirrabooka* was fast asleep when the shooting started on the main deck. His stateroom, in the crew's quarters, was just below the entrance to the salon on the stern. In the fog of his sleep, he thought he heard a commotion above his head. The sound of glass breaking and the captain's voice on the yacht's intercom system jolted him awake. When he felt the yacht slow down and heard the RHIB hit the stern, he thought they might have run aground. But when he heard shouting, the sound of running feet and gunshots above his head, he realized they were under attack.

The captain taught them all to load and shoot a shotgun during their initial underway training. Most of them had laughed at the thought they would ever need to use it but the training was kind of fun, so they didn't complain too much. After their shooting lessons, the captain took them to his stateroom and showed them where the loaded weapon was stored so they would know where to find it, just in case.

Now that the chef was fully awake, he moved swiftly and quietly to the captain's stateroom, grabbed the shotgun, and gingerly worked his way up the ladder to the salon. He could hear someone talk in a foreign language but he wasn't sure how many attackers were on the yacht. From the noise he heard earlier, he assumed they had weapons. He knew he would have to surprise them, if he was going to have any chance against them.

As he reached the top of the ladder, he peered over the top rung and looked back aft. He could see the shattered salon doors and the broken glass on the floor. To his horror, he could also see Chris's lifeless body on the deck right outside the doors. He caught his breath and muttered a quiet curse to himself. "Bastards. Somebody is gonna pay for that."

He spotted one of the pirates on the deck outside the shattered doors. He cradled his left arm close to his chest and was obviously in pain. He had a gun but it hung uselessly from its shoulder strap as he tended to his arm. He had his back to the chef and seemed to be focused on something in the wake.

As he peeked over the top rung of the ladder at the pirate on the stern, he caught some movement out of the corner of his eye. It was another pirate. He could see him through the salon window on the port side of the yacht. He moved forward on the outer deck. He had the same kind of gun as the guy on the stern. It looked as if he was stalking someone but he couldn't see any farther forward. Now he knew there were at least two pirates on the yacht. He hoped they were the only ones. After seeing Chris, he knew they would kill him if they found him. Based on that evidence, he decided he would have to kill them to have any chance of surviving.

While the chef pondered his next move, Amanda was being stalked on the bow by the two armed pirates who approached her. After seeing what had happened to the captain, she knew that these men would have already killed her if they didn't want something from her. She shuddered to think what would happen to her if they got their hands on her. She assumed they intended to rape her and then kill her, so she decided she would rather kill herself than fall into their hands. She took one look at the pirates as they walked toward her, said a quick prayer, and then stepped up on the lifeline on the starboard side of the yacht and threw herself into the dark sea.

In her haste to escape her attackers, Amanda forgot she was wearing a salt-water activated inflatable life jacket. The captain of the *Mirrabooka* required all crewmembers to wear them when they were on deck in the open ocean at night. Even worse, her life jacket had a salt-water activated strobe light that flashed as soon as she entered the water. Although she was now a bobbing beacon for the pirates, there was some good news. Along with the salt-water strobe on her vest, the captain had issued every member of the crew a salt-water activated Personal Locator Beacon, also known as a PLB. Amanda's PLB began broadcasting when she hit the water, and the international search-and-rescue satellite locating system immediately picked up her signal. The world now knew, through her PLB, that Amanda Anderson was in distress in the Strait of Malacca.

The pirate skipper of the RHIB cursed when he saw Amanda throw herself off the side of the yacht. He was surprised to see her pop back up to the surface and laughed when he saw her strobe light flashing. He throttled up the RHIB to come alongside her and fished her out of the water. She tried to put up a fight with the skipper and his first mate but they forced her head down under the water until she grew weak and lost consciousness. When she stopped struggling, they dragged her into the boat and tied her securely to the floor. She choked and gagged as she cleared the seawater from her lungs.

While they tied her to the floor of the RHIB, the skipper ripped the strobe light from her vest and threw it into the ocean. He didn't see her PLB. It was still attached to her vest, silently transmitting its distress signal, a signal that had been received and was now being tracked and analyzed by the International COSPAS/SARSAT Mission Communications Center in Singapore.

Shortly after Amanda jumped over the side of the yacht, all hell broke loose on the *Mirrabooka*. The two pirates who had tried to capture her ran back to the stern and joined their injured comrade as they watched the skipper of the RHIB and his first mate struggle to fish the feisty blonde out of the water and wrestle her into their boat. The men on the stern were unaware that they were being watched closely by the chef as he crouched down in the ladder well of the salon.

While the pirates were focused on the action off the stern of the mega-yacht, the chef decided to make his move. He quietly climbed up the last rung of the ladder and made his way through the salon to where he could get a clean shot at the pirates on the stern. As he moved slowly through the salon, he held his breath and prayed they wouldn't turn around and see him. He could plainly see the three men and hear them speak in a foreign language. He knew there was no turning back now. Just as he raised his shotgun, one of the pirates turned around. He could see the surprised expression on his face and realized he must have made quite a sight. There he was, a somewhat overweight and balding middle-aged man with a riot shotgun in his hands, standing in the salon in his bare feet with only his boxer shorts and a T-shirt on. It was the last thing the pirates would ever see.

The man who saw the chef shouted a warning and raised his gun but he was too late. An enormous blast filled the yacht's salon with noise as the chef pulled his trigger. The buckshot from the chef's first salvo hit two of the three pirates. They were instantly pushed back and fell to the deck as their upper bodies absorbed the hits from the twelve-gauge shotgun. The third man tried to move toward the starboard side of the yacht and take cover but he didn't move fast enough for the chef. After his first shot, he quickly pumped a new round into the chamber and pulled the trigger again. This time, the buckshot struck the third attacker in the legs and knocked him off his feet. The chef pumped another round into the chamber, steadied the muzzle of the shotgun, and ended the third man's life as he tried to swing his machine gun to get a shot off at the chef.

He continued to move toward the pirates. As the adrenaline coursed through his veins, he barely felt the shards of glass from the shattered salon doors as they cut into his bare feet. He just kept moving and firing into the bodies of the pirates until they stopped moving. The gunfight was over in less than fifteen seconds. But the time it took to kill the three men seemed like an eternity to the chef. As he watched the pirates die, he felt like he was watching a slow motion movie. Soon he realized it was quiet. The only sound he heard was the metallic click-clack of the charging bar and trigger of the shotgun. He still tried to shoot the gun but he was out of ammo.

When he realized he had run out of ammo, he started to panic. He wondered whether there were other men on the yacht. If so, where were they? And where were Amanda and the captain?

As he panicked about his lack of ammo, it occurred to him that he could use the three dead pirate's weapons. He stepped over their lifeless bodies and retrieved their weapons.

As he checked the pirate's weapons, he heard the sound of a boat motor behind him. He crouched down and turned around to see a small motorboat headed away from the *Mirrabooka* at high speed. He assumed, correctly, that the pirates had used the speedboat to attack the yacht. As he peered over the cockpit coaming, he realized he shook uncontrollably. He prayed they weren't coming back. Then he sat down and cried.

The skipper of the RHIB watched his crewmen get ambushed while he and his first mate tied Amanda to the bottom of the RHIB. He couldn't believe all three of them had gone down without a shot. How stupid could they be?

As he watched the carnage on the fantail of the yacht, he decided he wanted no more of whatever the crew of the *Mirrabooka* had in store for him. He had lost three men. They were replaceable but he could not afford to risk losing more. He now knew the crew of the yacht was armed, so he decided to cut his losses. He had the girl and he had the money from their deliveries. He slammed the engine throttles forward and headed back to the mother ship.

Chapter Seven

Hope's new boat sped across the water at almost sixty knots. It was a bright, sunny day and she smiled as the wind whipped at the ball cap that kept her hair from becoming a tangled mess.

Her father had picked up her boat a few weeks ago but this was the first time she had been able to take it out. She was impressed with the boat's performance. At around eighty percent of full throttle, she was already going faster than her old boat at full speed. The ride of this new, deeper V-hull was also much easier on her body as the boat sliced through the light chop on the Eastern Bay.

Hope was heading to Manchester's Seafood Packing House on Tilghman Island to pick up a bushel of live crabs for her mom and dad's Memorial Day party. Captain "Tiny" Manchester and his wife, Eunice, owned the business. Hope's mother and father had known the Manchesters for as long as Hope could remember. Hope's father went to kindergarten with "Tiny," who got his nickname when he played football on the local high school team. At six foot six and two hundred-forty pounds, he was anything but tiny and the coaches loved to tease him; hence the nickname. When Tiny graduated from high school, the nickname stuck. All the locals knew him as Captain Tiny or just Tiny.

Hope's father and Tiny were lifelong friends. They played together, worked together and generally grew up together before Hope's father joined the Army and moved away. After Hope's mother and father moved back to the Eastern Shore, Tiny's wife, Eunice, and Hope's mother became good friends too. Eunice never had any daughters and Hope had filled that void for her. Hope always enjoyed going back to Tilghman Island to visit with Eunice and her family.

Hope felt the winds pick up a bit but she was completely comfortable at the helm of her powerful racing boat. As a child, Hope rode with her father in his boats. He had taught her how to drive hard and, until her modeling career took off, Hope had enjoyed giving the male drivers a run for their money on the local racing circuit.

She checked her gauges and saw that the boat performed flawlessly; she felt the adrenaline course through her veins. A lot of the go-fast crowd compared driving speedboats with the rush of having sex. Whenever she heard that comment, she immediately knew that the person talking must have a pretty crappy sex life. Driving her boat hard was fun and she always enjoyed getting out on the water, but driving a speedboat was nowhere near comparable to having great sex with an adventurous partner. That thought reminded her, for a moment, that it had been far too long since she'd made love to a man who really took her breath away.

Her trip to the Manchesters' place on Tilghman Island was quick and uneventful. She made it there from her parents' house in less than twenty minutes. *Pretty impressive for a twenty-mile run.* When she arrived at the island, she eased up on her throttles and expertly piloted her boat down the narrow channel. The Manchester's Seafood Packing House and adjoining pier were on the channel, near the island's iconic two-lane drawbridge. She could see the drawbridge as she maneuvered her boat for the approach to the Manchesters' pier. She waved to the drawbridge operator, who watched her approach from his station on the bridge. He was a local guy. She didn't know his name but she had seen him before on her visits to the Manchesters'. He returned her wave by doffing his cap and smiling at her.

In addition to owning the packing house, Tiny Manchester was also one of the best hunting guides on the Eastern Shore. When Hope's father brought a party down to the island to go out hunting with Tiny, Hope would come along and visit with Miss Eunice.

Eunice loved to take care of Hope while the men were out in the fields. She taught the little girl how to cook and how to shoot. Hope was an excellent student and quickly became an excellent cook and an outstanding shot. Once she learned how to shoot, the men took her along on their duck hunting trips. She loved being out on the bay in the winter but she also loved being with Eunice, so she convinced the men to bring them both along. She and Eunice could out-shoot and out-cook most of the men in the hunting parties. Tiny and Hope's father made some extra money by making side bets with their clients on the ladies' shooting skills. They rarely lost their wagers.

Hope pulled up to the pier, threw one of Eunice's sons her lines, and shut down her motors. She looked up to see Eunice scurry down the dock to welcome her with a big bear hug and a smile. She was a big woman but she could move pretty fast when she wanted to.

Eunice said, "We heard you and those big motors coming down the channel, baby. I told Sonny that I knew it was you! We haven't seen you in ages, child! Where on earth have you been?"

Hope said, "It's good to see you, too, Miss Eunice. You're right. It's been too long!"

Miss Eunice hugged her again, and then stepped back and held her at arm's length. "Just look at you! I see you're still just as pretty as a new penny! When are you going to give up running around in that speedboat and find yourself a good man to settle down with?"

Hope could hardly get a word in but she smiled and hugged Eunice while being barraged by her questions. Hope always felt comfortable and at home with Eunice. Eunice was a wonderful person and had more personality, integrity, and common sense than many of the "successful" women Hope knew in Washington.

Life was hard on Tilghman Island but the people there were friendly and family-oriented. Once you earned their trust, you had a friend for life. Hope spent about an hour talking with Eunice as her boys offloaded crabs from the incoming watermen's boats. She asked Hope about her mother and father and they talked about

Hope's job working with her father at their construction company in Washington. When it was time to go, Hope gave Eunice a big hug and a soft kiss on the cheek. "It was wonderful to see you again, Miss Eunice. I promise I will be back to see you before the end of the summer!"

Just like a doting grandmother, Eunice held Hope's hands in hers for a moment and looked her in the eyes. "Baby, you know you are just like one of my own. You always will be. Please come back and see us soon. Tiny is going to be so sorry he missed you. You know we just love you to bits and you are always welcome here, sweetie."

After one more bear hug from Eunice, Hope stepped into her boat, cranked up her motors and turned her boat back up the channel to head back home.

Eunice's boys had stowed the bushel basket of crabs securely in a cooler in the stern of Hope's boat. They surrounded the basket with a very thin layer of ice to help keep them cool during Hope's ride back home. As Hope approached the entrance to the bay, she checked on the security of her cooler one last time and then pressed the throttles forward to get up on plane and head home. The giant Mercruiser engines roared to life and she rocketed up the Chesapeake Bay toward Eastern Bay. She looked down at the electronic chart plotter, checked her speed, and figured she would be home in about eighteen minutes.

About five minutes into her ride, as she was entering Eastern Bay, Hope decided to firewall the throttles to see how much speed she could wring out of her new boat. As she pushed the throttles forward, the boat surged forward on the water. The rapid acceleration pressed her back in her seat. She caught her breath and trimmed the bow back down with the hydraulic trim tabs as she watched her speed creep up past seventy-five knots, almost ninety miles per hour. She grinned as the boat screamed across the water, trailing a giant rooster-tail behind it.

Just as she was getting ready to throttle back, she heard a loud

bang from the engine compartment. She immediately reduced her speed and checked her gauges. At first, everything looked fine. But then she saw the starboard engine temperature start to creep up. She suspected the seawater pump that cooled the motor might have failed. She pulled the throttles back to idle and shifted into neutral to bring the boat to a complete stop. She shut down the starboard engine and grabbed a flashlight. Then she flipped a switch to hydraulically raise the engine compartment cover and headed back aft to see what was going on.

As the cover came up, she turned on the flashlight, and peered into the engine compartment. She noted that the serpentine belt that drove the seawater pump had jumped off its pulley. As she continued her inspection of the engine compartment, she uttered a curse. She saw that when the belt slipped off the pulley, it had somehow wrapped around the hydraulic lines that led to her power steering. When it wrapped around the hydraulic lines, it sheared through them like a hot knife through butter. With the help of her flashlight, she could see the red hydraulic fluid hemorrhaging from the hydraulic lines and dripping into her bilge. She knew this was a mortal wound for her steering system. Even if she could repair the lines, she wouldn't have any hydraulic fluid left to refill the reservoirs. She was stuck with one operable motor, no steering, and a bushel of live crabs that she needed to get out of the sun and into a live box. She wasn't happy that she was stuck, but at least she was close to home. She knew she could call her father on the cell phone and get him to come out and tow her home.

As she peered back down into the engine compartment, she heard another boat slowing down nearby. "Great," she said to herself. "Now I'm going to have to deal with some creeper who is gonna want to tow me in."

She turned to look at the fishing boat that approached her. She had already decided that she would wave this guy off and just call her father to ask him to come out and tow her back.

As the fishing boat's engines throttled back, she started to tell the approaching captain that her father was on his way. She knew it was a little white lie, but she really didn't want to be bothered by some well-intentioned Good Samaritan. However, her plan quickly changed when she saw the man at the helm of the fishing boat. He was a freaking hunk!

As the fishing boat slowed, the captain stepped away from the helm. "Good morning, ma'am. Can I help you?"

He was tall and muscular, with a nice tan and a friendly smile. He wore a dark visor and a pair of Ray-Ban sunglasses but she could see a full head of sun-bleached hair poke out of the top of his hat.

Much to Hope's delight, he wasn't wearing a shirt and she couldn't help but check out his tight abs and broad shoulders. He was fit but not muscle-bound. His pecs were nicely sculpted, not like some pumped-up gym rat but full and powerful looking, and not too hairy.

She felt a familiar tingling in her core that she hadn't felt for a very long time, too long in fact. *God, Hope, you need to get a hold of yourself. You don't even know this guy and you're going weak in the knees!*

Chapter Eight

As Mac headed back home from fishing, he spotted a go-fast boat off his starboard bow at the entrance of Eastern Bay. This go-fast was going nowhere fast. It was dead in the water with the engine cover raised up on its hydraulic rams.

Mac knew with the wind picking up, before too long, the skipper of the go-fast was going to be in for a rough ride. Without the engines to provide power and steering, the speedboat would get tossed around by the wind-driven waves. It would be a miserable ride for the boat's skipper and his crew. He saw someone working on the engine and, seeing no other boats around, decided to slow down to see whether he could help the skipper with his problem.

He pulled back on the throttles of his boat and began his approach to the drifting speedboat. It looked as if the skipper was the only one onboard. He saw his head lift up from looking down in the engine compartment. Mac caught his breath when he realized this skipper was no balding, heavyset, middle-aged man. This skipper was a woman. And, from what he could see, she was drop-dead gorgeous!

As he maneuvered closer to her boat, he saw she had a flashlight in one hand and what appeared to be the remains of a drive belt in the other. He surveyed her well-placed curves and admired her long, tan legs. She wore a Baltimore Orioles ball cap and it looked like she had a bikini on underneath her T-shirt. Mac was pleased to see that her sheer T-shirt didn't do much to hide the polka-dots on her bikini, or her figure. *This should be interesting.* He smiled as his boat slid up next to hers. "Good morning, ma'am. Can I help you?"

The go-fast boat's skipper put her hands on her hips. "Good

morning. I'm afraid I'm in a bit of a pickle. The serpentine belt on one of my motors slipped and, somehow, when it came off its pulley, it snagged the hydraulic lines on my power steering."

Mac chuckled. "A bit of a pickle, eh? I haven't heard that expression for a long time. Although, I guess I shouldn't be surprised to hear it coming from someone wearing an Orioles baseball cap!"

He was teasing her. Hope knew it. She liked it. She could tell he was looking her over as his boat nudged up against her speedboat. She took another look at his bare chest and felt a hot flash of color rush to her face. She hoped he couldn't see her blush.

Hope consciously took the bait. "Well, it seems to fit my current situation. As you may have noticed, I'm kind of stuck here."

Mac laughed. "I can see that."

He stopped for a moment as he surveyed her and her boat.

"I'm just giving you a hard time. Actually, I think you've summed up your situation pretty well. I have some tools and hydraulic fluid onboard my boat but nothing that can fix a hydraulic line."

While they talked, Moses decided to introduce himself to the go-fast skipper. As the two boats sat side by side, he jumped from Mac's boat to Hope's.

Hope laughed. As she petted the big dog, she said, "Well hello there, big boy! Are you tired of being ignored?"

Moses wagged his tail. Hope knelt down and gently held the big dog's head in her hands. She looked into his big brown eyes. "What's your name?"

Before Mac could answer, Moses thrust his head forward and licked her on the face. Hope and Mac both laughed as the big black dog wagged his tail.

Mac said, "Jesus, Moses! Would you mind your manners, just for once?" Then, as he tried to keep the boats from banging into each other, he said, "I'm really sorry about that! That's my dog Moses. He fancies himself as quite the ladies' man!"

Hope smiled and, as she scratched behind the big dog's ears, said, "Yes, I see that!"

Mac could tell this woman liked dogs, and Moses, who was a pretty good judge of people, seemed to like her too.

Mac said, "Now that Moses has introduced himself to you, I suppose I should do the same. My name's Mac. Mac Callaghan."

Hope smiled. "Well, it's a pleasure to meet you and your dog, Mr. Callaghan. My name is Hope, Hope Crosby."

Mac nodded. "That's a pretty name. Where are you headed, Miss Crosby?"

"Thanks. Unfortunately, as you can see, I'm not heading anywhere fast. I just picked up a bushel of crabs from some friends and was headed back to my parents' place on Tilghman Creek when this damn belt broke loose."

As Hope talked, she watched Mac move to the starboard side of his boat. He bent over, opened a locker in his cockpit, and uncoiled a couple of lines. As he leaned over and worked with his lines, Hope took an opportunity to check out his ass. She noted that he had strong legs with toned calf muscles. He moved easily around the cockpit of his boat and she caught herself wondering what he would look like without his khaki shorts on.

He turned around suddenly and caught her staring. He lowered his sunglasses and, with a handsome grin, winked at her. "Well now, we can't let those crabs go to waste, can we?"

Hope found herself blushing again. She couldn't believe he'd busted her while she checked him out. She grinned. "Why, no. Certainly not! What do you recommend we do about that, Captain?"

Mac tied a loop at one end of one of the lines he held in his hands. He tossed the line in the cockpit of Hope's speedboat. "Tilghman Creek isn't too far from here. As a matter of fact, it's right on my way home. I just moved into a place that's not too far from there. I would be happy to give you a tow back to your parents' place, if that would be okay with you?"

Hope looked down at the rope at her feet. *Baby, you could tow me all the way to Baltimore and it would be just fine with me.* As she bent down to pick up the rope Mac had tossed to her, she said, "Thank you, Mac. That would be very nice of you, if it's not too much trouble?"

Mac said, "No trouble at all. If you would be so kind as to slip the loop on that line I gave to you around the bollard on your bow, I will set up a harness to tow you home."

Hope climbed up on the bow of her boat to tie off the line while Mac set up the towing bridle on the stern of his boat. He moved back to the helm and maneuvered the stern around to attach the bridle. She watched him jockey the shiny silver control levers to shift the transmissions and open the throttles as he swung his stern around to get into a position to tow her. She could tell he was an accomplished skipper by the way he maneuvered his boat. He used the power of the big diesel engines to set himself up and then let the wind help him fine-tune his approach to her bow. He never once touched the helm. All he needed was the wind and the thrust from his props. Hope was intrigued with this tall, dark, and very handsome fellow.

Mac stopped his boat within a foot of her bow. As he walked back to the stern of his boat, Hope passed him the bitter end of the tow rope and he made it fast to the towing harness. As he cinched the harness tight, he turned to Hope and offered her his hand. "Would you like to ride back with us?"

Hope smiled, took his hand, and stepped onto Mac's boat. As she grasped his hand, she felt a warm shiver go through her. His grip was firm and reassuring. She reached out to steady herself with her free hand and touched his shoulder. As she expected, he was solid as a rock.

She looked down at him as she stepped down from the transom to the cockpit of his boat. "It's been a long time since I've been in the company of a real gentleman. Thank you for your help."

Mac smiled. "It's really no problem. I'm glad to help."

He motioned to the large upholstered seat next to the helm. "If you like, you can sit right up there."

He added, "But you're gonna have to move fast. Moses thinks that's his seat."

Sure enough, as Mac helped Hope step aboard, Moses jumped back in the boat and immediately returned to his customary position in the seat next to the helm.

They both laughed at the big black dog.

Hope said, "Oh my. It looks like Moses must have heard you!"

Mac said, "That's okay. You can sit right here in the helm seat next to me. There's plenty of room for two people in that seat. It will be easier for us to talk there anyway."

He helped her into the helm seat. *When we get back home, I'll have to thank you for taking that other seat, Moses.*

As they started the slow tow back to Hope's parents' house, he sat down on the helm seat beside her. He was curious to learn more about this woman and this was a perfect way to get to do it.

As he finessed the throttles to get the right speed for the tow, he looked over at Hope. "Do you live with your folks?"

Hope laughed. "No, thank God. No way! I adore my mom and dad but I don't think I could live with them again. I live in Georgetown. I'm just down here for the weekend. How about you? Where do you live?"

Mac said, "That's a great question. Up until now, I've lived in New York City most of the time. That's where I work. But I'm moving into a farm down here that I have been renovating for the past year or so. I'm hoping that I can live here and commute to New York during the week."

Hope said, "That sounds like a good plan, but don't you think that's an awfully long drive?"

Mac laughed. "Yep. It's a very long drive. I'm pretty lucky, though. I have a plane I can fly from Easton to La Guardia. It's only a thirty-minute flight for me. I just keep a vehicle at both airports and use the plane for the commute."

Hope immediately realized how dumb her question must have sounded to Mac. "Oh. Gosh, I'm sorry. That was a stupid question. I should have realized that no one in their right mind would try to make that commute by car! It sounds like you have a great set-up. It must be a lot of fun to fly into New York."

With his own plane and a place in New York City, she figured Mac must be a lawyer or some kind of financial industry guy. "What do you do for a living, if you don't mind me asking?"

It was a question Mac always dreaded. He had a good cover story but every time he answered this question, it reminded him of why he had never been able to settle down with anyone.

"I'm an investor," Mac said. "I'm a partner in a firm with another guy in New York. We invest in start-up companies."

Hope said, "Interesting. That's a pretty risky business, isn't it?" *He kind of hesitated to answer that question about his job. He must not like to talk about work. I wonder why?*

Mac could tell she understood the venture capital business. He said, "Yes. It can be. My partner and I have been pretty lucky, though. We have a good team of folks who work with us, and we do a lot of analysis before we do any deals."

Hope said, "No doubt. When I was younger, my dad taught me that you kind of make your own luck in business. Over the years, I've realized just how right he was!"

Mac laughed. "I think your father is dead on. We've made some mistakes along the way but, in the long run, we've done pretty well. What do you do?" He winked. "If you don't mind me asking?"

Hope laughed. "Okay, smarty-pants. I probably deserved that. I work with my dad in the construction business. We own a construction company up in DC."

Mac was surprised by her answer. When she said she lived in Georgetown, he had pegged her as a lobbyist or a lawyer. Construction was the last thing he expected to hear.

"Construction, eh? Well, I'll be damned."

Hope looked at him and, with a raised eyebrow, said, "And why does that surprise you?"

Mac immediately felt defensive. He guessed he must have hit a nerve. "Oh, no offense, Hope. When you said you lived in Georgetown, I just thought you might be a lawyer or a lobbyist or something."

Hope laughed. "It's okay. I understand. There are a lot of people who think only men can successfully run construction companies. I kind of like it when I surprise them."

Mac laughed. "No doubt! I bet you do."

Mac didn't mean to stereotype her. The words just kind of came out by accident. But he had to admit that he liked the way she gently pushed back.

Hope studied his hands as he worked the throttles to adjust his towing speed. His fingers were long and tan. She noticed that there was no wedding ring.

Hope said, "What were you and your buddy Moses doing out here this morning?"

"Fishing," Mac said.

"Did you catch anything?"

Mac smiled. "Yep. We were lucky enough to catch a couple of nice rockfish. I only kept one, though. That's all I need for dinner tonight." He gestured toward the stern of his boat. "It's in the icebox back there."

Now it was Hope's turn to smile. She guessed that he was probably a pretty good fisherman. She also liked the fact that he only kept what he needed.

She said, "Lucky, eh?"

She made a fist and gently punched his bicep.

"I thought we just decided that you make your own luck, didn't we? I'll bet you come out here all the time."

Mac laughed and shrugged. "Good point. I guess we did just kind of agree to that, didn't we? Actually, I haven't been out here fishing since I was a kid. This is the first time I've been out since I bought my new place over here. My parents lived here when I was younger and I was out here all the time but, when my dad died, my mom moved back to Baltimore."

Hope said, "I'm sorry about your dad."

Mac nodded. "Thanks. I appreciate that."

She wondered why he didn't say more about his mother and father but she decided to leave that line of questioning alone, for now.

Hope said, "I love rockfish—especially when they're broiled, with just a little crabmeat sprinkled on top."

Mac shrugged. "I haven't thought about the crab. That sounds pretty good. I like them broiled too. There's nothing better than fresh broiled rockfish with a little white wine, lemon, and Old Bay seasoning. I'll have to try your suggestion about the crabmeat sometime, though."

Hope smiled. "Trust me. I know. It's the best. The crabmeat really complements the fish."

She pointed her thumb in the direction of her boat. "If you want, I'll give you a couple of the crabs from my cooler when we get back to my parents' place and you can try it when you get home."

Mac nodded. "That sounds good. I may just take you up on that." He hesitated for a moment. "Why did you go all the way over to Tilghman Island to get your crabs?"

Hope smiled. "Because they're the best, of course! It's really not a long ride in my boat, and I love getting out on the water. I've been doing it for years now. There's a family over there who own a seafood distributor who are good friends of ours. I go over there every chance I get."

Mac watched her as she eased herself back in his helm seat and propped her legs up on his chart table. She looked perfectly at home. She was a freaking knockout. He also noticed that she didn't wear any rings. No wedding band. No engagement ring. Nothing. He wondered why she wasn't married. *Maybe she just didn't wear any rings today?* He admitted to himself that it didn't disappoint him to think that she might not be encumbered by another man.

He eased the boat into Tilghman Creek. Hope pointed to a huge house on the far shore. "That's my parents' house."

Mac had to catch himself before he laughed. What Hope pointed to was no house. It was a freaking castle! He had seen the home from the water and wondered who lived there. Now he knew.

The house was a magnificent brick structure with a slate roof. Mac guessed it must have been at least a twenty-five thousand square foot home. It was tucked away on the creek, as if it had always been there. It looked perfectly in place with the renovated crab shacks and other homes that lined the banks of the peaceful creek.

There was an empty boat lift at the dock where Hope's boat looked like it belonged and a boathouse that protected a Hinckley Talaria 55 swinging gently at its moorings. The Talaria was the flagship of the Hinckley line, with a price tag of well over $2 million dollars. From the looks of things at Hope's parents' place, it was pretty clear to Mac that business was good for Hope and her dad.

At the end of the dock was a very tall, deeply tanned man, with his arms crossed over his chest. Mac could see he had a full beard and a bright white ponytail poked out from under his hat.

Hope slid out of the helm seat, moved over to the port side of Mac's boat and waved at the man on the dock. She said, "That's my dad!"

Mac said, "I would have never guessed!"

She quickly turned to him, and cocked her head as she smiled. "Are you making fun of me, Mac Callaghan?"

He smiled and deadpanned, "No, Hope. I would never dream of doing such a thing. I just hope he's not mad at me for bringing you back. He looks like he could be a tough customer!"

Hope smiled. "Don't worry. He's really a big teddy bear. He'll be just fine."

As Mac maneuvered his boat, and the speedboat under tow, toward the dock, Hope's father waved. "Good afternoon there, Captain. Thanks for bringing my wayward daughter back to me."

Mac liked the guy already. Obviously, he had a good sense of humor.

Hope's dad looked at his daughter. "What happened, Hope?"

Hope stepped up on the dock and gave her father a big hug. "My boat broke down, Dad. Serpentine belt slipped on the starboard engine and tore up my hydraulic steering."

She turned and gestured toward Mac and Moses. "This gentleman, and his friend Moses, came along and rescued me."

By now, Mac had nudged Hope's boat up against the pier. He untied the towing bridle as Hope's father made it fast to the dock. Once the boat was tied up, her father stepped onto his daughter's boat and offered Mac his hand. "Thanks so much for helping her out. I was wondering where she was but I see she was in very capable hands."

Mac appreciated the compliment and noted her father's very firm handshake and warm smile. Her dad was an older guy, but he was still pretty damn strong! He seemed like a good guy to Mac. It struck him as odd that he seemed so at ease with her father. Mac didn't realize that this man had been an Army Special Forces operator. The two men shared a common bond; they just didn't know it, yet.

Mac knew it was time to go. He also knew he wanted to see Hope again but he didn't have a clue how to approach her about getting together with her while her dad stood there.

After he shook her father's hand, he turned back to Hope. "Well, Hope, it was a pleasure to meet you. I hope I will see you down here again some other time."

Hope wanted to see Mac again too. And she was frustrated that he was going to get away without knowing how to contact him. She realized that it was Mac who was now in a pickle as her father stood on the boat between the two of them.

She decided there was no way she was going to let this guy get away without giving him an opportunity to see her again.

She smiled back at Mac. "It was a pleasure to meet you too, Mac."

She moved to the back of her boat and culled a couple of crabs out of her cooler and put them in a bucket for him. As she passed him the bucket of crabs, she said, "Put these in the cooler with your fish. If you steam them and sprinkle the crabmeat over your rockfish, I promise you won't be disappointed."

Mac smiled as he took the bucket from her hand. He felt her hand linger on his forearm for a moment. "Thanks, Hope. I'll do that."

Hope grinned. "By the way, I'll be visiting with some friends at Shaunessy's tonight. Come on by if you're around?"

Mac breathed a sigh of relief. Shaunessy's was a little local bar and restaurant that was pretty close to his new place. He had been there a couple of times before and had made friends with the bartender and a couple of other guys there. He nodded. "That sounds like fun. I like that place. I will look forward to seeing you tonight."

And with that, he stepped aboard his boat, spun it around and pointed it back down the creek. He waved goodbye to Hope and her father, and headed back home with Moses.

It had been a long while since he had given much thought to dating anyone but something about this woman was different. *Who knows? Maybe this one's different than all the other ones?* Then he laughed at himself. Probably not, he figured. Up to this point in his life, he had decided that most women were wired pretty much the same. It always started out great, but in time, for one reason or another, his luck with them always seemed to run out. He had to admit that he was kind of tired of the baggage associated with good relationships gone bad but thought it might be fun to head over to Shaunessy's, just to spend some time with some new folks, and Hope too, of course. He chuckled and looked over at Moses. "What do you think, buddy boy?"

Moses just looked at him and gave him a big old Lab grin. Mac shook his head. "Yeah. A lot of help you are. You've already scored the first kiss!"

Chapter Nine

Amanda Anderson was terrified and in shock. Moments ago, she felt safe and secure on the bow of the *Mirrabooka*. Now, after nearly being drowned by her captors, she found herself tied face down to the bottom of a RHIB that violently bounced across the surface of the water at high speed.

When she leapt over the side of the *Mirrabooka*, she thought she would drown in the dark waters of the Strait of Malacca. As she scrambled to evade the armed men on the foredeck of the yacht, she had forgotten about her inflatable life vest. Unfortunately for her, it worked as advertised when she threw herself off the starboard side of the yacht. Along with her vest inflating automatically when she hit the water, the strobe light attached to it also flashed. It made her an easy target for the pirates. She tried to fight them off as they pulled her out of the water but they held her head under water until she passed out.

She thought for sure she had drowned until she woke up, choking and gagging, on the floor of the RHIB. A rope had been wrapped around her upper body and her legs, and effectively immobilized her. Another rope had been used to tie her down to the floor of the boat. She was wedged between a bunch of boxes that looked like suitcases. She had no idea who else was on the boat, where they were, or where they were taking her. All she knew for sure was that she was in serious trouble. After she had watched the captain of the *Mirrabooka* murdered before her eyes, she had no doubt that something far more sinister awaited her. She shuddered to think about what might happen to her. Then she realized she would probably never see Chris or her family again, and she wept. As the tears ran down her cheeks, she vowed she would find a way to survive this mess and then she prayed.

While Amanda contemplated her fate, the pirate skipper of the RHIB and his first mate were confronting a serious problem. The raid on the big yacht had gone horribly wrong for them. Their attempt to plunder the *Mirrabooka* was a spectacular failure. They lost three men and left at least one witness alive on the bullet-riddled yacht. They had captured the woman who was on the bow of the yacht but now they were worried about her being more of a liability than an asset. They talked about killing her and throwing her over the side but realized doing that would leave them with nothing to make up for their other losses when they returned back to the mother ship. The wet blonde tied to the floor of the RHIB might be the only thing that would save their lives when their bosses found out about their botched attempt to attack the *Mirrabooka*.

The skipper of the RHIB reluctantly pulled the satellite cell phone out of his pocket and prepared to call the captain of the mother ship. He didn't want to make the call but he needed to get the ship's current position to allow him and the first mate to find it in the pitch black darkness. He punched the numbers into the cell phone and made the call.

The captain of the mother ship answered. "How did it go?"

The skipper of the RHIB responded, "Not well."

"What does that mean?" the captain said.

The skipper hesitated. He knew his life and the life of the first mate depended on his answer.

"Our boarding party was ambushed by someone who came up from below decks. We lost three men but we got the woman."

There was silence on the other end of the phone. The skipper felt sick to his stomach as he realized his life was now at risk.

"Anyone left alive on the yacht?" the captain asked.

"Yes. At least one person. They ambushed our guys while we were pulling the girl out of the water."

The captain muttered a curse over the phone. "That's not going to be well received by our leadership. Is the woman in good condition?"

The skipper said, "Yes. She tried to get away from us by jumping overboard but we picked her up and tied her up. I think she will bring a good price."

"We'll see about that. Madame Tsao has pretty high standards— no marks, no bruises, no tattoos, no drugs. Will she pass that test?"

"She looks pretty clean. You can check her out when we get back."

"Okay. I'll do that. Do you have the money?"

"Yes sir."

The captain gave the skipper of the RHIB the coordinates, along with the course and speed of the mother ship, and then abruptly hung up on the skipper.

As the phone went dead, the skipper of the RHIB looked down at the woman at the bottom of the boat. He knew there was a market in Thailand for young, white women. If she was a virgin, her price could be astounding. Even if she wasn't a virgin, she could still fetch a hefty sum in the surrogate parent market or the prostitution market, as long as she was in good condition at the time of sale. At this point, he figured she was his only hope of getting out of this mess alive.

He keyed the coordinates to the mother ship into his GPS and set a course to intercept the it. At his current course and speed, it was only about ten minutes away.

The skipper and the first mate made the rest of the trip in silence. They picked up the shadowy outline of the mother ship when they were about a hundred yards away from her. The ship looked like it was moving at full speed. They guessed the captain was already working to put some distance between his ship and the *Mirrabooka*.

The skipper maneuvered the RHIB alongside the mother ship. He set his speed to match it and prepared to be hoisted back up onto the deck of the mother ship. The deck crew passed the hoisting sling to the first mate on the RHIB. Once the first mate attached the sling to the hard-points on the RHIB, he signaled the deck crew to hoist the RHIB up on deck.

When the RHIB was clear of the water, the skipper shut down the engines and moved forward to examine the woman on the floor of the RHIB. He untied the ropes that held her down to the deck and rolled her over.

He could see her eyes were open but she didn't make a sound. He thought for a moment how nice it would have been to take her for himself. He had never had a white woman. That thought quickly was overcome by the realization that she might be the only thing keeping him alive right now, so he went back to the task of getting her out of the RHIB.

The woman's life jacket was still inflated. It made it awkward for him to move her so he decided to remove it. He pulled his knife from the scabbard on his belt to cut it off.

As he pulled the knife out, the woman gasped. "Oh God, please. Please don't."

The skipper only knew a little English but he knew enough to recognize the words *God* and *please*. He guessed the woman thought he was going to kill her. He shook his head and held his finger to his lips. "No."

She obeyed his command and he continued to cut the life jacket off her. As the life jacket fell to the floor of the RHIB, a dim light caught his eye. He reached down and picked up the life jacket, turned it over, and saw the light glowing on the PLB.

It was lucky for Amanda Anderson that the skipper of the RHIB had never seen a PLB before. He thought it was some kind of a radio for communications on the *Mirrabooka*. She was tied up, so he knew she hadn't made any calls on it. So, without giving it a second thought, he crushed the radio under his boot, punctured the air bladders in the life jacket with his knife, and threw the whole assembly overboard.

Amanda saw the PLB too. During the attack on the *Mirrabooka* and her subsequent kidnapping, she had forgotten all about it. Unlike the skipper of the RHIB, she knew exactly what it was and what it did. More importantly, she now knew that she was not alone. Even though her direct link to the rest of the world had just been severed, she knew that her parents and their friends now knew she was in trouble. Hopefully, now that they knew her general location, they would be able to send someone to help her. She knew her mother and father would not rest until she was found, and she took great comfort in knowing that she was no longer alone. Amanda had begun to lose hope that she would ever be heard from again. That hope was restored when she saw the steady glow of the LED on her PLB.

The skipper and the first mate picked Amanda up and passed her to the deck crew on the mother ship. It was dark but when the crew saw Amanda, they shouted and hooted at their perceived good fortune. She did not understand what they said but she quickly felt their callused hands paw at her body as they transferred her to the deck. Most of them had never touched a white woman and they took every liberty with their hands to explore her body as they moved her. She felt their hands grope her and tried to go numb to it. She was glad her clothes and the ropes around her arms and legs kept them from reaching the prizes they all seemed to be after. Even so, the transfer from the RHIB to the deck was a shocking and degrading experience. She quickly realized what happened to her body now was no longer under her control, so she closed her eyes and muttered a silent prayer while the rough hands had their way with her.

She was startled by a loud shout and the crew's hands immediately stopped their rude inspection of her body. The men laid her down on the deck and everything grew quiet. She cautiously opened her eyes and was instantly blinded by a brilliant white light. Someone was standing over her with a flashlight. She assumed it was a man, but she couldn't tell for sure. She could hear a man's voice as the light played along her body. The light returned to her face. It hurt her eyes and she closed them for a moment. She heard another man's voice beside her and suddenly her head was lifted up and a blindfold was roughly tied around her face. Then she heard more voices and felt herself being picked up and carried again. She shuddered as she felt the hands take every liberty possible with her body again. She tried to squirm around to avoid the groping hands but the ropes made it impossible to protect herself.

She didn't know where they carried her but she felt herself being lowered down a series of stairs. She heard what sounded like a heavy metal door being opened and then, just as suddenly as she was picked up, she was laid back down on the steel deck. The groping hands were no longer all over her and she was left lying on her left side. She had no idea where she was but she heard the voices and the footsteps fade away. She heard the door close and what sounded like a key turning a lock. She was obviously somewhere below deck on the boat but she had no idea where. It was incredibly hot wherever she was and there was an overpowering smell of rotting fish, sewage, and diesel oil. She could hear an engine running somewhere underneath her and feel the vibrations of it through the deck under her side. She was still tied up and soaking wet but, for now, the hands were gone. She was scared to death but she now knew that she was not alone. Seeing the PLB had given her new hope and an even stronger will to survive. She closed her eyes, started praying again, and gathered her strength.

Chapter Ten

Mac wheeled his Toyota FJ40 into the parking lot at Shaunessy's bar. The jeep-like vehicle was one of the first things he bought after he purchased his farm. It was an old, rusted pile of junk when he bought it, but he had a friend at the Agency who specialized in restoring FJs. His buddy had done a terrific job. He had stripped the body off the frame and performed a total restoration. Everything in the FJ was now new, or completely restored. In addition to the new paint, lights, instruments, interior, and thirty-five-inch tires, Mac's buddy had completely rebuilt the suspension and drivetrain. The modifications to the drivetrain were needed because his friend had yanked the old motor out of the FJ and replaced it with a small-block Chevy V-8. The FJ not only looked good but it had a tremendous amount of excess horsepower. Every time Mac hit the starter, he got a rush of adrenaline as he listened to the big motor come to life.

It was a beautiful night and he had taken the soft top and doors off the FJ for the ride down to Shaunessy's. He loved driving down the country roads on a warm night with the top off. Moses was in his usual spot on the passenger seat. He loved to ride in the FJ too.

He turned in to the gravel parking lot of the bar and rumbled to a stop in a parking place near the front door. When Mac shut the motor off, Moses jumped out of his seat and proceeded to his newfound favorite place on the front porch of the bar. Although Mac had only been to Shaunessy's a couple of times, Moses had already established himself as the little bar's front porch dog. While Mac was in the bar, Moses would sit out on the front porch and greet the patrons.

Mac was pretty sure Moses's strategy allowed him to meet more girls than he did at the bar. The girls always stopped to fuss over him on their way into the bar and Moses loved all the attention.

Before Mac made it through the front door, a small posse of Moses's fans, mostly women, had come over to visit with his dog. As they patted his head and scratched his belly, Moses looked over at Mac as if to say, *Good luck in there, partner. I'll just stay here for a while!*

Mac winked at his four-legged buddy. "Be a good boy, Moses. Stay." He knew Moses heard him but he also knew the command was completely unnecessary.

As Mac entered the bar, "Red" Shaunessy greeted him. Red was the fourth-generation proprietor of the bar. He came from a long line of red-headed Irishmen who had owned the bar for the past eighty years. He was about six feet, four inches tall and weighed about two hundred-fifty pounds. At that size, he was a natural bouncer but he rarely had to use his muscle on any of his customers. A gentle nudge and a few well-placed words from Red were usually enough to convince even the most boisterous customer that crossing him would prove to be a very bad choice. Most of the folks who frequented Shaunessy's were locals. They liked their bar and they liked Red, so usually everyone got along just fine. When they did choose to challenge Red, they usually found themselves launched from the front porch of the bar with an invitation to come back, "after you sober up and get your shit together." And, after they sobered up and got their shit together, they were warmly welcomed back to the bar by Red with not a word spoken about their previous ejection from the local watering hole.

As Mac approached the bar, Red gave him a big smile and a wink. "Hey there, Mac! I heard you were moving in this weekend. Did you bring your buddy Moses with you tonight?"

Mac nodded. *News always travels fast around a small town. I haven't even got my boxes unpacked yet but the locals already know I'm here.*

He said, "Sure did, Red. He's out there with all his girlfriends. Hell, he does better with the women around here than I'll ever do!"

They both laughed. Red pulled a draft beer for Mac. "You here to play pool tonight?"

Mac looked around for Hope. He didn't see her so he paid for his beer, along with a generous tip for Red. "Actually, I was planning to meet someone down here, but it doesn't look like they're here yet. Go ahead and give me some change, please. I'll give one of the tables a try while I wait."

As Mac turned to survey the pool table, he passed Red a dollar, which was quickly exchanged for quarters for the pool table. Red passed the quarters back to Mac. "Good luck, my friend." He winked at Mac. "Try not to take all the other customer's money, okay?"

For fifty cents, Mac could usually spend the entire night on a table. The last time he visited Shaunessy's, he played all night and Red gave him a hard time about being a ringer. He loved to play pool and he could easily see how Shaunessy's could become one of his favorite weekend haunts after he got moved in.

Mac headed over to one of the two pool tables that had games going on and put his two quarters up on the rail of the first table. The two guys playing on that table were local guys. One was a lineman for the local power cooperative and the other was a carpenter. Mac met them the last time he visited the bar. They were both good guys and good pool players.

Joe, the lineman, smiled when he saw Mac. "Uh oh, look out, Nick. Mac's coming over here to take all your money again!" Mac laughed and shook hands with both men. Then he pulled up an empty barstool, sat down, and waited for his turn. While Joe and Nick played, the men caught Mac up on all the latest goings-on around town. They talked about where the best fishing holes were and continued the ever-persistent conversation about why the Baltimore Orioles couldn't seem to make it to the World Series. Mac thought it was the pitching. Bill thought it was the batting and Nick thought it was the owner. They laughed as they realized they were all probably at least partly right.

As they talked, Joe sank the eight ball and beat Nick. It was Mac's turn now. He stood up from his seat and walked to the table to insert his coins in the coin slot to start the next game. As he bent down to put his coins in the slot, he heard Joe say, "Holy shit! Look at the piece of ass that just walked through the door!"

Mac turned his head and saw Hope walk through the door with her friends. He smiled as he watched Red step around from behind the bar and give the beautiful woman a huge hug and a kiss on the cheek as he picked her up off her feet.

Nick laughed. "That damn Red. He knows everyone, doesn't he? Isn't he the lucky bastard tonight! What a knockout! Wonder who she is?"

Mac smiled. "I'm not sure who she is but I towed her home today. Her name is Hope and her parents live in a big ass house off Tilghman Creek."

Nick laughed again. "Well I'll be damned. That must be T.C. Crosby's little girl. She's not so little anymore! I did some of the carpentry work for T.C. on that house a long time ago. It's one of the nicest homes I've ever worked on. Everything in it is first class, and T.C. is a hell of an engineer and craftsmen. I only saw his daughter once while I was there. She was a lot younger then. Last time I saw her, she was using a D-4 dozer to grade the site around their house. I heard she was a model over in Europe for a while." He looked at Mac and Joe and said, with a wink, "Don't see too many heavy equipment operators who look like that, do ya?"

Mac nodded his head. "That's a fact, my friend. That's a fact." He watched Hope as she talked with Red. "I was coming back from fishing this morning and found her drifting around south of Bloody Point. I towed her back home. When I dropped her off at her parents' place, she said she might stop by here tonight."

Mac didn't want to let on just how happy he was to see her. He didn't have a chance to talk with her for long today but he was fascinated by this stunning woman who could handle a high-performance racing boat, drive a piece of heavy equipment, and look completely at ease in a local pool hall.

After visiting with Red and some folks at the bar, Hope and her friends came over to the table to watch Mac and Joe play pool. Mac watched her as she walked across the room. She was dressed casually in tight jeans and a loose-fitting white blouse that flattered her figure. Her hair bounced over her shoulders as she walked across the room. It was early in the summer but she was already glowing with a beautiful tan. She was absolutely gorgeous.

She spotted Mac looking at her and flashed him a smile. Mac felt a rush of color come to his face. It felt good to see her. He smiled back. "Long time no see!"

She laughed. "Hello there, Captain! I hoped you would be here tonight. I see you found the pool table. Can you save a game for me?"

Mac said, "Sure, I would be happy to. But I'm not sure I'm gonna be able to stay here for long."

He gestured at Joe and Nick. "These guys are pretty tough competition and I'm not sure how long I will hold up against them!" They all laughed and he introduced her to his friends.

He turned back to his game and prepared for his next shot. Out of the corner of his eye, he saw her move toward the table and deposit her two quarters on the rail. He had a feeling she had played on this table, and probably others like it, many times before. His intuition appeared to be on target as Red walked over, sat down on a barstool with a beer in his hand, and in a booming voice announced to the bar, "Now this I gotta see!"

Mac thought maybe he was the victim of a setup but he needed to focus on beating Joe before he thought about taking on Hope in front of a crowd. He liked the feeling of anticipation of playing Hope. It felt good. He liked a challenge and he had a feeling she was going to give him one.

Thanks to Moses, her new best friend, Hope knew Mac was in the bar before she ever stepped through the door. She saw the big black lab as she and her friends got out of their cars in the parking lot. As soon as Moses saw her, he bounded off the porch and greeted her with another sloppy kiss. Hope introduced her friends to Moses, too, and they all laughed as he proudly escorted them up to the front porch of the bar.

Hope was pleased that Mac was there. She had thought about him all afternoon and she was glad that he had decided to meet her here tonight. She saw him playing pool as soon as she entered the bar. He was on the back table with a couple of other guys. He looked good in his white T-shirt and jeans. She could tell he felt at home in the little bar. He was laughing and talking with two other men at the pool table. She liked his smile and noted the easy way he moved around the pool table. There was something about this guy. He seemed very calm and very confident—not arrogant, just confident. She was curious about him and wanted to get to know him better.

She pretended not to notice that he was there but she felt a rush of adrenaline course through her veins as she caught him looking her over from across the bar. It had been a long time since a man had made her feel this way. It felt good and she liked it.

Just then, her old friend Red Shaunessy greeted her with a big hug and a kiss. She loved Red. He was like a big brother to Hope. He had gone to school with her older brother and they were good friends. Red use to come by the house before he and her brother would go out to party. In those days, they would tease her and generally harass her about being a tall and skinny girl. Tonight was no different. As soon as she crossed the threshold of the bar, Red gave her a hard time about being so skinny she could blow away in a stiff wind. She loved the way he teased and doted on her. It felt so good to be back home again at Red's bar.

After she visited with Red for a while, she took her friends over to see Mac at the pool tables. Red saw where she was headed and said, "Hey, Hope! Watch out for that guy in the white T-shirt. He will take all your money!"

Hope laughed. "Is that so? I guess we'll just have to see about that, won't we?" She smiled as she walked over to the table. She loved to play pool, too, and, based on Red's warning, she guessed she was going to be in for a tight match with Mac.

Joe was no match for Mac tonight. As Mac worked his way around the table, he was conscious of Hope's eyes following his movements. He couldn't figure out whether she was checking him out or just sizing him up. Either way, he had to admit that he liked being the focus of her attention and the rest of the bar's too when Red came over and announced that this was a match they had all better watch.

As it turned out, Mac was right on both accounts. Hope was checking him out. She was slightly turned on by the way he crouched over each shot at the table and watched his long, tanned fingers as they supported the cue stick. He had a smooth shot and a steady hand. She could tell he was a good player. It was clear that he worked about three or four shots ahead of every shot in the game. Even when he missed, he left his opponent in a bad way. She also noted, again, that he had a very sexy ass. She could tell he was in great shape. He was toned and fit and she wondered what it would feel like to run her hands over the back pockets of his jeans. She blushed a little bit at the thought but couldn't help feeling more than a little turned on.

When Mac sank his last shot, he shook Joe's hand, turned to Hope, and said, "Well, Hope, I guess it's your turn." Then he smiled and winked at her. "Please be gentle with me."

Hope smiled and picked up her quarters. As she bent down to load the coin feeder, her blouse opened slightly to reveal her cleavage. She looked up as she released the coin feeder and caught Mac peeking down her shirt. She met his gaze and smiled at him. She realized that Mr. Callaghan might just be as interested in her as she was in him.

Mac realized Hope had caught him checking her out. Although he knew he had been busted, he recognized that, with her smile, Hope had given him the green light when she saw the focus of his gaze. This woman was confident and sexy. Mac felt his own rush of adrenaline as he prepared to compete with her. It had been an awful long time since any woman had made him feel this way.

Hope expertly adjusted the balls in the rack and Mac broke. It was a good rack and a good break. He sank the ten ball on the break and quickly started to work the table. Hope watched him set up his shots. He was good. Really good. She knew she was going to have to run the table to beat him, if he ever gave her an opportunity to shoot. She hated to lose at anything but she was impressed with the way Mac moved around the table and set up shot after shot.

Red looked over at Hope. "I told you, Hope. This guy is gonna take all your money, baby!"

Hope laughed and playfully punched him in the shoulder. "It's not over yet, Red."

That was when Mac missed his shot. It was a tough one. He tried to sink his last ball in the side pocket and set himself up for a winning shot on the eight ball in the corner. Unfortunately for him, he cut the angle too close; the ball bounced off the rail and slowly rolled down the table toward the corner pocket.

Mac said, "Damn, I thought I had you, Hope." He winked at her and smiled. She could tell he loved the competition and she wanted to beat him in the worst way.

Hope surveyed the table and tried to figure out how she could run the table herself.

Mac was disappointed he had missed his last shot but he was now transfixed by what he saw on the pool table. This woman could play pool! She moved around the table slowly and set up each shot deliberately. She was intensely focused on the task at hand and somehow, that made her all the more attractive to Mac. He could tell she was aware that he watched her. It made playing against her that much more fun. As he watched her, he realized he might be in trouble. Hope was down to her last two balls and now it was Red's turn to needle Mac as he said, "Mac, my friend, it looks like you're gonna go down in flames, brother!"

Hope smiled and lined up her shot. She sank her next to last ball but her cue ball rolled too far back up the table and was now stymied behind the eight ball. She tried to bank the cue ball off the rail to sink her last ball but missed it.

Red hooted and clapped Mac on the shoulder. "You'd better put her away, brother! Hope doesn't miss twice." He winked at Hope and she smiled.

Mac needed to make a long shot across the table to win. As he crouched down to make his shot, he noticed Hope step into his field of view. She positioned herself at the end of the table, right in line with his target. He knew exactly what she was doing. She was gaming him. She hoped that she might distract him enough to make him miss his shot. Mac saw right through what she was doing and smiled. *Not only beautiful but a hell of a competitor.*

Mac set himself up for his final shot on the eight ball. Hope knew she was done for. As Mac lined up the shot, she leaned over the table and whispered, "Double or nothing?"

Mac smiled and raised his head to look directly into Hope's eyes.

Hope felt her face flush. Then she felt a gentle heat flow through her body as he fixed his gaze on her. He lowered his head to turn his attention back to the table to set up his shot. Then he nodded and said, "Sure. But the next rack is winner takes all and if I win, you owe me dinner."

Hope watched him as he slid the cue stick through his fingers. She smiled back at him. "You're on, Captain!"

Mac sank the eight ball and Hope set up the next rack. This time Mac let Hope break. She had a good break but bad luck as none of the balls fell in the pockets for her. Mac didn't waste any time. He wanted a date with this woman and knew he had to win to seal the deal. He ran the table and never gave Hope a chance to take another shot.

As much as she hated to lose, Hope loved to watch Mac move around the table. He was confident, but not cocky. Self-assured, but in a kind and non-menacing kind of way. This guy not only challenged her, he kicked her ass and she loved every minute of it!

When he sank the eight ball, Hope extended her hand. "Nice game, Mac. I hate to lose, but you beat me fair and square."

Mac held her hand firmly as he shook it. "I think I just got lucky tonight. I hope we can play again sometime?"

"That would be wonderful. I promise to give you more of a fight next time."

He grinned. "I'll look forward to it."

Then he looked down at his beer. "I'm empty. Can I buy you a drink?"

Hope smiled. "I guess that's the least you can do if I'm going to buy dinner for you tomorrow night."

Mac said, "Oh, I was just kidding about that. But I would like to take you out sometime, if you're interested?"

Hope laughed. "A deal's a deal there, Captain. I would have held you to your bet, if I had won. I won't welch on mine. But instead of going out to dinner, why don't you come over to my folks' place tomorrow night and have dinner with me over there?"

Mac liked the sound of that. "That would be great."

Then he gently put his arm around her and guided her back toward the bar.

They sat at the bar and talked. She learned that he had never been married. He learned that she had never been married either. Neither one of them really gave a good reason for not settling down. Mac wasn't about to try to explain his biggest impediment to his long-term relationships and Hope didn't like to talk about her past relationships with men.

They talked about their families and friends and their favorite vacation spots. They had both done a lot of traveling and shared stories about their experiences overseas. Mac chuckled as he realized that most of his foreign travel involved being armed and covertly performing missions on behalf of the government of the United States. He knew he couldn't tell Hope any of those stories, so he pretty much let her talk and listened to her describe her experiences in different countries. It surprised him that, much like himself, she loved to travel but her best memories were formed by her experiences with family and friends here in the United States. He met a lot of people who loved to boast about their experiences abroad. He usually didn't have too much in common with those folks. It was refreshing to find someone who didn't need to brag. The more she talked, the more he realized how much they had in common. It was a fun and relaxed conversation and Mac lost track of the time.

At one a.m., Red announced that it was time to close down the bar for the night. Along with Hope, her friends, and Mac, there were only a few customers left in the bar but Mac and Hope were oblivious of them. They said their goodbyes to Red and Hope's friends and headed outside to the parking lot.

Mac and Moses walked Hope to her car, which happened to be parked near his FJ. Hope punched the button on her key fob and unlocked her doors. As Mac moved to open the door for her, Hope turned to Mac. "I had a really nice time tonight, Mac. It's been a long time since I've had that much fun."

She felt her heart beating strongly. She was drawn to this man. She really liked him and she wanted to kiss him.

Mac smiled and looked down at her as she stood by the door to her car. The lights from the bar reflected off her face and hair and as she tilted her head to look up at him, his eyes met with hers. "I had a good time too, Hope."

He didn't really know why he did what he did next. It just felt right. As he looked into her eyes, he moved closer to her and gently placed his hands on her hips. He felt her move toward him and watched as she raised her hands up to gently hold his face. They kissed softly and Mac felt Hope's arms circle around his neck. She pressed her hips into him and he felt the blood surge into his loins as his body responded to the pressure. Their lips met softly at first and then more firmly as they both committed to the kiss. He closed his eyes and inhaled the sweet smell of her perfume. As their tongues met, he caught a hint of the taste of her last beer. Her body felt so right and he was glad he had taken a chance when he reached out to her.

Hope was so happy to feel Mac's body press against her. He was a good kisser. She liked the feel of his whiskers against her face. She closed her eyes and felt his strong arms draw her into his chest. His body felt solid and safe. As they kissed, she gently pressed her hips against him and felt his body respond to her pressure. He was aroused and so was she.

Just then, Moses started to growl. Mac turned away from Hope and looked over at the bar. He quickly saw why the big dog was agitated. Two of Red's customers had apparently got into a fight inside the bar. Red was in the process of ejecting them from the bar. He had one over his shoulder but the other guy was still itching to fight the guy on Red's shoulder. Red was doing his best to protect the customer over his shoulder by deflecting the other drunk's punches. Both of the would-be combatants were kids and it was clear to Mac that Red was trying to defuse the situation without hurting either one of them. It was also clear that Red could use another set of hands to help him get control of the situation.

Moses barked. Red turned and saw Hope in Mac's arms. He laughed. "Hey, you two lovebirds. Could you break it up for a minute and help me with these two yahoos?"

Mac looked at Hope and shrugged. "Be right there, Red!" He looked back at Hope and said, "Hold that thought, please!"

He jogged up to the front porch of the bar and walked toward Red and the young pugilist. Moses followed closely on Mac's heels. The dog was trained to sense conflict and his training kicked in. Mac didn't want Moses to engage either of the customers so he commanded the growling dog to stay. The big dog sat down obediently but continued his low, throaty growl.

The customer who pursued Red heard Mac's command to Moses. He stopped chasing Red and turned to look at Mac. When he saw Mac and Moses, he said, "You need to mind your own business, mister."

Mac said, "No problem, buddy. Why don't you and I head out to your car while Red tends to your friend there?"

The customer laughed. "He's no friend of mine and you're not my buddy!"

He moved toward Mac and wound up to throw a punch. Mac didn't want to hurt the kid too badly but it was obvious that he needed to be restrained, at least for a little while.

As expected, the customer threw a punch at Mac's head. It was an easy punch to block. Mac pivoted away from his assailant, crouched down, and then quickly reached up and blocked kid's fist with the open palm of his hand. The speed of Mac's movement and the quick stop of his fist surprised the kid. He stared at his hand. As he tried to figure out why it had stopped so abruptly, Mac grabbed his elbow and used it to pivot the kid around in front of him. With Mac now behind his assailant, he used his free arm to put a choke hold on the now totally surprised and soon to be disabled customer.

It didn't take long for the drunk to pass out. As he went limp in Mac's arms, he gently laid him down on the front porch. Mac checked his breathing and rolled him over on his side to keep him from aspirating, if he got sick. Then he turned to see Red, the customer over his shoulder, and Hope all looking at him as if they had just seen a ghost.

Red laughed. "That's the damndest thing I've ever seen! You didn't kill him, did you?"

Mac chuckled. "No. I just put him to sleep for a little bit. He will be fine." Then he looked up at the kid on Red's shoulder. "Do you think you can behave yourself now?"

The kid looked at Mac and Red and profusely apologized to both of them. It was clear he did not want to experience the same fate as his buddy on the porch. Red put the kid down and walked over to the now slowly moving and groaning victim of Mac's choke hold. As he looked over the kid on the porch, Red said, "Thanks for the help, Mac. I think I can handle it from here. You're gonna have to teach me that move sometime, though. It might just come in handy around here."

Mac said, "No problem, Red. I'm glad I could help. Are you sure you're gonna be okay?"

Red laughed. "Yep. I will be fine." Then he winked. "Sorry I interrupted you two lovebirds. You guys make a nice couple!"

Mac looked over at Hope, who now blushed. "Thanks, Red. We'll be on our way then." He looked at Moses. "C'mon, Moses. It's time to go home."

Moses lumbered down the stairs of the porch and jumped up in the passenger seat of the FJ. Mac turned and walked back to Hope, who waited by her car.

She smiled. "That was quite a show you put on there, mister!"

Mac said, "Oh that. That's no big deal. Just something I learned in a self-defense course in college." He guessed she knew he was lying but it was all he could think of to say.

Hope laughed. "Right. Self-defense course, eh? It looked like a little more than self-defense to me!" She was amazed at how quickly Mac had subdued the drunk customer. She didn't know too many venture capitalists who could fight.

She pulled out her cell phone. "What's your cell phone number, Mac?"

He smiled. *I like where this is headed.*

As Mac gave her his number, she keyed it into her phone and hit the call button. Mac's phone rang in his pocket. He pulled out the phone and pressed the answer button as he looked into her eyes.

Hope hung up her phone. "There, now you have my number. Call me tomorrow morning and I will give you directions to my parents' place. I will cook you some dinner to pay you back for beating me at pool." Then, with one of her eyebrows raised, she said, "If you're up for it, after dinner, we can take my dad's boat out for a sunset cruise, if that sounds okay with you?"

It was an invitation Mac couldn't and wouldn't refuse. "That would be great, Hope. I will give you a call tomorrow morning."

With that, he put his arms around her one more time and kissed her softly. "I had a great time tonight. Sorry we were interrupted."

Hope said, "Yes. Red's timing could have been a bit better. Perhaps tomorrow night we'll have better luck?"

She winked at Mac, kissed him softly one more time and then got in her car and headed back home.

Mac watched her taillights fade away as she headed down the road. He let out a slow whistle and looked over at Moses. "That was quite an evening, my friend. I think we're gonna like it down here."

He hoisted himself into the driver's seat of the FJ, fired up the motor and headed back home.

Chapter Eleven

The Operations Center at CIA Headquarters in Langley, Virginia was always a busy place. It was the data fusion and analysis center for the director of the Central Intelligence Agency. The director, also known as the DCI, was responsible to the president of the United States for all intelligence matters. The DCI's deputy director and the foreign desk officers in the Ops Center were the people who prepared the DCI's intelligence briefings and monitored current intelligence operations around the world. The Deputy DCI and the desk officers were some of the CIA's most experienced personnel. They were carefully screened for their jobs after they had gained extensive operational experience and demonstrated superior analytical judgment. They were the "go-to" guys and gals in the Agency.

The Ops Center was divided into foreign desks that aligned to the various geographic regions of the world: a South America desk, an Africa desk, a Europe desk, a Russia desk, a Southwest Asia desk, an East Asia desk, a China desk and a North America desk. The North America desk was established shortly after the terrorist attacks on 9/11.

Unless there was an active operation in progress, it was usually pretty quiet on a Saturday night in the Ops Center. Tonight was no different for most of the desks but there was a flurry of activity around the East Asia desk. Even more unusual, Mr. Henry Burnside, the Deputy DCI, had just arrived from home for a briefing from the East Asia Desk Officer. His presence was a sure sign that something hot was going on in that area of the world.

The East Asia Desk Officer who stood the watch on the

Memorial Day weekend was a woman named Tuyen Nguyen. She had been an operative for the CIA in Southeast Asia for twenty years before being assigned to her current job at Langley. "T," as she was known to her colleagues at the Agency, was the only daughter of a Vietnamese couple who had immigrated to the United States during the Vietnam War. She was educated at Stanford University and recruited by the Agency after she graduated with honors. She was a brilliant scholar who, as an operative, was also well-schooled in the Agency's covert operations.

The Deputy DCI had been with the Agency for over forty years. Unlike the current DCI who was a retired Air Force general, he had cut his teeth in the field as an operative. His early assignments had been on special operations teams in Vietnam, Laos, and Cambodia. Later, he was tasked to manage the selection and training for members of the Agency's Special Operations Teams, which were now known as Kinetic Risk Management Teams. T had been one of his earliest recruits. He had been her mentor and, over the years, they had become close friends.

Burnside was all business tonight as he sat down at the end of the conference table at Tuyen's desk. A bank of projectors above his head displayed a chart of the Strait of Malacca, along with pictures of the bloodstained decks of the *Mirrabooka* and file photographs of Amanda Anderson. He grimaced and rubbed the back of his neck with one of his big, meaty hands. "Okay, T, give it to me straight. What kind of a mess have we got here?"

Tuyen sat down next to the Deputy DCI. "It's not looking good, boss. We have a trail to follow but it's tenuous at best."

She pointed her laser pointer to the projector screens and walked the point of light across the pictures as she talked.

"Secretary Anderson's daughter, Amanda, was a crewmember on this yacht. It's called the *Mirrabooka*. Mirrabooka is an Aboriginal name for the Southern Cross. The owner is an Australian golf pro. He and his family were not onboard. The yacht, with its crew of four, including the captain, was attacked while it was en route to Port Blair, in the Andaman Islands, to meet the owner."

She advanced the presentation on the screen to a picture of the bloody mess on the stern of the yacht. She designated Chris Foster's body with her pointer and continued, "The captain and the first mate on the yacht are confirmed dead. The captain's body was found on the bridge. The first mate's body was found here on the stern. They were both killed with bullets from the automatic weapons that appear to have been carried by the attackers."

She advanced the presentation to the next slide, which was a picture of the bodies of the attackers sprawled across the stern. "These three were killed by the only survivor, the yacht's cook."

She flashed a picture of the chef on the screen and continued. "He was asleep in his stateroom below deck when the attack started. Somehow he had the presence of mind to get a riot shotgun from the captain's cabin and waste these three while they were standing together on the stern. Two of them were shot in the chest. The other one took a load of buckshot in the chest and in the legs. The cook says he never saw Ms. Anderson after he woke up. There is no other evidence on the yacht that indicates she might have been killed. We have confirmation that SARSAT picked up a signal from her Personnel Locator Beacon that appears to confirm she was alive after the attack, or at least her PLB was functioning. Unfortunately, the COSPAS folks lost track of the signal about half an hour after they picked it up and started tracking it."

Burnside looked at the picture of the chef and chuckled. *Jesus, this guy doesn't look like he could punch his way out of a wet paper bag.* But he obviously had the balls to wax those three dirtbags, at close range no less. It always amazed him how courage manifested itself in so many different ways in different people.

Tuyen continued, "We have asked the owner of the yacht and the chef to not disclose that Ms. Anderson was a member of the crew. It's only a matter of time before the media gets the story but, if we can keep Ms. Anderson's name out of the press, we have an outside chance of recovering her before her kidnappers realize they have kidnapped the secretary of state's daughter."

Henry held up his hand. "Okay. Got all that. Tell me more about the signal from her PLB."

Tuyen nodded. "The SARSAT tracked it for less than thirty minutes. It initially moved directly south, toward the Indonesian coast, for fifteen minutes at about thirty-five knots. Then it started tracking to the west for the next fifteen minutes, along the Strait of Malacca, at ten knots. Then it went dead. COSPAS in Singapore are cooperating with us and have agreed to withhold release of Ms. Anderson's name."

She switched screens to another display and continued with her briefing. "The Singapore Coast Guard picked up the captain of the yacht's distress call at roughly the same time as Amanda Anderson's PLB was detected. The first mate was wearing an inflatable life vest with a PLB attached to it but his device had not been activated. We are assuming Ms. Anderson was wearing a life vest with a PLB attached to it like the first mate. We aren't sure how her beacon was activated. She could have manually activated it or it could have been activated by immersion in salt-water."

T advanced her briefing to another display. "We have received permission from a federal judge to monitor and track cell phone calls in that area. The satcom cell phone provider, who serves that region, is working with us to provide tracking data and transcripts of suspicious satellite cell phone traffic in the vicinity of the *Mirrabooka*. We have isolated one of the satcom cell phone tracks of interest with the track of Ms. Anderson's PLB, before it went dead. We are now actively monitoring and tracking that cell phone number and other numbers that have been contacted from that phone since the attack. The analysis of that data indicates that Ms. Anderson is alive and is most likely being transported to Phuket, Thailand."

T had to take a deep breath before she delivered the rest of her analysis. The information she was about to share with the Deputy DCI was not surprising but it was grave. She composed herself, looked the Deputy DCI square in the eyes, and said, "Our analysis of the phone conversations indicates they are making plans to sell Ms. Anderson in the prostitution or surrogate parent markets. It's not clear at this time who will be the highest bidder. The only good news in all of that is they will keep her alive, but if we lose the cell phone trace, we will lose her track."

Burnside shifted in his seat. "Yep. This could get really ugly. If they find out they have the secretary of state's daughter, they will either try to ransom her or publically execute her. Is there any indication they know her identity?"

T shook her head. "It doesn't look like it. They are marketing her as a young, Caucasian woman, in excellent condition. I'm hoping she stays that way until we can get to her."

Burnside nodded in agreement. "If they figure out who she is, I don't think they will try to ransom her directly. They will either kill her outright or try to sell her to a terror organization and let them use her to put pressure on Secretary Anderson and the United States."

He shifted in his seat. "This is a lose/lose situation, T. I think your analysis is spot on." Then it was his turn to look directly at T. "What's your recommendation?"

Tuyen switched screens to display an electronic map of the Strait of Malacca. It showed the track of Amanda Anderson's PLB and the subsequent cell phone hits they were receiving. She said, "We are positioning an unmanned surveillance aircraft in international airspace outside the Strait of Malacca in the Andaman Sea. If we can cross-fix the satellite cell phone conversations to a surface contact in the area, we can track the target until it pulls into port. If we can get to the ship before they make landfall in Phuket, we might be able to save Ms. Anderson. Right now, the track looks like it's moving to the west at ten knots. That gives us a max of seventy-two hours to make a grab. We are going to have to move very fast."

She continued, "I agree with you, Henry. If we alert the local authorities, I think Ms. Anderson's life will be in more danger than it is now. If the pirates think they are being tracked, they will kill her and dispose of her body.

"Based on my analysis of the situation, I think we should deploy one of our teams to rescue Ms. Anderson. If we can get to her before her ship gets into port, we have a chance of rescuing her before she is sold. Once the boat makes port, our chances of keeping track of her and getting her back alive are slim to nonexistent."

She stopped talking and looked at the Deputy DCI. He looked down at the electronic displays laid out in front of him and drummed his fingers on the glass top of the conference table.

He pushed his chair back and ran his fingers through his hair. Then he nodded his head. "I agree with your recommendation, T. This is a freaking mess. We really only have one chance to get her back alive." He hesitated for a moment while he looked at the screen. Then he turned back toward T. "You and I know there is only one team that we can send to get this job done right. Where's Mac?"

T said, "He's at his farm on the Eastern Shore this weekend."

Burnside nodded. "Call him and tell him to get his ass out of bed. Get his team to meet him at the airport. They need to get their gear, get on an airplane and get in theater now. They can get briefed up on the way."

He stopped and looked up at the clock. It was almost four a.m. "Does the DCI know about this yet?"

T said, "No, sir. I was waiting to brief you before we contacted him."

"Let's call him now, please. He's going to need to talk with the president before we authorize this operation. We also need to decide who is going to break the news to Secretary Anderson and his wife."

Chapter Twelve

Mac was fast asleep when his cell phone rang. It was a different ringtone than the normal one. As soon as he heard it, he was instantly awake. This ringtone was the one he set for calls from the Agency. As he rolled over and reached for the phone, he looked down at his watch and noted the time: 0407. Hell, he had only been asleep for two and a half hours!

He grabbed his phone and selected an app that immediately turned his phone into a secure communications link to the Agency. When the app completed the link, he said, "Callaghan."

"Mac, this is T. We have a situation that needs your immediate attention."

He immediately recognized the voice at the other end of the phone and felt a familiar surge of adrenaline as she spoke.

"Hi, T. Where do you need me to be?" He knew T was the Southeast Asia Desk Officer so he didn't have to ask her where he was going. Besides, she wouldn't be likely to give him too many details over the phone anyway.

"A helicopter will be waiting for you at the Easton Airport."

"Okay. I'll be there in twenty minutes. What's the status of my team?"

"We're calling them now. They will meet you at the rendezvous point."

T had known Mac for a long time. She had worked with him in clandestine operations before. She knew that, as usual, she was sending him on a mission that could very well lead to his death. Before she hung up the phone, she said, "Good luck, Mac, and be careful."

"Roger. Thanks, T. Watch my back, please."

T smiled. "You know I always do that. Just try not to precipitate an international incident this time, okay?"

Mac laughed. "You know me, T!"

"Yes, Mac. I know you and your band of merry men. That's what I'm worried about!"

She hung up the phone and looked up at the chart of the Andaman Sea displayed on the computer. It showed the projected track of the ship from its last known position to Phuket, Thailand. Based on their knowledge of the overseas prostitution market and the intelligence they had gleaned from the satellite cell phone calls, they assumed Phuket was the intended port of call. Time was short. She turned back to her desk, picked up her phone and punched the speed-dial button to connect her with the Current Operations desk officer.

The Current Ops desk officer answered the phone and T said, "I've got permission from the DCI to execute a mission to recover the secretary of state's daughter. Mac Callaghan and his team are being notified. They will be meeting at a rendezvous point at Dover Air Force Base. My briefing team will meet him at Dover and prepare his team for their operation during the flight."

The Ops officer said, "Roger that. Based on our earlier conversation, I've coordinated with the Air Force for tanking for our transport aircraft. The little birds and the RHIBs are being staged and will be on their way to Singapore shortly. The SID is aware that we are inbound to Changi. They have cordoned off a hangar at the airport and will provide on-site security for us when we get there. They are also pulsing their folks in the field to see if there is any new chatter related to marketing Ms. Anderson."

T nodded her head. That was good news. SID was the abbreviation for the Singapore Security and Intelligence Division. They were Singapore's equivalent of the CIA in the United States. The CIA and the SID had a good working relationship and T had worked with many of their operatives in the past. She knew they worked fast and their intelligence was well vetted.

T said, "Excellent. The team's tropical and urban weapons containers are on the way to Dover. They should be there in plenty of time to get loaded before the team arrives." The containers T referred to were special containers that were uniquely stocked for each member of the team. They were pre-staged at Langley and continuously maintained to be ready to perform in the various climate conditions the teams could encounter around the world. There were arctic containers, jungle containers, desert containers, tropical containers, and temperate area containers that were further tailored for urban and field operations. Each container was uniquely packed with tactical clothing, weapons, ammunition, explosives, communications gear, survival gear, and helmets and body armor for each man in Mac's team. There was an entire staff at the Agency dedicated to maintenance and upgrades of the gear in the containers but before they could change anything in a container, they were required to obtain the express permission of the owner of the container. Every member of the team had a different specialty and they tailored their containers to optimize the gear required for their specialties.

While T and the Current Ops officer at Langley put the logistics support chain for the mission in motion, Mac and his team made their way to Dover.

Immediately after he hung up with T, Mac called Sean in New York. It took a few seconds for the call to be answered but after a couple of rings, he heard Sean's sleepy voice on the phone.

"Hey boss," Sean said. "What's going on?"

"I have to go on a trip, Sean. My flight leaves in a couple of hours. I need you to cover for me at the office and I need someone to come down here and pick up Moses."

Sean didn't hesitate. "No problem, boss. Ben and I can come down there today and pick him up. He's gonna miss you. Any idea how long you will be gone?" Sean knew it was unusual for Mac to know the answer to that question but it helped if he had a general idea of when to expect Mac back. He knew better than to ask where he was going.

Mac shook his head. "No. I'm afraid I don't have a solid idea about when I'll be back. Please tell Will to press on with whatever we have going on and help him make decisions as best as you see fit. You know I trust you to do whatever you think is right."

Mac laughed a little bit at himself when he made that statement. In many ways, he thought Sean was more capable to run the company than he was. Someday, when Mac finally decided to retire, he thought Sean would be a perfect selection as the new partner in the firm. Mac knew it, Sean knew it, and Will supported it. Mac only hoped that his future adversaries didn't find a way to send him into early retirement before he was ready to step down!

Sean said, "Thanks, Mac. I've got it. Is there anything else you need me to do?"

Mac thought for a minute about his dinner plans with Hope. It was way too early in the morning to call her but he knew once he set foot on the helicopter at Easton, he would officially be on a private communications lockdown. He thought about asking Sean to call her and tell her he wouldn't make it to dinner tonight but he didn't think it was fair to put him in the middle of his bailing on their date. He decided he would bend the rules and call her himself, when he had a chance. He knew he would have to break lockdown to do it but he wanted to talk to her personally and explain, as much as he could, his no-notice departure overseas.

He said, "No. I think I'm okay down here. I didn't get much unpacked but I guess it will all be here when I get back. Make sure the place is all buttoned up before you guys head back home, okay?"

Sean laughed. "I knew you wouldn't get very far without me and Ben anyway! We will plan to spend the night tonight. While we're there, we'll spend some time getting the place in order before we head back home on Monday."

Mac nodded. "Yep. You were right about that. I don't know where the time went." He decided to skip the fact that he spent most of the previous night shooting pool and talking with Hope.

Sean said, "Don't worry about it, boss. We'll get it squared away. Do me a favor and take care of yourself, okay?"

"You know I will. Thanks, Sean."

Mac hung up the phone and rolled out of bed. Moses jumped up too. He thought they were going fishing again and ran down the hallway to get his breakfast. Mac headed to his closet and pulled on a pair of jeans and a T-shirt. He grabbed a sweatshirt from a shelf above his head and headed down the hallway to feed his dog. He could feel himself make the internal shift from his "normal" life as a venture capitalist to his "real" life as a Special Forces team lead. It was a familiar feeling and a good one. Mac knew he and his guys were going to be challenged to go in harm's way. He knew they were ready and fully expected they would accomplish the task at hand, whatever it was.

He fed Moses and then walked from the kitchen to his study. Just as Sean had predicted, Mac had finished unpacking the study first. As he entered the study, he hit the switch on the wall that illuminated the cut glass chandelier over the pool table. He walked over to the table and gently rolled the cue ball down the table. It bumped softly against the rail and slid into the corner pocket with a satisfying clack as it came to rest against another ball that was already in the pocket. He smiled as he recalled the look on Hope's face when he beat her at pool last night. He knew she didn't like getting beat and he looked forward to their next match at Shaunessy's. The next time they played, he might not come out on top. He loved the way she challenged him. Then he wondered how she would react to him bailing out on their dinner date tonight. He shrugged and breathed a heavy sigh as he headed over to the bookcase beside the fireplace.

When Mac started his renovations at the farm, Henry Burnside required him to have a secure space built into the house to accommodate Agency communications and store weapons. One weekend, while the general contractor doing the renovations was off, the Agency sent a group of their own contractors to his house to construct a vault within the walls of the old house. They picked a spot in the study behind a bookcase because it backed up to the closet in Mac's master bedroom. The vault had two entrances. One was through the bookcase in the study and the other one was through the closet in Mac's bedroom. Unless you knew precisely where to look, it was almost impossible to tell that there was a vault between the two rooms.

Access to the vault was controlled by a retina scanner hidden behind a fake light switch on the wall next to the bookcase. Mac rotated the light switch cover and placed his eye against the rubber cup of the scanner. A dim green light examined his retina and, as he expected, he heard the resounding click of the deadbolts being electrically thrown in the access door. Once the latches were unlocked, the bookcase opened like any other interior door. As the bookcase swung back, he briefly scanned the bank of monitors over his desk in the vault. The monitors continuously recorded imagery from his remote security cameras on the property. He wasn't the only one who saw the imagery. Feeds from all his cameras were monitored by analysts at the Agency. When the cameras detected movement, they would automatically send a signal to the analysts, who would identify and track the target, if necessary. Most of the time, the targets were quickly identified and dismissed by the analysts as erroneous indications from wildlife. Although one of the analysts, who was also an avid hunter, had spotted a ten point buck roaming Mac's property and had immediately put in a request to come down and go hunting at the farm.

Mac picked up a cell phone that was in the charging dock on his desk in the vault. It was his secure Agency cell phone. He would be using it on his way to the airport to stay in contact with T and to touch base with the rest of his team. He turned the phone on, noticed he already had a couple of voicemails and text messages, and put it in his pocket. Then he turned to his gun case on the opposite wall and surveyed the weapons behind the glass doors. Mac stored his "go-to" weapons in the vault. He had a variety of weapons in the gun case. There was an AK-47, an M-14, a twelve-gauge riot gun, a couple of sniper rifles, including a Barrett M 107 .50 caliber weapon that he loved to shoot, and various compact machine guns and handguns that he had collected over time. In the cabinets under the gun case, there were boxes of ammunition and bandoliers loaded for each weapon in the display. He didn't expect he would ever need to use any of the weapons in the vault, but you never really knew when you would need access to firepower in his business, so he kept them there, just in case.

He never left home on a mission without one specific weapon. It was a .40 caliber Glock Model 23 pistol. The Model 23 was small enough to conceal easily in his waistband and the .40 caliber bullet had enough energy to stop bad guys in their tracks. It had saved Mac's life on numerous occasions. He picked up the gun from the case and slid back the charging handle. A round from the gun's magazine slid easily into the chamber. He set the safety, placed the weapon in its holster, and headed out of the vault. As he re-entered the study, he closed the bookcase door behind him. As the door closed, he heard the reassuring click of the deadbolts locking. Then he turned off the light over his pool table and headed back down the hallway.

He brushed his teeth, grabbed his shaving kit and headed back into the kitchen. Moses had finished his breakfast and, by now, had figured out something was up. He greeted Mac in the kitchen but his usual jubilance upon welcoming the new day had been replaced by a more inquisitive look.

Mac bent down and held the Lab's head in his hands. "I've gotta go, Moses. Sean and Ben will be down here in a few hours to take care of you while I'm gone. Be a good boy, and I will be back before you know it, buddy."

Moses looked up at him with his big brown eyes, licked him on the face and then headed over to his dog bed on the floor of the kitchen. Moses was a veteran of these missions too. He knew Mac was leaving and he assumed he would be back, sooner or later.

Mac watched his dog lie down. Then he turned out the lights, closed the kitchen door and locked it. He walked down the driveway to his beat-up, old Ford pickup truck, got in the driver's seat, fired up the motor and headed to the airport.

Chapter Thirteen

As the main rotor blades of Mac's helicopter came to rest, he saw a Humvee roll to a stop just outside the helicopter's rotor arc. A very tall woman, dressed in black fatigues, stepped out of the passenger side of the vehicle and waited by the hood of the truck. Her long red hair was pulled back into a ponytail and she wore dark sunglasses. He smiled when he saw her. *It looks like they sent the big guns on this one. I wonder what the hell is going on.*

The woman who waited by the front of the Humvee was Mo Sumner. Mo was the intelligence team lead for all the Operations Desks at the Agency. Her real name was Maureen but everyone at the Agency called her Mo. She was not usually sent on field ops. Normally, one of the members of her staff would be here to brief Mac and his team. If she was here, the DCI or his deputy, Henry Burnside, were making sure that all their bets were covered.

Mac was glad to see Mo. He had worked with her many times before and trusted her completely. She was smart, pragmatic, and experienced. He knew if she was here, his intelligence would be accurate and fully vetted. He also couldn't help but admit that he found her pretty damn attractive too. She had beautiful, long hair and a rockin' body. She was a smoking hot brainiac. *A very nice combination.*

He jogged over to the Humvee and gave her a big hug. There wasn't an ounce of fat on her body. She felt good in his arms. As he enjoyed gently crushing her breasts against his chest, he said, "Well hello there, Mo! What a nice surprise. I wasn't expecting to see you here, but I'm glad you came."

Maureen had known Mac for a long time. She had worked with

him on a couple of overseas operations and heard the stories about some of the other feats he and his team had pulled off on others. It was hard for her to believe that a man who seemed so easygoing was capable of such incredible violence. Perhaps that was what drew her to him. She really didn't know why, but from the moment she first met him, she had harbored a secret desire to make their professional relationship into something much more personal. The opportunity for them to get together had not yet manifested itself, but she relished the thought of spending the next couple of days with Mac Callaghan and his team.

Mo returned Mac's hug. He felt good. Her hand brushed the pistol in the holster that was tucked into his belt. It was a quick reminder that she was getting ready to brief a team that was going to go in harm's way.

She smiled and looked up at Mac. "Is that a Glock in your pocket, mister, or are you just really happy to see me?"

Mac broke out laughing. "Why yes, ma'am. As a matter of fact, it sure is. Hugging you always seems to have that effect on me, Mo." He moved his hand to the holster and raised his eyebrow. "You of all people should know that I don't leave home without proper protection."

She quickly picked up on the underlying tone of Mac's comment. She liked it. She raised her sunglasses up above her eyebrows and winked at Mac. "I wouldn't have you any other way, Mr. Callaghan." She loved the easygoing banter and hoped to herself that someday, somehow, it would become something more. Then she remembered they had a job to do.

She turned and gestured to the rear door of the Humvee. "Come on, funny man. Let's get going. We're loading the vault into the back of the C-17 right now. As soon as they get it powered up, I can start briefing you." Then she said, "By the way, Rosie and Chuck are inbound and Billy is already here."

Mac nodded. Rosie, Chuck, and Billy were the other members of his team. Rosie and Chuck lived in the Baltimore/Washington metro area. Billy lived in the mountains of West Virginia. Mac knew Billy had planned to spend the Memorial Day weekend at Ocean City, Maryland. He looked at her. "Sounds good, Mo. I was wondering how long it would take you guys to find Billy down in O.C."

Mo looked at him and laughed. "Oh, he's here all right. He's a little bit hungover. But he's here."

Mac wasn't surprised. Billy O'Neill was one of the best demolition men in the business, but he did like to party a bit.

He nodded. "Well, we have a long flight ahead of us. We'll put him on one hundred percent oxygen once we get airborne. That should help him sober up." Then, with a more serious look, he said, "Based on the fact that you're here, I'm guessing this is a hot one?"

As Mo climbed into the Humvee and closed the door, she nodded. "Yep. This one's going to be a challenge. The timeline is super tight. I will tell you all about it as soon as we get into the vault."

Mac opened the rear door of the Humvee and took his seat. It was a short ride to a remote hangar on the far side of the base. The doors to the hangar were closed when they arrived and there was a guard at the door. He could tell it was an Agency guy by the black fatigues and the H&K MP7 that hung loosely by his side. Seeing the guard reminded Mac that it was time to get down to business. When he walked through the hangar door, he would need to cut himself off from his normal life and go on lockdown. Mac asked Mo to give him a second to make a quick call before they went through the door to the hangar.

He walked a short distance away from her to get a little bit of privacy. Then he pulled his cell phone out of his pocket and punched the keys to call Hope. He knew it was still too early, around 0630, to expect her to answer. But he wanted to let her know how sorry he was to miss their dinner. He heard the phone ring and then smiled as he listened to her voice on her voicemail greeting. She sounded good, even on voicemail. She was still sleeping, no doubt. He did his best to come up with a reasonable sounding excuse for reneging on her dinner invitation and then he ribbed her for allowing herself to get beat at pool last night. He grinned as he hung up the phone. He knew that teasing her about losing at pool would make her crazy and, he had to admit, he liked knowing it would have the desired effect on her. Then he turned off his cell phone and turned back toward the hangar. He rejoined Mo and showed his ID to the guard at the hangar door. Then he stepped through the door of the hangar into his other life.

As Mac walked through the hangar door, he could see the enormous fuselage of an Air Force C-17 being loaded in front of him. The rear doors of the giant aircraft were open and the loadmasters oversaw the loading of a tractor-trailer sized desert camouflaged box into the rear of the aircraft. The large brown box was known as the Vault. It was a secure briefing and operations center that mirrored the capabilities of the Operations desks at Langley. From the outside, this aircraft looked like any other C-17 operated by the Air Force. However, this particular aircraft had been modified with special communications systems that allowed the Vault to communicate directly with the Agency and oversee operations in the field. Once the gaping jaws of the C-17 swallowed the box, it could be connected to the aircraft's electrical system and the special communications systems. At that point, it was a fully operational command center that was capable of directing operations and communicating with the Agency anywhere in the world.

Mac could see the team's weapons containers stacked up on the hangar deck near where the Vault was being loaded. On top of one of the containers was the motionless form of his partner and demolitions man, William "Billy" O'Neill. Billy was a former Navy SEAL. He was at home in any environment. He lived in the mountains of West Virginia but was just as comfortable in the jungles of South America or, for that matter, the deserts of Africa. Right now though, he was fast asleep on the top of his personal weapons container. Mac thought about waking him up but decided to leave him alone. They would wake him up soon enough.

Out of the corner of his eye, he saw two familiar figures walk through the hangar door. One of them was a hulking figure while the other one was shorter and more slender. They looked like Stan Laurel and Oliver Hardy walking together and he smiled as he saw them approach Mo. The big guy hugged Mo and then picked her up off the hangar deck and spun her around in the air. As Mac heard her shriek, he smiled. The rest of his team had arrived. Douglas Roosevelt, known to most as just Rosie, was the big guy who spun Mo around in the air. At six feet seven inches tall, he was a mountain of a man. He was also one of the most accomplished snipers in the world. He was a former Marine who was a member of the Marine Corps' infamous Force Reconnaissance Battalions, where he honed his skills in combat. He was widely regarded as the best sniper at the Agency. His partner, the guy who looked like Stan Laurel, was Charles "Chuck" McKnight. Chuck was the communications and electronics expert on the team. Like Mac, he had been trained by the CIA but he also had extensive training at the NSA, where he became an expert in electronic surveillance and computer hacking. Chuck was the smallest member of the team physically but his ability to throw a knife with deadly accuracy coupled with his ability to harness the latest technologies to achieve the team's mission was eye watering.

When Rosie and Chuck finished spinning Mo through the air, they put her back down on her feet and headed to where they saw Mac standing over the inert form of their demolitions man.

They shook hands and warmly embraced one another. These men had been together for a long time. Each of them, at one time or another, had saved their teammate's life. Their bond was stronger than blood and you could tell they all keenly anticipated their next mission.

As Rosie finished giving Mac a hug, he looked down at Billy's sleeping form. "Well now. I see the mad bomber of West Virginia is getting his beauty sleep." With a wink, he continued, "Want me to give him a special wake-up call?"

Just as Rosie finished talking, Billy's eyes opened up and he let out a rebel yell that could easily be heard above the noise of the equipment loading the Vault. Startled by the noise, the Air Force loadmasters stopped loading and looked over at Mac and his team. People always got a little jittery around Mac's team. Even Mac had to admit that they made quite a sight. Rosie had a full beard and a head full of dreadlocks, Billy had long blond hair and a full beard, and Chuck looked like he had just graduated from high school. All in all, they must have made quite an impression on the Air Force enlisted men. Mac laughed. He waved to the loadmasters. "Sorry about that. It's okay, guys. Nothing to worry about over here."

Then he looked down at Billy. "Look who rose from the dead!"

Billy grimaced and rubbed his eyes. "Yep. I'm awake. With all the racket you knuckleheads were making, how could anyone possibly get any sleep around here anyway?" Then he rubbed his head. "My damn head is killing me. Anyone have any water?" He rolled upright on the container. "A couple of aspirin probably wouldn't hurt either."

The whole team laughed. They were together again. Although it had been a couple of months since their last operation, it seemed like they had just gone out yesterday. They rarely had many opportunities to get together when they were home, but when they were on a mission, there was no one who could come between them.

Chapter Fourteen

Hope missed Mac's phone call. When she woke up, she saw the message alert on her cell phone. It indicated he had called her at six thirty a.m. She wondered why the hell he had called her so early in the morning, until she listened to his message.

He said he was sorry to be calling so early but that he had been called out of town unexpectedly. He said he had to travel overseas to meet with an unhappy investor. He also said he wasn't sure when he would be back but that he would call her as soon as he got back in the country. He told her how sorry he was that he was going to miss their dinner together and then the bastard had the brass to remind her about her loss to him at pool before he hung up! Although she was bummed that she had missed his call, she had to admit the last part of the message kind of made her laugh.

She tried to call him back and give him a hard time about standing her up but her call went right to his voicemail. She left him a message and tried to sound as if it was okay that he couldn't make it for dinner but it was hard for her to hide her disappointment. She wished she hadn't had the presence of mind to silence her phone when she came home from Shaunessy's. If she had heard the phone ring, at least she would have been able to talk with him, even though she knew she would have been annoyed that he was calling her at the crack of dawn.

Maybe he got cold feet about their date? She went through their conversation from last night in her mind and remembered the way he held her when they kissed. He sure seemed to be genuinely interested in her and, she had to admit, she was really turned on by him too. Then she thought about the way he subdued the drunk customer at the bar and started to wonder more about what Mac really did for a living. Was he really a venture capitalist or was he up to something else? Could that explain why he suddenly had to leave the country? She didn't have any answers to her questions, so she spent the day being generally perturbed about Mac's apparent overnight change of heart and subsequent disappearance. She started to think he was just like all the other men who had made promises to her they never intended to keep. This one just seemed to be so different, though; at least she thought he was.

While Hope tried to figure out what Mac was up to, Amanda Anderson confronted a far more serious challenge. Not long after the pirates had left her, the lock in the door turned again. Then the hinges on the heavy door creaked as someone entered the room and turned on a light. She still had her blindfold on so she couldn't see who came into the room, but she could hear a lot of footsteps and at least two male voices. One of them sounded similar to the voice she heard on deck that, with his command, made all of the hands stop their torturous assault on her body. Her mind raced as she wondered why he had come back. Blindfolded and still bound tightly with the ropes, she realized she was powerless to stop them from doing anything they pleased to her. As she felt them start to move her, she tried to steel herself against what she was sure to be another, more intense assault on her body. She felt them roll her on her back and start to untie the ropes that held her arms. She fought them off as best as she could but soon shook uncontrollably as her body reached its physical limits and fear overcame hope. As her arms were freed, she felt two sets of hands grab each of them, pull them out straight, spread them away from her sides and hold them firmly to the hard steel of the ship's deck. Then she felt her legs being untied and knew her worst fears were about to be realized. She cried and begged the men to stop. As the ropes on her legs were untied, more sets of hands held her legs down on the floor. She tried to kick the men away with her now freed legs but she was no match for their strength. She realized there was nothing she could do to keep them from assaulting her and tried to prepare herself for the inevitable.

Then the familiar voice said something and something tugged against her shirt. She heard and felt the fabric give way as someone cut off her *Mirrabooka* crew shirt. Her shirt fell away and then someone lifted her bra and cut it away from her shoulders. Her breasts were now fully exposed and she felt someone's callused hands roughly feeling her up. At the same time, someone put his hand down her shorts, lifted them up away from her body, and cut them away from her skin. She had given up wearing underwear a long time ago and as the men cut away her shorts, it wasn't long before they had an unobstructed view. She heard them talk and laugh and someone roughly rubbed her crotch.

As her pants were torn away, she tried to take her mind away from the horrific onslaught that she was sure would follow at any minute. She felt the men force her legs open and, as her world opened up to them, someone's hand groped her between her legs. She recoiled in horror and panicked as her body's self-defense mechanisms took over. She tried to kick her assailant away from her and managed to free one of her legs for a moment. But before the assailant could continue, she heard a shout from the familiar voice. Thankfully, as suddenly as it started, the assault on her body stopped once again.

As she struggled to comprehend what was happening to her, she saw a flash of light through her blindfold. Then she saw another flash and heard the familiar voice give another command. Someone took off her blindfold and roughly held her head up. She couldn't believe her eyes when she opened them and saw a man standing over her taking pictures with his cell phone! It was all too surreal and her mind could not grasp what was happening to her.

As quickly as the blindfold was taken off, it was put back over her eyes again. Amanda heard the familiar voice give commands again and her legs were forced back together as the rope bindings to her legs were reapplied. After her legs were bound, the familiar voice spoke again and she was dragged across the floor. They rolled her into a sitting position and pushed her against something hard. She couldn't really tell what it was but it was solid and cold. It felt like a column or a pole but she couldn't be sure. The familiar voice said something again and they pulled her arms behind her and tied her wrists together around the object that she was leaned up against. Then they draped something—it felt like a burlap bag—over her shoulders and left.

The light in the room where she was being held was turned off and she heard the door creak closed. The lock clicked in the door and it was quiet again in the room that had become her dungeon. She collapsed against the column behind her. A flood of emotions overcame her and, as she sobbed, she thanked God for sparing her from the savage attack on her body that she expected when the men tore off her clothes. She didn't know how she had avoided being raped by them. She also didn't understand why they were taking pictures of her naked body. Why would they be doing that? Maybe they were trying to use the pictures to blackmail her parents? What would they do when they saw her? How was she ever going to get out of this mess?

She shuddered as she thought about what might happen to her. It was all too much for her to understand. Instead of harboring her fear about what might happen to her next, she decided to try to regain her composure and prepare herself for her next ordeal. She adjusted the burlap bag, or whatever it was, with her teeth to try to cover herself up. She was determined to survive. She knew there would be more tests of her mental and physical toughness and she needed to rest and try to regain some of her strength.

Chapter Fifteen

Henry Burnside and T Nguyen sat along the outer wall of a small conference room at CIA Headquarters in Langley. It was the director of the CIA's private conference room. They had been invited to join the DCI, General "Catfish" Hunter, to brief him on the proposed operation to recover Amanda Adams. The president of the United States, the secretary of defense, and Amanda's mother and father were also planning to attend the briefing. While Henry and T waited to start the brief, the secretary of state and his wife were escorted to the conference room from the Agency's underground garage. The president and the secretary of defense planned to join the meeting via secure teleconference link from a room in the basement of the West Wing of the White House.

It was almost eleven a.m. on Sunday morning. T had been up for most of the night with her staff to prepare the briefing. Over the past twenty-four hours, the intelligence agencies of the United States and their counterparts in Singapore had gathered an immense amount of information about Amanda's location, the intentions of her captors, and the options that were available to attempt to rescue her.

With the cooperation of the region's satellite cellular phone service provider, the Agency had obtained copies of the marketing photographs of Ms. Anderson taken by her captors, along with translations of the conversations that were taking place between the pirates on the ship, their leadership ashore, and the potential customers who were now actively competing to purchase Ms. Anderson. The pictures confirmed two things for T's team. First, and most importantly, Amanda Anderson was still alive and in relatively good condition. Second, she was being offered for sale to a major player in the human trafficking business in Malaysia. Her captors were negotiating with two brokers. At this point, the price for Ms. Anderson was over three hundred thousand dollars. Her generally good condition and striking good looks sparked a bidding war on the mainland. Her rising market value was the only factor keeping her alive and relatively unharmed. Although it was incredibly disturbing to T and her team that this type of business thrived in Southeast Asia, it was a reality they understood, and hoped to leverage to their benefit, in their attempt to rescue Amanda. As long as the bidding continued, and the bidding price remained high, her odds of survival remained good.

Shortly after T's first meeting with Henry Burnside, she received approval from the Agency to launch a high-altitude surveillance drone that now maintained an active track on the suspected pirate ship. The drone provided them with continuous surveillance of the ship. In addition to the surveillance by the United States, the SID had arranged to position picket boats, disguised as fishing dhows, along the expected course of the pirate's ship to provide periodic visual surveillance and tracking.

T received the initial assault plans from Mo Sumner on Saturday afternoon. Mac and his team were developing them in the Vault during their flight to Singapore. It didn't take them long to formulate their plan but the range of the pirate's ship from Singapore required them to ask for some assistance from the US Navy. They needed a place to refuel and stage their OH-58 Kiowa helicopters they planned to use for the raid. The DCI called his friend and colleague, Benny Ramirez, the secretary of defense, and asked for his assistance. There was no hesitation on Benny's part. He immediately ordered the Navy to get one of its littoral combat ships (LCS), the USS *Independence*, underway to support the raid. The LCS was a relatively small coastal patrol craft but it was extremely fast. It also had a helicopter landing area that could support landing and refueling the four little birds that would be used on this operation. It now steamed at full speed to close on the pirate ship and provide a landing spot, also known as a lily pad, to Mac's team. It was almost midnight in Singapore. Although Mac and his team had flown aboard shortly after the ship got underway, there was not enough time for the LCS to get close enough to the pirate ship to launch a raid before sunrise. Amanda Anderson would have to survive for another twenty-four hours before the team could get close enough to attack the ship at night and attempt to rescue her. That twenty-four hour delay would put the ship another two hundred forty miles closer to Phuket, Thailand. They would only have one shot to rescue Amanda before her captor's ship pulled into port.

The DCI was dressed in casual clothes for the meeting with secretary and Mrs. Anderson. He welcomed them into the conference room, introduced them to the staff, and then showed them to their seats at the head of the table. T was impressed by the way they seemed to hold it all together. She had seen them both on television but had never met them in person.

After everyone took their seats, the DCI asked T to join him at the end of the conference table. His face was grim but his voice was firm and resolute when he said, "John and Sarah, thank you for coming over here this morning for this briefing. We know you have both been under a tremendous amount of pressure for the past thirty-six hours and we want you to know that we are doing everything in our power to rescue Amanda." He gestured toward T. "This is Tuyen Nguyen. We all call her T. She is the director of the East Asia Operations desk here at the Agency. She and her team have been tracking your daughter since the attack on the yacht on Friday night. She is also overseeing the operation we currently have underway to rescue her. She is one of our very best and brightest desk officers. She is also a veteran Agency operative who has served with distinction in this area of operations. I have every confidence that she and her team are capable of successfully getting Amanda back home to us. As soon as we have been connected to the president and SECDEF, she will start the briefing."

After a short delay, the secure video-teleconference screen came to life. T could see the president and the secretary of defense sitting at the end of a conference table at the White House. She had never briefed the president before. The whole scene seemed somewhat surreal as she waited for the signal from the DCI to proceed with the brief.

The DCI greeted the president and SECDEF. "Good morning, Mr. President."

The president was dressed in a polo shirt. It looked like he was either coming back from, or about to go out on, a golf outing. He nodded to the DCI. "Good morning, Catfish. Thanks for setting up this briefing for us." He paused and then looked toward the secretary of state and his wife. "John and Sarah. I want you to know how concerned Ann and I are about Amanda. Our hearts are with you during this extraordinarily difficult time, and I want you to know that we will exhaust every avenue to get Amanda back home safely."

Secretary Anderson looked at his wife and reached out to hold her hand. He looked back at the video monitor. "Thank you, Mr. President. Sarah and I are so grateful to you for your willingness to help us. We know Amanda's situation has put you and our country in an extremely delicate position."

The president nodded. "It's going to be okay, John. Based on what I'm hearing, it looks like we have a window of opportunity here to get her back. I'm looking forward to hearing the plan. I'm looking even more forward to hearing that Amanda is safe again." Then he shifted his gaze to the DCI. "Okay, General, let's see what you and your team have come up with."

The DCI nodded at T and she began her briefing. "Good morning, Mr. President, Secretary and Mrs. Anderson, Secretary Ramirez, and General Hunter. My name is Tuyen Nguyen. I am the East Asia Desk Officer here at the Central Intelligence Agency. I am responsible for overseeing development of the operational plan to rescue Ms. Anderson."

She paused for a moment while the teleconference facilitator switched from a view of the conference participants to a view of the

Malaysian Peninsula. The Strait of Malacca was blown up and displayed at the center of the screen.

T knew this was going to be a very difficult briefing for Secretary Anderson and his wife. She wanted to be sure to very clearly articulate the risks associated with this operation but she also did not want to add to the emotional burdens they were already carrying. Keeping this brief at the right level of detail while being sensitive to the Andersons' concerns for their daughter's safety was going to be a real challenge, especially considering the fact that she was also briefing the president of the United States!

T used the computer cursor on the screen to designate the current location of the pirate ship. "Based on our collection and analysis of intelligence from various sources, we have confirmed that Ms. Anderson is alive and being held captive on a ship that is currently heading toward Phuket, Thailand."

She looked over at Mrs. Anderson and saw her sigh with relief at the news that her daughter was still alive. That was the good news. T and Henry Burnside had already decided not to show the Andersons the pictures of their daughter that confirmed she was still alive. None of them wanted to put the couple through the agony of seeing their daughter naked, physically restrained and obviously terrified while lying on the filthy deck of the ship.

T went on with her brief. "We believe the crew of the *Mirrabooka*, the yacht Ms. Anderson was working on, were victims of a random attack by a group of drug-running pirates who came across the yacht while they were making deliveries to their distributors on the mainland. Ms. Anderson was kidnapped with deliberate intent to sell her to the human trafficking market in Thailand. It's not clear to us how she was captured or how she managed to activate her Personal Locating Beacon but tracking her PLB allowed us to precisely determine where she was taken after the attack on the *Mirrabooka*."

She advanced the presentation to a collage of very high quality photographs of a rusty ship. "Based on our track of Ms. Anderson's

PLB and subsequent analysis of intelligence, we have determined that this ship was a vessel of interest in our search." She placed the cursor over the RHIB on the deck of the ship and zoomed the presentation to show the damage to the fiberglass bow of the boat. "This RHIB on the deck of the suspect ship shows damage that correlates with the evidence of an impact on the stern of the *Mirrabooka*. Our teams found evidence of black paint and fiberglass on the swim platform of the yacht that appears to be similar to the materials that would be found on this RHIB. It also explains the high speed of Ms. Anderson's PLB track shortly after her device was activated and the subsequent change in course and speed of the PLB track after it was detected."

T turned and looked at the audience. "Based on evidence obtained from Ms. Anderson's PLB track, the subsequent analysis of the damage to the bow of the RHIB, its correlation to damage on the stern of the yacht, and our ongoing tracking and analysis of satellite cell phone communications from this vessel of interest, we believe that this is the ship being used to transport Ms. Anderson. Our colleagues at the Singapore Security and Intelligence Division have used their sources in country to help us confirm our assessment. Both agencies have independently confirmed that she is being held onboard this ship. That assessment has given us the confidence to launch a covert operation against this ship to recover Ms. Anderson."

T advanced the presentation again to a high-definition image of the ship. It was a small freighter with a boom over the RHIB on the cargo deck. There was a deckhouse on the stern that contained the bridge and what appeared to be quarters for the crew. It looked like thousands of other rusty cargo ships that plied their trade on the Andaman Sea. T continued, "We have dispatched a team of special operators to Singapore. They are preparing four specially outfitted helicopters for a night assault on the ship."

She advanced the presentation to show a picture of an OH-58 helicopter that was specifically modified for CIA operations. "Thanks to Secretary Ramirez, our team plans to fly out to the USS

Independence and rendezvous with them as they steam toward the location of the pirate ship."

She advanced the presentation again to show a picture of the USS *Independence*. "The *Independence* is one of the Navy's littoral combat ships. We call it the LCS. She is fast and she has extensive capabilities for handling helicopters. There is also a corpsman onboard who can provide first stage medical assistance in case Ms. Anderson or any of the special ops team members are injured during the rescue."

T advanced the presentation again and showed the group a close-up photograph of the deckhouse of the pirate's ship. "Our assault force will commence their operation from the *Independence* at approximately 0100 hours, Singapore time. We intend to use the darkness to maintain the element of surprise for as long as possible. Also, based on our surveillance, it appears that after midnight, there are only one or two pirates on watch on the bridge of the ship. We plan to neutralize the bridge watch first. Once the bridge team is neutralized, our assault force will close on the ship and fast-rope from the helicopters to the deck. Once onboard the ship, they will eliminate any further resistance they encounter, rescue Ms. Anderson and then destroy the ship. We expect our element of surprise to be lost when we approach the ship by helicopter. Our team is trained, equipped, and prepared for close-in combat with the crew of the pirate ship. Based on analysis of the attack on the *Mirrabooka*, we know they have automatic weapons and we assume they will be using them to repel our team. The DCI has placed no restrictions on the assault team's rules of engagement. In other words, our team will neutralize anyone on the ship they perceive to be a threat to them or Ms. Anderson."

T advanced the presentation to a picture of the LCS again. "Once our team has rescued Ms. Anderson, they will board the helicopters and return to the LCS."

She advanced the presentation to the CIA seal. "That completes my brief, Mr. President. Do you have any questions, sir?"

The president leaned forward in his chair and folded his hands on the conference table. He looked at the secretary of defense. "What do you think, Benny?"

The secretary looked over at the president and shook his head. "This is a tough one, Mr. President. It's high risk to Amanda and it's high risk to the Agency's team. That being said, I don't see a better way to get her back. If we try to attack the ship using conventional forces, they will almost certainly kill her or use her as a human shield. If we wait until the ship pulls into port, it's highly likely they will have already transferred her ashore with their RHIB, or by some other means. In my mind, this is our best chance to get her back safely."

The president nodded and looked back at the group assembled in the DCI's conference room. He looked at the DCI. "Catfish?"

The DCI looked around the room and then looked back into the teleconference camera. "Mr. President, I believe that this course of action gives us the best odds of getting Amanda back safely. I acknowledge the risk is high but know of no better way to rescue her under the current constraints. We have rock solid intel. We have our very best team in theater to perform the mission. I think we can be successful and leave very minimal tracks behind us."

The president nodded and then looked back in the camera. "John, Sarah, what do you guys think?"

Mrs. Anderson looked at her husband, squeezed his hand and nodded. T could see the tears in the secretary's eyes as he tried to compose himself and answer the president's question. He cleared his throat. "Mr. President, we understand the risk to Amanda and the risks to the men and women who we don't even know who will perform this mission. We understand the situation that our little girl is in. We know if she makes it to the mainland that we will probably never see her again. We can't bring ourselves to imagine how she is being treated. We know that she would want us to do whatever we can to try to rescue her. We know this attempt may cost her and other brave souls their lives and we are humbled by your, and others, support to help us get her back. Bottom line—we believe this may be our only chance to bring our daughter back home. We support going forward with this plan and thank you, Catfish, Benny, Henry, Ms. Nguyen and their teams for their efforts to save our daughter's life."

The president listened to the secretary of state intently and then, without any hesitation, said, "Okay. Let's go forward with execution of the operation, Catfish. I will be on Air Force One during the predicted time of the assault. Please ensure the communications officer has a link available for me to monitor the operation in real-time. I will leave it to you to provide specific direction to your team on the details of the raid."

The last statement by the president seemed innocuous enough but General Hunter knew exactly what had just been said, or, more accurately, what had not been said. Without saying anything directly, the president had just reminded the DCI that if the operation failed, ownership of the failure would rest directly on the shoulders of the DCI. General Hunter understood and accepted the responsibility. He looked back at the president without flinching. "Yes, Mr. President. I understand. We will make sure the comms links are set up for you."

The president nodded and looked into the camera. "John and Sarah, our thoughts and prayers are with you during what must surely be a horrific time for you and your family. Please let Ann or me know if there is anything else we can do to help ease your burden over the next twenty-four hours."

Secretary Anderson looked back at the president. "Thank you, Mr. President. Sarah and I can't thank you enough for all your help."

At that point, the conference feed was terminated. The DCI looked at Henry Burnside and Tuyen. "Good job, T. You and Henry need to get to work now. Looks like it's time for Mac and his gang to pull another rabbit out of the hat."

Chapter Sixteen

The four Kiowa helicopters, two in the attack configuration and two in the utility configuration, skimmed the surface of the dark waters of the Andaman Sea. The attack birds were armed with Hellfire missiles and 7.62 mm miniguns. The utility birds were configured for hauling Mac's special operations team. It was 0130 local Singapore time, and they headed to the last reported position of the pirate ship. They had launched thirty minutes ago from the deck of the LCS and were now less than twenty miles from the target.

Mac and Chuck McKnight were in one utility bird. Rosie Roosevelt and Billy O'Neill were in the other one. The two attack helicopters flew in loose formation on the chopper that Rosie and Billy rode in. Using their advanced targeting FLIR turrets, with pencil beam lasers installed, the pilots of the attack birds would be designating the targets for Rosie and Billy's .50 caliber laser-guided sniper rounds. Rosie and Billy's helo had been specially modified with padded tables that looked like stretchers above each of the skids on the aircraft. The tables had special mounts to isolate vibrations and stabilize the night-vision equipped Barrett M-107 .50 caliber long-range sniper rifles that Rosie and Billy intended to use to neutralize the watch team on the bridge of the pirate ship. Once the bridge watch was neutralized, Rosie and Billy would provide close-in covering fire support until Mac and Chuck were safely aboard the ship. When Mac and Chuck secured the deck, Rosie and Billy would join them on the ship to assist with the search for Ms. Anderson.

When they were ten miles from the reported position of the target, they picked up the infrared signature of the ship. The attack pilots used their FLIRS to confirm the identity of the target and prepared for the attack.

Mac, his team, and the pilots of the helicopters used headsets that were tuned to the same tactical frequency. The headsets all had voice-activated microphones that allowed them to maintain hands-free communications with one another during their mission. Their tactical frequency was also being monitored, via a satcom link, by Mo Sumner, T Nguyen, Henry Burnside, the DCI, the secretary of state, his wife, and the president of the United States.

The tactical frequency had been eerily quiet since the initial comm check after the assault force took off from the LCS. Now that the pilots had detected the ship, the headset circuit would be the primary means of communication for the team.

Mo Sumner and the rest of the folks listening to the tactical circuit heard Mac's voice pierce the silence on the radio as he calmly reported, "Target detected. Execute split. Energize video. Lock and load."

In addition to the communication links, Mac and his team's helmets were also outfitted with low-light television cameras. The images from the cameras were being instantaneously transmitted back to Mo and her support team at the Vault.

On Mac's command, the members of the team reached up to their helmets and flipped on the switches on the battery packs that energized the video cameras. Mo Sumner monitored the video feeds from each helmet at her desk. As the grainy video from each camera was displayed on her screens, she called out the status for each member of the team. "Callaghan—Check. Roosevelt—Check. McKnight—Check. O'Neilll—Check." Once she confirmed the feeds were active and stable, she said, "All video feeds check four-oh." Then she hesitated for a moment and added, "Good luck, gentlemen."

Mac came back almost immediately and said, "Roger. Thanks, Mo!"

She closed her eyes and imagined what Mac and the rest of their team looked like in their blacked-out night assault gear as the helicopters carried them to their intended target. They were a formidable team and the odds were good they would all come home safely. But Mo knew that you never really knew what you were up against until the shooting started. She closed her eyes, whispered a silent prayer for the men's safety and then went back to monitoring her intelligence feeds.

After the video feeds were confirmed, Mac checked the status of his team and their equipment by saying, "Team status. Rosie?"

Rosie responded, "Green."

"Chuck?"

"Green."

"Billy?"

"Green."

Mac nodded his approval. He expected them to lock and load without any problems. They had checked and re-checked their weapons before they left Singapore. They did it again when they arrived at the LCS and once more before they took off tonight on their mission. This was the last check. It was a routine formality that was necessary to ensure they were absolutely ready to engage the enemy. They were all green. It was now time to execute. Mac pulled the nylon stocking mask down over his face and checked his weapon. "Roger. I'm green too. Let me know when you're in position."

Mac and Chuck's helicopter turned north. Their pilot flew to a position at just inside five miles from the stern of the ship. Once they were in position, they orbited in place while they waited for the other three helicopters to position themselves at that same distance off the bow. Once they were in position, they would simultaneously close on the ship. When they closed to within three-quarters of a mile, the maximum range of the .50 caliber sniper rifles, the snipers would commence targeting the bridge watch.

After a short wait, Mac heard Rosie's voice on the circuit. "We're in place, boss. Ready to move on your command."

Mac said, "Roger. Wait. Break. Break. Mo, any changes to

status at the target?"

Maureen Sumner took one long final look at all her displays. Then she picked up a red phone. It was a direct line to T Nguyen at Langley.

T answered after one ring. "Go ahead, Mo."

"I'm not seeing any changes on any of my feeds, T," Mo said. "I'm ready to press unless you see any reason to abort?"

T put her hand over the mouthpiece and looked over at Henry Burnside and the DCI. "Sirs. The team is ready to go. All intelligence indicators appear normal. It does not look like the enemy is aware of our presence. I recommend we execute the plan."

Henry Burnside nodded and looked over at the DCI. General Hunter looked at the secretary of state and his wife. "Thanks, T. I agree with you and Henry. Let's go."

T removed her hand from the mouthpiece of her red phone. "I concur with your assessment, Mo. Let's execute the plan."

"Roger that." Mo hung up the phone and picked up the satellite radio phone. She keyed the mic. "Permission is granted to execute the mission as planned."

Mac could hear the tension in Mo's voice. He knew she would be watching this one closely. He knew T, Henry Burnside, and probably the DCI were listening in too. He had no idea that the secretary of state, his wife, the secretary of defense and the president also sat on the edge of their seats as they listened in too. He said, "Roger that." He paused for a moment, took a deep breath, and said, "Break. Break. We're cleared to engage. Report one mile."

The assault force proceeded inbound from their positions at the bow and the stern of the ship. Rosie and Billy assumed the prone position on their sniper tables, lit-off their long-range starlight scopes and chambered the .50 caliber laser-guided rounds in their rifles. The laser-guided slugs in their rifles were modern marvels of technology. They eliminated any concern about the adverse effects of helicopter vibration and the movement of the target on the sniper's aim. All the snipers had to do was put their aimpoint in the vicinity of the intended target. Once they fired their weapons, the bullets would home in on the gyro-stabilized laser beam that was transmitted by the FLIR on the OH-58s. As long as the pilot held the laser dot on the target, the .50 caliber bullet would ride the beam until impact. It was a devastating capability that married the long-range of the Barrett sniper rifle with the precision accuracy of a laser-guided weapon.

The attack birds lined up on either side of Rosie and Billy's helicopter. Rosie was on the right sniper table and Billy was on the left. The attack bird on the right would designate for Rosie's rounds and the one on the left would designate for Billy's rounds.

Mac listened to the calm dialogue between the snipers and the pilots as they acquired their targets on the ship.

Rosie started it off when he said, "Rosie has one on the port bridge wing."

His designator pilot said, "Roger. Tracking same. Two miles."

Then he heard Billy say, "I've got one on the bridge. Not moving. Think he's at the helm. Can't tell for sure. Don't see any others on the bridge."

The pilot on Billy's side said, "Tracking him now. Concur with your assessment. No other targets on the bridge or weather decks. Ship's course and speed are steady."

It was quiet until they were one mile from the pirate ship. Mac's pilot came up on the circuit and said, "Assault force at one mile."

That call was followed very quickly by the pilot in the sniper's helo. "Sniper's at one mile."

Mac positioned the fast-rope at the right door of his helicopter. He would kick out the bag with the fast-rope in it and descend down the rope first while Chuck covered him. After Mac hit the deck, he would provide supporting fire for Chuck's descent.

The snipers made their final adjustments as the helicopters continued to close on the ship. Rosie locked in first at a thousand yards, just inside one-half mile from the bow. He said, "I'm ready to fire."

Not to be outdone, and reassured by the fact that all he needed to do was get the bullet close to his target and let the laser designator do the rest, Billy also declared his readiness to pull the trigger in his weapon too. "Billy's ready to pull too."

As briefed, the pilot in the starboard attack helicopter started the countdown. "Countdown to fire in five, four, three, two, one. Lasers on."

Just as the lasers came on, the snipers pulled the triggers on their weapons and sent two .50 caliber rounds streaking toward their targets. The pilots in the helicopters saw the muzzle flashes from the sniper's rifles and increased their concentration as they worked to keep the gyro-stabilized laser dot in the center of mass of their intended targets.

Rosie and Billy relaxed for a moment, pulled the bolts of their rifles back to eject the expended cartridges and then slid them forward to chamber new rounds in their weapons. Once they were locked and loaded again, they looked back in their scopes to prepare for their next shot, if it was needed.

Not surprisingly, it was not. The bullets found the soft flesh of their targets almost simultaneously. The force of the massive .50 caliber slugs was astonishing, even for men who had seen the deadly effects before. The target on the bridge wing was nearly vaporized by the bullet that hit him squarely in the chest. What was left of him crumpled to the deck in a sodden heap. The helmsman met a similar fate. The bullet that was aimed at him smashed through the Plexiglas on the bridge and tore through him as it continued through the exterior wall of the cabin at the rear of the bridge.

Mac heard Rosie's voice come up first. "Target one eliminated. No other targets in sight."

Billy was on the radio right after that. "Target two eliminated. No other targets in sight."

Mac said, "Roger. Good job. We're heading in now. Engage anyone you see on deck."

Mac heard both men confirm receipt of his order and turned his attention to his and Chuck's approach to the ship. He knew his guys had his and Chuck's back. Now it was their turn to get onboard and secure the ship.

The pilot of Mac and Chuck's helicopter began his approach to the stern of the ship. Mac could see the phosphorescence in the wake and momentarily had a flashback to the early morning fishing trip on his boat Saturday morning. Now, less than forty-eight hours later, he was half a world away from home and about to board a ship full of armed men. He quickly dismissed the thought and got back to business.

Mac felt the helo slow down and arrest its rate of descent as the pilot aligned the starboard door over the stern of the ship. He gave a thumbs-up to Mac—the signal from the pilot that he was ready for Mac to deploy the fast-rope. Mac kicked the bag containing the thirty-foot fast-rope out the door. He watched the rope deploy and then connected his harness to it. Just as he clipped into the harness, he heard Rosie's voice on the radio. "Target on the bow. Moving toward the stern. Must have heard us coming. He's armed."

Mac said, "Roger. I'm about to head down the rope. Be nice if you guys would make him go away before I get there."

Mac knew whoever it was would not be around to bother him much longer. He waited until he saw the deck stabilize below the fast-rope. He was ready to make his move. As soon as the pilot gave him the signal, he would go. He checked his weapons quickly and looked over at the pilot who said, "Go, Mac!"

Mac didn't hesitate for a moment. He pushed off into the dark and used his harness and gloves to manage his descent on the fast-rope. Within seconds, his feet found the deck. As soon as he hit, he crouched down, released his harness, stuffed his gloves in his vest and brought his MP-7 up into the firing position. He scanned the deck with his night-vision goggles. It looked like it was clear, so he called Chuck down by saying, "Mac's on deck. It's clear. Come on down, Chuck."

He looked up and saw Chuck start down the rope. He moved out of his way and scanned the deck for movement. He heard gunfire erupt from the bow of the ship. The crew must have heard the helo. It was only a matter of time before they engaged him and Chuck. Just as Chuck touched down, Mac heard Rosie again on the radio. "Target on the bow eliminated. New targets coming out of the forward entrance to the crew's quarters now. They're armed. We're taking fire."

Mac noted the matter-of-fact tone in Rosie's report over the radio. He could see him calmly lying on the sniper table over the skid of his helicopter. Mac was sure that even though the enemy shot at him and his partner, Rosie was calmly identifying, targeting, and eliminating targets as quickly as he could. He could hear him coordinate shots with Billy and their pilots to ensure that none of their rounds were wasted. It was easy to tell he had been under fire many times before. It was easier still for Mac to trust that between Rosie and Billy, the deck would be cleared of all threats in just a few minutes.

The pirate skipper of the RHIB was asleep when Mac's helicopter made its approach to the stern. At first he thought he was having a dream but when he woke up and realized a helicopter hovered over the ship, he knew they were under attack. He knew the captain was on the bridge. He rolled out of his bunk, slipped into his trousers, and headed down the passageway. The skipper banged on the doors of the crew's quarters to wake them up as he made his way to the bridge. He knew the ship was carrying close to fifteen million dollars in cash. It was locked in the ship's hold, along with the girl. Someone was either coming to arrest them or rob them, or both. Either outcome would spell death for the skipper and his fellow crewmembers. If they were captured, they would be executed by the government. If they were robbed, they would be executed by the drug syndicate. This was a fight to the death, no matter who was in the helicopter.

He sprinted up the ladder to the bridge and found the captain, or more accurately, what was left of the captain, behind the helm. The captain was the first target of Billy's sniper rifle. He was sitting at the helm when the slug from Billy's rifle drilled through the bridge window and killed him. The skipper quickly realized he, too, was now potentially a target on the bridge. He ducked back down the ladder and headed for his stateroom to pick up his weapon. As he entered his stateroom, he heard the sound of more gunfire as the crew engaged the attackers. He guessed there must be at least five or six of them, judging from the sounds of automatic weapons fire he heard above his head. *How did they find us?*

He grabbed his AK-47 and his cell phone. Before he headed back down the passageway, he punched in the number for their support team lead in Phuket. As the phone rang, he heard more gunfire from the bow of the ship.

A sleepy voice answered the phone, "Yeah."

The skipper said, "We are under attack! Not sure how many are onboard but they came in a helicopter."

The voice on the other end of the phone was now completely awake. "A helicopter? Where the hell did that come from?"

The skipper said, "Don't know."

"Where's the captain?

"Dead. Killed on the bridge."

"Where are you?"

"About a hundred miles south of Phuket. Still below deck."

"Keep us informed. I will call the mainland."

The line went dead. The skipper put the phone in his pocket, pulled back the charging handle on the AK, pushed the selector switch to full automatic and headed toward the stern to defend the ship.

Back in the Operations Center at Langley, a phone rang at T Nguyen's desk. She picked it up and said, "Nguyen."

T nodded. "Roger."

She hung up the phone and picked up her red command phone. "Mo, this is T. I'm getting reports of cell phone activity on the ship."

Mo Sumner acknowledged her call. "Roger. Got it, T. I'll pass the info along to Mac."

Mo hung up her red phone in the Vault and picked up the phone for the tactical radio circuit. "Mac, we're getting reports of cell phone comms coming from the ship."

"Roger. Thanks, Mo. We're engaged. We're about to start our search now." Mac now knew there was at least one person still alive on the ship. If they had a cell phone, it was probably someone who was senior in the chain of command. He suspected if he found the person with the cell phone that he would probably find Amanda Anderson too.

After Mac and Chuck were safely on deck, their helicopter retreated back into the darkness. They scanned their surroundings on the deck as the noise from the helicopter subsided. They could now hear the sounds of AK-47s on the bow followed by the sharp crack of the sniper rifles in the distance. He assumed the pirates were trying to shoot down Rosie and Billy's helicopters. Mac knew the pirates couldn't see the helos at night. By firing blindly at the noise in the distance, all they were really doing was highlighting their own positions for the snipers. As he expected, one by one, the pirates were quickly and efficiently eliminated by Rosie and Billy. They really never stood a chance.

The shooting on the bow stopped and it was now relatively quiet. Mac and Chuck started to carefully make their way from the stern of the ship to the bridge. Over the tactical circuit, Mac heard Rosie say, "You've got company, boss. There's movement behind the bridge. Next to the smokestack on the starboard side."

As Mac looked up, he saw muzzle flashes from the upper deck. Then he heard the unmistakable sound of an AK-47 on full auto. He and Chuck ducked behind a ventilation duct as they felt and heard the bullets thud into the metal that protected them.

Mac said, "Good timing, Rosie! We're engaged. He's got us pinned down. Sounds like an AK. Need some covering fire."

Then he heard Billy say, "We've got another one heading up the starboard side toward the bow."

It was like chasing cockroaches in the kitchen, Mac thought. They popped up all over the place now. He knew they had to move fast to have any chance of rescuing the girl. With him and Chuck pinned down, he worried that time was getting away from him.

He barked into the radio, "Take him down, Billy. Rosie, any chance you can get this guy by the smokestack off our ass?"

Before he could say another word, he heard Billy say, "Bull's-eye on mine."

Then he heard Rosie say, "I'm trying to target your guy now. He's covered by the smokestack. We'll keep his head down while we maneuver over to the other side of the ship."

The next thing Mac heard was another crack from a Barrett sniper rifle. Then he heard screaming from behind the smokestack. What he didn't know was that while Rosie was talking, Billy had taken an educated guess on the position of the man who had Mac and Chuck pinned down while he hid behind the smokestack. Billy couldn't see his target but he had a rough idea about where he was. He aimed the crosshairs of the scope on his rifle at an area low on the smokestack and pulled the trigger. It turned out Billy made a good guess. The .50 caliber slug ripped through the thin sheet metal of the smokestack and hit the skipper of the RHIB in the wrist. The impact of the bullet spun him around as it traumatically amputated the lower portion of his arm. Not surprisingly, this resulted in significant consternation to the skipper, who was now the source of the high-pitched scream.

Chuck made the most of Billy's lucky shot. He left the relative safety of the ventilation duct and scrambled up and over the smokestack. He found the screaming skipper, who was now so busy tending to his recent amputation that he never had time to look up and see Chuck pull the trigger on his MP-7. In less than two minutes, seven members of the crew of the pirate ship were dead.

Mac rejoined Chuck behind the bridge. He leaned over the dead body of the skipper and checked his pockets. Inside the front pocket of his pants, he found a satellite cell phone. He put the phone in his pocket and reported back to Mo on the tactical circuit. "Mo. I found a cell phone on the guy we just took down."

"Roger. I saw it through your camera. Bring it back with you."

"Done."

Mac and Chuck held their positions for a moment and listened for any further signs of pirates. Hearing nothing but the sounds of the helicopters in the distance, Mac made the call to get Rosie and Billy onboard. "Rosie. Billy. Let's get you two onboard now."

Mac heard Rosie and Billy confirm receipt of his command and turned to see the other utility helo begin its approach to the stern of the ship. From their covering fire positions on either side of the bridge, Mac and Chuck watched the men slide down the fast-rope and take their positions on deck. Once they were safely aboard, their helicopter disappeared back into the night. As silence returned to the ship, Mac said, "Chuck and I are up on the bridge."

Rosie and Billy quickly joined them at the entrance to the bridge. They positioned themselves to begin their penetration of the interior spaces of the ship. The tactics they used were similar to how they trained to fight in high-rise buildings. Chuck was up front. He was responsible for opening the door, or breaking it down, if necessary. Mac had the point. He was the first one through the door. Once Mac made his move through the door, Chuck would follow immediately behind him to provide covering fire. Rosie and Billy provided support to Mac and Chuck but also kept an eye out for any kind of an ambush that might come from behind them.

Mac crouched at the door of the bridge. He watched Chuck turn the dog on the hatch. It appeared to spin freely in his hand and he watched him crack the door open. He waited for a moment to see whether anyone inside would start firing. They all knew this was when they were most vulnerable. When they didn't hear anything, Chuck started a silent countdown with his fingers. He held up three fingers, then two fingers, then one finger and then paused and yanked open the door. Mac threw himself through the door. His heart raced as he rolled across the deck of the bridge and came up in a crouched position with his weapon ready to fire.

As many times as he had practiced this tactic and implemented it in real life, it still made him anxious. He never knew who he was going to meet on the other side of a door. He knew he needed to be instantly prepared to engage a threat or recognize a non-threat. It was a split second decision that could save a life or take a life. In this case, it appeared that he was alone. He scanned the room quickly and determined there was no one left alive on the bridge. Mac whispered into his mic, "Bridge is clear."

He stood up as the rest of the team entered the bridge. "Rosie. Stay up here and keep an eye on things."

"Roger that." As he answered Mac, Rosie moved to the forward port corner of the bridge and scanned the deck for indications of other pirates. As he moved into his position, he used the butt of his MP to break the bulbs of the lights on the bridge. Darkness brought them cover and a tactical advantage over the crew. He had no intention of improving their odds on targeting him, or one of the members of the team.

While Rosie secured the bridge, Mac looked down through the hatch to the crew's quarters. The passageway was dimly lit. He crouched down into a push-up position and peered over the lip of the hatch to see the farthest end of the passageway. He didn't see anyone in the passageway but, like Rosie, he didn't like the lights. He used his MP to shoot out the lights in the passageway. Then, using his NVDs, he scanned the passageway one more time to ensure no one waited for him down below. Seeing no movement, he slowly lifted himself up and made his way down the ladder to the crew's quarters below the bridge.

As he and the rest of the team descended down the ladder, Mac heard movement down the passageway to his right. He couldn't tell exactly where the noise was coming from but he whispered a warning to Chuck and Billy. "Movement on our right."

Chuck and Billy assumed their combat positions along the wall of the passageway as Mac moved forward. As he passed one of the doors in the passageway, he saw the door open slowly. He watched as the barrel of a weapon protruded through it. Before the pirate holding the weapon could react, Mac grabbed the barrel and yanked it, along with a completely surprised pirate, into the passageway. As the pirate came through the door, Mac yanked the weapon out of the pirate's hands and used his elbow to crush the pirate's windpipe. The pirate gasped and clutched his throat. Before he could react, Mac stepped behind him, cradled his head with his elbow and snapped his spine. The pirate was dead before he hit the floor.

As he lowered the lifeless body of the pirate to the deck, he quickly checked the body for any artifacts that might help them locate Ms. Anderson. Finding nothing on the dead pirate's body, he pushed him alongside the wall. "This one's dead. Let's secure the rest of these cabins."

Back in the Vault, Mo Sumner now counted eight dead pirates. She shuddered as she watched Mac's ruthlessly effective hand-to-hand fighting skills.

After their encounter with the pirate in the crew's quarters, Mac and his team systematically cleared all of the cabins to make sure there was no one left who could offer them any resistance in the crew's quarters. As they completed their search, Mac was concerned. He wondered where they could be holding the girl. He had expected to find her in the crew's quarters. If she wasn't in the crew's quarters, where was she? *Maybe he was too late. Was it possible they had been tipped off? Had they already killed her? Or, maybe they had already transferred her ashore?*

He whispered into his mic, "Crew's quarters are secured. No sign of the girl." They approached another ladder that would take them farther down into the engine room and cargo hold. He turned to Chuck and Billy. "Chuck. Stay here and cover the passageway. Billy and I will keep looking."

Chuck nodded and took a position at the end of the passageway where he could cover the entrances to the crew's quarters, the entrance to the main deck, and the ladder to the bridge.

After extinguishing the lights with their weapons again, Mac and Billy descended the ladder to the next deck and repeated the process they used in the crew's quarters to open doors and secure spaces while they looked for the girl. Unlike the crew's quarters, the doors on this deck led to compartments that contained food, tools, and other supplies. They were not designed to accommodate the crew. Not surprisingly, they didn't find anyone behind any of the doors as they worked their way forward.

As they approached the end of the passageway, they found a watertight door at the entrance to what looked like the cargo hold. He twisted the handle on the watertight door and felt the dogs on the hatch release. When the dogs were fully retracted, he slowly opened the hatch and found another door behind it. He turned the knob on the door and gently pressed inward on it to open it. It wouldn't budge. It felt like it was locked. He tried the door handle again. The doorknob turned freely but the door would not move.

He looked back at Billy. "I need a little something to pick this lock."

Billy smiled. "I've got something here that will do the trick, boss. Step back for a second."

While Mac and Billy exchanged places, Billy reached into a pouch he carried and pulled a tiny shape charge out of one of the pockets. He pressed the charge up against the door handle. Then he looked back at Mac. "Stand back. This is gonna make a little noise."

Mac nodded and said into his mic, "Fire in the hole below deck."

Rosie and Chuck both acknowledged the heads-up. Mac turned back to Billy. "Do it."

Billy pulled a tab on the front of the shape charge and they both stepped back, away from the door.

The tab initiated a five-second fuse on the charge. After the advertised five seconds, the charge blew open the door with a muffled bang. As the smoke cleared, Mac and Billy were almost knocked over by the overpowering stench of rotten fish and diesel oil. They guessed they had blown the door to the main hold but it was so dark, they couldn't be sure. Mac held his breath and looked into the hold. It was pitch black. Even with his NVDs, it was hard to make out shapes. He carefully pulled out his NVD compatible flashlight and shined it into the compartment. Much to his surprise, his light illuminated the naked body of woman! It had to be Amanda Anderson. She sat upright but she was blindfolded. Her arms and legs were bound with ropes and she was secured to a pipe that was welded to the deck. There was a filthy blanket lying next to her on the deck but her clothes were nowhere to be seen.

Mac quickly spoke into his mic. "We've got her. She's alive. Cover me while I go in."

Far away, in the Vault at Singapore, the Operations Desk at Langley, and in Air Force One at thirty-one thousand feet over Kansas, there was a huge sigh of relief.

He slowly entered the stinking hold while carefully looking around for booby-traps. He shined the light around Ms. Anderson but couldn't see any wires.

He moved across the deck to where the woman was seated and whispered, "Ms. Anderson, I'm here to help get you out of here. I'm going to take your blindfold off now."

He watched her body sag against the ropes and heard her whimper. She shook as he gently removed the blindfold. When the blindfold came off, he saw her look up at his face. He realized he still had his face mask on so he pulled the face mask up so she could see his face. "Hold on for a second. It's gonna be okay."

Her eyes filled with tears. She tried to speak through her cracked lips but the emotions were too much for her.

Back in the Vault, Mo Sumner watched the grainy video of Mac's attempt to calm Amanda Anderson. She was glad the video feed only went to her analysts and not to the Operations Desk at Langley. It was hard enough to hear the audio of the rescue but it would have been too much for her parents to see their daughter in her present condition. Mac did his best to calm her down and Mo hoped it was having the same effect on her parents. She wondered how Mac did it. He could transition from breaking a guy's neck with his bare hands to becoming an empathetic rescuer in the blink of an eye. She had seen him do it before. At first, it had surprised her. On later reflection, it had impressed her. She didn't know how he did it but she was glad that he did. He certainly was a different breed of cat. She blushed for a moment as she thought about how good he felt in her arms back at Dover and then realized she needed to get back to work.

Mo continued to watch them through the video feed, she heard Mac continue to try to reassure Amanda. He said, "Easy now. Try to stay calm. We're gonna get you out of here, I promise." He realized that no matter what he said, it might be too much to expect Ms. Anderson to settle down. He knew she had been through hell during the past three days, but he didn't want to have to sedate her to keep her from panicking.

He pulled his mask back down to cover his face and retrieved his knife from the scabbard on his ankle. He used the knife to cut through the ropes that bound her arms and legs. When she was free, she tried to get up but fell back down to the deck. Her arms and legs were too weak to hold her weight. Mac wasn't surprised. He figured she must have been tied up for the entire time she had been held captive. Her muscles had atrophied. He leaned over her and gently scooped her up off the deck. "It's okay. Try to be still. I'll carry you out of here."

He picked up Amanda Anderson and the filthy blanket that was next to her and carried them both out of the hold. As he passed through the watertight hatch, he gently set her down on the deck in the passageway and covered her up, as best as he could, with the blanket. He pulled a water bottle out of his harness, opened it up, and offered it to her. She took the bottle and started to drink it but coughed and gagged as the cool water hit her parched throat. Then she regrouped, slowed down and drank again, more slowly this time. She stopped for a moment, looked up at Mac, and quietly said,

"Thank you."

Mac looked back at her. "No problem. Try to take it easy. We have a couple of things to do before we get you out of here. Just sit tight for a few minutes. We won't leave you alone but we can't take you off the ship just yet."

Then he looked over at Billy. "Let's blow this tub of shit."

Billy nodded. "Happy to do that, boss." He patted the pouch that, until a few minutes ago, held the shape charge he used to blow the door to the hold. "I've got some C-4 here that should make short work of this garbage scow. Do you think fifteen minutes is enough?"

Mac thought about his response for a second and then nodded. He knew there might still be combatants left onboard the ship but he hoped Rosie or Chuck would find them and neutralize them before he and Billy got back to the main deck of the ship. Even if they had to fight their way through them, he and his team should still be able to get off the ship in fifteen minutes. All he really had to do was get Ms. Anderson on a helicopter and get her out of here. He knew the rest of them could be pulled out of the water, if worst came to worst. He looked back at Billy. "Fifteen minutes should do it."

Billy moved back into the ship's hold to place his charges. He turned on his flashlight and shined it into the bilge to find a soft spot along the keel. If he placed the charges correctly, the explosives would break the spine of the ship and fold it up like a lounge chair.

He removed two blocks of C-4 from his pouch and molded the soft putty-like material along both sides of the keel of the ship. Then he inserted detonators in each block and set the digital timers for fifteen minutes. He set the countdown timer on his watch for fifteen minutes and then simultaneously pressed the triggers on the timers. When he verified that the timers were functioning, he said, "Charges are set. We have fifteen minutes to get outta here boys!"

As Billy came back through the main hatch of the hold, Mac picked up Amanda Anderson and put her over his shoulder. Her blanket fell on the floor and he felt her try to retrieve it. He said, "Don't worry about that, Ms. Anderson. We have a flight suit for you in one of the choppers."

He looked at Billy. "Okay, Billy, lead me out of here."

Billy nodded and made his way up the ladder to the crew's quarters, which were still secured by Chuck. Then, with Billy in the lead and Chuck following Mac, they made their way up the ladder to the bridge.

They were met by Rosie on the bridge. When they got there, he gently took Ms. Anderson out of Mac's arms and held her as they made their final preparations to leave the ship. His massive frame dwarfed her tiny features and she settled easily into his arms.

Mac sent Chuck and Billy down to the main deck to destroy the RHIB. He wanted to make sure no one got off the ship alive and he also wanted to minimize floating debris. They were gone for only a few moments when he saw a flash of light through the bridge windows and heard the sound of a muffled explosion.

Billy reported, "RHIB is toast."

As soon as the RHIB was destroyed, Mac called for the helicopters to make their approach to the stern of the ship. He checked with Billy, who confirmed they still had ten minutes to go before the charges on the keel were detonated. Then he sent Billy and his partner Rosie, who still held Ms. Anderson, back to the stern to get them off the ship first.

He and Chuck watched as they propped Ms. Anderson up on the sniper table over the starboard skid of their helo and then climbed aboard themselves. He knew once they got her settled on the stretcher that was pre-placed in the chopper that they could get her dressed and start an IV to help replenish her fluids on the way back to the LCS. Once their helicopter departed from the stern of the pirate ship, Mac called down the other helo. He and Chuck quickly made their way to the stern and climbed up on the skids and gave the pilots a thumbs-up.

As they flew away from the ship, Billy held up two fingers to signal Mac that they had two minutes left before the charges on the keel would detonate. Mac gave him an okay signal with his hand and then came up on the tactical circuit. "Let's pick up an orbit here and wait for her to go down."

The assault force helicopter pilots complied with his request and turned their aircraft back toward the ship while they waited for the charges to detonate. Billy started the countdown at ten seconds. "Ten, nine, eight, seven, six, five, four, three, two, one, zero."

Less than a second after Billy's countdown, the ship lifted slightly up and out of the water and settled back down. There was no fire and no visible explosion. Mac wondered, for a moment, whether Billy had used enough explosives to get the job done. He should have known better than to harbor any doubts though because, shortly after the charges detonated, they could see the ship settle as the sea rushed into the hold. Then it broke in half. The stern sank before the bow but the whole ship was completely gone in less than five minutes. Mac directed the pilot of his helicopter to fly low over the area where the ship went under. They saw some debris in the water but no survivors. The drug lord's mother ship had disappeared beneath the surface of the Andaman Sea. Now it was time for Mac and his team to disappear too.

Mac scanned the surface one more time. "Okay, folks. This mission is a wrap. Let's go home. Break. Break. Mo, we have Ms. Anderson onboard and we are heading back to the LCS. I will have the corpsman examine her when we get back to the *Independence* and give you an update on her status then. The ship has been destroyed and there are no signs of survivors."

Mo responded, "Roger. Nice job to you and your team, Mac. We'll debrief you guys when you get back on deck here."

Mac settled back in the web troop seat and rolled up his face mask. He let out a long sigh and stretched his muscles. He could feel the tension drain out of him. He was happy to have successfully rescued Ms. Anderson and even happier that none of the members of his team had been injured during the raid. Now he could look forward to getting back home. As he thought about going home, he started thinking about Hope Crosby again. He hoped she would forgive him for standing her up. And, if she did, he looked forward to watching her eyes flash as he kicked her ass on the pool table again. He smiled as he thought about her and realized it had been a long time since anyone had caught his attention quite like she did.

His thoughts of Hope were interrupted by a sudden tingling in his right leg. He couldn't figure out what was going on at first and then he remembered he had put the dead pirate's cell phone in the right pocket of his trousers. He pulled the cell phone out of his pocket and studied the numbers displayed on the screen. He knew better than to answer the phone. Mo and her analysts would most certainly want to examine it and use it for more intelligence. If he answered it, the person on the other end would instantly know something was wrong. After a while, it stopped. Somewhere, someone wondered why the phone's owner didn't pick up. Only Mac and the members of his team knew the answer to that question.

Chapter Seventeen

It had been over a week since Hope had received Mac's voicemail. Since then, she had heard nothing from him. She started to call him again but stopped. She had already left him a voicemail. Why leave him another?

She was embarrassed to admit that she had gone by his place by boat on Memorial Day. Although she had never been there before, she recognized his boat up on the lift in his boathouse. It was a beautiful property. She could see the house had been renovated but it still had the look of an old farmhouse. It looked pretty nice.

From the water, she could see Moses running around near the pool up by the house. A couple of guys lounged by the pool, but neither one of them were Mac. She felt like such a creeper for doing a drive-by at his place but she really wanted to see him again and she was curious why he had vanished so quickly. She was kind of glad that she didn't see him. If he had been up there, she would have really been angry. At least he wasn't home. Or at least it looked like he wasn't there, so she headed back to her parents' place and tried to be patient.

After heading back to her place in Georgetown and waiting for almost a week to hear from him, she was a little pissed off. How could someone, in this day and age, just disappear off the face of the earth?

She tried to keep her cool because she really thought Mac was different. He didn't strike her as the kind of guy who made promises and then broke them but it was hard for her to understand how he could seem so interested in her and then just vanish. Her intuition told her something else was going on. Something about the way he handled the drunk at Shaunessy's told her he wasn't just some rich venture capital guy. This guy had something else going on. What the hell could it be? Every time her cell phone rang, she hoped that his number would be displayed on it. And every time someone else's number was there, she became more anxious. It was obvious that something, or someone, had a bigger priority in his life than Hope. She didn't like that feeling, at all.

When she was just about ready to give up on hearing from her again, he called her. It was a Sunday night. She sat in the study at her house in Georgetown and watched the Orioles play the New York Yankees on television. She thought for a moment about not answering his call. Then she decided she didn't feel like playing games, so she picked up the phone and punched the answer button on the glass.

"Well, hello there my long-lost friend," she said. "I wasn't sure if I was going to ever hear from you again."

She knew she was being kind of a bitch but she couldn't help herself.

Mac winced on the other end of the call. He knew she was going to be pissed. He had been through this drill too many times before. He hated it. Now he was going to have to lie and he knew he wasn't really good at that. He had finally finished his debrief from his mission to Singapore. The Agency helicopter had just dropped him off at the Easton Airport. He called Sean first to check in and tell him he was back. After he got a data dump on what was going on at the firm from Sean, he called Hope. He wished there was some way to tell her the truth about where he had been but he knew he couldn't do that. He took a deep breath and laid down his cover story.

"Hi, Hope. I am so sorry I had to leave town so unexpectedly. We have a client in China who needed to see me right away. I had to jump in the G-5 right after I got his call. I just got back this evening. We don't make calls back to the States from mainland China because everything is monitored there, so I couldn't get back to you until now."

Hope listened to Mac's excuse. It was plausible but something in his voice just didn't seem right. She decided to give him a pass, for now, until she got to know him better. She had to admit that it was great just to hear his voice again, even if his story wasn't completely convincing.

"Client in China, eh? I wish I would have known you were heading there. I've always wanted a custom-fitted cheongsam from there. Next time you go, give me a heads-up and I will give you my measurements."

Mac smiled. He knew he wasn't going to get out of this one easy. He also knew he didn't have a clue what a cheongsam was. "Well, I would be happy to pick one up for you, if I knew what a, what did you call it, was? Is it legal?" He hoped his lame attempt at humor would get her to laugh a little bit.

Hope chuckled. She knew he wouldn't have any idea what a cheongsam was. "Yes, Mac. It's totally legit. It's a dress, for God's sake. The newer designs are called qipao but I like the more traditional cut of the cheongsam."

Mac chuckled to himself. *Of course you do.* Then he said, "Well, I'm kind of hoping I don't have to go back there for a while but, when I do, I will be happy to pick one up for you."

"Well, that would be very nice of you, Mr. Callaghan. So, did you get your client settled down in China?"

Mac thought about his answer for a second and smiled. "Well, it was kind of an explosive situation but, after the visit, I don't think he will be giving us too much more trouble in the future." He couldn't help himself. He knew he should have just waved off her question but figured, what the hell, if he had to lie, he might as well make it fun.

"Hmmmm. That sounds like a tough one. Well, I'm glad you got it worked out and made it back safely. I was wondering if I was ever going to hear from you again." Hope couldn't help it. She was still a little angry about the way he disappeared. She knew he must have had something come up unexpectedly, but it still torqued her off.

Mac knew he was going to get wire-brushed a little bit. He had expected it. At the same time, he didn't feel like spending the rest of the time on the phone playing cat-and-mouse so he changed the subject. "What are you up to tonight?"

"Well, right now I'm sitting at home watching the Orioles do their best to lose another game to the Yankees. Why do you ask?"

Mac smiled. There weren't too many women he knew who watched baseball, at least by their own choice. He thought that was kind of cool. "Yankees, eh? That's no damn good. If the Orioles could just get their bullpen squared away, they would have another chance to make a run at the pennant."

Hope nodded. "Yep. They need to make a lot of changes, but at least they're fun to watch again."

Mac smiled. She was right. "I just landed at Easton Airport a few minutes ago. I'm heading to my farm now."

"Moses will be glad to see you."

"Unfortunately, he's not there right now. He's up at my place in Long Island. I asked a friend of mine to take care of him when I found out I had to head out of town."

Now Hope knew who she had seen at his house on Memorial Day. She decided not to reveal that she had seen them while she did her drive-by in the boat. "Well, once you get him back, I'm sure he will be happy to see you."

Mac nodded. "Yep. I suspect you're right. I'll be happy to see him too. I'm heading back up there tomorrow morning." He paused for a moment. "I'm planning to be back down here on Friday. I was wondering if you were going to be free this weekend. I would like to take you out to dinner to make up for my short-notice cancelation of our dinner date last week. I would be happy to come up there and meet you, if you're interested?"

Hope was glad to hear he was coming back into town this weekend. Even though she was mad at him for pulling his disappearing act, she had to admit that she really wanted to see him again. "Well, as a matter of fact, I haven't made any plans for the weekend. Why don't you come up here and meet me for dinner?"

Mac was glad to hear she wanted to meet him. "That's great. Do you have any place in particular that you like?"

She thought for a minute. "How about Milano's? You can park your car here at my place and we can walk there from here."

"That sounds great. I've been there before and liked it. I will make a reservation for seven and plan to get to your place at six thirty, if that works for you?"

"Why don't you come by at six and we can have a drink before we go?"

"Sounds like a plan. Send me a pin with your address and I will be there at six."

Hope smiled. "I will. It's pretty easy to find. Just park in my driveway and I will look forward to seeing you."

They said goodbye and hung up. Hope followed up their conversation with a text message that contained the address to her house. Mac responded almost immediately with a short note that said, "Thx. C u soon."

Hope had to laugh at herself a little bit. A few hours ago, she was pissed off that she hadn't heard from him. Now she was glad he called back and, as much as she hated to admit it, already looked forward to seeing him again. She wished she didn't have to wait for another week but knew there wasn't much she could do about it. She went back to watching her baseball game and thought about what she would wear to their dinner on Saturday night.

Half a world away in Bangkok, Thailand, there was an entirely different kind of telephone conversation going on. From a dingy office in the back of a warehouse in Phuket, the Far East leadership of the region's drug distribution ring was on a secure phone call, trying to explain to their bosses in San Francisco how their ship, and the roughly $15 million in cash that was stashed in the hold, had vanished without a trace. The conversation was not going well for them. They had just explained the botched attack on the *Mirrabooka* and the subsequent kidnapping of the woman on the yacht when the phone erupted with a scream from the San Francisco end of the line.

Their boss sat at his conference table on the top floor of an office building in San Francisco's Chinatown. His name was Chen Yiu. He was the president of Yiu Shipping Lines. Yiu Shipping was an international shipping firm that he had inherited from his father, who had inherited the business from his father. It was a huge shipping conglomerate and he was a well-known and very powerful man in San Francisco. Unbeknownst to his friends and business associates, he was also the chief operating officer of an international drug manufacturing and distribution consortium.

Chen was used to getting bad news. In the shipping business, he learned to roll with the punches and find suitable alternatives to complex problems. The same was true of his leadership and management of the drug distribution business. In this case, however, he was furious to find out that his leadership in Thailand had made a complete mess of the raid on the *Mirrabooka* and subsequently lost one of his ships and over fifteen million dollars of his cash.

After he heard the news over the phone, he stood from his chair, leaned over the speakerphone and screamed, "Are you fucking kidding me? You guys attacked a yacht, lost three men, left a survivor, kidnapped a woman from the crew and didn't think there might be repercussions? You didn't think someone would notice? Then you risked the secrecy of our entire operation, lost my ship and, with it, lost fifteen million dollars all over a piece of ass? This has to be the stupidest thing I've ever heard. I should jump on a plane right now and come out there to kill you all myself."

The men on the call in the Phuket shuddered when they heard Chen Yiu speak. They had never met him personally but had heard about his ruthlessness. They had no doubt that he could easily have them killed. They also knew that when he killed someone, he liked to make them suffer before they died.

The voice in San Francisco, now dripping with sarcasm, continued, "What did you think the authorities were going to do when they found the yacht? Throw you a party?"

It was quiet on the phone. The men in Phuket were afraid to speak. Chen continued, "Where was the yacht registered?"

"Our sources tell us it was from Australia," answered one of the men in Phuket.

"Who owns it?"

"Grant Bailey."

"The golfer?"

"Yes, sir."

"Great. Really great. This won't take long to hit the press."

"Yes. We're actually kind of surprised that it hasn't already."

"That's probably the smartest thing you've said during this whole conversation. Who put the clamp on the press?"

"We aren't sure. We think it's the government of Singapore."

"That's probably true." He snarled, "What else do your sources tell you?"

"They are telling us the captain of the yacht and the two crewmembers, including the woman, were from the United States. The cook was from Australia. The yacht was transiting the Strait of Malacca when our men attacked them. The cook was the only survivor of the attack. Unfortunately, before he was killed, the captain of the yacht made a distress call. The Singapore Coast Guard responded to the call and found the yacht the next morning."

"Do your sources know the identity of the girl?"

"No, sir."

"Do they know who attacked our ship?"

"They don't know for sure but they think it was the United States."

"Why would the United States attack one of our ships?"

"Our sources think they were after the girl."

"How did they know where she was?"

"We don't know."

"So, why do they think it was the Americans?"

"Because a US warship left Singapore unexpectedly right before the attack and returned to port shortly after we lost contact with our ship."

"Interesting. But not conclusive. Anything else?"

"Yes. The SID hosted an American Special Operations Force in a hangar in Changi Airport. The team arrived in a C-17 two days before our ship was attacked and left two days after we lost contact with them. We are being told that several small helicopters flew out of Changi around the same time the American ship left port. We're not sure when or if they came back. That's all we know right now. We are trying to put resources in place to get information from the crew of the US warship."

"How do you plan to do that?"

"When they come into town, we will use our people on the street to gather information from them about why they left port so suddenly. Hopefully, we can also get information from the crew about what they were doing while they were at sea."

"Okay. Anything else?"

"No, sir."

"You have forty-eight hours to get back to me."

The phone went dead as the boss in San Francisco hung up the phone.

The men in the warehouse in Phuket looked at one another glumly and then quietly planned how they could get the boss the information he needed. If they were successful in finding out who attacked the ship and why they attacked it, they might save their own lives. If they failed to meet the boss's expectations, they had two choices. They could kill themselves or wait for the boss to kill them. If they tried to hide, the boss would torture and kill every member of their families. It was a no-win situation and they knew it.

After he hung up the phone, Chen turned away from the conference table and walked over to the wall of glass windows that overlooked the Oakland Bay Bridge. He watched a huge container ship make the turn in the Outer Harbor Entrance Channel at Treasure Island to start its final approach to the Container Terminal at the Port of Oakland.

He uttered a heavy sigh, turned around, and sat down at his desk. Bobby Chong, one of Chen's chief lieutenants, stood in front of Chen's desk. He was present during the boss's meltdown during his telephone conversation. He knew the boss was angry and there was nothing he could say to make him any happier. He knew he didn't have to speak. When Chen was ready, he would tell him what his next move should be.

Chen looked up at him. "I don't want to wait two more days for the morons in Phuket to get back to me."

Bobby nodded. "What would you like me to do, boss?"

"I want you to tap into our network in Washington, DC. I want you to figure out what the hell really happened out there. I want to know why our contacts at DEA did not tip us off. I want to know how the United States found out about our ship and why they chose to attack it. If it was them, I want to know how they found us. Then I want to know who the girl was and I want to know who rescued her. Then I want you to find them and kill them both."

Bobby nodded. "Yes, boss."

"When Phuket calls me back, I want someone to already be over there in place and ready to eliminate every one of them after the phone call. Their stupidity must be punished. I obviously need some new blood in the leadership over there. We have a lot of work to do to get this operation back in business again."

"Yes, boss."

The boss turned around and resumed his observation of the San Francisco Bay.

Sensing that he was no longer needed by the boss, Bobby excused himself and headed down the hall to his office. He had a lot of work to do.

Chapter Eighteen

Mac's cell phone rang while he was on his way to Georgetown to meet Hope. He looked down at his phone and recognized the number immediately. It was T. *Shit, not again. She's never going to believe me if I bail out on another date.* He toggled the secure app on his phone. "Yes, ma'am."

T said, "Where are you?"

"I'm in my truck right now. Heading to Georgetown."

"Have you been listening to the radio?"

"No. What's up?"

"Someone from the Associated Press picked up the story on Amanda Anderson's rescue. It's all over the radio and TV now. They don't have any significant details but they know about the attack on the *Mirrabooka* and Amanda's subsequent rescue. Not sure but we think the leak might have come from one of our sailors in Singapore. We're working with the State Department and Defense to create a cover story. Think we'll blame this one on the Delta Force guys. The SEALs have been getting all the press these days. We might as well share the wealth."

Mac laughed. "Okay, T. Thanks for the heads-up. I'll do my best to ignore the news."

T said, "Actually, the news is the least of our problems."

Now she had Mac's full attention.

She continued, "It appears that the folks who ran the drug business from the ship you sank are looking for the people responsible for the attack. Our colleagues in Singapore are seeing a lot of chatter on their networks. Now that the news has put out the story on Amanda Anderson, we think she's in danger."

"What's the threat?"

"We've received some information that a hit is being put out on her. We think it's coming from someone in the US."

Mac nodded. "That's not good. Is she still back home with her parents?"

"Not right now. The White House asked the Federal Protective Service to temporarily relocate her."

Mac grimaced. "Those guys don't have a great reputation, T."

T laughed. "I knew you were going to say that, Mac. That's why I'm calling you!"

Mac realized he had probably just walked into a trap.

She continued, "Actually, Secretary Anderson is not wild about the FPS's track record either. He's keeping her at his place for now. However, he just called the DCI and asked him to help them out. It seems as though you and your team made quite an impression on Ms. Anderson. Her father has asked for you to personally provide her protective services until this thing blows over."

Mac grimaced. He was on his way to a date in Georgetown and now he was being asked to babysit a college girl. But, he knew the DCI wouldn't have asked T to call him unless the threat was credible. He had a chance to get to know Amanda during their trip back to the States, and during their debrief. She was a nice kid. She deserved a break.

"Okay, T." He groaned. "Where do you need me to be and when?" He stopped for a moment and said, "And please don't tell me you need me tonight!"

T laughed. "No. I don't need you tonight. But I would like you to meet her tomorrow at Easton Airport."

Mac nodded. He could see where this was going but he asked anyway. "Okay. I can meet her at the airport. Where is she going to stay?"

"Why Mac, I've seen the video of your new place on the Eastern Shore. It looks really nice. It's already wired to the Agency and if you're there, I think we can keep our finger on the pulse of any eminent threat to Ms. Anderson. Would you mind keeping an eye on Ms. Anderson from your home over there on the shore? I know it's kind of unusual but I think it would work in this situation."

Mac could almost see T smile on the other end of the phone. He knew she'd carefully set a trap for him. But he also knew Amanda Anderson was in a rough spot. He knew the press, and anyone else who looked for her, would have a rough time finding her at his place. She was a good kid. He decided he would do it. For her and for T.

"Okay, T. I will take her in. When will she arrive at the airport?"

"She'll be there around ten a.m., if that works for you?"

"Yep. I will be there. How long do you think she will need to stay?"

T said, "Okay. Thanks, Mac. It's kind of hard to say how long we will need to keep her over there. I will keep an eye on the threat and the press and then let you know what's going on." Then she paused and said, "Have fun tonight!"

Mac laughed. "Thanks, T! I'll try to behave myself."

T chuckled and said drily, "No doubt. Just be waiting at Easton Airport at ten o'clock tomorrow morning, Mac!"

He hung up the phone just as he made his way through Roslyn. He crossed the Key Bridge to Georgetown and turned up 33rd Street NW toward Hope's house. After driving a couple of blocks on 33rd Street, he turned right on N Street and scanned the houses for Hope's address. Her place was easy to find. He pulled into the driveway and grabbed the flowers he'd picked up on his way up the road. Then he walked up her sidewalk to the front porch and rang the doorbell.

It didn't take long for her to answer the door and when she did, she took his breath away. He had never seen her with her hair up. To say that he liked it would be a gross understatement. She looked beautiful. She wore a halter top dress and he could tell she had been out in the sun since he had seen her last. She looked good and he found himself momentarily at a loss for words.

She flashed him a grin as she opened the door. Then she moved to him and gave him a hug and a soft kiss on the cheek.

Mac offered her the flowers. She smiled as she took them from his hands. "Oh, Mac. These are beautiful. I love flowers. It was so thoughtful of you to bring me something."

Mac smiled. "I'm glad you like them. I figured it was the least I could do after my no-notice departure on Memorial Day weekend."

"Yes. I have to admit that your voice message caught me a little off guard." Hope motioned for Mac to come inside. Then she said, "But I figured it caught you just as off guard too. I was glad to hear everything was okay when you called me on Sunday."

As Mac walked through the entryway to her home, Hope motioned for him to follow her into the kitchen. He liked the way her place was decorated. It was an older, Georgian style home but it had been renovated. The kitchen was flooded with natural light from a solid wall of windows. The afternoon sun framed her figure as she bent down at the cabinet under her sink to retrieve a vase for the flowers. He watched her as she filled the vase with water, cut off the bottoms of the stems and then arranged the flowers in the vase. Her hands moved deftly and he watched her face as she studied the arrangement and moved the flowers around until their locations met with her approval. Her slender figure and the curve of her neck reminded him of Audrey Hepburn with her hair up. She was a bombshell and Mac was mesmerized by her beauty.

As Hope tended to her flowers, his eyes roamed from the kitchen to the family room. A beautiful fireplace on the far wall was framed by a bookshelf and a gun cabinet. In the center of the family room, his eyes were drawn to a beautiful antique pool table. Now he knew why she was so damn good at pool. She had her own table in her house. Just like him! She turned around and saw him smiling as he looked at the pool table. She grinned at him. "What?"

"Now I know how you gave me such a run for my money at Shaunessy's!

Hope laughed. "Well, after dinner tonight, we might just have to have a rematch. I still can't believe I missed that shot!"

Mac smiled too. "I couldn't believe you missed it either. I thought you had me. And when you opened the door for me, I knew I better sink the eight ball before you had another chance!" He winked and bowed at her. "I would be honored to give you a rematch, mademoiselle."

Hope smiled and batted her eyes. "Be careful what you ask for, mister. You might just get your ass kicked the next time we play. Now, what would you like to drink?"

Mac smiled. He had no doubt that she would figure out some way to play him again tonight. He was looking forward to it. "I'd like a beer, please. Anything cold."

She said, "That sounds good. I'll get one too." She reached into the refrigerator and pulled out two bottles of beer. Then she opened the freezer and pulled out two ice-cold mugs. She filled them up, handed one to Mac and lifted her glass. "Cheers. Here's to getting to know you better, Mr. Callaghan."

Mac nodded. "I'm looking forward to it."

They clinked their mugs together in a traditional toast and drank. Mac grinned as he noticed the foam from her beer clung to her upper lip. It was cute. She saw him look at her funny and said, "What now?"

He pointed to the top of his lip. "It looks like you're saving some of your beer for later…or, perhaps you've decided to grow a mustache?"

She reached up to her mouth and wiped the foam away from her lip. "It's considered the best part of the beer, you know. I was just checking to see if you would notice!" Then she nodded toward the backyard. "C'mon, Inspector Clouseau, let's head out to the courtyard, shall we?"

Mac followed her to the courtyard. On his way to the back door, he stopped in front of the gun cabinet by the fireplace. "I didn't know you were a shooter?"

Hope said, "Oh. Yes. Well, I guess we haven't had a chance to talk about that yet. I love to shoot. My dad was in the Green Berets and he taught me how to shoot when I was a little girl." She motioned toward the gun cabinet. "Those guns don't get fired much anymore. I keep the ones I use most of the time down at my parents' place."

Mac admired the weapons in the case. There were a couple of Browning and Beretta shotguns, a Remington bolt-action deer rifle and a Winchester Model 94 lever-action rifle. It was a pretty impressive collection.

Hope said, "Are you a hunter too?"

Mac nodded. "I used to do a lot of hunting when I was a kid. Nowadays I spend most of my time target shooting." He paused as he thought about the targets he and his team shot at a week ago but decided to let that thought pass. Then he said, "I have an indoor shooting range in the old barn at my place. You'll have to come over some time and check it out."

Hope smiled. "Why, I would love to come over and see your place sometime. I wouldn't mind taking you on in a friendly shootin' match either!"

She winked at him and then turned to open the French doors to the courtyard. "Welcome to my garden, Mr. Callaghan."

He followed her into the courtyard where he saw she had a beautiful garden surrounding a koi pond, with a small fountain in the middle of it. They sat together in an antique free-standing porch swing and listened to the muted gurgle of the fountain. Even though her house was in the middle of Georgetown, it was remarkably peaceful and quiet in her backyard. They sat in the porch swing and talked about where they went to college and how they got into the businesses they were in. Mac was fascinated by her experience in the construction business and told her about his recent renovation of his home on the Eastern Shore.

Hope watched him as they talked. He was relaxed and confident. She liked how he listened to her and seemed to be genuinely interested in what she did and where she grew up. He laughed when she told him stories about her mother trying to set her up. When he laughed, she studied the laugh lines around his eyes. She couldn't quite put her finger on what it was but this guy was different. She instantly felt comfortable with him. It was as if she had known him for a long time, even though they had really just met. It was a different feeling for her. She liked it.

They finished their beers and headed down the street to dinner. It was a beautiful summer night and they enjoyed the short walk to the restaurant. By this time of day, the sun was low on the horizon and the neighborhood cooled off as twilight descended on the city.

They entered the restaurant and the maître d showed them to the bar while they waited for their table. They sat down at the bar and ordered a glass of wine. As they waited for their drinks, Mac looked up above the bar and saw Amanda Anderson's picture on the television. Then they cut away to a shot of the blood-soaked stern of the *Mirrabooka*. A senior administration official had confirmed that American Special Forces had participated in the rescue. Mac found it interesting that there was no mention of the ship, or any survivors. He made a mental note to call the rest of his team to alert them about his latest tasking to keep an eye on Amanda.

Hope watched the news report too. She nodded toward the television. "Oh my God, that poor woman. Hasn't she already gone through enough? Now the media will hound her to death!"

Mac nodded. "Yep. Just confirms once again that the world is full of wackos."

"It sure is." She looked at him inquisitively. "It will be interesting to see who actually pulled off the rescue."

Mac looked away from her and shrugged. "I suspect it will be an interesting story. Sounds like the Special Forces guys did a good job."

He wondered how T and Henry Burnside would spin it. He had no doubt they were busy working on a cover story while he watched the news with Hope. The conversation made him uneasy; when Hope looked at him, he felt as if she looked right through him. He wondered why she asked the question the way she did. It was almost as if she knew something about him and probed him to see what he would say. He decided he better change the subject but, before he spoke again, the maître d did it for him as he approached them and showed them to their table.

After they finished dinner, they headed back to her place. They laughed and talked as they walked and, before they knew it, they were back at Hope's house. As they turned and walked up the sidewalk to her house, Mac hoped that she would invite him in, but he didn't want to seem presumptuous so he said, "I want you to know I had a great time tonight, Hope. Thanks so much for going out to dinner with me."

She stopped on the sidewalk and turned to him. "That sounds like you're getting ready to head home, Mac. If you think you're getting out of here before I get a rematch on the pool table with you, you're freaking kidding yourself, buddy."

Her words were music to Mac's ears. He really wasn't ready to go yet. He just hadn't figured out a way to get invited inside. Not surprisingly, Hope made it easy for him.

After they walked through the door, she slipped off her heels and headed back toward the kitchen. She gestured to the family room. "Go ahead and rack 'em. I'll get us another drink."

He walked into the family room and flipped on the lights. He admired the antique pool table as he collected the balls from the leather pockets. He picked up the triangular rack and arranged the balls as Hope came back into the room with two more frosty mugs of beer.

As she deposited the beer on an end table by the couch, he smiled. "You're not trying to gain an advantage over me by getting me drunk, are you?"

She laughed. "I'd say the playing field is pretty level, wouldn't you? If anyone has grounds for concern, it's probably me! I have a lot less body weight to absorb it than you do!"

Mac laughed. "You're probably right. Okay. Then for that

reason, I'll let you break this time."

She selected a cue stick from a stand in the corner and from his perspective, very suggestively applied a thin layer of chalk to the tip. He could tell she knew he watched her. When she finished with her cue, she looked at Mac and, with a wink, said, "You're on!"

While Mac selected his cue, she calmly moved to the head of the table and set up her cue ball. He watched her as she took aim, steadied herself, drew back her cue stick and drilled the cue ball down the table. The balls jumped on impact and bounced around the table. Mac saw the green and white striped fourteen ball slide into one of the corner pockets. It was a good break.

He watched her as she moved around the table. He could see her plan ahead for her next series of shots. As she leaned over the pool table, the green felt contrasted with her long, tan fingers. He could see the gloss of her clear nail polish under the lights and watched as she crouched over her next shot. Her halter top dress exposed her back to him and his eyes followed the gentle curve of her spine down to her hips. She launched the cue ball again and sank another ball, the ten this time. As she continued to sink the "high" balls, Mac wondered whether he was ever going to get a shot in. He smiled as she worked her way around the table, stopping every now and then for a sip of her beer. Just as he was about to give up, she missed a shot on her second to last ball, the nine. As it bounced off the bumper next to the side pocket, she muttered a curse. "Damn it! I can make that shot."

Mac smiled as he surveyed the table. Then he raised an eyebrow at her. "Pressure getting to you?"

She started to laugh. "Damn you, Mac Callaghan. You've got a lot of nerve! This game is far from over, my friend."

As he looked at the table, he thought, *I sure hope you're right.*

He winked at her. "I'm kind of hoping our game has just begun."

She looked at him, smiled and quietly said, "Perhaps."

Hope watched Mac as he started to run the table. She was a little drunk and more than a little turned on by this handsome pool shark who was crouched over her pool table. She wanted to beat him in the worst way but her passion for competition was overtaken by a not so subtle feeling of attraction. She felt a familiar sensation in her core as her body reacted to the scene before her. It had been awhile since she had felt like this around a man. It felt good and it felt right being in her home and playing pool with Mac.

To her delight, Mac missed his next shot and she was back in control again. She looked across the table at him as she chalked up the tip of her cue. "Now who's feeling the pressure, buddy?"

Mac smiled. He loved competing with her and he loved the way she pushed back at him. "The game's not over yet."

She felt his eyes follow her as she sized up the table for her last two shots. She could easily see the path to victory. One shot to drop the nine ball and then a shot on the eight. She lined up her shot and gently stroked the cue ball to put the nine in the side pocket. After the cue ball clipped the nine, it rolled a short distance up the table and came to rest in a perfect position for her last shot on the eight ball. She stepped back from the table and took another look at the shot. "Eight ball in the corner pocket."

Mac acknowledged the call. He knew he was in trouble. He watched her as she leaned across the table for her final shot and felt himself getting aroused as he watched her dress rise up around her hips while the curve of her breasts strained the fabric of her halter top.

She softly stroked the cue ball and it rolled in a perfect line to the eight. The balls gently clicked together and the eight ball rolled into the corner pocket like it was on rails. The game was over. She had beaten him fair and square. She laid her cue stick on the table and walked toward Mac with her hand extended to shake his hand. She was thrilled to beat him but now her heart beat strongly in her chest as she approached him.

He reached out to her and shook her hand. Her handshake was firm but her hand was soft. He held onto her hand and looked down into her eyes. She returned his gaze and turned her face up to his. They didn't say a word. They didn't have to.

He lowered his head to kiss her and their lips met. They kissed each other gently as their bodies came together. She reached her hands up, circled his neck with her arms, and murmured through their kiss, "Sorry to have to kick your ass like that."

Mac chuckled. "Somehow, with you in my arms, I'm not feeling too bad about losing. Besides, I think we're going to have many more opportunities to test each other, my dear."

Then he wrapped his arms tightly around her and kissed her deeply. She opened her mouth and welcomed his tongue while she wrapped her arms more tightly around his neck and pressed her hips against him. She could feel him hardening against her waist and she dropped her hands to his hips and pulled him firmly against her.

He felt warm and strong and full as he reacted to the pressure of her hips. She felt him press himself into her while his hands ran up her back to her neck. He ran his fingers through her hair and she felt the pins holding her hair up give way to his strong fingers. As her hair tumbled down around her shoulders, she felt his hands move to caress the sides of her breasts. His thumbs found her nipples and they reacted to his touch as they strained against the sheer fabric of her dress. It wasn't long before she felt his hands move down below her waist. His fingers lifted the hem of her dress and worked their way up her inner thighs. The dress she wore did not pair well with her underwear. In truth, not many of her dresses did. Consequently, she wasn't wearing any panties tonight. She was glad she had decided to leave them in her dresser drawer as she opened her legs to him and felt his fingers gently explore her. She moaned softly and gently bit his lower lip as he found the soft center of her core.

While Mac drove her crazy with his fingers, Hope decided it was time to release him from the fabric prison of his trousers. She reached down to unbuckle his belt and found the zipper on his trousers. As she unzipped him, she felt him pressing against her fingers through the fly of his underwear. She unbuttoned his trousers and they dropped to the floor. Then she carefully slipped his boxer shorts down his long, tan legs.

When she first met Mac on the Bay, she had wondered what he would look like out of his shorts. She no longer needed to wonder as she pressed his underwear down his legs and admired his package on her way down. After she helped him step out of his trousers, she gently took him into her hands. She heard him inhale instinctively and felt him shiver as her hands enveloped and caressed his throbbing shaft. She felt him harden fully in her palms. Then she looked up and kissed him hard again. "Take me now, Mac. I need you to take me now."

Mac was beyond holding back at this point. He ran his hands up along her sides and lifted her dress up over her head. As she shrugged the dress from her shoulders, he placed his hands under her armpits and gently lifted her up off the floor. She was light and she was ready for him. As he lifted her up, she raised her knees and arched her back. Then, as he slowly lowered her back down, she gently positioned him to help him glide into her core. She gasped breathlessly as she felt him enter her and, as she aligned her hips to allow him to completely fill her up, she kissed and nibbled his neck.

He backed her up to the pool table and eased her down on the soft green felt. She laid back, stretched her arms out over her head, and smiled up at him as he slowly and deliberately poured himself into her.

Mac gazed at Hope as their natural instincts synchronized the rhythm of their bodies. She was absolutely beautiful. Her body was strong and firm. Her long, dark hair was sprayed across the felt as she rocked back and forth with him. It was all happening so fast but it felt as if they had been together forever. She looked back up at him and gazed directly in his eyes as she raised her knees, hooked the heels of her feet in the small of his back, and rocked back into him. Then she pressed herself harder against him and reached behind him to grip his hips to pull him hard against her. She felt the muscles in his legs flex as he responded to her and he felt her inner core hum with pleasure.

Their passion, now fully unleashed, exploded from within them. Hope rode the waves of her desire to a gasping crescendo as she let herself go completely. She felt her body shudder as her core contracted and pulsed over and over again. Then, when Mac finally let himself go, they both collapsed on the green felt of Hope's pool table.

Hope felt Mac's full weight press down on her as he collapsed into her on the table. She welcomed his release by fully enveloping his body with her arms and legs. As the waves of his passion slowly subsided, she could feel his body continue to pulse inside her. She ran her fingers up along his spine and massaged his shoulders and neck. Then he was still.

As Mac's body recovered, she felt his arms relax and his chest pressed down against her breasts. He felt strong and good and right, and Hope smiled and nuzzled his neck as his breathing returned to normal and he settled down in her arms. While they recovered, they giggled and laughed about how much fun it was to play pool together. Then, with a soft kiss on his ear, Hope whispered an invitation for Mac to follow her upstairs to her bedroom, where they racked them up again, and again.

Chapter Nineteen

It had been almost a week since Chen Yiu had given the order to terminate his leadership team in charge of Far East operations. Per his orders, the men had been tortured and executed. Their naked and emasculated bodies had been left in the streets of their neighborhoods for all to see the penalty for losing over $15 million dollars of the syndicate's money. Chen sent a clear message to those who engaged in the business of trafficking narcotics for him. Failure to keep the drug pipeline open and/or a loss of revenue for the syndicate would not be tolerated. To do anything that affected both was a fatal mistake. The new leadership team was acutely aware of the fate of their predecessors. They knew they could expect to suffer similar consequences if they failed Chen again.

Chen now had a different problem to deal with. His bosses in the syndicate had expressed a desire to send a clear message to the people who attacked their ship. Chen knew it would be a challenge to find the people responsible for the attack. He suspected that the government of the United States had a hand in the raid, but he couldn't figure out why.

Fortunately for him, CNN broke the story about the rescue. The news confirmed the story about the attack on the *Mirrabooka* and the subsequent raid by the United States on the syndicate's ship. It also confirmed the identity of the woman. She was Amanda Anderson, the daughter of the US Secretary of State. Now it was clear to him why the United States had gotten involved. The news reported that the US Army Delta Force had conducted the raid but that report was not confirmed by the Chen's sources at the US Drug Enforcement Agency. Further, Chen's contacts in Singapore indicated that there had been a high level of involvement by the SID in the raid. He knew that normally the SID coordinated closely with the CIA. He also knew that the CIA had assault teams composed of men and women who were capable of pulling off a raid like this one. He guessed the CIA was the agency involved in sinking his ship, not the Army Special Forces. If the operation was conducted by the CIA, it was going to make it harder for him to find the bastards who sank his ship. The CIA was notoriously difficult to penetrate and he knew he had no contacts on the inside.

Chen decided to change his strategy. If he couldn't get on the inside of the CIA, perhaps he could solve this problem in another way. He thought he might be able to get his hands on Amanda Anderson and, through her, get the attention of some people at the CIA. He knew it would be easy to find her. The news media thought they knew where she was and they were camped out in front of her parents' house in Washington, DC. Although the secretary of state and his wife had granted interviews to the press, no one had interviewed their daughter. She was reported to be recuperating at her parents' home but no one had seen her. Chen was willing to bet that the media was right about where she was, so he directed his people to stakeout the secretary of state's house in Washington. It was relatively easy to do that right now. His people could blend in with the media circus and could follow anyone who left the residence. In the meantime, he put a full-court press on his contacts in Washington at the DEA and other law enforcement agencies to try to determine the identity of the raiders.

While the drug syndicate tried to figure out how to get their hands on Amanda Anderson, Mac Callaghan sat in the parking lot of the Easton Airport and waited for a CIA helicopter to deliver her to him.

It was early on Sunday morning. He was still dressed in the clothes he had worn on his date with Hope the night before. He had reluctantly left her in her bed in Georgetown this morning after a spectacular night of lovemaking. She was not happy when he woke her up with a soft kiss as he got dressed and prepared to leave her. He told her he had an appointment with a contractor back at his farm that he had to get back for. Thankfully, she hadn't asked too many specific questions about what he was having done at the house. He was glad she didn't. He hated to have to lie to her. He didn't protest at all, though, when she coaxed him back to bed for another mind-blowing roll in the hay before he left.

He hadn't expected their date to result in his spending the night in her bed but he was damn glad it had. She was an incredible lover with an insatiable appetite and an uncanny ability to keep him going long after he thought he was spent. She seemed totally at ease with him and took him to places where, he had to admit, he had never been. She had surprised him and he liked it. Making love to her was exhilarating and fun.

As he sat in the cab of his truck, he could still smell her perfume on his shirt and feel the tingling in his muscles from the strenuous activities of the night before. While he waited for the chopper to arrive, he closed his eyes and smiled as he remembered his date with Hope. She was smart, she was funny, she was beautiful, and she was a dynamo in the sack. *Damn near perfect*, he thought. He couldn't wait to see her again and feel her body move against his.

His dream-like trance was interrupted by the distant sound of a chopper. He looked to the west and saw the black shape of the approaching helicopter. He looked down at his watch. It was five minutes after ten. He figured this must be the chopper from the Agency. He reached across the cab and opened the glove compartment of his truck. His Model 23 was in its holster there. He picked up the holster and slid the gun out of it. Then he slid back the slide to chamber a round, set the safety, and returned the weapon to its holster. It was time to get back to work. He slid the holster into the waistband of his trousers and pulled out the tails of his shirt to cover up the gun. Then he stepped out of the cab of his truck, put on an old ball cap, and headed toward the transient line. As he walked, he felt some soreness in his muscles. He realized they were muscles he hadn't used for a very long time. He smiled again as he thought about Hope and then looked toward the helicopter as it set down on the tarmac.

As the chopper's blades slowed to a stop, Mac walked toward the copilot's door. He saw Amanda next to the pilot. She smiled and waved as she saw him approach the helicopter. When the main rotor blade stopped, the door opened and Amanda stepped out to greet Mac. She gave him a big hug. "Hello there, Mac! I never thought I would ever see you again and now, here you are!"

He smiled and gave her a hug back. "Hello, Amanda. It's good to see you. Welcome to the Eastern Shore. I'm glad you could come down here and get away from all the madness up there in the city for a while."

She nodded. "No shit. It's unbelievable up there right now. My dad had to smuggle me out of the house this morning in the trunk of his car!"

Mac received Amanda's luggage from the helicopter pilot. Amanda had only packed a backpack and a small suitcase. It was obvious that she didn't plan to stay too long. Mac hoped her planning was on the mark. He wasn't really sure what to expect. It was unusual for him to take on a protective custody gig. He knew they could be kind of open-ended arrangements. Fortunately, he had plenty of room and she seemed to be a good kid, so he hoped for the best. He grabbed the backpack and handed it to her.

"Here. You take the backpack and I will put your suitcase in the back of my truck."

He shook the pilot's hand. "Thanks for bringing her down. I've got it from here."

The helicopter pilot grinned. "Glad to be of service, Mac. I needed some flight time anyway and it's a beautiful day. Also, T asked me to pass along to you that she hasn't heard anything different than what she talked about with you yesterday."

Mac nodded. "Roger that. I may need to get some flight time myself over the next couple of days." He turned and looked at

Amanda. "Do you like to fly?"

She said, "Sure. I've only ever flown in an airliner, though. The first time I ever flew in a helicopter was when you guys came to get me off the ship and today, of course."

Mac pointed to the G-5 parked across the ramp. "Well, I think you're in for a treat. That airplane over there can take us just about anywhere we want to go. Think about what you would like to do while we head back to my place and we can talk about where you want to go. After a week or so, I'm sure you'll be ready to get away from the farm for a while."

She looked at the airplane and then looked at Mac. "Wow! Really? That's totally cool!"

Mac laughed. "Really. Let's head over to the truck now and get you back to my place."

As they headed back to Mac's place, Amanda caught him up on all the things that had happened to her after she got back to the States. As expected, she had been admitted to Bethesda Naval Medical Center for a full physical and mental evaluation. She passed both with flying colors, although she admitted to still having trouble sleeping. They had given her some sleeping pills and sent her home after a couple of days. Everything had been okay at home until the news broke the story about her kidnapping and rescue. Then things got a little crazy for her and her parents. There were newsmen and paparazzi all over the place. The president had authorized additional Secret Service agents to protect Amanda and her mom and dad but they all knew Amanda would be a captive in her own house until all of this blew over. When they realized that Amanda was going to go crazy in her house, her father called Henry Burnside and asked for help.

Now Mac understood how he had got into the mix. He and Henry had known each other for a long time. Mac knew there were plenty of agency safe houses scattered around the Washington, DC metropolitan area. Henry could have easily put Amanda into one of those. Something else must be going on. Something that indicated to

T and Henry that Amanda needed more than just normal protection. As he headed back to the house with Amanda, his cell phone beeped with an incoming text message. He pulled his cell phone out of his pocket and checked his messages. A smile crossed his face as he saw the message was from Hope. He opened the text and laughed. She sent him a picture of her pool table. The balls were neatly racked on the table and centered on the foot spot. The cue ball was centered on the head spot. The text message read, "Thx for last nite…n this morning. Missing u n rdy for another rack."

Amanda saw him smiling as he read the text. "Someone special, Mac?"

"Sort of."

"Are you married, Mac?

Mac laughed. "No. Not by a long shot. This line of work is not conducive to long-lasting relationships. At least, it hasn't been for me."

Amanda nodded. "That's too bad. You seem like such a nice guy." She chuckled and looked out the window as she said, "I mean, when you're not killing people."

Mac looked over at her and raised an eyebrow. "Well, that's very nice of you to say, I think?" Then he smiled at her and rubbed his chin. "I like to think the people I've had to kill during my career needed it. Otherwise, I probably would have left them alone."

Amanda chuckled. "Yes. I kind of noticed that." She turned and looked back at him. "I hope you don't think I'm prying. Please tell me to shut up if I'm asking too many questions. Do you have a girlfriend?"

Mac looked over at her. "You're not bothering me. Actually, I just started seeing someone. Before that, it had been a long time since I had seen anyone. I found it kind of hard to maintain a relationship with anyone when I routinely get called away at a moment's notice."

"I can see how that would be problematic. I just think you must get lonely sometimes."

"Yep. Sometimes I do. But, believe it or not, I have a real job that keeps me pretty busy."

"Oh yeah? What do you do?"

"I'm a partner at an investment firm in New York."

Now it was Amanda's turn to smile. "Interesting. How in the world do you keep your business running when you are running all over the world rescuing damsels in distress?"

He laughed. "I have a very understanding partner and really good people on the staff who help keep me out of too much trouble."

Mac enjoyed his conversation with Amanda. She had still been pretty shaken up on the ride back home from Singapore. He and the other folks on his team had given her some room to decompress after her ordeal with the pirates. She seemed much more at ease and willing to talk now.

As Mac talked with Amanda, he replied to Hope's text message. He said, "Me too. How bout nxt weekend?"

It didn't take long for her to respond. All she said was, "Deal."

He read her response and smiled again. He wondered whether Amanda would still be staying with him by then.

Mac turned his pickup truck down the long gravel driveway that led to his farm.

Amanda let out a small whistle. "Is this all yours?"

Mac nodded. "Yep. And you are my first visitor since I moved in a few weeks ago. I just finished a major renovation on the house and outbuildings. Once you get your stuff unpacked, I'll give you a tour." In the distance, he could see Moses running down the driveway toward them.

He pointed through the windshield at Moses. "I hope you like dogs?"

"Yes. I do. My folks have a Golden retriever."

"Good. I have a Lab. His name is Moses. That's him coming down the driveway to greet us."

Moses had obviously heard them coming up the driveway and was now rendezvousing with Mac's truck to provide them with an escort back to the house. The big dog was happy to see them after spending the night on the farm alone. As they got out of the truck, he greeted Amanda in his customary fashion with a sloppy, wet kiss on her face.

Mac pulled Amanda's suitcase out of the bed of the pickup and walked her to the front door. He opened the door for her. "Come on inside. We can make some lunch and go for a boat ride, if you like. Or you can just hang out by the pool, if that suits you better?"

Amanda walked through the front door and looked around. From the entryway, she had an unobstructed view of the river through the windows in the back of the house. It was a sunny day and the sunlight sparkled and danced off the water. "Oh my God, Mac, this place is absolutely beautiful. Yes. Let me unpack my stuff and then we can get some lunch. I'm kind of hungry. I didn't get much for breakfast this morning."

He showed her to her room on the second floor. When he renovated the house, he designed the second floor specifically for guests. There were three guestrooms and a bunkroom with six bunk beds upstairs. All of them had their own bathrooms with showers and whirlpool tubs. As he showed Amanda to her room along the back of the house overlooking the water, she smiled. "Wow! This is really nice, Mac. I had no idea I was going into protective custody in paradise!"

Mac smiled. "Well, I'm hopeful that you will have a very peaceful and relaxing visit. You'll be safe here. And while you're here, I'll do my best to keep you busy."

Amanda patted Moses on the head. "Thank you. I know this is unusual but I already feel safe here. I know you and Moses will take good care of me, and I promise I will try not to be a bother and intrude on your life too much."

Mac said, "Don't worry about that. We'll all be fine. I will head downstairs and find something for us to eat."

Mac and Moses headed back downstairs to the kitchen. He was glad Sean and Ben had come down to finish unpacking the house.

He had to agree with Amanda. The place looked great. All the boxes were gone and the pictures were hung. It really did feel like home and he was proud to show off his new house to Amanda. She was a good kid and he hoped he could help her find some peace.

Chapter Twenty

It was a good week for Mac. He enjoyed having Amanda around the house. She was a fitness buff, so he had a ready-made workout partner. And she loved being out on the water, so he and Moses took her fishing. She was more of an outdoorsy kind of girl than he had expected. Every time he turned around, she asked him to take her out on the boat, which was just fine with him. He was impressed by how well she handled his boat and it wasn't long before Mac let her take the helm of the *Kestrel* on their fishing trips. He enjoyed sitting back and watching her as she conned the boat. She was a natural skipper and he saw a lot of himself in her when they headed out to go fishing. Contrary to what he heard about young people, she seemed perfectly happy to roll out of bed early and leave the dock at 0600 every morning. They caught quite a few fish during the week and Mac was pleased to find that she had become an accomplished chef while she served as a crewmember onboard the *Mirrabooka*. She treated him to some spectacular meals. After dinner, they would sit on the back porch and talk about her life experiences, before and after her ordeal in the Strait of Malacca. She was still recovering from her kidnapping and assault. The experience had shaken her confidence but she seemed to be trying to put it all behind her. He was surprised at her maturity and hoped her time at the farm could help her decompress and get on with her life.

One evening, while they played pool in the study, he saw her looking at the guns he had on display in his gun cabinet. When he asked her whether she was interested in shooting, she confessed that she had only fired a gun once before, when the Captain of the *Mirrabooka* trained the crew to fire a twelve gauge shotgun. Mac told her he had an indoor firing range on the farm and asked her whether she wanted to learn how to shoot.

She said she was interested in learning more, so the next morning, they went to the range. First he taught her about basic firearms operations, safety, and cleaning and then he cut her loose on the range. He started her out with a small caliber rifle. She took to it very well and seemed to enjoy the challenge of precision target shooting. Then he taught her how to shoot a shotgun and a pistol. She really took to the pistol and he gave her a Smith & Wesson M&P Shield 9 mm that, because it was designed for concealed carry, seemed to fit her hand and eye quite nicely. He was impressed with her progress and, after a couple of visits to the range with her, he told her it was okay for her to go there by herself and practice. After that, she spent a lot of time on the range. Mac could tell she liked to shoot but he also suspected she had another motive for learning. He sensed that since her experience in the Strait of Malacca, she had decided to never let herself be a victim again. After Mac inspected the bullet groups on the targets she showed to him, as long as she was armed, he figured that would never be a problem for her.

When she wasn't out on the boat or on the shooting range, Amanda spent much of her time by the pool. She loved to read and the weather in June was perfect for working on her tan while she devoured every book she could get her hands on.

Moses seemed to like having her around too. He spent a lot of time under her chaise lounge, shielding himself, while she baked in the sun. When she did go into the pool for a dip, Moses was happy to join her there. Mac had designed a ledge at one end of the pool for people to sit on and remain partially submerged. Moses had discovered the ledge and decided it was perfect for assisting him with his ingress and egress from the pool. Consequently, Moses spent almost as much time in the pool as Amanda. They both seemed to be happy.

Mac had checked in with T a couple of times for updates on any threats to Amanda. Her sources did not have any higher fidelity information on the nature of the threat to her, but the news media had found out about her covert escape from her parents' house. They now hounded her mother and father wherever they went. The network news anchors and the morning show hosts all clamored for the opportunity to have an exclusive interview with her, and Mac knew how resourceful they could be. He knew they would not stop until they got their story. It was only a matter of time before someone tipped them off. He had forbidden Amanda from using her cell phone and only allowed her to contact her parents from a secure phone in the vault in his house. He hated to cut her off from her friends but recognized the risk associated with anyone, other than her parents, knowing her exact location.

While he provided protection to Amanda, he talked with Hope about their date on Saturday night. He planned to pick her up at her parents' house on Saturday afternoon and take her out to dinner. There was one problem with his plan, though. He knew he couldn't leave Amanda at home by herself while he went out with Hope, and he certainly didn't intend to bring her along. He needed someone to keep an eye on her while he was gone. He thought about it a little bit and decided to give Rosie Roosevelt a call to ask for some help. Amanda liked Rosie, and Rosie could be entrusted with her safety. T and Henry Burnside would split a gut if they knew what Mac planned to do but he figured it would be okay for just one night.

He called Rosie on Thursday afternoon to see whether he would be available to come down for the weekend. The big sniper answered the phone with a hearty laugh. "Mac, my brother! How the hell are you?"

"I'm good, Rosie," Mac responded. "How about you?"

"I'm good. All is well. Staying busy. What are you up to?"

"I have a favor to ask of you."

"Uh oh!" Rosie feigned mock horror. "You're not going to ask me to go on a double date with you again, are you? The last time we did that, it didn't work out too well!"

Mac started laughing. "No, thank God! I'm not asking you to do anything like that. Besides, I really don't feel the need to get arrested, like we almost did the last time."

"No shit," Rosie replied. "If that moron hadn't tried to pick a fight with you, it actually would have been a pretty nice night. Although, I have to admit, it was kinda funny when we put that bozo and his buddy in the beer cooler!"

Mac laughed. "Yep. I thought that would get them to chill out a little bit…"

"Very funny, wise guy," Rosie said. "Okay, enough with the trip down memory lane. What do you need, Mac?"

"Well, I have an unexpected houseguest. You met her on our last trip together. She's staying here for a while to help keep her off the skyline, if you get my drift."

Rosie said, "Got ya. I've been watching the news. I was wondering where she was holed up. Okay, I'm following you. What do you need me to do?"

"I need someone to be here at my place to keep an eye on her on Saturday night. Would you be available to help me out? I'll take you fishing on Sunday!"

Rosie laughed. "It appears to me that you are in somewhat of a jam, eh my friend? Would there be a woman involved in this jam by any chance?"

Mac knew this was coming. Rosie would probably help him out but he wasn't going to let him off the hook too easily. He chuckled. "Perhaps. Is that a problem?"

Rosie shouted, "I knew it! Damn, Mac, you've had one hell of a long dry spell! How long has it been for you? Are you sure you still know what to do?"

Mac laughed. "Very funny, wise guy. Yes, it's been a while but I think this one might be different. I think I can still figure it all out. So, what do you say? Do you think you can hook me up?"

"Of course I can. It will be nice to see your place now that it's finished off, anyway. I can be there sometime in the morning on Saturday, if that will work for you?"

Mac said, "That will work perfectly." Then he stopped for a minute and said, "Hey, Rosie. I really appreciate your help."

"Don't give it another thought. I hope you enjoy your time out. Do me a solid and try not to beat anybody up while you're out with this babe, okay?"

Mac chuckled. "Too late. I already had to put the sleeper hold on some guy at a local bar on our first date!"

"No doubt," said Rosie. "What a surprise—NOT! Make sure you've got plenty of grub for me. You know how I like to eat! Oh, and I will bring my own hardware, if you catch my drift?"

Mac said, "Okay, man. Roger the hardware. You know I have plenty here but I understand why you want to bring your own. Thanks again, Rosie. I will see you on Saturday." He hung up the phone and smiled. *This was all coming together quite nicely.*

He walked out to the pool and saw Amanda and Moses in their usual positions. She was sprawled out on a chaise lounge and he was asleep underneath her chair. She was a cute kid. In reality, she was a beautiful young woman. Mac couldn't help but notice how well she filled out her white bikini. Then he reminded himself that she was just a kid. *Stop it, Mac; she's only twenty-one years old, for God's sake.*

He regained his composure, walked over to Amanda, and stood beside her. She put down her book. "What's up there, Mr. Callaghan?"

"Not too much, kiddo," Mac said. "I have a question for you. Would you mind terribly if I invited Rosie Roosevelt down here on Saturday night?"

"Rosie Roosevelt? That's the sniper guy on your team, right?"

"That's the one."

"Oh Mac, it would be so nice to see him again. He's such a big old teddy bear. Of course I would like to see him!"

"Well, I'm glad to hear that because I invited him down to spend the night here at the farm with you, if that's okay?"

"Of course it's okay." Then she looked at him and cocked her head quizzically. "Did I hear you say, 'Spend the night with you'? Where are you going to be?"

Mac shuffled his feet and looked down at the ground. "Well, I'm planning on going to dinner with a friend on Saturday night, if that's okay with you?"

Amanda laughed. "Why Mac, I believe you're blushing! That's too funny! You're one of the toughest guys I've ever met and now you're standing here looking like a prep student!"

Mac laughed. "I am not!" Then he looked at her quizzically. "Am I? Really?"

"Yes, you are!" She laughed and then looked up at him. "It's okay, Mac. Really! I'm glad for you. I think it's great that you're going to get a chance to go out and have some fun. I wish I was going with you." Then she winked at him. "Can I assume your friend is a girl?"

Mac laughed. "Why yes, as a matter of fact she is. I just met her a few weeks ago."

Amanda smiled. "Good for you, Mac. I'm glad. You seem like such a nice guy, and I wondered why there wasn't a woman in your life. Do you ever think about getting married? You would be such a great dad."

Mac looked out over the creek and thought for a minute before he answered her question.

Amanda said, "I'm sorry, Mac. I didn't mean to ask too personal a question. If you don't want to talk about it, I understand."

Mac looked back at her and smiled. "No, Amanda, I don't mind talking about it. I just needed to collect my thoughts a little bit before I answered your question." Then he looked back out on the water. "I've never seriously considered getting married. In all honesty, I've never had a relationship with a woman that was serious enough to talk about marriage. I've had what I thought might become a few serious relationships but my work with the Agency always seemed to be a deal-breaker. As you now know, my life is not totally under my control. I'm okay with that arrangement but I've found it's pretty hard on relationships."

Amanda listened to his response. She thought for a minute. "I can understand that. But there must be someone out there who could deal with your shadow life, I mean, if you're really interested?"

"I don't know, Amanda. Maybe it's me. Maybe it's them. I don't know. This lady I'm planning to take out to dinner on Saturday night seems different, though. I know it's way too soon to really say I know her well, but I really do like being with her."

"Does she know what you do? I mean, what you really do?"

Mac shook his head. "No. I don't know her well enough to tell her. I mean there are some things, things you know, that I could never tell her."

"Why?"

"It's kind of complicated, Amanda. You're only here because you were personally involved in the rescue operation. There are only a handful of people in the country, including the president, who even know what I do." He looked at her seriously. "Most folks who see us in action don't live to tell anyone about it. That's one of the reasons we sank that ship you were on. We try very hard to not leave our fingerprints behind us."

Amanda took her sunglasses off and looked him dead in the eye. "Mac, I know what you do is classified and terribly important. Hell, I'm living proof that you guys exist and I'm glad you killed those bastards and sank their ship. I don't know you that well but you seem like such a wonderful man. Don't let your job keep you from meeting an equally wonderful woman. If she's really meant for you, she'll want all of you, including your crazy job. And, if she's as smart as she should be and loves you unconditionally, she will figure out what you do and let you do it without asking too many questions."

Mac didn't know what to say. He was kind of shocked. He didn't expect such candor from someone he barely knew, especially from someone so young. As he thought about what she said, he realized she was probably right. But how could she see right through him so easily? Was he really that transparent or was she just that damn smart? Either way, he had to admit she was on the mark. He hesitated for a minute and then said, "Thanks, Amanda. That's very nice of you. Maybe I just haven't found the right woman yet. Frankly, I haven't met anyone, besides Moses, who loves me unconditionally. I'm not even sure that kind of love really exists."

Then he jokingly said, "Who knows? Maybe you're right. Maybe my soul mate is somewhere out there after all? Maybe I just haven't found the one yet who can love me and handle all my baggage too!"

Amanda smiled and looked up at him again. Then she put her sunglasses and her book on the table next to her chair and stood up in front of him. Suddenly, he became aware of how close she was to him and how good she looked in her white bikini. Before he could react, she wrapped her arms around his neck and gave him a warm hug. Then she turned her head and whispered in his ear, "She's out there, Mac. I know it. Stop pretending like it's next to impossible for you to find her. You need to open up your mind and believe that she exists, that she's really out there. Then you'll need to open up your heart and let her in."

She softly kissed his cheek. "You'll know her when you see her and she'll know too."

As Mac stood there dumbfounded, Amanda released him from her embrace, walked to the edge of the pool, and dived in. He was surprised when she hugged him. He was even more surprised by her words. *What a great kid, er, woman. Her parents must be very proud of her.*

He looked back and watched her glide through the water in the pool. She was smart and she was beautiful. He was so glad he and his team had been able to bring her back home safely.

Mac wasn't the only one who was surprised by Amanda's actions. Hope watched their exchange through a set of binoculars from the wheelhouse on her father's boat. She had decided to come home early on Thursday morning. Work was slow at the construction site and the weather was beautiful, so she decided to head down to her folks' place to work on her tan and spend some time with her mother before she saw Mac on Saturday. While she was headed down Route 50, her father called her and asked her to take the big boat out for a run. He had been so busy that he hadn't had a chance to run it as much as he wanted to, so he thought Hope could take it out for him.

She assumed Mac was working in New York. When she turned up his creek and started her slow-cruise toward his place, she didn't expect to see anyone around the house. She really just wanted to go by his place to feel a little closer to him. Right as she turned the corner to make her approach to his dock, she saw a man come out of Mac's house. It looked a lot like Mac but she was too far away to see him clearly. She pulled a set of binoculars out of a compartment under the helm and sure enough, it was him! Her heart leapt with joy at the thought of seeing him again and being with him. She watched him as he walked to the patio and saw that he talked to a bikini-clad woman, with long blonde hair, who was seated on a chair by the pool. She saw the woman stand up and give him a huge hug and a kiss. She couldn't believe her eyes! She felt as if she had been kicked in the stomach. All of the wind passed out of her lungs and her heart felt as if it was breaking. *What an asshole!* The man she made love to just a week ago was with another woman! How could she have read him so wrong? She wouldn't believe it if she hadn't just seen it. It couldn't be true. How could he have asked her out on a date and confirmed his plans to take her to dinner on Saturday when he was down here kissing some blonde bimbo!

She was furious and humiliated. She looked back through the binoculars one more time. The image was blurred by the tears that now filled her eyes. She saw him stand there while the blonde walked away from him and dove into the pool. *Who was she? What the hell was she doing there? And why was Mac asking her out on a date on Saturday night when he was screwing someone else during the week here at his house?* It was all too much for Hope. She wheeled her dad's boat around and firewalled the throttles. She wanted to get as far away from Mac's place as quickly as she could. The engines surged; the boat rose gracefully on plane and sped around the corner of the creek.

While Mac thought about Amanda's comments, he heard the throaty roar of motors spooling up on a boat down the creek. Although the boat was pretty far away, he saw it just as it disappeared around a bend in the creek. *Funny*, he thought; *the boat looked just like Hope's dad's Hinckley*. He wondered what he was doing over this way today. After he watched the boat disappear, he walked back toward the house. *Maybe Amanda is right. Maybe Hope will be different than all the others. Maybe I am ready to try to have a real relationship with her.*

He had no idea that he had just unwittingly cut the stem and pulled out the roots on the flower of his blossoming romance.

Chapter Twenty-one

Chen Yiu sat at his desk in the study of his home in Sea Cliff. The oak logs in the massive stone fireplace crackled softly behind him. Sea Cliff was one of the most exclusive neighborhoods in San Francisco and Chen's property sat on a cliff overlooking Baker Beach. To his right was a spectacular view of the Pacific Ocean and the Golden Gate Bridge. To his left was Bobby Chong. Chen leafed through a set of grainy photographs of Amanda Anderson that Bobby had just personally delivered to him. The pictures were obviously taken at long range and were not very high quality but they were good enough to positively identify the young woman as she climbed out of the trunk of her father's car.

Per Chen's orders, his men followed both Amanda's mother and father. On Sunday morning, they had resigned themselves to accept the fact that, once again, they were going to be following Amanda's father as he ran errands. But this time, instead of going into town like they expected him to, he headed south from the Andersons' home in Arlington and ended up at the Manassas Regional Airport. When he arrived at the airport, he drove past the terminal and, from a more secluded spot, let his daughter out of the trunk of their car. When Chen's men saw Amanda get out of the trunk, they closed on the pair as they walked through the terminal. They photographed them as she waited to be picked up by a light civil helicopter. Then, after the helicopter departed the airfield, they convinced one of the tower employees to let them into the tower for a "tour," where they pretended to learn about flying while they watched the track of the helicopter as it passed over the Chesapeake Bay and disappeared in the vicinity of the Easton Airport. The tower operator was kind enough to tell them the radar return had vanished because "the helicopter had probably landed at the airport there."

With the digital photographs of Amanda Anderson in their camera and a tip on where she was headed, they left the airport and immediately reported their findings to Bobby Chong. Bobby knew Chen would want to see the photographs immediately so he ran copies off in his office and called Chen. As expected, Chen asked Bobby to bring the pictures to his home. As Chen looked through the photographs, he noted the suitcase that Amanda carried with her to the helicopter. She obviously planned to spend some time somewhere. The question was, where?

He looked at Bobby. "This is good work. How are we planning to figure out where she went from the airport in Easton?"

Bobby said, "I'm working on that now, boss. I'm going to hire a local private investigator in Easton to do some snooping around at the Easton Airport to see if we can find out who met her when she landed there. I think a local guy will be less intrusive than if one of us go over there and start asking a lot of questions."

Chen nodded. "Yes. I agree. What's the cover story?"

Bobby smiled. "I'm using the jealous boyfriend cover. I'm going to tell the PI that I think my girlfriend is cheating on me with some rich guy in Easton. We'll see how that works."

Chen said, "Okay. What next?"

"If the PI can get a lead on who picked her up, he may be able to figure out where she went. I'm also using a couple of our folks in Washington to check with their contacts to see if we can identify any potential CIA safe houses in the area. They may have put her up in a protected location to get her out of the media spotlight. Once I get a report back from the PI, we can decide whether it's worthwhile for us to send some of our folks down there to check things out."

Chen nodded. "That's good but I'm not convinced it's good enough."

"What do you mean by that, sir?"

"I don't think any of the members of our teams on the East

Coast are capable of making a clean hit on her when we find her."

Bobby nodded. His boss was probably right. He had harbored the same concerns but had been reluctant to voice them to the boss. In all honesty, he thought the whole idea of trying to make the hit was a bad one to begin with. Sure, they had lost a ship, their men, and a ton of money, but trying to take on the CIA was a pretty risky task. He said, "Well, we could reach out to some people to arrange a contract hit. Would you like me to start making inquiries?"

Chen looked away from Bobby for a moment while he weighed the potential risks and rewards of his decision. He knew that taking out a contract on Amanda Anderson would put a lot of things in motion that would significantly raise the stakes in the game. He wasn't afraid of the government of the United States. He knew there would be a short-term uproar over her death but that news would quickly be forgotten when the next celebrity scandal hit the press or another politician was caught with his pants down. If he made the hit on Amanda and the people who rescued her, his peers and subordinates would be intimidated by his boldness and his bosses would be assured that he was still in control. The press would quickly forget Amanda Anderson but the people who ran the various international crime syndicates would be put on notice that Chen Yiu was a force to be reckoned with. Still, he wasn't comfortable with contract hits. There were too many variables that were out of his control.

Chen looked back at Bobby. "No. I don't want you to make any calls. I want you to lead a team to make the hit for me."

Before he came to work for Chen in San Francisco, Bobby was one of the most accomplished hit men in Thailand. He was a veteran of many high-profile hits on politicians and businessmen in Southeast Asia. He knew how to infiltrate security, eliminate targets, and escape undetected. He had never gone up against anyone in the American CIA, though. He assumed that if Amanda Anderson was in a safe house, that she was probably being guarded by a second-tier Agency contractor. He figured all the first-tier contractors were most likely involved in front-line field operations. He weighed the risk in his mind and realized that, if he could pull off this hit, he would be a "made man" in the Yiu crime syndicate for the rest of his life. He looked at Chen. "I appreciate your confidence. It will take me a day or two to get a team together. Once I get everyone together, I will leave for Washington."

Chen nodded his head. "Take my jet and use whatever resources you need to get the job done, Bobby. I need this to happen quickly and I don't want to leave any tracks."

"As you wish, sir." Bobby nodded and gave Chen a solemn bow. Then he turned and departed the study.

Chen watched Bobby as he left. Then he looked back out the window at the Pacific Ocean. *Those people back in Washington have no idea what I have in store for them.* He muttered softly, "This will teach them not to screw with me." Then he got up from his chair and headed out to the backyard of his estate to practice his putting.

Chapter Twenty-two

It was late on Friday afternoon when T called Mac. He answered the phone and, after toggling his secure app, said, "Callaghan."

"Hi, Mac! It's T."

"Hey, T! It's Friday afternoon. Aren't you supposed to be out on the golf course, or something?"

T could imagine him smiling at the other end of the phone. He just loved to poke fun at her, and usually, she would return the favor, but not this afternoon.

"Very funny, wise guy. Hey, we have a problem. I just got a tip that someone is looking for Amanda Anderson down your way."

T's tone and the information she relayed to Mac instantly got his attention. All the fun and humor was gone from his voice when he said, "Okay, T. How do they know she's down here?"

"We're not sure. Our tip came from a private investigator in Easton. He used to be one of our contract employees. He worked as a driver and provided security at the old safe house we had there in St. Michaels. He got a call from some guy who said he wanted to hire him to find his girlfriend. The client said he thought his girlfriend was shacking up with somebody down your way. He also said he thought she had flown into the local airport there recently. When the client faxed a picture of Amanda to him, the PI recognized her right away from seeing her on the news. He told one of his buddies who still works here about it on Wednesday. The information is just getting to me now. Have you seen any unusual activity down there?"

"No. Nothing going on down here. But we haven't left the farm since Sunday. Where's the client from?"

"San Francisco."

"Sounds like it might be a connection to our Far East friends, eh?"

"Yep. I think you're right. We're tracing the fax information down now."

"Did the PI take the job?"

"Yes. I called him back right before I called you. I'm afraid your cover may be blown. He went to the airport and sniffed around a little bit. Someone at the hangar there saw you pick her up in your pickup truck on Sunday. They had seen you there before when you flew in on your jet."

"How do you want to play it? Do we need to get Amanda out of here?"

"Well, I guess we could do that." T hesitated for a moment. "But Henry and I were thinking you might want to consider another option."

Mac laughed. "I should have known there was gonna be a hook buried somewhere in this conversation." He shrugged. "Okay, T. What do you guys want to do?"

"Well, we were talking about some possible scenarios up here and came up with a couple of options. We think having a link to these guys through the PI might be an opportunity for us. We also think it might be useful to let this play out a little bit more. It's possible, if they make a move on you and Amanda, that they would leave us a trail to follow back to their leadership in San Francisco."

Mac listened to T's rationale. "Okay. It's twisted, but I'm following your logic. Go on."

"We know we have a good security system set up down there at your place. None of our safe houses are wired like your farm and, with a trained security team on-site, we think we can manage the risk to Amanda. If we ask someone from your team to come down and stay there for a while until we sort things out, would you be okay with that?"

Mac hesitated for a minute. He knew Rosie was already coming down to his place this weekend but he didn't want to tell T about it. She would blow a gasket if she figured out what he was trying to do. He decided maybe he could kill two birds with one stone. "I guess we can do that. Let me give Rosie a call to see if he can come down and visit with me for a couple of days. I think the two of us can take pretty good care of Amanda, unless it looks like they're bringing a herd. In that case, we need to get Amanda out of here and bring in some of our own reinforcements."

T said, "That sounds good to me, Mac. Give Rosie a call and let me know if he would be willing to help you out."

Mac hung up the phone and let out a sigh of relief. He hated to lie to T but it seemed innocuous enough. He would call T back in an hour or so and let her know that Rosie was in.

In the meantime, Mac wrestled with another problem. He couldn't figure out why Hope wasn't talking to him. On Thursday, after he had talked with Rosie and Amanda about covering for him while he went out, he tried to call her to confirm their date. She didn't answer her phone when he called. He figured she was probably busy, so he left her a voicemail. He thought she would call him back later that evening but now it was late on Friday afternoon and he still had not heard back from her. He wondered whether she had received the message. Then he started second-guessing himself about what he should do next. Should he call her again? Should he send her a text? Should he just leave her alone and wait for her to get back to him? This was one part of the dating game that Mac absolutely hated. Instead of waiting around and wringing his hands, Mac decided to try to call her back again. He picked up his phone and punched her number. The phone rang again but there was still no answer. He left her another voicemail and then hung up and waited for her to call back.

At dinnertime, he still hadn't heard anything back from her. It must have been apparent that he was worried about something because Amanda said, "Is there something bothering you, Mac? You seem awful quiet tonight."

He looked at her, shook his head, and smiled. "You are an awfully perceptive young lady."

She laughed. "It's not too much of a challenge with you, Mr. Callaghan. For some strange reason, I feel like I'm on the same wavelength as you. And I can tell something is bothering you. Come on, give. What's going on?"

Mac thought for a minute and then responded, "Amanda, I need some advice. I'm gonna sound like a freaking high school kid here in a minute but I'm really perplexed by something. Would you mind listening to what's going on in my head?"

Amanda smiled. "This ought to be interesting." Then she chuckled. "You know I'm just kidding. Sure, I would be happy to help, if I can. What's on your mind, Mr. Tall, Dark, and Handsome?"

He hesitated for a moment while he collected his thoughts. "Well, I've called this woman who I'm supposed to go out with tomorrow night a couple of times now. Normally, when I call her, she either picks up or calls me back pretty quickly. I haven't heard anything back from her for the past two days now and I don't really know what to do about it. Do you have any ideas?"

Amanda frowned. "Oh, Mac. That's not a good sign. Something is definitely wrong. Is this the one who lives in that big ass house down the creek?"

Mac had shown her the house when he took her fishing earlier in the week. He nodded. "Yep. That's the one. Actually, that's her parents' place."

"She's not in the same line of work as you are, is she?"

"No." Mac laughed. "She's not. But it sure feels like she is right now!"

"What's her name, Mac?"

"Hope. Hope Crosby."

"That's a pretty name."

"Yes. It is. And she is a pretty terrific woman but I don't get why I'm suddenly getting the silent treatment."

Amanda thought for a minute. "Well, it sounds to me like she's sending you a signal. Do you know her well? Is it possible that she has changed her mind about going out with you? If she hasn't confirmed your date and she's not answering the phone, it sounds like she's backing out. Not very cool of her not to tell you, though. Why don't you try to text her?"

Mac thought about it. "I guess I can text her. That seems kind of weak to me but I'm out of ideas. I mean, it's not like it's our first date. We got to know each other pretty well, if you know what I mean. I can't figure out what happened to change everything so suddenly. Let me give the text a try."

He pulled out his cell phone and composed a text message to Hope. It said, "Hi. Tried to call but haven't heard back from you. Are we still on for Saturday?"

He hit the send button on his phone and watched the face of the phone while the message was sent. Then he put the phone down on the dining room table. "This sucks. I hate feeling jerked around like this."

Amanda nodded. "It seems odd to me too, especially if she was really into you, or, you were really into her." She gave him a knowing wink that left no doubt that she completely understood what he was talking about.

Mac blushed, again. He felt as if he were talking to his kid sister, and she had the goods on him!

Right about then, his phone beeped. It was an incoming text message.

Amanda raised her eyebrow. "Hope?"

Mac looked down at his phone and smiled. "Yes!"

His elation at seeing her text come in quickly turned to astonishment and then bewilderment when he read it. "Can't make it Saturday night. Besides, it looks like you already have your hands full."

Mac showed his phone to Amanda. "What the hell does that

mean?"

Amanda shook her head. "I don't know, Mac. That seems kind of strange. It sounds like she thinks you're seeing someone else. Are you?"

"No."

"Well, why don't you ask her what she meant then?"

Mac nodded and then typed the question into his phone. "What do you mean by hands full?"

He hit the send key and waited for Hope's response. In a few seconds, his phone beeped again. He looked down at the message and felt his heart sink. It said, "Who's the blonde?"

As soon as he saw the message, he knew what had happened. He remembered the boat that looked like Hope's father's boat out on the creek on Thursday when he was with Amanda. Hope, not her father, must have been on her father's boat! She must have been down here this week! *How in the hell am I going to explain this without blowing my cover?*

Amanda looked across the table from him. "What did she say?"

He showed her his phone and watched her face. He could tell she still didn't get what was happening. "Well, who is the blonde?"

As soon as the words left her lips, he saw that she got it. She immediately got a panicked look on her face and looked back at him. "Oh my God, Mac! Am I the blonde?"

He nodded to her. "It has to be you. Honestly, I'm not seeing anyone else. You're the only woman who has been around me for the past two weeks, I mean, besides Hope. The other day when you and I were out by the pool, I saw a boat on the creek that looked like her father's boat. It must have been his boat but I guess Hope was on it too. She must have come down here from her house in DC and seen you and me together here at the house."

He stopped for a minute and rubbed his face with his hands. "Ugh." He groaned. "What a freaking coincidence. I had no idea she was going to be down here this week. Now I'm not sure how I'm going to wiggle my way out of this."

"What do you mean, Mac? What is there to wiggle out of? Why don't you just tell her who I am?"

"It's not that simple. There are two problems with telling her who you really are. First, I have to protect your identity. Second, I also have to protect my cover down here. If I blow my cover, I might as well put a for sale sign on the farm."

"Well, what are you going to do?"

"I'm not sure. Let me try this."

He picked up the cell phone again and typed, "I take it you saw me at my place. I have a friend staying here but she's not my girlfriend."

He hit the send button, passed the phone over to Amanda, and grimaced. "Typical. I knew this was all too good to be true. I never saw this coming but it just confirms my feelings about relationships and this job."

Amanda shook her head. "Oh, come on, Mac. You can't be serious. You can't let her go that easily. At least wait until you see what she says!"

As if on cue, Mac's phone beeped. Amanda picked it up, looked down at it, and frowned.

Mac said, "That doesn't look good. What's it say?"

Amanda's shoulders slumped forward as she looked at the message. "It's not good, Mac. She says she's shocked that you are denying it. She says she saw you. Then she says she doesn't need the drama and doesn't want to see you anymore."

Mac looked at Amanda and exclaimed, "Shit! Well, I guess she's partly right. I don't need the drama either. If she's not willing to let me explain myself, then why should I bother? Besides, I'm not inclined to be whipped like a cur dog when all I'm doing is trying to protect you, her, and me. I'm probably better off to just stay single. It will be easier in the long run anyway."

He reached across the table and picked up the phone. Amanda watched his face as he read the text from Hope. She could tell he was hurt. She wished there was some way she could explain what

Hope had seen. Then she watched as he stood, slid the phone in his pocket and walked over to the refrigerator. He opened the door, pulled out two bottles of beer and cracked off the bottle caps. "C'mon, Amanda, let's go play some pool."

She looked across the kitchen at Mac. "Oh, Mac. I can't stand to see you feeling this way. Isn't there some way you can tell her what's going on without blowing your cover?" She stood and followed him into the study, where he racked the balls for a game of eight-ball.

"No. I don't know how I can really finesse that one, Amanda," Mac said. "Besides, this is just the first of many lies that I would have to tell her. I'm getting really tired of lying to people. It's easier to just keep to myself than to have to deal with all the questions." He decided not to tell her about his call from T. He had seen her finally begin to relax during the course of her stay with him, and he didn't want to do anything to set back her recovery.

Amanda picked up a cue stick, chalked the tip and lined up her break. She could tell that Mac really liked this girl. She hated to see him get stood up for no good reason, especially when it was because of her. Before she hit the cue ball, she said, "I think you should sleep on this tonight. If she really means that much to you, or if you think she might, there must be a way to explain all of this to her."

Mac nodded and smiled. "I'll think about it. Now go ahead and break. I don't think I want to talk about this anymore tonight."

Amanda leaned over the pool table and broke. She was learning fast and Mac was impressed when two balls dropped into the pockets of his pool table. She looked up and smiled at him. He winked at her. "Nice break, rookie."

Then he watched her as she worked her way around the table. While she studied her next shot, he couldn't help but think about playing pool with Hope. He realized just how quickly he had fallen for her and it hurt to know that, as quickly as their relationship had started, it now looked like it was already over.

Meanwhile, about two miles down the creek from Mac's house,

Hope sat on the plumped-up down comforter of the rice bed in her bedroom at her parents' house. She watched the screen of her cell phone. She had sent Mac her response to his last text over a half hour ago. His lack of response indicated to her that he was done talking. She still couldn't believe he was seeing someone so soon after they had made love at her place in Georgetown. She felt as if she had been sweet-talked and used. She couldn't believe that she had fallen for another guy again. Worse than that, she had slept with him after only one real date. She had fallen for him and broken all of her own personal rules. *How could she have made that mistake? How could she be so stupid?*

Even more hurtful to her was the way he tried to lie his way out of it. She thought he was more of a man than that. If he would have just come clean and told her the truth, maybe she would have given him another chance. She wanted to believe him but she already had all the proof she needed. She had seen him embrace that woman in the bikini with her own eyes. That was proof enough for her.

She heard her mother call from downstairs. Dinner was ready. She took a deep breath, wiped her eyes, and headed downstairs for dinner.

Meanwhile, across the country, Bobby Chong was on the phone, finishing his conversation with the private investigator he hired to find out where Amanda Anderson was holed up on the Eastern Shore. He held the phone to his ear and listened intently to the report. The PI had done some poking around at the Easton Airport and had come up with a lead. He found an aircraft mechanic at the airport who saw a woman who fit Amanda Anderson's description at the airport last weekend. He saw her fly into the airport in a small helicopter. When the helicopter dropped her off, he said she was picked up by some guy in a pickup truck. The mechanic thought it was the same guy who owned an airplane there at the airport, but he wasn't sure.

After his conversation with the mechanic, the PI talked one of his buddies in security into showing him the tapes that were taken by the surveillance cameras located around the ramp. Sure enough, the footage that was recorded on Sunday confirmed the mechanic's story. The truck that picked up Amanda Anderson was registered to a guy named McCrae S. Callaghan. The PI told Bobby that, according to Google, Callaghan was a venture capitalist. He also confirmed that Callaghan owned an airplane that was hangared at Easton. It was a Gulfstream G-5. The PI said Callaghan had recently bought and renovated a farm that was not too far away from St. Michaels, a small town near Easton. The PI borrowed a friend's boat and took a cruise by Callaghan's place. Low and behold, he saw a young woman who fit Amanda Anderson's description by the pool and snapped some pictures of her from long range through a telephoto lens. He told Bobby that the girl looked like Amanda Anderson and promised to fax him the pictures as soon as he hung up from the call.

As he listened to the PI, Bobby jotted down the address for McCrae Callaghan's farm. He gave the PI his fax number and his address, a post office box in San Francisco, and asked him to send him a final bill. They finished their conversation and he thanked him for his services. After he hung up, he dialed Chen Yiu.

Chen answered the call almost immediately. "Yes, Bobby?"

"We found her. I'm waiting to get confirmation right now. If it's her, I'm going to need to take a trip to the East Coast."

"That's very good news. Have a safe trip and keep me informed."

"Yes, boss."

The fax machine in his office started to whir. He assumed the pictures of the girl were coming in. As he heard the boss hang up, he dialed another number on his cell phone. While he waited for the party on the other end to pick up, he walked over to the fax machine and studied the grainy image that was being spit out of the fax. He smiled as the voice at the other end of the phone said, "Hello."

"This is Bobby. We have a job. It's on the East Coast. In Maryland. Grab your gear and meet me at the boss's jet in two hours."

"Is it just the two of us?"

"No. We will pick up some more guys when we get there."

"Okay. I'm on my way."

Bobby hung up the phone and made two more calls. The first one was to the airport. The airplane was fully fueled and the pilots were ready to go. His second call was to one of his people in Washington. When they answered his call, he said, "I'm coming in tonight, leaving in about two hours. I want the team ready to go tomorrow. We'll need at least three vehicles, two for the team and one for support. Make sure they have four-wheel drive. I don't want to get stuck down there in that godforsaken place. Let's plan on making our move on Sunday morning, before daybreak."

The voice on the other end of the phone said, "Got it. Is Charlie coming?"

"Yes. He will be with me."

"Good. Always like to work with that guy. He's a little crazy but sometimes crazy is good. It will be good to see you again, Bobby. It's been too long!"

Bobby chuckled. "Yep. I was thinking the same thing. We'll call you when we're an hour or so out."

"Okay. See you soon."

Chapter Twenty-three

Mac and Amanda had just finished their breakfast on Saturday morning when Rosie Roosevelt arrived at the farm with his usual flair. He had just purchased a new diesel Dodge Ram pickup truck, so he decided to bring it down to the farm to show off.

Moses was the first one to hear him coming. The big dog got up from his bed, ran to the kitchen door, and bolted through the dog door. At just about the same time, the driveway alarm on Mac's property beeped. Right after that, Mac received a text from the Agency announcing that a potential intruder had been detected on the driveway.

Amanda picked up on all the commotion. She looked across the kitchen table at Mac. "Is everything okay?"

Mac smiled as he stood up. "When I moved down here, my boss at the Agency made me get the place wired. He put motion sensors and cameras all over the property. The feeds are continuously monitored back at the Agency. That beeping you hear is an alarm that says someone is coming down the driveway. The text message was from an analyst who just wanted to confirm that we were expecting visitors. I think our friend Rosie is making his way up the driveway but I need to run into the study to take a peek just to be sure."

Amanda nodded. "That's pretty cool. Would you mind if I tag along?"

Mac laughed. "Sure thing." Then he looked at her and joked, "Before you know it, you're gonna be a full-fledged member of my team."

Amanda said, "That would be fine with me!"

They got up from the table and walked into the study. Mac moved over to the bookcase, slid open the light switch cover next to it, and pressed his eye against the retina scanner. When the bookcase opened automatically, Amanda exclaimed, "Whoa! That's way too cool!" Then, she saw the bank of monitors on the wall. "Oh my God!" She pointed at one of the monitors. "Look, there he is!"

Sure enough, one of the cameras tracked Rosie's new truck as it rumbled down the gravel driveway with a cloud of dust trailing in its wake. Mac quickly shot an "All clear" text back to the analyst at the Agency and then he showed Amanda how to switch between the electro-optic and infrared camera as it tracked Rosie's approach. They zoomed in on Rosie, sitting in the cab with his arm hanging out the window. They both chuckled as they watched him come to a stop outside where he jumped out of the truck and wrestled with Moses as the trailing cloud of dust enveloped them both in a gritty gray fog.

Mac looked at Amanda and winked. Then he said, "We better get out there before Moses tears him apart!"

They walked down the main hallway to the front door and greeted their friend as the dust subsided. Moses ran ahead of him, proudly showing off that he was the first to greet the biggest member of the team.

Amanda ran to Rosie and jumped into his arms. She planted a big kiss on his cheek and, as she disappeared in his arms, said, "It's so good to see you, Rosie! I'm so glad you could come down and help take care of me!"

Rosie picked her up off the ground and twirled her around. "It's good to see you, too, kid! I'm glad I could come down. Looks like you're doing well!"

"Yes, I am, Rosie. I'm doing so much better now that I got away from the city. I really like it down here at Mac's place, too, and he's been taking good care of me."

Rosie looked over at Mac. "Was there ever any doubt?"

He put Amanda back down on the ground and greeted Mac with a firm handshake and a giant bear hug. As he squeezed Mac and patted him on the back, he said, "How goes it, my brother?"

Amanda watched as the two warriors held each other for a moment. She could tell they were close friends. It made her happy to see Mac happy too. Sometimes he seemed kind of distant and aloof but not today.

Mac responded, "Fine as frog's hair, Rosie! You?"

Rosie laughed. "No doubt. I'm gettin better by the minute!" He turned around and gestured toward the big truck in the driveway. "So, how do you like my new wheels?"

Mac whistled through his teeth. "My oh my. That's a beast. When did you pick that thing up?"

"Got it right after we came back from our last trip. C'mon over here and help me get my gear out of it."

Mac, Amanda, and Moses walked over to the truck. It had probably been very clean and shiny this morning when Rosie left his house. Now, it was covered with a fine layer of dust. Rosie opened the back door of the crew cab and passed his bags to Amanda and Mac. There was one small suitcase and then five different gun cases.

Mac laughed as Rosie handed him the weapons. "Well, Rosie, I see you've brought enough clothes for the weekend and enough firepower for the Vietnam War!"

Rosie grinned. "Well, you never know when you're going to need them, so I just figured I would bring along a couple of 'friends.'"

Mac gestured toward Amanda. "Speaking of friends, you should see our friend Amanda on the firing range, Rosie. She might just be one of your students at the next sniper school!"

Rosie put his arm around Amanda's shoulder and gave her a squeeze. "So you like to shoot, eh?"

Amanda looked up at the hulking former Marine. "Yeah, Rosie. I really do. Mac's been teaching me a lot and I've really enjoyed it. He told me you were the best. Maybe when he goes shopping this afternoon, we can go down to the range together?"

Rosie's eyebrows shot up and he looked over at Mac.

"Shopping? I thought you were going on a date this afternoon?"

Mac shrugged and shook his head. "Unfortunately, that's not happening, dude. We had a little change of plans late last night. It's kind of a long story but, as usual, my romantic batting average remains firmly rooted in the cellar."

Rosie looked over at Amanda. She shook her head and gave him a look that let him know he needed to cool it with the girlfriend talk. He looked back at Mac. "Well, partner, I'm sorry to hear that. I guess we'll just have to have our own party here then!"

"Precisely," Mac said. "I decided not to wave you off because I knew you wanted to see Amanda, and I figured since you were already coming down, we could have our own little party here tonight and then go fishing tomorrow. I'm picking Sean and Ben up at the airport and then going in town for a little shopping. We're gonna have a big old Southern-style barbecue here tonight!"

He cocked a thumb and pointed it over at Amanda. "By the way, it turns out that Amanda is a damn good cook, too. Between her and Sean, I think we are in for some mighty fine eats!"

Mac didn't want to tell Rosie about his call from T while Amanda was with them. He didn't see any reason to worry her. He figured he and Rosie could keep her safe here at the farm. After he got the call from T, he decided to ask Sean and Ben to come down to the farm too, just in case he needed some help. Both Sean and Ben were proficient marksmen and he knew he could count on them, if he needed them, in a pinch.

Mac, Amanda, and Moses helped Rosie carry his gear up to his room on the second floor and then watched as he unpacked it. As Mac had expected, Rosie had brought along an assortment of his 'go-to' weapons. He had two sniper rifles, a customized Remington Model 700 and an Accuracy International L115A3 AWM. Both rifles were chambered in .300 Winchester Magnum and Rosie had registered kills with both weapons at over a thousand yards. His other two long guns were a7.62 mm Knights SR-25 semi-automatic rifle with a twenty round clip and a .12 Gauge Remington Model

870 tactical shotgun. His last gun case contained his pride and joy, a matched set of Heckler &Koch HK45 semi-automatic pistols in .45 ACP. While he left his rifles and the shotgun in the study, he strapped a twin Desantis Patriot holster rig over his broad back, chambered a round in each pistol and securely nestled them into their holsters under his arms. Then he smiled, looked at Mac and gave him a hand salute. "I am ready to relieve you, sir!"

Mac laughed. "Of course you are!" Then he came to attention and returned Rosie's salute. "I stand relieved of the watch, sir." He looked over at Amanda, smiled and winked at her. "I'm heading into town to pick up some stuff for dinner. You and Moses stay here with Rosie. Don't let him get into too much trouble around here while I'm gone, okay?"

Amanda batted her eyes at Mac, took on her best mock Southern accent, and did her best Scarlett O'Hara impression from *Gone with the Wind*. "Oh Mac, where will I go? What will I do? Why, I believe I'll just go out to the firing range with Rosie and blow some shit up!"

Both Mac and Rosie laughed. She really was like a kid sister to both the men and they enjoyed how quickly she picked up on their frat boy banter.

Mac grabbed his keys. "Okay, you two. I'm outta here." He looked at them both. "Ribs and brisket okay tonight?"

Both Amanda and Rosie nodded their agreement.

As he headed out to the truck, he yelled back to Rosie, "Rosie, I will tell the home office you're on call so they can reach you, in case something comes up. Give me a call on the cell, if you need me for anything."

He climbed up into the cab of his truck, fired it up, and headed down the driveway. As they watched him drive away, Rosie looked at Amanda. "What the hell happened with his date?"

Amanda shrugged. "It's all my fault, Rosie! I just feel terrible about it."

"Huh? How could it be your fault?"

"Well, it's kind of bizarre actually. We were out talking by the pool on Thursday. I gave him a hug and his girlfriend saw us from out on the river." She stopped and looked directly at Rosie. "I swear to God it was just a hug! I wasn't trying to make a move on him, or anything!"

Rosie laughed. "Geez, I leave you kids alone for a couple of days and look what happens!"

As soon as he said it, he wished he hadn't. Amanda's eyes welled up with tears and she started to cry. He realized he had stepped on his crank so he quickly regrouped and put his arms around her. "Oh, come on, kiddo. Don't cry. I was just kidding around. It was a bad joke on my part. I know you weren't putting the moves on Mac."

As Rosie worked to settle Amanda back down, he looked out the back window at the river. "How the hell did she see you guys out there by the pool? Does this chick live around here? Hell, I can't even see any houses from here!"

Amanda sniffled. "No. Her parents live down the river."

She pointed down the river. "Their house is down that way. Apparently she came home early this week and took her dad's boat out for a spin. I guess she decided to swing by here, and when she did, she saw me out by the pool with Mac. She thought Mac was two-timing her so she canceled their date! It's such a shame because I know how much Mac liked her but—"

Rosie interrupted her, "Mac's afraid of blowing your cover and his, isn't he?"

"Yes. I told him I don't care. Hell, I'll go somewhere else if it will make it easier for him! I just feel awful."

Rosie said, "That sucks. Talk about bad timing!" Then he looked down at Amanda's tear-streaked face, pulled a handkerchief out of his back pocket and gently dried the tears from her eyes. He put his arm around her shoulder and walked her outside, where they sat down on Mac's porch swing. As they rocked back and forth on the swing, he said, "Look, Amanda, I know you feel bad but there's really nothing you can do about this. I understand why Mac did what he did. He knows what's at stake if he tells this girl who you are and he's probably not real interested in letting everyone in the community know what he really does either."

He sighed. "It's probably hard for you to understand but it's really hard for us to live normal lives. Nobody likes to live a lie. Nobody likes to be left in the dark. You've had a pretty unique view of what we do. You can probably figure out that, unless you're on the inside, it's hard to establish and maintain any kind of real relationship. Mac will be okay. He probably just decided to cut her loose before things got really hard for him."

Amanda shook her head. "I just can't buy that, Rosie. You guys are all such great guys. It's such a waste of good men. There just have to be some good women out there who can deal with your shadow lives."

Rosie smiled. "Well, let me know when you find one for me, girlie! Up until now, I've come up dry too!"

Then he ran one of his giant hands across her head and rumpled her hair. He laughed. "C'mon, kiddo. This is depressing. How about we head over to Mac's shooting range and bust a few caps?"

Amanda nodded. "That sounds like fun. Before we do that, though, let's take Mac's boat out for a quick spin."

Rosie looked at Amanda quizzically. "Are you allowed to take it out without him?"

"I don't see why not," Amanda said. "He's been letting me run it with him onboard. I feel pretty comfortable with it. I don't think he would mind if we took it out for a quick spin. Do you wanna go?"

Rosie looked at her and thought about it for a minute. "What the hell. I guess we can take it for a quick spin. Are you sure you know what you're doing?"

Amanda laughed. "Thanks for the vote of confidence, Rosie!" She winked at him. "Don't forget, I was a deckhand on the *Mirrabooka*. I think I can handle Mac's boat okay. Besides, I think it would be fun."

Rosie laughed and gave her a mock salute. "Okay, Skipper.

Let's just not do a re-creation of the three-hour cruise of the SS *Minnow*!"

"Very funny, wise guy. You should be impressed that I even know what you're talking about at my age." She winked at him. "Let's do it!" With that, she started down the path to the boathouse with Rosie and Moses trailing behind her.

She wasn't buying any of this crap about it being "too hard" for Mac, or anyone else on his team, to have a relationship with a woman. She saw the disappointment on Mac's face when he found out Hope wouldn't go out with him. Even though he wasn't willing to admit it, she could tell he was looking for someone to share his life with. She could tell he really liked this girl and she was going to be damned if some woman was going to use her as an excuse to not go out with him. In the back of her mind, she wondered why Hope never responded to Mac's calls. She thought that was kind of a bush-league play on her part but she was willing to give her a second chance for Mac's sake. Besides, if she was one of those women who needed to be constantly courted and pursued, Mac would quickly find out that she wasn't worth his time anyway. Amanda had never understood nor cared much for women who played those kinds of games.

As she stepped aboard the *Kestrel* and started the two big diesel engines, Amanda made up her mind. She was going to take Mac's boat down the creek to Hope's parents' house to see if she could talk to Hope. She knew Rosie would blow a gasket when he figured out what she was doing, but she hoped that she could convince him to become a willing accomplice. If this woman was really worth Mac's time, Amanda and Rosie would figure it out soon enough.

Chapter Twenty-four

T Nguyen had just finished her breakfast at home when her cell phone chirped. It was the distinctive ringtone of a call coming in from the Agency. She picked up the phone, toggled the secure app and said, "This is T."

"T, this is Henry. Can you talk?"

"Yes. I'm secure on this end."

"What's the status on Mac? Has he seen anything down there that looks suspicious to him?"

"No. Not yet. We did ask Rosie Roosevelt to go down there and supplement him this weekend while we try to figure out what this guy in San Francisco is up to."

"Good. Because the cell phone number we got from the PI down on the Eastern Shore is now transmitting and receiving in Alexandria."

T nodded. She figured it was only a matter of time. "Well now. Isn't that an interesting development?"

"Sure is. I need you to get that info to Mac as soon as possible."

"Okay. I will give him a call." She hesitated for a moment and then said, "Henry, do you think we should move her?"

The other end of the line went silent for a minute. T could tell that Henry was thinking about his options.

"No. I don't think I want to move her. I think this is our chance to nip this thing in the bud. I will direct our analysts to increase our monitoring of the sensors down at Mac's farm. I'm also going to put a team on a sixty-minute alert here at Langley. If we need to move quickly, we can augment Mac and Rosie by helo."

"Do you think sixty minutes is enough, Henry?"

"I think so. If we get any further indication that these guys are on the move, I'll press it up to an Alert-30."

"Okay. That sounds like a good plan. I don't think anyone could get into Mac's place undetected anyway and, frankly, when Mac and Rosie get finished with them, there probably won't be much left of them anyway. I will give him a call and let him and Rosie know what's going on."

"Thanks, T. If this thing heats up, I'm going to need you to come in and supplement the North American Ops desk."

"Roger that, Henry. I will be close to the phone, if you need me."

"Thanks."

T heard Henry hang up the phone and immediately dialed Mac's number.

She heard him pick up the phone and waited for the customary delay as the encryption software connected them to each other.

Mac said, "Hello, T! What's the good word?"

T laughed. "Mac, when have I ever called you with good news?"

She heard him chuckle too and he said, "You know me, T. I'm forever the optimist. Who knows? Someday you may call me and just say hello."

T shook her head. "I'll keep that in mind, Mac. Sadly, that's not the case today. Henry just called me. It looks like our friend in San Francisco is on the move. His cell number is now being tracked in Alexandria, Virginia."

The line went quiet for a minute. T could tell that Mac was trying to figure out his options. "Okay. I'm glad Rosie is here. I'm also picking up Sean and Ben today from the airport. You met them at my Christmas party. They will be here for the rest of the weekend. They're not Agency guys but they can both handle themselves pretty well."

"Yes. I remember them. I know they're good guys but I'm not wild about you deputizing your friends as Agency contractors."

He laughed. "I knew you would say that. Trust me, they're not too bad and believe it or not, it turns out that Amanda Anderson is a damn fine shot too. I seriously think we should consider recruiting her for our sniper school. I think she might even be interested in doing it."

T raised her eyebrows. "What the hell have you been doing down there, Mac? You're supposed to be protecting her and letting her decompress, not recruiting her for your next mission!"

"It's okay, T. Really. She's a good kid. Once we get through all this stuff, I will bring her up there to meet you."

"Okay, Mac. Okay. But let's keep her alive long enough to arrange for a meeting, okay?"

"I'm on it, Ms. Nguyen. Let me know if you're hearing anything else, okay? We'll stay close to the house and keep our eyes peeled."

"Good. By the way, Henry is putting a Quick Response Team on standby at Langley. If you need them, they can be there in twenty minutes by helo."

"Okay, T. That sounds good. Hey, thanks for the heads-up. I'll stay in touch with you over the weekend, okay?"

"That would be good, Mac. Please let us know if you get any indication of something going on down there."

"Will do, T. Thanks again for the call."

T heard Mac hang the phone up on the other end. She sighed as she put her phone down. She hoped that she and Henry Burnside played their cards right. Only time would tell for sure.

Chapter Twenty-five

While T and Mac were on the phone, Hope and her mother sat down for lunch on the back porch of her parents' house. Hope was recovering from one too many glasses of Merlot and a lack of sleep from the previous night.

As she sat down with her mother, she was still trying to figure out where she had gone wrong with Mac. She thought she had finally found someone who had the perfect combination of physical attraction and stimulating companionship, qualities which she had begun to believe were only in her dreams. Then, in an instant, her dream was shattered by the revelation that he was seeing someone else. Seeing Mac with another woman surprised and shocked her. She wouldn't have believed it, if she hadn't seen it with her own eyes. Then, to make matters worse, the way he seemed to casually dismiss her when she caught him really pissed her off.

As angry as she was with him, she was also disappointed in herself. She knew she had allowed it all to happen too fast. She should have known better. She shared at least half of the blame. It had all felt so right, though.

When she finally got out of bed in the morning, she decided to just put him out of her mind and enjoy the rest of the day with her mom and dad. While she and her mom ate their lunch, they heard the intermittent sounds of her dad's rifle firing from his perch in the loft in the barn.

He loved to use his old sniper rifle to eradicate the ever-present groundhog population on their property. He would periodically set up his rifle on its tripod in the loft of the barn where he could get a commanding view of his property. Then, he would wait until the little varmints poked their noses out of their holes and dispatch them with a single shot from ridiculously long ranges. After every shot, her mother and Hope would hear a victorious shout or a curse, an audible signal of the outcome of his shot. Being a former Green Beret, they didn't hear too many curses.

She and her mother had just finished praying for the soul of another poor varmint when Hope looked out in the creek and saw Mac's boat barreling down the creek. She did a double-take and looked again. Sure enough, it was his boat and his bow was pointed right at her dock!

She couldn't believe it! She was just starting to get over him and now, here he was, right at her back door!

Her mother saw her reaction when she saw the boat. "What's wrong, Hope?"

Hope looked at her. "It's nothing, Mom. Just some guy I met at Shaunessy's a couple of weeks ago."

Her mother looked at the boat and then looked back at her daughter. "Well, he certainly is a big fellow, isn't he? Are you seeing him?"

"No, Mom. Not anymore."

"I only asked because I was just wondering how your father was going to react if you were going out with a black man. I'm certainly okay with it. I think your dad would be okay with it too. But I thought we might just be about to see a sequel of Spencer Tracy's role in *Guess Who's Coming to Dinner*."

Hope looked quizzically at her mother. She couldn't understand how she could make a leap from Mac to Spencer Tracy. She looked back out on the creek at Mac's boat as it came closer and quickly realized why her mother had asked the question. Mac wasn't on the boat. Instead of Mac, there was a very tall, very well-built black man on the stern of the boat with Moses. He appeared to be very agitated with the helmsman, who also wasn't Mac. The helmsman on Mac's boat was the woman who she saw in Mac's arms on Thursday afternoon! *What the hell is she doing here?*

She looked back at her mother. "No. That's not him, Mom. Actually, I'm not sure who that guy is. I don't know the woman either. The only thing I recognize is the boat and the dog."

Her mother looked back at her. "Well, that sounds interesting. Would you like to invite them up for lunch?"

Hope couldn't believe her mother. She was such a Southern lady. She didn't even know these people and she was ready to invite them up on the back porch for lunch! She shook her head and answered, "No, Mom. I don't think they will be staying for too long. Let me run down to the dock and see what they want."

She walked down the path toward the dock while the people on Mac's boat tied up alongside the floating dock. Moses saw her coming and leapt off the boat onto the dock. He made a beeline up the path toward her and greeted her with his customary big, sloppy kisses. She knelt down and rubbed the big black dog's ears and petted his giant head as he wagged his tail. She hadn't seen Moses for a while. Seeing him reminded her of Mac. As much as she loved his dog, she had to admit that she was still pissed off at Moses's master. Now she looked down the path as the blonde and the huge black man walked up the path toward her. She couldn't hear what they were saying but it sounded like they were arguing about something. As they got closer, Hope stood up and waited for them to get closer. She wondered again to herself what would possess them to come here. Then she started to think that something must have happened to Mac.

The blonde approached her first and said, "Are you Hope?"

"Yes. I'm Hope." She looked back toward the boat. "Where's Mac? Is he okay?"

The blonde looked at her colleague. "He's not with us." She hesitated for a moment and said, "Yes. He's okay. But, he doesn't know we're here."

Hope said, "That seems a bit odd. I have to tell you that I'm more than a little bit surprised to see you here."

Amanda nodded her head and looked at Hope. She extended her

hand. "My name is Amanda Anderson and this is my friend Rosie."

Hope shook the girl's hand and then turned and shook the hand of the giant man who stood on the path. She felt her hand disappear in his huge hand. He had a firm grip, but it was gentle, almost comforting. She wondered what this guy did for a living.

Hope heard a sound behind her. She turned around and looked back up the yard to the house. Moses had found his way up on the porch. He had "introduced" himself to her mother who, fortunately, loved dogs. Hope cupped her hands over her mouth and shouted, "That's Moses, Mom. He fancies himself as quite the ladies' man." Then she turned back to Amanda and Rosie and sarcastically said, "Kinda like his master, I guess."

Amanda shook her head. "No. Not really. Actually, that's exactly why we're here to talk with you, Hope."

She hesitated for a moment, looked over at Rosie, and continued, "Well, I guess to be honest, I should say that's why I'm here to talk with you. Rosie, bless his heart, only agreed to come along when I threatened to scream and pout like a two-year-old. That being said, I think he'll vouch for most of what I'm going to say to you but you need to know that both of us are doing this for Mac without his knowledge."

Hope watched Amanda carefully while she talked. She could tell the girl was nervous but the tone of her voice and the look in her eyes convinced her that she was telling the truth. As she talked, Hope felt as if she had seen her before. She couldn't quite figure out why, but the blonde who stood in front of her looked awfully familiar.

She also watched the big man named Rosie as he stood beside Amanda. He looked kind of uneasy. She wasn't sure whether it was because he didn't want Amanda to be talking to Hope or whether something else bothered him. He sure was fidgety. He kept looking off into the distance as if he looked for someone, or something. *Maybe he thinks Mac's going to catch them or something?* He reminded Hope of a Secret Service agent. He sure looked like one, with his dark jacket and sunglasses on.

She looked back at Amanda and shook her head. "Well, it's mighty noble of you to come down here for Mac to talk to me but I've already seen you in action, Miss Anderson. I don't think there's much you can say to me that will undo what I've already seen for myself."

Amanda put her hands on her hips and looked Hope directly in the eyes. "I know you saw me with Mac by the pool but I want you to know that it's not what you think. I'm not seeing Mac, and if you would just take a minute to excuse yourself from your own personal little pity party, I'll tell you the real story, at least as much of it as I can tell you."

Hope was completely taken aback by Amanda's words. She wasn't use to people talking to her like that and she didn't see herself as someone who would have a pity party. She started to tell this woman and her burly friend to get off her property, but something in the back of her mind stopped her. She shifted her gaze and looked back at Rosie. She noticed that he had cracked a thin smile. When he saw she looked at him, he looked away. Obviously, he thought she was being a bitch too.

She looked down at the ground for a moment. *Maybe I should hear her out.* She held up her hands. "Okay. You've got my attention now. Those are pretty strong words for someone you don't even know. Go ahead. Get whatever you have to say off your chest."

She watched as Amanda gathered her thoughts and talked. She had to admit that for such a young woman, she was very confident and very well spoken. She realized that she kind of reminded her of herself when she was younger.

Amanda said, "First, I want to apologize to you for what you saw at Mac's house on Thursday. I know how it must have looked but I can assure you that I am not having a relationship with Mac Callaghan. What you saw was a spontaneous display of affection from me to a man who literally saved my life just a few weeks ago." She pointed toward Rosie and continued, "I can't tell you exactly how he, and Rosie, and a couple of other guys did it, but I can tell you that they literally rescued me from the bowels of hell. If you've been watching the news lately, you can get the gist of what happened but I'm not here today to rehash that story."

Hope now realized why the girl in front of her looked so familiar. This was the girl who she had seen on the news. The girl who was kidnapped at sea and who was rescued by some Special Forces dudes a few weeks ago! She held her hand up. "Sorry to interrupt you. I was wondering where I'd seen you before. Now I know. You're the girl who was rescued by the Delta Force guys, aren't you?"

Amanda nodded. "Well, yes, kind of. I mean, I am the woman who was rescued. The rest of the story doesn't really matter."

"What do you mean by that?"

"I can't really explain the details of my rescue. I hope you will understand and accept that and not ask me any more questions about it. I know that's hard to do but you have to trust me. There are a lot of people's careers and lives I could really screw up by telling you the whole story." She looked over at Rosie. "His is one of those lives and the last thing I want to do to the men who saved me is screw them over."

Hope nodded. "Okay. I guess I can understand that. Thank God you're okay."

"Thank you," Amanda said. "Yes. I thank God every day for my life and my freedom. I will never forget the men who saved me." Her eyes welled up with tears and she stopped for a moment to get control of her emotions.

Hope suddenly felt tremendous empathy for Amanda. "I'm sorry. I didn't mean to open old wounds. Are you going to be okay?"

Amanda nodded. "Yes. I will be fine. Thank you. It's all still pretty fresh in my mind and it's still hard for me to talk about it."

She wiped her eyes. "But I'm not here to tell you my story. I'm here to ask you not to give up on Mac. There are a bunch of good reasons why he can't tell you why I'm staying at his house right now. He's probably not even supposed to tell you who I really am. What I can tell you though is, during this past week, I've heard him talking about you. I know he wants to be with you. I saw the look on his face when he talked about how much he was looking forward to going out with you this weekend. I saw him coordinate with his friend Rosie here to make sure I was safe while he was out with you. I watched him consider the possibility of having a relationship with you, something he's told me he could never seriously consider before, and then I saw how disappointed he was when you told him you wouldn't see him this weekend. I'm here to tell you that Mac is a wonderful man. He's a man worth pursuing. A man worth waiting for. Frankly, I think he was falling in love with you, and it breaks my heart to see him and you miss an opportunity to be together because of me. If you really have any feelings for him, I'm here to ask you to give him another chance. Please."

Hope looked at Amanda and then looked at Rosie. "It didn't make sense. I couldn't believe it when I saw you guys. But I saw you with my own eyes. Was I really that far off-base?"

Rosie's face broke into a huge smile. "It's not that you were that far off-base. It's just that this is all pretty complicated stuff. It's really hard to explain. We are absolutely forbidden from talking about what we do and where we go. Since we can't tell you anything, we're kinda here asking you to take a leap of faith for a very good friend of ours."

He winked at Hope. "I've known Mac for a long time. I have put my life in his hands many times and never questioned his integrity. I think you'll find out he's worth it, if you can just be patient with him and let him find his way."

Then he winked at Amanda. "Although, when he finds out we came here to talk with you, he may find his way down a path to kill both of us!"

Amanda laughed and playfully punched the big man on one of his massive biceps. "Stop it, Rosie! You're going to scare the hell out of her."

They both looked back at Hope. She was very quiet. She thought back to the night she saw Mac put the choke hold on the drunk at Shaunessy's. Then she remembered Mac's no-notice trip out of the country the next day. It must have had something to do with Amanda Anderson. She realized now that he wasn't just a venture capitalist. He had another life. It all started to make sense now. She knew something was different about him but never in her wildest dreams did she believe he was some kind of hostage rescue dude.

She looked back at them. "I've been such a fool. I assumed way too much and failed to give him the benefit of the doubt. What should I do?"

At the same time she asked Amanda and Rosie her question, Hope heard the sharp report of her father's rifle. In the back of her mind, she guessed he must have dispatched another groundhog but what happened next seemed like something out of a movie. Before she could react, Rosie reached around her and Amanda's waists, picked them up off the ground like two sacks of potatoes, and carried them across the yard to a brick wall that bordered one of the Crosbys' gardens. When they reached the wall, he dropped the two women to the ground, stepped in front of them, and pulled two pistols out from under his jacket. As Rosie scanned the barn, Hope heard her father curse and watched Rosie turn and aim his pistols toward the sound coming from the barn.

Hope shrieked, "Stop. Stop it, Rosie!" She looked up the yard to the house and saw her mother on the porch with a terrified look on her face.

Rosie looked back at her and said sternly, "Who's the shooter?"

Hope brushed herself off. "It's my father, dammit. He's not shooting at you! He's up in the barn, shooting groundhogs."

As quickly as Rosie had pulled the guns out from under his jacket, he returned them to their holsters. He bent over both women, picked them up, and dusted them off while he apologized. "I'm so sorry, ladies. I hope I didn't hurt you guys. Sometimes my training and reflexes get the best of me."

Amanda Anderson had a horrified look on her face. She looked up the yard and saw Hope's mother and then looked back at Hope. "Oh Hope, I'm so sorry. I had no idea anything like this would happen!"

Hope adjusted her hair and looked back at Rosie and Amanda. She completely surprised them both when she said, "It's okay. Really. I get it now and I'm glad you came to see me today."

She looked up at her mother on the porch and shouted, "Sorry, Mom. It's okay. I'll explain what's going on in a minute."

Then she looked at Amanda and Rosie. "Why don't you two come on up to the house for lunch? I'd like to introduce you to my mom and dad." Then she winked at Rosie. "I have a hunch you and my dad will get along just fine. He was a Green Beret in Vietnam."

Rosie smiled. "He sounds like my kind of guy."

The three of them headed up to Hope's parents' house where Amanda, Hope, and her mother had lunch and spent some time getting to know one another. The Crosby women instantly became a support group for Amanda when she shared her story with them. The two Eastern Shore ladies took her in and made her feel like one of their own.

Meanwhile, Rosie and Hope's father continued with her dad's groundhog population reduction plan as the former Force Recon Marine and Army Green Beret competed with each other to see who could make the longest range kill. It came as no surprise to either one of the men that they got along very well. Before they left Hope's parents' house, Rosie and T.C. Crosby had exchanged cell phone numbers and agreed to get together again for an upcoming sniper reunion and competition at Quantico, Virginia. They shared a common bond that had been tempered in their own blood, sweat, and tears.

Chapter Twenty-six

While Hope and her parents got to know Amanda and Rosie, Bobby Chong and his team were assembled in an old warehouse just off Highway 1 in Alexandria, Virginia. A portable projector, connected to a laptop computer, projected an overhead photo of Mac's farm on a piece of paper that was taped to the wall. Pictures of Amanda Anderson and Mac Callaghan were taped beside the makeshift projection screen. Charlie Phat, a hit man Bobby had brought along with him from San Francisco, briefed the team. Charlie was an Amerasian orphan who was recruited by the KGB after the Vietnam War. He never knew his parents but he knew he had been abandoned by an American and he would never forget it. His hatred of his father's country made him a perfect KGB recruit.

After his training in Vietnam, he had been assigned to San Francisco as a KGB operative, where he and Bobby Chong had done a couple of jobs together. Although he was still a member of the KGB on paper, he had not done a job for them since the breakup of the Soviet Union. Consequently, he was available for freelance jobs like the one Bobby had called him about. He was a trained professional who was widely recognized for his proficiency in martial arts. He was also a trained sniper.

Charlie used a Sharpie to draw up the plan for their attack on a piece of paper that hung from the wall. He had three arrows drawn on the paper. The arrows started at the perimeter of Mac's property and converged on the main house. Charlie's plan was to split the initial assault team up into three groups of two men to make a coordinated assault on the main house. A reserve group of five men would be positioned in a van, just past the main entrance to Mac's property, to seal off the driveway and neutralize any leakers or external threats that might materialize after the attack on the house. If the initial assault team made it to the main house undetected, they would simultaneously breach the front and back doors and then move from room to room and kill everyone inside the house. Once the house was secured, each of the men would carry thermite grenades that would be used to torch the house to help cover their tracks. Their plan was to make it look, at least initially, like a fire had broken out and killed the occupants of the house. There was little doubt that the fire inspectors and the subsequent autopsies of the bodies would indicate otherwise, but, by then, they would be long gone from the scene of the crime.

Charlie knew there was always a chance things would not go as planned. If that was the case, he briefed the men on a contingency plan too. If they could not make it to the main house before coming under fire, they would use M32 grenade launchers to lob thermite grenades into the house. Once the dwelling was consumed by fire, the teams could wait to pick off Amanda Anderson and her guards as they attempted to escape the smoke and flames.

Bobby and Charlie were the most experienced members of the assault team. The others were local operators from the Baltimore/Washington metropolitan area. Most of them specialized in local hits on drug dealers and customers who were behind in their payments. This would be the first time many of them had participated in a para-military type of hit. Because of that, Bobby and Charlie briefed the operation in excruciating detail. They checked and double-checked their weapons and used a darkened storeroom in the warehouse to check and sight-in their night-vision goggles and laser sights on their weapons. By 1600 on Saturday afternoon, they were as ready as they were going to be.

Bobby sent them home and told them to get some sleep. They planned to meet back at the warehouse at midnight to finalize their plan and make the trip across the Chesapeake Bay Bridge. Their target time was 0400.

Chapter Twenty-seven

When Mac brought Sean and Ben back from the airport, they were gleefully met by their buddy Moses as they came up the driveway. The big dog raced along the driveway as Mac circled around and backed the pickup toward the side door where they could unload the groceries. When the truck stopped, Sean opened the door and stepped down from the passenger side of the truck. Moses greeted him right away. He nuzzled Sean's right front pocket and, as usual, Sean produced a dog treat for his friend. Moses, having achieved the objectives of greeting his friends and getting fed, immediately retreated back toward the pool where they guessed Rosie and Amanda enjoyed the late afternoon sun.

While Sean and Ben unloaded the truck, Mac walked around to the back porch to check on Rosie and Amanda. Sure enough, they lounged by the pool. Amanda was stretched out on her favorite chaise lounge and Rosie sat at a poolside table under an umbrella.

Rosie looked up and waved when he saw him. "Well, well, well. We were starting to think you guys must have got lost."

Mac smiled. "I see you guys are holding down the fort here. Assume it's been pretty quiet?"

Rosie nodded and looked over at Amanda. "She's been sitting here soaking up the sun and I'm catching a little nap. All is well, sir."

Mac looked out over the pool at the river behind his house. It was one of those beautiful, sunny, early summer kinds of days when the sky was clear and the air was still. He let his mind wander for a moment. *It sure would have been a good night for a boat ride with Hope.* Then he reminded himself to let go of that thought. He knew that kind of thinking would only bring him down and he wanted to enjoy the party tonight at his place with Amanda, Rosie, Sean, and Ben.

He pointed back up to the house. "Rosie, I know you've already met Ben and Sean but I want to introduce them to Amanda. They're up in the kitchen now, unloading groceries. Why don't you guys come on up for a minute?"

Amanda sat up from her chaise. "That sounds good. I'll be right up, Mac."

Mac turned and went back into the house. Amanda hesitated for a moment by the pool. She looked over at Rosie and whispered, "How are we gonna tell him?"

Rosie looked at her. "Don't even try to go there, young lady. You cooked this one up all by yourself, Amanda. You're gonna have to figure out the answer to that question on your own!"

Amanda grinned. "I knew you were going to say that. But she's going to be here at six, Rosie. Should I tell him before she gets here or just wait until she pulls up to the house?"

Rosie got up from his chair, stretched his massive frame, took off his holsters, removed his shirt and performed a flawless cannon ball into the pool. He made an enormous splash and Amanda had to jump to get out of its way. Moses, not wanting to be left out, performed his own spirited belly flop and joined Rosie in the pool. He swam circles around Rosie while the big man floated on his back and sprayed water out of his mouth into the air like a giant whale.

Amanda laughed. "You know, for a former Marine, you are one big freaking chicken, Rosie Roosevelt!"

He looked over at her and winked. "You got to learn to choose your battles, ma'am. I'm keeping my distance on this one to avoid the frag. Don't worry. It will all work out okay. He may kill us when he finds out...but it's highly unlikely that he'll eat us!"

With that, he rolled over on his belly, lifted his legs straight up into the air, and plunged down to the bottom of the pool. Moses looked down into the water, watched his swimming partner sitting on the bottom, and wisely decided to retreat to the shallow end of the pool.

Amanda took that as her signal that Rosie was finished with this particular conversation so she put on her cover-up and headed up to the house to meet Mac's assistant and his partner.

As she walked through the door, she saw two very tall, very handsome men in the kitchen, unloading groceries. One of them turned toward her and smiled. He said, "Well, you must be Amanda Anderson!" He moved toward her with his arms outstretched and, before she knew it, swallowed her in a huge, warm hug. As he squeezed her in his arms, he said, "You poor thing. Mac told us all about your situation. I hope you won't have to stay here too long. If it turns out you do, I told him you should come up and stay with Sean and me in Long Island. Oh, by the way, I'm Ben and this is Sean."

Ben turned her loose and, before she knew it, she was being welcomed in the same manner by Sean. She couldn't remember feeling more welcome in any home she had ever been to, including her own! It was amazing to her how these men had opened their hearts and provided her with a safe place to stay. She hugged Sean back. "It's a pleasure to meet you, too, Sean. Mac has told me so much about you guys. It sounds like he would be lost without you!"

Sean laughed and pointed at Mac. "Oh him, he can take pretty good care of himself, you know. We just help keep him fed, dressed properly and pointed in the right direction, most of the time!" He laughed and punched Mac in the shoulder as he walked back toward the kitchen.

Then he looked over at Ben. "We're just glad to be able to come down and meet you. Besides, we haven't been down here for a few weeks. We thought we better get back to restock the shelves with some decent food. I was afraid Mac was filling you up with Pop Tarts and TV dinners!"

With a look of mock horror, Mac looked over at Ben. "Hey! I've been feeding her pretty well!" He hesitated and continued,

"Well, actually, I've been pretty good at getting groceries and she's been really good at feeding me!"

He laughed and looked over at Amanda, who nodded and said, "Yep. That's pretty much the way it's been working. And I'm okay with it."

Sean looked over the pile of grocery bags on the counter. "It sounds like you're a great cook, Amanda. Would you like to help Ben and I get the ribs and chicken ready for our little barbecue?"

Amanda nodded. "Absolutely! Let me change out of my bathing suit and I'll be right back to help you." Then she looked over at Mac and said with a wink, "I just know this is going to be a wonderful evening."

Mac smiled at her. "Oh, you do now? Well, I guess we'll see. If we can keep Rosie from drinking too many margaritas and falling into the pool again, I will call it a raging success."

Amanda headed off to her room while Ben and Sean finished unloading the groceries. When she came back to the kitchen, she had showered, dried her hair and put on some makeup. She was dressed in a pair of cutoff jean shorts paired with her white bikini top that was loosely covered up by a sheer, white, short-sleeved peasant top.

Ben looked up and saw her when she was walking down the hallway. "Oh, Amanda. You look hot, baby! I just love that top! And your hair looks beautiful! That's a perfect combination for our party tonight." Then he poured a glass of wine for her and pulled a freshly starched chef's apron out of a drawer. He handed the wine glass and the apron to Amanda.

"Okay, boys. What do you need me to do?"

Sean pointed to a pile of freshly washed vegetables drying by the sink. "If you can cut those up for the salad, that would be great."

The two men and Amanda worked together as if they were in a chef's kitchen in New York. As they prepared the meal, Sean basted the ribs. "I think we bought too much food. I guess I can freeze these extra ribs for another time."

It may have been the wine, or it may have been the fact that

Amanda just felt so comfortable with the two men in the kitchen because, before she knew it, she blurted out, "No, Sean, go ahead and baste them. We're going to have another guest for dinner tonight."

As soon as she said it, she knew she had inadvertently let the cat out of the bag. Ben reacted first. "Did you invite your boyfriend down here without telling Mac?"

Amanda chuckled. "No. I invited the girl Mac was supposed to take out on a date tonight over for dinner. Only problem is, I haven't got up the courage to tell Mac yet!"

Ben raised his fist to his mouth. "Shut up! He's going to kill you, Amanda!"

Sean looked at her. "Was it Hope?"

"Yes," Amanda said. "I couldn't help it, Sean. I hope you guys won't be mad at me. I just couldn't stand seeing Mac get stood up because of me!"

"Because of you?" Ben said quizzically. "Why because of you?"

Amanda told them the whole story. When she was finished, the men were silent. Their silence didn't last for long.

She watched while Ben looked over at Sean and smiled. Then Sean laughed and Ben walked over and gave Amanda another big hug. He said, "That's the best news we've had all day. When we heard about Hope, we thought she must be a pretty special woman for Mac to spend so much time talking about her. When we found out he had spent the night with her in Georgetown, we thought he might have finally found someone for the long haul. Then, when we heard he wasn't going out with her tonight, we figured he had screwed it all up again somehow."

"Screwed it up?"

"Yes." Ben nodded and looked at Sean, who silently confirmed his partner's comment. "We've been watching Mac screw up his relationships for quite some time now. Frankly, most of the women we met who he has gone out with were not much of a challenge for him. We figured those relationships wouldn't last long anyway. But this girl, this girl seemed to have captured his interest in another way. Neither one of us has met her but we're glad you had the courage to go down and talk with her."

Sean nodded his agreement with Ben's comments. "You know he's going to freak out when he finds out you went to her house and invited her here, don't you?" He hesitated, and then looked at Ben. "Not that there's anything wrong with that! At least we'll be here to help you through it!"

Amanda smiled deviously. "Thank God! I'm so glad you guys are okay with my plan. I know it's a risk but I'm even more convinced, after meeting Hope and her mother and father, that she's the real deal. I think you guys will like her too."

Sean pointed out the back window toward the pool. "Here he comes. When are you going to tell him?" They turned to see Mac make his way across the patio to the back door.

Amanda whispered, "I think I'm just going to wait until she gets here."

They all laughed and just then, Mac opened the back door. He saw them working in the kitchen and heard them laughing. He looked at them and said, "Don't believe a word they say about me, Amanda. These two guys know way too much about me, I'm afraid!"

Amanda and her two new accomplices laughed together. Sean said, "Yes. We've been together for way too long. We have to stay friends forever, Mac. We know way too much about one another's dirty laundry to be anything but the best of friends."

Amanda nodded. "That's an understatement." She looked over at Mac. "You've definitely seen me at my worst. I'm so grateful to you for saving my life and now for giving me a place to hide out for a while."

She picked up her glass of wine and held it in the air. "Here's to great friends and dirty laundry!"

After a rousing, "Hear, Hear!" they carried the food outside to the back porch to join Rosie and Moses and start the barbeque.

Chapter Twenty-eight

Shortly after Mac and his friends started the barbecue, the driveway alarm went off in the house. It was immediately followed by a text on Mac's cell phone from an analyst at Langley. She reported, "Late model BMW heading your way. Single female occupant. Expected guest?"

Mac texted back, "No." He looked over at Rosie. "Someone's coming down the driveway. BMW with just the driver, a woman."

Rosie nodded. "You want me to check it out?"

"No. Let me take a look."

He got up and headed into the study. As he waited for the door on the safe room to open, he instinctively reached for his pistol and confirmed it was tucked in his waistband, beneath his shirt. Once the door opened, he walked to the wall of monitors to get a look at who was coming down the driveway.

There was still plenty of daylight at this hour of the day and the long-range electrooptic camera was locked on and tracked the car as it approached the house. Mac reached down to the control panel and toggled the zoom button to zoom in on the occupant. When he saw who was driving, he gasped, "What the hell? What the hell is she doing here?"

It was Hope! He was shocked but excited to see her. His mind raced as he watched her car approach the house. *Why didn't she tell me she was coming? Why didn't she ever call me back? Why is she coming over here?*

His phone buzzed again. It was the Agency. They waited for an answer. He reached for his cell phone and texted the analyst at the Agency, "Vehicle and occupant is friendly." After he sent the text, he thought, *at least I hope so!*

He walked out of the study and watched her car pull into the parking area in front of the house. Before she opened her door to get out of the car, Moses had already positioned himself at her door. The black Lab's tail wagged furiously. Mac smiled as he walked out the front door and watched her step out of her car.

Moses danced around her as if he had just found a new toy. She was dressed in a sleeveless dress that accentuated her narrow waist. Her hair was up and she carried a sweater and her sandals in her hand. She raised her sunglasses as he walked out the door; she smiled at him. "Well, hello there, Mr. Callaghan. Bet you're kind of surprised to see me, eh?"

Mac wasn't quite sure what to say, or for that matter, what to do. He suddenly felt unsure of himself as he approached her. He really wasn't sure where he stood with her. But she was here and she looked beautiful. *Oh, what the hell*, he thought. *Who cares why she's here. She's here!*

As he got closer to her, she solved his dilemma about what to do for him. She opened her arms wide and gave him a warm hug. As he pulled her into his chest, he smelled the perfume in her hair and felt her breasts press against his chest. While he enjoyed the feeling of her pressed up against him, he whispered in her ear, "I wasn't sure if I was ever going to see you again."

Hope leaned back in his arms and smiled. Then she cupped his face in her hands and looked up at him. "I owe you an apology, Mac. I made an assumption and jumped to a conclusion. I assumed the worst and never really gave you a chance to explain yourself. I'm sorry. I acted irrationally and I apologize."

With that, she stepped up on her tiptoes, wrapped her arms around his neck and softly kissed his lips.

Mac didn't know what to say. He thought maybe he should try to explain what was going on. He realized Amanda, Rosie, Ben, and Sean were all in the backyard and he couldn't figure out how he was going to explain what they were all doing at his place. He looked at her. "Well, I'm just glad you are here." Then he hesitated for a moment and said, "Although, things are still kind of complicated around here..."

Hope interrupted him by gently pressing her finger to his lips. She grinned at him. "Don't worry about it, Mac. No explanation needed. I know you've got a lot going on right now and I'm just happy to be here with you."

Mac shook his head. "Well, I'm not exactly sure how to explain all this to you anyway." Then he gestured toward the back of the house. "I have some friends out back. We're having a little impromptu barbecue tonight. Would you like to meet them?"

Hope nodded. "I would love to meet them."

They walked around to the back of the house with Moses proudly leading the way. As they descended the steps to the patio, Mac mentally prepared himself for how he would introduce Hope to his friends. He wasn't quite sure what kind of reaction he was going to get when he introduced Hope to Amanda. Then, while he thought about that, he noticed that Rosie had taken off his jacket, which allowed the entire world to see his two pistols proudly displayed under his arms. Before he could figure out how to explain the assortment of guests on the patio, some of them armed, Amanda walked toward them, extended her arms toward Hope, and said, "Hi, Hope! I'm so glad you could come over to see us!"

Mac was completely caught off guard by Amanda's approach to Hope. He opened his mouth to say something but couldn't find any words to express his surprise. *How the hell did she know Hope? What in the hell was going on?*

As Amanda hugged Hope, she looked over her shoulder and winked at Mac. Then to his utter amazement, after Amanda finished greeting Hope, Rosie ambled over to her and lifted her completely off her feet and twirled her around in the air. She laughed as the big man swept her off her feet. Then she looked down from her elevated perch and said, "Oh, Rosie! What nice guns you have!"

Rosie laughed and, as he gently returned her feet to the ground, flexed his huge biceps. "Yep. Seems like all the women have the same reaction when they see these babies!"

Hope laughed at the big man and winked at him. "Well, those guns are pretty nice too. But I meant those H&Ks under your arms!"

At this point, Mac couldn't take it anymore. He stepped back and looked at all of them. "Okay you guys. What the hell is going on?"

Before he could get an answer, Sean looked over his sunglasses at Mac. "Hey boss, before you get your knickers in a wad, why don't you introduce this beautiful woman to Ben and me?"

Mac was still trying to figure out how Amanda and Rosie knew Hope. Before he uttered another word, Ben walked over to Hope. "You must be Hope. We're so glad to meet you. I'm Ben and this is my partner, Sean. We've both heard so much about you and have been dying to meet you."

The two men exchanged hugs with Hope. After he planted a kiss on Hope's cheek, Sean held her at arm's length and looked her over from head to toe. He smiled broadly and exclaimed, "I just love your dress, Hope! It's perfect for a summer night and you look sensational in it."

Hope smiled. "Why, thank you, Sean. That's so kind of you to notice. I see you have an eye for fashion. I bought it ages ago from the J. Peterman Company. It just seems to work on a warm summer evening."

Sean nodded his head. "I love the J. Peterman catalogue. The clothes are fabulous and the stories are even better. It's a beautiful dress, Hope. You look fabulous."

Then he looked at Mac. "Why don't you offer her a drink and then we can all sit down and help you get that deer in the headlights look off your face!"

Mac laughed and looked around at his friends. "I don't know what you've done but it's obvious that all of you are in this together. Since I'm clearly the odd man out here, I'll take your advice, Sean. But after I get her a cocktail, you knuckleheads have some serious explaining to do!"

He turned and cocked his head at Hope, who now smiled from ear to ear. He ran his hand casually through his hair and rubbed his forehead. "I see that you're in on this too."

Hope laughed and with a mock Southern drawl, said, "Who me? Little old me? Why, I can't imagine what you're talking about, sir!" Then she winked at him and continued, "I just happened to be in the neighborhood and thought I would stop by and say hello."

Mac laughed. "Okay, Miss Scarlett. Well, since you're here, what can I get you to drink?"

"I would love to have a glass of red wine. Do you have any Merlot?"

"Absolutely!"

Mac headed up to the house and retrieved the glass of wine for Hope. While he was gone, Hope sat down with Amanda and Rosie, while Sean and Ben worked at the grill on the patio.

Amanda looked over at Hope. "Did you see the look on Mac's face when I hugged you?"

"Yes, I did. I thought he was going to go have a heart attack!"

Rosie piped up. "You can bet your ass he's up there right now trying to figure out how all this went down!"

Hope nodded. "I hated to surprise him like that but it was kind of funny. You guys should have seen his face when I got out of my car up on the driveway! I'm guessing none of you told him about your little visit to my parents' place this afternoon?"

Amanda looked over at Rosie. "Neither one of us could figure out how to tell him without getting him all stressed out about us going to see you. We decided to just let you show up and surprise him and then tell him after the fact."

"Well, I guess you succeeded with your plan!" Hope looked up toward the house and saw Mac return with her drink.

As he approached the patio, the three co-conspirators stopped talking. He walked down the stairs to the patio with a grin on his face. As he placed the glass of wine in Hope's hand, he turned around and raised his glass. "Here's to the guiltiest-looking bunch of friends a man could ever have."

Then he looked at Hope and said, "And here's to you, Hope. I'm so glad you could come over here tonight and join this merry band of miscreants. Cheers!"

Hope and Mac's friends stood up and shouted a resounding, "Cheers!"

Then, while Ben and Sean continued to cook their dinner on the grill, they told Mac the story about how Amanda and Rosie snuck away to visit Hope at her parents' house.

Mac was initially annoyed that Amanda had disobeyed him by telling Hope about who she was and how she came to stay at Mac's house. But his annoyance at her quickly faded to laughter when Hope recounted how her father's gopher hunting had turned Rosie into an impromptu G.I. Joe in her parents' backyard, while her mother looked on in horror.

As Mac wiped the tears from his eyes, Hope told them the story of Rosie's gopher hunt with Hope's dad while the girls and Hope's mother got acquainted over lunch. According to Hope, T.C. Crosby claimed to have outshot Rosie from their perch in the hayloft of the barn. In his mind, the Green Berets had bested the Marines, yet again.

Not surprisingly, Hope's version of the story was not quite the same way Rosie saw it. In his version of the story, the former Force Recon sniper had easily triumphed over the elder Green Beret, although he did admit to being quite impressed with Hope's father's marksmanship. Mac made a mental note to invite T.C. Crosby over to the house for a rematch in the future. He sounded like a good guy and Mac was now more curious than ever to meet Hope's mother and father.

The group spent the rest of the evening getting to know one another better. Mac watched Hope as she talked with his friends. She had such an easy way about her. She had a great sense of humor and easily fit in with his crew. Although he knew Amanda and Rosie had exposed her to some risk, he was glad they had gone to see her. It was all so easy having her here at his place with his friends. It felt like they had known one another for a long time. It all felt so comfortable. It felt the way it was supposed to feel when you're with people you know and trust. It was a feeling he hadn't felt in a very long time. He was grateful and he was content.

Before he knew it, it was almost midnight. Ben and Sean decided it was time to head up to the house for the night and said their goodbyes to Hope. As Ben reached across the table to give her a hug, he inadvertently knocked over Hope's glass of wine. She wasn't fast enough to get out of her chair before the wine splashed on her dress. Ben reacted with horror as he looked at the red stain that spread across her lap.

He held his hands up to his face. "Oh my God! I can't believe I just did that!"

Hope looked down at her dress. "It's okay, Ben. I just didn't move fast enough. But I need to get out of this thing and soak it in some cold water!"

Ben grabbed her hand and led her up the path to the house. "Come with me," he said. "I'll help you soak it and find something else for you to wear."

Mac, Rosie, Amanda, Sean, and Moses followed Hope and Ben up to the house. While Ben helped Hope soak her dress, the rest of his guests said their goodnights and headed off to bed. Mac and Moses waited in the kitchen until Hope came back from the laundry room with Ben.

When they came back into the kitchen, Mac turned to see her and caught his breath. Ben had put her in one of Mac's white dress shirts. The tails of his shirt just barely covered the tops of her thighs and his French cuffs flapped around her wrists as she walked into the kitchen.

Ben smiled at Mac and Hope. "Well, my work here is done. I'm off to bed. You two kids be good now, you hear!" Then he headed up the stairs to bed.

Mac looked at Hope. The shirt was opaque and he could make out the curve of her breasts and see the faint contrast of her nipples through the cotton fabric. There was something incredibly sexy about seeing a woman, especially this woman, in a man's dress shirt. He made a mental note to himself to thank Ben for his selection of shirts. It was perfect and she looked incredible in it.

Hope saw him looking at her. She raised her arms and did a pirouette. Then she walked toward him. "You like?"

He watched her move as she walked toward him and studied her long tan legs as the tails of his shirt brushed against them while she walked. His shirttails were just long enough to cover her bottom but short enough to let him see that she didn't wear any underwear. He felt a familiar surge of blood race to his hips.

He smiled back at her. "I like. I like it a lot. You look very hot in my shirt, Ms. Crosby."

"I'm glad you like it, Mr. Callaghan. I suspected you might."

They moved toward each other and Mac opened his arms to receive her as she folded her body into his chest. She reached her arms up around his neck and stepped up on her tiptoes to present her face to him for a soft kiss. He kissed her and, as they both felt the passion course through their veins, their tongues met. Mac ran his hands across her bottom and gently pressed her up against his hips. He felt her press back into him and, as he ran his fingers up her sides, he felt her shiver as they brushed along the sides of her breasts. Her hips pressed harder into him as he reached up into her hair and gently released the pins that held her hair up. As the hairpins ricocheted off the tile floor in the kitchen, her long hair cascaded down around her shoulders. Mac brushed back the hair from her neck and nuzzled her ear. He took a deep breath and smelled her perfume as it filled his sinuses and his lungs.

Hope kissed his neck and whispered in his ear, "My mom and dad are going to think you took advantage of me when I show up at home in one of your dress shirts."

Mac chuckled as he kissed her chin and nibbled on her lower

lip. "Hell, I haven't even met your mom and dad yet, but I suspect they don't worry too much about you being taken advantage of."

Then he stopped talking and kissed her again deeply. She responded to his advance and, as their tongues danced together, she ran her hands up under his shirt. He felt her fingers run through the hair on his chest as she massaged his pecs with her soft palms. Now it was his turn to shiver as her fingers teased him. He was fully aroused now and he pressed his hips harder into her again and stopped kissing her for a moment. "Well, you could always stay here until your clothes dry off."

"Why, Mr. Callaghan, I thought you would never ask."

She moved one of her hands back down across his belly and gently inserted it between his flat stomach and the top of his trousers. Her fingers quickly found his hardness and softly wrapped around him. She looked up at him and smiled. "I think it's time for you to show me to your bedroom so I can help you with this."

That was the signal Mac was looking for. He stepped back slightly and reached behind her to softly pick her up in his arms. She was as light as a feather. As he carried her down the long hallway to his bedroom, she laid her head against his chest and listened to the strong, steady beat of his heart.

As they passed through the doorway, Mac turned and used his foot to close his door. Right before the door closed, Moses poked his nose through it and tried to follow them into Mac's room. They both chuckled at the big dog and then Mac said, "No, Moses. Not tonight. You stay, boy." The big dog was accustomed to sleeping in Mac's room but he seemed to understand the command. As the door closed, they heard him flop down on the floor outside the door and breathe a heavy sigh.

Hope ran her hands through Mac's hair and kissed him again while he carried her over to his bed and gently laid her down on the mattress. The bedroom windows on either side of his bed were open and the late-night summer breeze gently parted the curtains. He could hear the rhythmic chirping of the crickets outside his windows as he looked down at the beautiful woman who was now framed by the sheets on his bed. His shirt had ridden up slightly over her back when he laid her down on the bed. He could clearly see the soft curves of her hips as she rolled over on her side and waited for him to get undressed.

Without shifting his gaze from Hope, he lifted his shirt over his head and tossed it over the blanket chest at the foot of the bed. Then he slid his web belt through its buckle, unbuttoned his shorts and with one tug, dropped his trousers to the floor.

The streaming moonlight clearly revealed his tan lines. It also revealed the fact that he was well past ready to make love to Hope as his manhood clearly signaled his arousal. As he knelt down on the bed, she rose up to meet him. She gently kissed his chest and ran her hands down his stomach to caress him as he unbuttoned her shirt. As she shrugged the shirt from her shoulders, he slid his hands behind her back and gently returned her to her back. Now that her shirt was off, he had unobstructed access to her body. He lowered his head and engulfed her with his mouth, gently kissing and nibbling her skin. While he focused his attention with his mouth on her breasts, his hands slid down across her stomach and stroked the insides of her thighs. He felt her open up to him as his fingers brushed across her lips. She was warm and wet and, like Mac, beyond ready to make love. He could feel her core open up to his fingers as he curled them up inside her and she arched her back. He found her G-spot and felt the first shudder course through her body as she let herself go.

While she still shivered from the effects of his long, strong fingers, he rose up on his arms and maneuvered himself over her. He felt her shift her legs and raise her knees to fully prepare herself to receive him. He felt her fingers deftly move him into position. Then he slowly dropped his hips as she fed him into her soft, wet core. He drove the entire length of his shaft into her and settled down into her saddle as he kissed her deeply. He ground himself hard against her and felt her shiver as he filled her up with his body.

After his initial penetration, he drew back up and teased her lips with the tip of his manhood. He hesitated as he prepared to drop down deep inside her again. Her hair was splashed across his pillow and her eyes were wide open and locked in his gaze.

She smiled at him and he felt her legs wrap around his thighs as her hands pulled hard against his ass. Then she dug her heels into his back and breathlessly urged him on. "Don't tease me, Mac! I need all of you. I want all of you inside me right now!"

Mac had no problem obliging her request. He slowly dropped his hips and felt his body completely enveloped in her warm, wet core yet again. The feeling was indescribable as she smothered him with her warmth. It didn't take them long to instinctively fall into a natural rhythm that was as old as time itself. After only a few minutes, their bodies took over all of the conscious thought processes of their brains as they lost themselves to their most basic instincts and ground hard into each other's bodies. Hope was small but she was incredibly strong, and Mac loved how she used her hips to push back hard into his body. The pleasure of being joined together was now being replaced by the animal intensity within each of them to drive harder and harder into each other until the pulsating waves of their releases crashed over their bodies. Mac felt Hope's body tighten around him as she reached her final peak.

She shuddered and cried out softly as her body surged and bucked against him. He held her tightly and rode her waves of passion as she gave herself completely to him. He was only moments away from his own release now and as he felt the adrenaline course through his veins, he knew there was no holding back. With one final thrust, he drove his hips hard into the glorious soft wetness that surrounded him and surrendered to a body shaking release that squeezed every ounce of passion out of his body. As the waves of his passion subsided, he collapsed into her arms. Then their bodies relaxed and their breathing returned to normal. They rolled in unison onto their sides. Mac drew Hope tightly against his chest and held her in his arms while their bodies recovered.

They laid together in the moonlight, enjoying the afterglow of their union. Their bodies were warm and slightly damp from their exertion. Mac used one of his hands to brush the tousled hair away from Hope's face.

He kissed her softly at the base of her neck. "I'm so glad you decided to come over tonight."

She smiled at him and ran her hand down across his hip. Her fingers brushed along his inner thigh and then she gently held him. "Me too. Baby, that was incredible!"

She shivered as the night breeze blew through Mac's open windows across their sweat-soaked bodies. He reached down and pulled the sheet, along with a light summer blanket, up over them. Hope sighed and rolled over. She pressed her body gently back into her lover and murmured, "I don't want this night to end."

Mac conformed his body to hers and once again felt the warmth of her warm skin against his. She fit perfectly in his arms and, as he drew her up close to him again, he allowed himself to think how nice it would be to have someone to share his bed with him on a regular basis. "Don't worry. I'm not going anywhere."

Hope reached over his arm and pulled it tightly around her. She took a deep breath, and said, "It just feels so right, Mac."

Mac nodded. "Funny, I was just thinking the same thing. It feels like I've known you forever, Hope."

She chuckled. "Yes, I know. Maybe you have?"

"How's that?"

"Oh, I don't know, Mac. It just feels like you and I were meant to be together somehow. I can't really explain it. It feels like I've been waiting so long to find someone like you, and now that I have, it feels like I've known you forever."

Mac thought about what she said for a minute. "Maybe so. But if Amanda and Rosie hadn't intervened, it might not have turned out quite so well!"

They both laughed. Mac looked at his watch and saw it was almost one a.m. He pulled Hope closer to him and felt her warmth against his legs and chest. As she snuggled up against him, he kissed her softly on her cheek and said, "Good night, baby."

Hope closed her eyes and rubbed his arm softly. "Sweet dreams."

It wasn't long before she felt the steady rise and fall of his chest against her back as Mac drifted off to sleep. She grinned as he started to snore softly. The sound wasn't objectionable to her at all. It was kind of soothing, actually. She realized that she might have finally found a man who could match her in the boardroom and blow her mind in the bedroom. She had begun to think her hopes and dreams of finding someone like him would never come true. She said a silent prayer to thank God for putting her in this man's arms and then quietly drifted off to sleep.

Chapter Twenty-nine

Bobby Chong and his team arrived on the outskirts of Mac's farm at three o'clock in the morning. The trip from Alexandria to the Eastern Shore had been uneventful. Traffic was light and they had actually made better time than they expected. Bobby and Charlie Phat rode in the back of the lead Suburban. There was another Suburban and a panel van behind them. The Suburban contained the rest of the assault team and the panel van had the reserve team in it.

Bobby signaled the driver of his truck to stop on the shoulder of the road on the west side of Mac's property. He turned around and looked at the two men in the back of the truck. "This is your spot. Once you get out of the truck, take your positions. Stay inside the tree line until I give you the signal to move in."

The men both acknowledged Bobby's orders. Then they reached up and turned on their night-vision devices, stepped out of the truck and gently closed the doors behind them.

Charlie grimaced as the truck pulled back onto the road. "Moon is too damn bright, Bobby."

Bobby nodded. "I know. But I can't wait to make our move. By the time the conditions are better, they might decide to move her again."

"Well, we just better hope the guys who are guarding her are not players."

"Don't think so. She's staying with some venture capitalist dude. Probably doesn't know the front end from the back end of a gun."

Charlie nodded. He didn't say anything more. He felt uneasy about this job. They were moving too fast and they really didn't have any intelligence on the guy who owned the property, or the place they were staying in. He sighed momentarily. *If they weren't paying so damn well, he never would have taken this gig.*

They reached the entrance to Mac's driveway. The driver pulled off the road and turned off his lights as the other Suburban continued past them on its way to the eastern side of Mac's farm. As Bobby and Charlie got out of the truck, the panel van pulled in behind the first Suburban. The driver of the van turned off his lights and gave Bobby a thumbs-up.

Bobby returned the gesture, reached up and turned on his goggles and then reached down and cycled the bolt on his Russian AS Val silenced 9 mm assault weapon. His weapon, along with the weapons on the rest of the team, had been fitted with silencers to help attenuate the sound of gunfire when they attacked the farm.

Charlie was a professional. He had carefully prepped his weapons for this job. He had three with him: his Val, a .30-06 Remington sniper rifle—not too different than Rosie Roosevelt's—and a .45 ACP Colt Combat Commander. The Colt was Charlie's personal favorite. He had the Remington on a sling across his back while he carried the Val loosely in front of him.

The team had assumed that the farm was equipped with some kind of surveillance system, so they avoided the driveway. Bobby and Charlie made their way to the left of the driveway and settled down in a soybean field in front of the house. They waited until the third team was in place on the east side of the farm. While they waited, Charlie unslung his 30-06 and used his sniper scope to scan Mac's house and outbuildings. They were still pretty far away but he could see a car and a couple of pickup trucks in the driveway. There weren't any lights on in the house and there didn't appear to be any movement around the house. It looked like a soft target. No lights and no sentries.

It didn't take long for the third prong of the assault force to get in place. They checked in over their headsets. "Team Three's in place."

Bobby acknowledged with a terse, "Let's go."

On Bobby's command, the teams moved toward the house. Team One left the woods and started across a field toward the back of the house. Bobby and Charlie worked their way through the soybean field and Team Three moved forward through a cornfield.

Bobby felt completely unprotected. He knew that he and Charlie were in a bad place, along with the men in the other teams. It was almost as if this place had been designed to be defended with open fields of fire all around the house. He realized the only guys who had any cover at all were the men in Team Three. They had a cornfield to give them some cover but at this time of the year, the corn was only waist high.

Just as Bobby fretted over their lack of cover, he heard a flock of geese start honking to his right. Team One had inadvertently stumbled into the geese, who were roosting overnight in the field. Not surprisingly, the geese were raising a hell of a racket. Bobby hissed into his headset, "What the hell are you guys doing?"

"It's the damn geese." The Team One lead responded, "We're going to have to go back to the woods and work our way around them."

Bobby nodded and hissed, "Damn right you are! Do it now before you wake up the whole fucking farm!"

It was already too late for Bobby and his team. Mac heard the noise through the open windows in his room. It wasn't the normal nighttime muttering of the geese that he was used to hearing as he slept. Something was wrong. Either a predator closed in on them, or something worse caused them to make a fuss.

He carefully disentangled his arm from Hope's grasp and rolled out of bed. His movement woke her up. She looked up at him dreamily and asked, "Where are you going, baby?"

"Something's stirring up the geese. It's probably nothing but I want to check it out. I'll be right back."

Hope nodded and smiled. "Okay. When you come back, I'll be ready for round two, darling."

Mac smiled. "In that case, I'll be back before you know it!"

He pulled on a pair of shorts and walked to the bedroom door. As he opened the door, he saw Moses still dutifully guarded his bedroom door. The big dog stood up and followed him as he walked down the hallway into the study.

As he turned to open the safe room door to the study, the cell phone in his pants pocket buzzed. He put his eye up to the retina scanner on the safe room and, as he opened the bookcase, answered the phone.

"Callaghan."

"This is Langley. We have detected an intrusion."

Mac felt a shot of adrenaline surge through his body. "I heard the geese out in the field. I'm just walking into the safe room now. What are you seeing?"

As he walked into the safe room, he looked at the bank of monitors on the wall. Two cameras, the ones on the east and west sides of the farm, tracked the heat signatures of four men. The two men to the east walked away from the cameras. It was easy to see why as the distinct infrared signatures of the geese in front of them had undoubtedly slowed their approach to the house. The other two men were crouched down. Mac could see their shoulders and heads above the emerging crop of corn in the field. All of them appeared to be armed with assault weapons and he could tell they wore night-vision devices.

The analyst at the agency said, "I'm seeing four guys right now. They look like they are armed and wearing NVDs."

"Are there any others?"

"I don't know. These are the only ones I've seen so far."

"Okay. Keep tracking those four for as long as you can. Use the other cameras to sweep the rest of the farm and see what you come up with. I need to wake everyone up and get them down here to the safe room. Call T Nguyen and Henry Burnside, too. Tell them I've got company."

Mac didn't wait for an answer. He hung up and stuffed the

phone in his pocket and reached behind the door to the safe room. He pulled an armored vest off the hook on the back of the door and threw it over his head. When Moses saw the vest, the demeanor of the normally friendly Lab completely changed. The hair stood up on his neck and he growled. Mac reached down and petted his head while he said, "Easy, boy. Let's go to work."

He grabbed another, smaller vest, and put it on his dog. Then he grabbed his Model 23, stuffed it into a shoulder holster and threw it over his armored vest. As he headed out the door, he picked up an M-14 and a belt that was stuffed with full magazines of 7.62 mm rounds for the rifle. Then he headed back through the study and up into the upstairs bedrooms to wake up his friends.

The first door he came to upstairs was Rosie's. He nudged open the door and saw Rosie by his window with his sniper rifle in his hands. He used the starlight scope on the rifle to scan Mac's front yard.

As Mac walked toward the window, Rosie said, "Took you long enough to get up here. I was thinking I was going to have to come downstairs and wake you and your girlfriend up!"

Mac laughed. "I bet you did. I should have known you'd be up."

"I heard the geese."

"Me too. Then Langley called. There's four of them out there. Two groups. One group spooked the geese."

"I'm seeing six in three groups. And they have a couple of trucks parked out on the road by the driveway. Looks like there are a couple more in there."

"Six?"

"Yep. And there's a sniper in one of the groups. What do you want to do?"

"Huh. Sounds like they brought a small army. Guess this is gonna get ugly. I need to get everyone down to the safe room. Then I guess we take them on."

"Good plan. Got a headset?"

"Yep."

"Get it. Set it to channel one and call me when you're ready to rumble."

Mac stepped back out the door and went to Amanda Anderson's room. He opened the door quietly and walked over to her bed. He planned to gently wake her up but Moses took care of that for him. He laid his big head on her bed and licked her face. She grimaced and rolled on her back and opened her eyes with a start when she saw Mac standing there.

He held his fingers to his lips and whispered, "Shhh. Someone's here, Amanda. I need you to get dressed as quickly as you can and get down to the study. Put on some shoes, too, in case we have to make a run for it."

She looked at Mac. "Who is it? What do they want?"

"Not sure. Doesn't matter. They're armed. Don't have time to talk. We need to get moving."

He turned and walked toward Amanda's door while she rolled out of bed. Out of the corner of his eye, he noticed that she was buck naked. He chuckled. *That girl never ceases to surprise me.*

The next door he came to was Sean and Ben's room. He opened the door quietly and walked into their room. The two men slept in a huge antique bed Mac had bought during a trip to Charleston, South Carolina. Mac moved over to Sean's side of the bed and lightly touched his shoulder. Sean's eyes immediately opened and he looked up at Mac. "What's going on?"

"Someone's coming, Sean. You and Ben need to get up and get dressed quickly. There are at least six of them and they are armed." While Mac talked to Sean, Ben woke up. Ben was moving before Mac finished his sentence and Sean was getting dressed before Mac moved back out through their bedroom door.

By the time he made it back downstairs, his cell phone buzzed again. He pulled it out of his pocket. "Yes?"

The analyst on the other end said, "I see six of them now. Three groups of two. One of the groups is joining the middle group by the driveway. Looks like they are about two hundred yards out now."

"Okay. We're on it. Rosie's tracking them, and I'm gathering everyone up."

An easily recognizable female voice cut in. "Mac, this is T. I'm on my way into work."

"No time to talk, T. I've got at least six coming at me and a truck full of them at the end of my driveway."

T said, "Understood. We're activating the emergency response team now."

"Good. We might need them."

Mac walked down the hallway to his bedroom. Hope lay in bed, wide awake, waiting for him. As he walked in the door, she saw the bullet-proof vest and the rifle in his hand.

"What's going on?" she asked.

"Bad guys. At least six of them. Coming to get Amanda, I guess." He turned and grabbed a pair of his gym shorts and his dress shirt from last night. "Put these on now and follow me down the hall to the study. We don't have much time."

She quickly jumped out of bed and got dressed. While she pulled on his shorts, Mac put on a pair of boots and laced them up. When they were both dressed, Mac walked to her and held her in his arms for a moment. He kissed her softly. "Don't worry. Rosie and I can hold these guys off until we get some help."

She nodded. "Give me something to shoot with, Mac. I can help too."

He looked down at her and hugged her again softly. "Exactly what I was thinking." They walked down the hallway and met Amanda, Ben, and Sean in the study. Mac motioned for all of them to follow him into the safe room. He saw Hope's expression as she walked into the room. "I promise I will tell you about all this stuff later."

Then he reached into his gun cabinet and grabbed his Model 870 riot shotgun and handed it to Hope. He smiled as she expertly cycled the forearm stock and chambered a round of buckshot. He draped a bandolier with twenty-five rounds of buckshot around her neck and then turned to Amanda.

He gave Amanda an M-16 with another bandolier of clips full of ammunition. Ben and Sean got H&K MP-7s. He gave them ammunition, too, and then told all of them to wait for him in the safe room until he came to get them. Then he grabbed his headset and headed out the door, with Moses by his side.

On his way out, he tossed another headset to Sean and pointed to the bank of monitors on the wall. "Keep an eye on what's going on outside, Sean. Let me and Rosie know what you're seeing. If they get into the house, you can escape through this door or through the closet to my room."

Then he looked at all of them and said, "These guys are here to kill us. Don't hesitate to shoot them, if you get the chance."

They nodded and Sean put on his headset as Mac closed the door to the safe room behind him.

Mac headed out of the study with Moses. He clipped on his headset. "I'm ready, Rosie."

"Good. Cuz they're getting close and my trigger finger's getting mighty itchy."

"Where do Moses and I need to be?"

"East side of the house. Two of them coming up through the cornfield. You take them and I'll take the four in the soybean field."

"Overachiever." Mac couldn't help poking fun at his friend.

He could hear Rosie chuckle in the headset. "Uh huh. Just trying to keep you from screwing this thing up, boss."

Mac smiled. "No doubt. And that's what I love about you, my brother."

He checked his weapons one more time and clipped on his night-vision goggles. Before he stepped outside, he did a quick radio check with Sean. "Sean, are you up on channel one?"

"Yep. I've got you and Rosie. I'm also talking to Langley. The analyst says they called in the quick reaction team but it will take them at least thirty minutes to get airborne and another thirty minutes for them to get here."

"Okay. There's no way they can get here in time to neutralize these guys. Rosie and I are going to take out the guys in the field. Keep an eye on the cameras and let us know if anything changes."

"Roger."

The eyes of the group in the safe room were riveted to the displays on the wall. They could now see the features of the men in the assault group as they got closer to the house. The infrared cameras highlighted their faces. Their exposed skin was hotter than their clothing and the vegetation around them. Conversely, the weapons they carried were cooler than their surroundings. They stood out clearly too.

Mac quietly opened the kitchen door and he and Moses slipped out into the pre-dawn darkness. As Mac moved across the patio, the big dog fell in behind him. They moved silently together along the side of the house to ensure they were not silhouetted by the moonlight. Mac crouched down and worked his way into a garden on the east side of the house. He and Moses stopped there and established a concealed position in the bushes. From their camouflaged vantage point, they had an unobstructed view of the cornfield. Without any command, Moses sat down by Mac's side and quietly waited for the attackers in the cornfield to come into view.

Rosie was ready to engage his targets. He had a clear shot on all four of the guys who approached the front of the house. He studied each of the men through the scope of his rifle as they approached the edge of the soybean field and decided to take the one with the sniper rifle on his shoulder first. The rest of the guys looked as if they only had one weapon, so he figured this was the high-value target. He suspected they all might have bullet-proof vests on so, he settled his aimpoint just below the neck of the sniper. He whispered through his headset. "I'm ready. Need to get this show on the road before they get too close."

Mac had just picked up the team that came from the cornfield. They were well within range. He shouldered his M-14 and picked both men up in his scope. Moses saw the rifle come up and quietly growled. Mac whispered, "Easy, boy."

Then he aimed his rifle at the attacker closest to the tree line, centered his aiming dot at the center of his chest below his throat and whispered into his headset, "I'm ready, too. Give me a three-count, Rosie."

Mac took a deep breath as he waited for Rosie's firing command. Then he used his trigger finger to release the safety on the M-14 and rested it on the trigger. He listened to Rosie as he began to count. "Standby. Three, two, one, fire."

As Rosie counted down, Mac slowly exhaled. When he heard Rosie's command to fire, he squeezed the trigger. He felt the impact of the gun against his shoulder and watched the bullet travel downrange. During his career, he had seen the look of surprise and shock on the faces of many other men and women as his bullets found their aimpoints. The look on this man's face was no different than the others he had seen as he crumpled into the dust of the cornfield. Mac knew right away it was a perfect shot. The man was probably dead when he hit the ground.

The dead man's partner was caught off guard as his comrade crumpled to the ground beside him. While his mind tried to comprehend what had just happened to his colleague, he was further distracted by a barrage of gunfire that erupted from the front of the house as the members of his team were engaged by Rosie. The sudden noise distracted the man long enough for Mac to target him and squeeze off another shot. This man was no less surprised when Mac's bullet ripped through the base of his neck.

As he watched his second target crumple to the ground, Mac listened to the sound of automatic weapons firing at the front of the house. Then he heard bullets break the glass in his windows and thud into the wood siding. He shook his head. *So much for my remodeling job.*

As he completed the countdown with Mac, Rosie squeezed off his shot. Not surprisingly, Rosie's bullet tracked perfectly to his aimpoint and ripped through Charlie's chest, just below his left collarbone. The impact of the bullet knocked Charlie onto his back. Like Mac's first target, Charlie was dead shortly after he hit the ground.

Unlike the team on the east side of the house, the men who were with Charlie did not hesitate when they saw their colleague fall. Bobby Chong was looking at the house when Rosie fired his first round. He instantly recognized the muzzle flash from the window and immediately dropped to his knees, raised his weapon, and fired into the second-floor window of the house. While Bobby provided covering fire, the other members of his team ran toward the house at full speed. They took cover next to a garage, near the front of the house, and poured gunfire into the upstairs window of Rosie's bedroom.

As soon as Bobby's rounds worked their way along the roof to his firing position, Rosie abandoned his perch in his bedroom window and hit the floor. He snapped the scope caps shut on his sniper rifle and slung it across his back. Then he crawled across the floor and grabbed his SR-25 and his riot shotgun from the boxes on the floor. He chambered rounds in both weapons and set the safeties. Then he grabbed two bandoliers of ammo, one for each weapon, and crawled out the door as more bullets from outside smashed through the windows and thudded into the walls above his head.

While Rosie ducked for cover, Mac came up on the headset and reported, "Both targets engaged on this side. Think they are KIA. Heading back inside now."

Sean replied, "Roger. We saw it. Confirmed KIA."

"Roger. How's it looking out front?"

"One KIA out front. Two guys are over by the garage and one of them is hunkered down in the soybean field out front."

Rosie joined the headset conversation. "Roger. I'm heading downstairs. Track those guys as long as you can and keep an eye on the driveway. If the guys in the van by the driveway start heading our way, we're gonna need to know where they are too."

With all the gunfire at the front of the house, Bobby didn't hear the sound of Mac's rifle firing on the eastern side. Through his headset, he directed the two men in Team Three to attack the east side of the house. There was no response. "Team Three. Are you up?"

When he didn't get any response from either member of Team Three, he thought there might be something wrong with his headset. He did a quick communications check with the other team to see whether he was transmitting. "Team One, radio check?"

"Team One Alpha, loud and clear."

"Team One Bravo, loud and clear."

Bobby now feared that Team Three had either been neutralized or was cut off from communication. He decided to flex to Charlie Phat's Plan B at this point and fire the thermite grenades into the house. After assuming that he had already lost half his team, it was obviously too dangerous for him to continue his assault on the house. He decided to call his reserve force into action and directed what was left of his remaining assault force to prepare their grenades.

Bobby made the call over the headsets to get the reserve team moving. "Team Four, this is Team One Lead."

"Team Four Alpha here. Go ahead."

"Team Two Bravo and Team Three are KIA. We're flexing to Plan B. We'll need you guys to support us on the flanks."

"Roger. We're heading out now. We'll be in place in five mikes."

Bobby now had five minutes to set up his grenade launchers while the reserve forces took their positions. He shifted his position in the field and prepared his grenade launcher. While he waited for the team to get in place, he called on the members of Team One to prepare their launchers too.

As soon as Bobby Chong's reserve force left their truck, Sean and the analyst at Langley picked them up on the camera that was focused on their vehicle. Sean called Mac and Rosie. "Looks like the bad guys are calling in reinforcements."

Mac was just coming in the house when he heard the news. "Okay. What's the ETA on the QRT?"

"Not sure. Let me check." Sean picked up a phone on Mac's desk and pressed the speed-dial button marked Langley.

The voice on the other end said, "Go ahead, Mac."

"This isn't Mac. It's Sean. He's still outside the house. He wants to know the status of the QRT?"

"Roger that, Sean. Tell him they're getting the team loaded and the aircraft started. They should be wheels in the well in ten minutes. Once they get airborne, they should be there in thirty minutes."

Sean nodded his head and said, "Roger."

Then he gave Mac and Rosie the news on the headset. "Langley reports the QRT ETA is about forty minutes from now."

Rosie was the first to respond. "So much for the Q in QRT, eh?"

Mac acknowledged the call too. "Yep. That's not gonna help us too much. I'm coming in the house now. It's awful quiet. Where are the bad guys, Sean?"

Sean took a look at his screens. "There are two groups of three men, each fanning out to the east and west sides of the house. The two guys over by the garage are maintaining their position and the guy in the field is maintaining his."

"Okay. I'm inside. Rosie, cover the front. I'm heading to the safe room. Sean, open the door in the study."

"Roger. It's too quiet, Mac. They must be up to something."

"Yep. I'll give it a look. We need to buy some time for the QRT to get here."

Mac and Moses walked through the safe room door as it opened. He could tell by looking at the faces of his friends that they had watched the killings of the attackers through the television monitors on the walls of the study. They all looked frightened but, he was pleased to see that no one panicked.

Sean sat at the desk in front of the bank of television screens. Mac walked up behind him and put his hands on his shoulders. "Okay, Sean. Show me what's going on."

Sean pointed to the top screen. "Here is one of the two groups that got out of the van by the driveway. It looks like they're heading to the east side of the house. They split up after they got out of the van. The other group—there were three of them, too—headed the other way. I'm guessing they went to the west side but we don't have enough cameras to cover everyone."

"You're probably right." Mac studied the two monitors in the middle of the bank. "These are the guys I'm really worried about. Can't figure out why they are holding their position, unless it's to wait for the reinforcements."

He got back on the headset. "Rosie, are you seeing anything?"

"Nope. It's quiet. Too quiet. I'm thinking we go out and engage them instead of waiting. What do you think?"

Before Mac could answer him, he saw a bright flash of light from the area around the guy in the soybean field. When the gains from the camera reset and the picture stabilized, he could see he held something that looked like a big Nerf gun. He instantly recognized the silhouette as an M32 grenade launcher. Then he saw another flash. And another.

"Heads up, Rosie!" he shouted through his headset. "Incoming grenades!"

Before he got the words out of his mouth, he heard the first grenade hit the side of the house and explode. Fortunately for them, the guy in the field was a crappy shot. However, the concussion of the first blast was strong enough to blow out the windows at the front of the house.

The second and third rounds came through the windows in the bedroom and living room on the west side of the house. When Mac heard them break through the windows, he shouted, "Get down, hold your ears and open your mouths."

He hit the floor and assumed a ready position for the others to mimic. He waited for a moment but heard no explosion and felt no concussion. Then he heard a sharp hissing. At first, he thought it was gas but then he heard Rosie call out, "Those bastards brought thermite, Mac! We've got fire out here. Lots of it. We're gonna have to make a move, brother."

Mac realized now that he didn't have any more time to wait for the QRT. He thought about trying to escape through the back by boat but realized they would be sitting ducks in the boathouse while they waited for the lift to drop the boat in the water.

He looked at Hope. "Do you have your keys?"

"No."

"Where are they?"

"They're in the car."

He raised an eyebrow and looked at her quizzically. "In the car?"

"Yes. Everybody down here leaves their keys in their cars. My cell phone and my purse are in there too." Then she looked at him and gave him a sheepish grin. "We don't normally worry too much about robberies, much less terrorist attacks down here…at least until you moved into the neighborhood, Mr. Callaghan."

Mac laughed. "Point well taken. Do you know somewhere we can go that's relatively safe? I need a place for us to hole up until the QRT gets here."

Hope nodded her head. "There's only two ways you can go on the main road from here: St. Michael's or Tilghman Island. I'm assuming St. Michael's is too populated. I guess we could head down to Tilghman Island but there's no way out of there once you cross the drawbridge."

Mac had been to the island before. He remembered the rows of warehouses and fish-packing houses along the Narrows. He looked at Hope. "I think Tilghman is the best plan. More remote. Will minimize collateral damage and casualties. Do you think you could get your friends down there to help us out?"

"Well, if we can get to my cell phone, I can call my mom and ask her to call our friends down there. I know they will help us if they can."

While Mac and Hope planned their next move, Rosie watched

the two attackers by the garage as they continued to launch a barrage of thermite grenades into Mac's house. The west side of the house was now fully engulfed in flames but the light from the fire silhouetted the attackers as they stood up to fire their grenade launchers. Rosie positioned himself behind one of Mac's shattered windows and unslung his sniper rifle from his shoulder. He rested the forearm of the weapon on the windowsill and used it to steady his rifle as he targeted the closest member of the assault team beside the garage. He took a deep breath, held the rifle steady and, as he released his breath, squeezed off his first shot. The bullet streaked through the night sky and impacted the attacker about two inches above his breastbone. The impact of the bullet spun the man around and violently slammed him on the ground. The dead man's partner saw the results of the impact of Rosie's bullet. After he watched his colleague's life terminated before his eyes, he immediately took cover behind the garage.

But, shortly after he disappeared from view, he got curious about what was going on at the front of the house. While he shielded his body behind the garage, he tried to peek around the corner to get a view of the house. Rosie suspected the man would put himself at risk again. He knew it was human nature for the man to want to see what was going on. He had seen many other targets exhibit the same behavior. They all met similar fates.

He watched the man poke his head out from behind the garage and then duck back under cover. To Rosie, it looked like a high stakes game of "Whack-a-Mole." Rosie watched him and, with a devilish grin, quietly said, "You're not even going to make this hard for me, are you, son?"

Just as Rosie predicted, the curious attacker peeked around the corner again. Rosie timed his shot perfectly. He squeezed the trigger as the top of the man's head appeared from behind the garage. As his eyes cleared the corner of the garage, Rosie's 180 grain bullet bored through the center of the attacker's forehead.

"Take that, you son of a bitch," Rosie said. Then he reported to

Mac, "I've got two KIA by the garage. That leaves the guy in the field and the rest of the crew."

"Good. House is burning down. We need to get out of here."

"Wanna try to make a break for it now?"

"You got the keys to your truck?"

"Right here in my pocket."

"Okay. Let's meet in the kitchen. I'll ride with Hope and Moses in the Beemer. We'll take the lead down the driveway. You bring Sean, Ben, and Amanda in your truck. Let Ben drive while you and Sean lay down covering fire. I think we're gonna have to fight our way out of here now."

"Agreed. Let's go for it now. If we can pin down the guy in the field, we should be able to do it before the other guys are close enough to target us."

The fire spread to the study now. Mac knew it was time to get out. He looked at his friends. "Grab your weapons and ammo belts. We have to get out of here, fast." Then he turned to the wall monitors, picked up his phone, and hit the speed-dial to T Nguyen. She picked up on the first ring.

"Go ahead, Mac."

"We've gotta get outta here, T. They set the damn house on fire."

"Yes. I'm watching on the monitors. Watch the guy in the field out front! The QRT is airborne but still at least thirty minutes out."

"Okay, T. We're heading out. I'm going to try to head to Tilghman Island. I will call you when we get clear of these guys."

"Roger."

Mac turned to his friends. "Lock and load your weapons. Hope and Ben will be driving. You guys will need to sprint to the cars, get them started and lower all the windows while the passengers load up and lay down covering fire. Once we get moving, keep firing your weapons at anything that moves until we get out on the main road."

Then he looked at Ben. "When we get to the end of the driveway, turn left and follow Hope and me to Tilghman Island."

He watched as each one of his friends chambered a round in their weapon and smiled as he recognized that the guys out in the front yard were in for one hell of a surprise. Mac took one look back at his house. It was now almost completely engulfed in flames. It really pissed him off that these bozos had destroyed his dream house. With that thought in mind, he pushed open the kitchen door and said, "Let's go!"

The six friends, led by Mac and Rosie, broke from the house and ran to their vehicles. All six of them fired their weapons as they ran. Mac and Rosie focused their fire in the general vicinity of the man they had seen in the soybean field at the front of the house. The rest of the group laid down a barrage of covering fire on either side of the driveway until they reached Hope's car and Rosie's truck.

Chapter Thirty

Bobby Chong was caught off guard when Mac and his friends made their sudden dash to the vehicles parked in front of the house. Although he and his men had achieved their objective of starting the fire and flushing the occupants out of the house, his assault force was totally out of position to target them effectively. With his initial assault force decimated and his reinforcements out of position, there wasn't much he could do to stop them.

As Bobby watched Mac and his friends come out of the house, he swore under his breath. He couldn't believe there were six of them! Out of the six people who ran out of the house, two of them were women. One of them was definitely Amanda Anderson. But, as he knelt to take a shot at them, he was greeted by a hail of gunfire from the two men at the front of the group. All he could do was dive into the dirt as the bullets snapped the air over his head. While he attempted to bury his body into the soft soil in the field, he came up on his headset and said, "Targets are moving. They're heading to the cars out front. Do not let them get off the property!"

He heard the roar of the truck's diesel engine and peeked up above the top of the soybeans. The truck was following a sedan—it looked like a BMW—down the driveway. They both accelerated quickly. He knew if he didn't stop them now that he would miss his opportunity to keep them on the property. He aimed his weapon at the lead car and squeezed off a burst of automatic weapons fire. He heard the rounds make impact with the car but it didn't seem to slow down. Just then, he saw the twinkle of muzzle flashes come out of the back window of the truck and felt the bullets whiz around him again. As he ducked for cover, a bullet struck his rifle and ripped it out of his hands. By the time he found his weapon and tried to reacquire his targets, all he saw were the brake lights of the truck at the end of the driveway.

He screamed into his headset for what was left of his team to get back into their vehicles and told the driver of the Suburban at the head of the driveway to tail the cars as they escaped. He figured they might still have a chance to kill them all, if they could catch them.

Unfortunately for him, the driver of the Suburban misunderstood Bobby's orders. He thought Bobby wanted him to block the driveway. He started the truck and parked it in the center of the driveway to try to block the vehicles coming from the house.

As Mac, Hope, and Moses accelerated down the driveway, they were briefly engaged by Bobby Chong from his position in the soybean field. Bobby's shots ricocheted off the hood of the car. One of them penetrated the front right tire of the M5. Another two came through the passenger side door but somehow miraculously missed Mac and Hope.

Hope saw the tire advisory displayed on the dash but kept her foot to the floor as she rammed through the gears. She wasn't planning on slowing down, until she got the hell out of here anyway. Besides, she knew the M5 had run on flat tires. They weren't exactly designed for bullet penetration but they should get her far enough down the road to get away from these guys.

As they approached the end of the driveway, they saw the silhouette of a large SUV that blocked their path.

Instinctively, Hope hit the brakes and her car skidded. Mac came up on the headset and said, "Driveway's blocked, Rosie."

Rosie didn't hesitate for a second. He came back on the headset and said, "Jink left, Mac."

Then he looked at Sean. "Think you can push him out of the way?"

Sean looked at the truck in the middle of the driveway. "You bet your ass I can!"

Rosie shouted, "Check your seat belts!"

They all looked ahead and saw Hope swerve to the left as the big Dodge truck roared past her. Rosie unloaded his magazine into the windshield on the driver's side of the vehicle as they approached from head-on. As the driver succumbed to Rosie's barrage of gunfire, Sean jerked the wheel to the right and then back to the left to strike the SUV obliquely on the back right side of the vehicle. The trucks slammed together with enormous force and, as the glass shattered and the metal twisted, Rosie's new monster truck easily crushed the rear of the SUV and pushed it out of the way.

Amanda, and the men in Rosie's truck, cheered as they roared past the now disabled SUV with its recently deceased driver.

Rosie came up on the headset and laughed. "Driveway is clear! I believe we just Dodge RAMMED that tub of shit out of the way! Tell Hope it's safe for her little Beemer to come on through now!"

"Roger. I'll tell her. As soon as we get out on the road, we'll take the lead, brother."

"You got it."

"Everyone okay in your truck, Rosie?"

"Yep. A little shook up but okay. How about you?"

Mac looked around the car. Hope seemed okay and Moses sat in the back, looking out the window with his tongue hanging out, just as if he were out on a casual Sunday afternoon drive. "Yep. We're okay here too. Took a couple of rounds in the car. Not sure how long she'll last." As he talked to Rosie on the headset, he raised his left hand and massaged the back of Hope's neck. Then he looked at her and said, "Nice driving, baby doll!"

"Did you just call me baby doll?"

Mac chuckled. "Yes. I guess I did." He looked over at her. "Does that bother you?"

She smiled as she reached her hand over the center console of the car and stroked Mac's knee. She took her eyes off the road for a minute and looked at him. "No. Actually, I think I kinda like it."

Then she stabbed the phone button on her steering wheel with her finger and called her mother. Even though it was five a.m.,

Catherine Crosby answered her phone.

Her mother's groggy voice came up over the car's stereo speakers. "What's going on baby girl?"

Hope looked at Mac and smiled. Then she looked back out at the road ahead and focused on her conversation with her mother. "I need your help Mom."

Her mother's voice immediately took on a serious tone. "What do you need, Hope?"

"Mom, I'm with Amanda Anderson. She's the girl you met at our place yesterday."

"Yes. I remember."

"Mom, I don't have much time and it's really hard to explain but we need a place to hide her. I'm heading to Tilghman Island right now. Can you call Miss Eunice and ask her to help us?"

"Of course I can, darling." She hesitated for a moment. "Honey, your dad is awake too. He wants to know if Mr. Rosie is with you guys."

"Yes, he is, Mom." She looked over at Mac and winked. "There's also a Mr. Callaghan and a couple of other guys too."

"Okay. He says he's going to jump in your boat and head over there. He thinks he can help, darling. He says he wants you to tell Mr. Rosie that he's on his way."

"Okay, Mom. I will tell him."

"Be careful, Hope. I love you."

"I love you, too, Mom."

She punched the phone button on the steering wheel again and hung up on the call with her mother.

Mac looked over at her. "She sounds like a nice lady."

"She is."

Mac hesitated for a moment. "I hope you won't be offended by this question, but why is your dad coming?"

"Because he met Rosie yesterday and he knows what you guys are up to with Amanda. By the way, he used to be a sniper with the Green Berets."

Mac turned and looked out the window at the early morning sky. "Oh great. How many more civilians can I get involved in this fiasco?"

Hope shook her head. "My dad's no civilian, Mac. Don't worry. He won't do anything to slow you down."

While Hope talked to her mother, she caught up to the crew in Rosie's truck. She pressed the M button on the steering wheel and floored the accelerator. The car surged forward and passed the guys in Rosie's monster truck. Then she led the mini-convoy down the road toward Tilghman Island.

None of them saw the other Suburban that trailed them from a distance. This driver was smarter than the other guy. He kept his lights off and stayed way back at a distance to keep from being observed. No one in Hope's car or Rosie's truck saw him as he followed them down the highway. The driver called Bobby on his cell phone. It took a couple of tries but Bobby finally picked up.

"Yes?"

"Bobby, this is Joe. I'm trailing them. They're heading west. Do you want me to keep following them?"

Bobby didn't hesitate when he heard the driver's call. "You're damn right I do! I want to personally supervise their executions. Keep calling me with updates."

Before he hung up the phone, the driver heard Bobby scream, "Get in the van! Now! We need to mount up and run those bastards down. C'mon. Let's move!"

Chapter Thirty-one

Eunice Manchester stood on her dock, checking her crab floats, when her cell phone rang. In the early summer, she and her family made half of their living by selling soft-shell crabs. They separated the crabs that were ready to shed their shells from the other crabs they caught and put them in tanks on their docks where they could circulate water from the creek through them to keep the crabs alive until they shed. They had to check the tanks every two or three hours to pluck the soft-shelled delicacies out of the water as soon as they squirmed out of their hard shells. Crabs were unbelievably cannibalistic. If Eunice, or one of the other members of her family, failed to get the soft-shelled crabs out of the tanks quickly enough, the other crabs would eat their temporarily defenseless cousins.

While it wasn't unusual for Eunice to take a call at five-thirty a.m., it was unusual for her to receive a call from her good friend, Cathy Crosby, at this time of day. When Eunice looked down at her cell phone and saw Cathy's number displayed on her phone, she immediately thought something must be wrong.

As she wiped her hands on her apron, she said a short prayer, and answered her phone. "Good morning, Cathy. What in the world are you doing up so early, hon?"

"Eunice. I hate to bother you but I need to ask for your help."

Eunice could tell by Cathy's voice that something was wrong. "What's wrong, Cathy?"

"It's Hope. She's in trouble and she's heading your way."

Eunice thought Hope might be having trouble on her boat. She looked down the channel to see whether she could see her but all she saw was the sun cresting over the eastern horizon. "What's going on,

Cathy? Is she out in her boat?"

"No, Eunice. She's coming in her car from a friend's house near St. Michaels. They should be getting to your place in about fifteen minutes."

"Okay. What's going on?"

"Well, it's kind of complicated. To make a long story short, she's helping a woman who is in the government's protective custody. Apparently, the people who were looking for her found her at her friend's home over in St. Michaels. They tried to kill her, along with Hope and her friends. They're in a bind, Eunice."

"How can we help her, Cathy? You know if this girl is a friend of Hope's, then she's a friend of ours."

She thought for a minute and said, "I'm sure we can find a place down here to keep her safe. Let me call Tiny to see if we can hide her here in the warehouse."

"That would be great, Eunice. Hope should be there shortly. By the way, T.C. is already on his way. He took Hope's boat and is heading over to your place right now."

Eunice laughed. "Oh Lord, Cathy! I should have known the cavalry would be on its way. No doubt he'll come barreling down the Narrows at sixty knots, too."

Cathy chuckled. "You know him as well as I do, Eunice. There was no holding him back. He's worried about Hope and her friends."

"It's okay, Cathy. I'll just have to ride herd on him and Tiny to keep them from gumming up the works too badly over here!"

It was Cathy's turn to laugh now. "I know exactly what you mean, Eunice. Once those two big boys of ours start flexing their muscles, there's no tellin' what will happen next!" Then her voice took on a serious tone. "Please be careful, Eunice. I'm not sure how all this is going to play out but I'm grateful for your help."

"It's no problem at all, Cathy. I will take good care of Hope and her friends. They'll be just fine here. I'll have her call you when they get here safely."

She said goodbye to her friend and scurried back down the pier to the warehouse. While she headed into the building, she called her husband to fill him in on what was going on.

He answered the phone quickly when Eunice called. She rarely bothered him, unless it was something important.

"Yes, Momma?"

"Where are you, Tiny?"

"I'm out in the yard fixing some crab pots."

"I need you to meet me in the office. Cathy Crosby just called me. She says Hope needs our help. She's on her way over here in her car with some of her friends."

"What's wrong?"

"It's a long story. It must be something big, though, 'cause T.C. is hightailing it over here too, in Hope's boat."

Tiny listened to his wife describe the situation. He knew T.C. Crosby very well and he knew he wasn't a person who was prone to overreacting, about anything. He knew if he was headed over here in a hurry at this time of morning that Hope must be in a heap of trouble.

He nodded. "I'll be right there, honey. Let me get Sonny first and then we'll head on over."

While Tiny Manchester and his son headed over to the warehouse to meet with Eunice, Hope and her friends slowed down to cross the perforated iron grates that supported their vehicles as they crossed over the drawbridge at Tilghman Island. The narrow bridge was the only way to get on the island by car. According to the *Washington Post*, it was one of the busiest drawbridges in America. But at six a.m. on a Sunday, boat traffic through the Narrows was nonexistent. It was a day of rest for the watermen who, at this early hour, would normally be heading out to earn their living. The drawbridge operator wasn't busy, so he took some time to study Hope's car and Rosie's truck as they crossed the bridge. He immediately knew the vehicles weren't from around Tilghman Island. Not too many people on the island drove M5s and, while many of the watermen had jacked-up trucks, none of them could compare with Rosie's rig. He shook his head when he noticed that the front end and front left fender were badly damaged on the truck and wondered how a rig that looked like it was almost brand-new could already be trashed.

He started to wonder where the two vehicles were headed when he saw their brake lights illuminate. They turned left and headed down toward Manchester's Seafood Packing House. Then they disappeared from his view and he went back to scanning the Narrows for boat traffic.

As Hope pulled up to the Manchester's business, she saw Eunice and Tiny walking out on the wide porch at the front of their building. She could tell they had talked with her mom by the concerned look on their faces. She drifted to a stop in front of them, set the parking brake, and turned off her engine. She saw Tiny look at the front end of her car. His eyes quickly scanned the damage and then shifted over to Rosie's truck. She suspected he also noticed that the man in her passenger seat was heavily armed and wore body armor.

Hope and Mac got out of the car and approached the Manchesters.

As she stepped off the porch and gave Hope a hug, Eunice looked at her. "Your mom called me, Hope. Are you and your friends okay?"

"Yes. We're okay, Eunice. A bit shaken up but we're okay."

She looked over at Mac. "Eunice, Tiny, this is Mac Callaghan. He is a friend of mine."

Mac shook Eunice and Tiny's hands. "I'm pleased to meet you both," he said. "I'm so sorry to have to impose on you but grateful that you are willing to help us."

Tiny Manchester looked him over carefully as he shook his hand. "Well, young man, it sounds like you're in a pinch and any friend of Hope's is a friend of ours. What can we do to help you, son?"

Before Mac could answer the big waterman's question, Hope

gestured toward the truck parked behind her car. "Mac and one of his friends are guarding the woman in the truck over there. Her name is Amanda. She is being hunted by a group of men who tried to kill her at Mac's house up the road about an hour ago. The other guys in the truck are also friends of Mac's." She looked over at Mac. "We had a dinner party at Mac's last night and after we went to bed, the house was attacked by a bunch of guys who were trying to kill Amanda."

While Hope explained the situation, Eunice moved toward her and put her arm around her shoulder. "It's okay, baby. Tiny and I understand. Your mom filled me in on what's going on."

Then she looked at Mac. "What do you need, Mr. Callaghan?"

Mac looked around the parking lot of the packing house. He was uncomfortable. He didn't like having his vehicles in the open and he didn't see a really good spot to land the incoming helicopter from the Agency.

He looked back at Tiny and Eunice. "I have a helicopter coming across the bay right now to pick up Ms. Anderson. I need to find a place for them to land and, until they get here, I need to find a place to hide her and protect her. I'd also like to get these vehicles off the street and out of view, if that would be possible?"

Tiny looked back at Mac. "I'm way ahead of you on getting the vehicles out of sight." He pointed to an open garage door at the far end of the packing house. Mac saw a young man by the door.

Tiny continued, "That's my boy Sonny down there. We've moved our trucks out of the garage to make room for your vehicles. Once we get them out of sight, we can work on figuring out where to land a helicopter here on the island."

Mac nodded. "I like how you're thinking, sir."

He turned to Hope. "Let's put your car in first. Back it in please, in case we need to get out of here in a hurry."

Hope nodded her agreement and jogged down the steps from the porch to her car.

While Hope started her car, Mac walked over to explain his plan to Sean and the passengers in Rosie's truck. Under the watchful eyes of the Manchesters, they backed Hope's car and Rosie's truck into the packing house garage. Once the vehicles were safely tucked away, Sonny closed the garage door.

When the vehicles were safely hidden, Eunice Manchester looked at the assembled group. "How long do you think you'll need to stay here?"

Mac shrugged. "I'm not sure. It shouldn't be too long, though. Once we figure out where to set down the helicopter, it shouldn't take very long for us to get out of your hair."

Eunice smiled. "You're not bothering me at all, hon. I'm just trying to figure out whether to make breakfast for you or not?"

Before Mac could say anything, Rosie piped up. "That would be mighty kind of you, ma'am."

Mac looked over at Rosie and laughed. "I should have known the big man would be hungry."

Then he looked at Eunice. "That would be great, Mrs. Manchester. It's been kind of a long morning."

Eunice looked back at Mac. "It would please me if you would call me Eunice, young man." Then she nodded toward the parking lot. "We've got some coffee, eggs, sausage, and biscuits up in the kitchen by the office. I'll go up there and see what I can put together."

Mac smiled. "Yes, ma'am. I mean, Miss Eunice. Thank you."

The sudden sharp ringing of a bell surprised all of them momentarily. Mac and Rosie both instinctually reached for their weapons and looked around to locate the origin of the noise. It took them all off guard. Then, as soon as the ringing started, it stopped. Then it rang again.

Tiny Manchester saw that Mac and his friends were unnerved by the sound of the bell. He held up his hands. "No worries, folks. That's just a repeater of our office telephone ringing. We have a bell out here in the packing house to let us know when it's ringing up there in the office. We have an answering machine up there too. If it's anything important, they can leave a message."

After a couple of more rings, the bell fell silent.

When the phone stopped ringing, Eunice looked at her husband and her son. "Tiny, why don't you and Sonny find some chairs and make these people feel more comfortable?"

Tiny nodded. "We can do that, Momma. Let me know when breakfast is ready and we'll head on up to the office."

Eunice headed out the side door of the packing house. Before she left, Hope said, "Miss Eunice, let me come up there and help you."

Before Eunice could respond to Hope, Ben chimed in, "Me too. I would like to help too."

Eunice turned and smiled at Hope and Ben. "That would be nice." She looked at Hope and winked. "Let's go up there and teach this handsome city slicker how to cook an Eastern shoreman's breakfast."

She paused for a minute. "It will also give me some time to find some clothes for you to wear, dear."

She then refocused her gaze on Ben. "And, having you come up to help us with breakfast will help me get a handle on what's really going on with Hope and her friend Mac."

Ben laughed and Hope blushed. She realized she still wore Mac's shirt, and not much else, from the night before. She had been so busy that she didn't even think twice about what she was wearing.

Ben looked over at Eunice. "I have a feeling that you've already figured all that out, Miss Eunice. But I will be happy to help you fill in the blanks while you teach me how to make some Tilghman Island biscuits."

Mac looked at Ben and in a mock stern voice said, "Hey Ben! Remember, you're supposed to be on my team there, dude!"

Ben smiled. "Don't worry, Mac. I'm betting Miss Eunice has already pretty well figured out what's going on anyway."

Ben and the two women left the packing house and made their way across the parking lot to the office. It wasn't long before

Eunice's huge cast-iron skillet sizzled with bacon grease as the two women taught the Long Island city slicker how to make biscuits properly.

They didn't realize that their trek across the parking lot from the packing house to the office was watched carefully by one of Bobby Chong's drivers.

Chapter Thirty-two

The Tilghman Island drawbridge operator was concerned. He had watched the black Suburban move across the bridge and park down the street near Manchester's Seafood Packing House. Then he saw a white van cross shortly after it and park alongside the Suburban. Something didn't look right to him. He called the Manchester's to see whether they knew anything about the two trucks but didn't get an answer. Right when he was about to leave a message, a sailboat sounded its horn down the Narrows. It was the signal for the drawbridge operator to open the bridge. The sound diverted his attention away from the vehicles parked outside the Manchesters' driveway. He made a mental note to call Tiny after the sailboat passed through the draw and then completely forgot about it when he began the process of activating the warning signals, lowering the vehicle and pedestrian gates, and raising the draw span.

While Eunice, Hope, and Ben prepared breakfast, Mac called the Agency on the cell phone.

Not surprisingly, T Nguyen answered the phone on the first ring.

"What's going on, Mac?"

"We're okay, T. We had to fight our way out of my house but we made it."

"Yes. We were watching you guys through the security camera feeds. Apparently one of your neighbors called the fire department."

"Well, that was mighty nice of them. Did they get there in time?"

"Doesn't sound like it. I'm sorry, Mac. Unfortunately, the firemen found a couple of dead bodies down there too. Some of your and Rosie's handiwork, no doubt. The local sheriff is asking some questions, so we're sending a team down there right now to help tamp things down a bit."

"Okay. Thanks, T. Where's the QRT?"

"Holding over the Chesapeake Bay. Just west of Tilghman Island."

"Can you patch me through to them?"

"Yep. Hold on a second; I will conference them in."

Mac listened as T established comms with the helo. As soon as he heard the voice on the other end of the circuit, he smiled. It was a very familiar voice—Chuck McKnight!

T signaled the connection was made and turned it over to Chuck, who said, "T tells us you and Rosie have got your asses in a crack again."

Mac laughed and toggled the phone to speaker so Rosie could hear the conversation. Then he said, "Well, good morning, Chuck. I wasn't expecting to hear your voice. Sorry to drag your ass out of bed so early, but we could use some help."

He could hear laughter on the other end of the phone. Then Chuck said, "We heard there was a party going on down your way so we figured we would just drop in, literally. We're orbiting to the west of Tilghman Island now. Where are you guys?"

"We're in a warehouse on the south side of the Narrows. Just east of the drawbridge."

"I see it. You guys wearing headsets?"

"Yes. Channel one."

"Standby."

The next thing Mac and Rosie heard on the headsets was Billy O'Neill's West Virginia accent, dripping with sarcasm, as he said, "So you bastards had a party and forgot to invite Chuck and me? Serves you right that someone tried to crash it!"

Rosie and Mac both smiled. Even with all the bullshit, they knew they had the help they needed now. It was good to hear their friends' voices.

Rosie came up on the headset. "It's about time you bozos showed up. Took you long enough, didn't it?"

Mac hung up his phone and spoke into the microphone on his headset. "Okay, you two. We need to get Amanda Anderson out of here as quick as we can. Why don't you guys turn inbound and I will work on finding you a place to land."

Chuck responded, "Roger that, Mac. We're turning in now."

Mac turned to Tiny and asked him for some advice on where to land the helo. After conferring for a minute, Tiny made a quick call to one of his buddies down the street and confirmed a good landing spot.

Mac came back up on the headset and said, "Chuck, Billy, the owner of the warehouse says there's an open field a couple of blocks west of our position. It's actually some guy's front lawn. We called ahead for you so they know you're coming. Once you set her down, c'mon up here and we'll figure out our next move."

"Wilco."

Unbeknownst to Mac and his team, while they formulated their plan, Bobby Chong formulated his. When he and the rest of his team caught up with the driver of the Suburban, they got a full debrief from him. They now knew that their primary targets were in the packing house with their vehicles. They also knew that some of the group had split up from the main force. This was a welcome surprise for Bobby. He realized there was an opportunity to gain leverage on the men who guarded Amanda Anderson. If he could take some hostages, he could use them to try to force Callaghan's hand.

Bobby and the rest of his men checked their weapons, left the van, and headed toward the Manchesters' office.

When the door to the office opened, Hope, Ben, and Eunice didn't give it much thought. They heard footsteps in the office but assumed it was Tiny, or one of the boys, looking for breakfast. Eunice called out, "Tiny, is that you?"

When they didn't get an answer, Ben walked to the entrance of the kitchen to see who had come in. He was looking down, wiping the flour off his hands, as he walked through the door, so he never had a chance to see the person who pistol-whipped him.

Both women screamed when the attackers leapt over Ben's body and wrestled them to the floor. Although they tried to fight them off, the surprise and overwhelming force were too much for them. As the men pinned them to the floor, they wrapped plastic tie straps around their wrists.

As his men finished binding Eunice and Hope, Bobby Chong helped himself to a hot biscuit. He looked out the window overlooking the Narrows. "These biscuits are mighty good. Yes sir. They sure are."

He walked across the kitchen and pressed the barrel of his weapon against Hope's forehead. "If you ever want to taste another one, I recommend you keep your mouth shut and do what I tell you to do. It would be such a waste to blow the brains out of such a beautiful thing."

He traced Hope's jawline with his flash suppressor and then placed it in the center of her chest. Then he looked at Eunice. "That goes for you too, Grandma. I would hate for you to have to watch me blow this sexy thing up in front of you."

He used his weapon to open the loosely buttoned collar of the dress shirt Hope wore. He took a moment to admire her breasts. "Nice. Very nice. After I kill your buddies, I think you and me are gonna to go for a little ride in the country."

He ran the muzzle of his weapon down her stomach and crudely pressed it into her crotch. As Hope shuddered, he said, "Yes indeed. You and me are gonna go for a nice long ride, baby. And after that, I think I might just keep you around for a while."

Hope glared at him but didn't say a word. She knew she had to wait for a better time to make her move. The one thing she knew for sure was that she would die before this asshole would ever have a chance to "take her for a ride" anywhere!

As he taunted Hope, Bobby ordered his men to tie up Ben too. A large pool of blood formed around Ben's head now. Hope noticed he still wasn't moving.

As Bobby's men yanked on the free end of the zip tie to finish tying Ben's hands behind his back, she heard him moan softly.

Well, at least he isn't dead...yet, Hope thought. Then she wondered how in the hell she and Eunice were going to get out of this jam.

After his men finished tying up Ben, Bobby grabbed Hope's arms and roughly lifted her up off the floor. He motioned to one of the other men to do the same with Eunice. Bobby pulled out his pistol, pulled the hammer back and held it against Hope's head. His colleague did the same with Eunice. They marched them out of the kitchen at gunpoint. Then they continued through the door of the office, guided them across the porch, and down the stairs to the parking lot.

When they got to the bottom of the stairs, Bobby ordered Eunice's captor to spread out. He didn't want the two hostages to be too close together, in case Mac Callaghan decided to fight it out.

As they walked toward the warehouse, they heard the obnoxiously loud sound of a speedboat's engines pierce the morning silence. The boat made a tremendous racket as it headed down the Narrows toward the drawbridge. It was still a ways away but Bobby could clearly see the man who drove it. He was an older guy with a beard and a long white ponytail. The boat was still too far away to tell whether the driver could see Bobby and his men. He decided to wait to make his move until the boat passed by. As the boat grew closer, Bobby was amazed at how loud it was. The noise was deafening. He watched as the boat passed behind the packing house. As far as he could tell, it didn't look like the old dude with the ponytail saw them.

Bobby didn't pick up the hint of a smile and the glint in Hope's eye as she recognized the sound of her boat. Nor did any of the men see her glance at Eunice, who gave her a curt nod, when the boat made its way past the Manchesters' dock on the Narrows. The ladies both knew that the cavalry had arrived.

Shortly after the speedboat passed by, it pulled into the marina, near a restaurant at the drawbridge. Bobby heard the engines cut off but just assumed that the old man was coming back from an early morning boat ride on the bay. He didn't think about it anymore as he turned his attention to the garage door of the packing house.

He grabbed Hope by her wrists and turned her to face the garage door. He held her closely in front of him, pressed the muzzle of his pistol against her temple, and broke the silence of the morning with a loud shout. "Callaghan. I have something out here that you need to see!"

Mac and Rosie sat with Amanda, Sonny, and Tiny on the tailgate of Rosie's truck when they heard Bobby's shout. The hair on the back of Mac's neck stood straight up when he heard Bobby's voice. He jumped off the tailgate and ran to the side door of the packing house and looked through the window. Rosie, Moses, Amanda, and Tiny were right behind him.

"Shit!" Mac cursed and then held his arm back to keep the others from being seen.

Tiny saw his wife out in the parking lot. He moved toward the door and reached for the knob. Rosie knew what he was trying to do. He gently grabbed the big man's shoulders. "No, Tiny. Don't. Don't try to be a hero. Let Mac and me handle this one. I promise you, we will get her back for you."

Tiny looked at the big stranger who he had just met less than an hour ago. He nodded. "Okay. I'll give you guys a chance. What do I need to do?"

Before Rosie could answer, Mac cut him off. "Raise the bridge, Tiny. Get someone to raise the damn drawbridge. And then tell the operator to get the hell out of there!"

Tiny looked at Mac and nodded. He pulled his cell phone out of his pocket and dialed the number to the drawbridge operator.

The operator answered, "Tiny. Shit. I meant to call you earlier but I got busy and forgot about it. There are a couple of trucks—"

Before the bridge operator continued, Tiny cut him off. "I know,

Junior. I know. I need you to do me a favor and not ask any questions."

"Sure thing, Tiny. Are you guys okay?"

Tiny's voice cracked but he composed himself and said, "Yes. We're okay, Junior. But I need you to open the drawbridge and leave it open. Now. Then get the hell away from the operator's station and stay away until I call you back."

The operator hesitated for a second. "Tiny, I can't leave my station."

Tiny said, "I knew you were going to say that, Junior. But I need you to do it to save Eunice's life and probably your own."

"Eunice's life? What the hell is going on, Tiny?"

"I don't have time to talk about it right now, Junior. Just do it. Please!"

"Okay, Tiny. Okay. I understand. I'm opening the draw now. I'll wait for your call. Be careful, man!"

"Thanks, Junior. I owe you one."

While Tiny talked to the drawbridge operator, Mac and Rosie developed their plan. Rosie grabbed his sniper rifle and followed Sonny, who knew a quick way to get him up to the roof. While Rosie and Sonny got into position, Mac checked in with Chuck and Billy on his headset.

"Chuck, Billy, we have a problem."

Chuck quickly came back. "What's up?"

"Bad guys showed up. They must have followed us somehow. Surprised us. Took two hostages." Mac looked at Sean. He knew he was thinking the worst had happened to Ben. "One of our team is missing. It's Ben. Not sure where he is. They have the hostages out front, in the parking lot."

"Roger. We're working our way up the street now."

"Okay. I need you to flank these bozos and get ready for a call for covering fire." Mac looked back at Sean and Amanda and continued, "I'm going out to talk with them. You'll need to coordinate fire with Rosie when he gets in position."

"Okay. Billy and I will flank. Will be ready to shoot on Rosie's command then."

"That's the plan."

Mac looked at Sean. "I need you and Tiny to stay here to help Amanda. I'm going out."

Sean looked back at him. "Okay. Do you think they killed Ben?"

"I don't know, Sean. I don't know."

He turned away from his friends and walked toward the door. Before he turned the knob, he pulled his Model 23 out of its holster and stuffed it in his waistband. Once the weapon was secured, he turned the knob and walked out the door with his hands high in the air.

While Rosie got into a firing position on the roof, his cell phone buzzed in his pocket. At first, he just ignored it. Then it buzzed again. He set his rifle down, pulled the cell phone out of his pocket, and looked down at the origin of the call. It was Hope's father! *What the hell was he doing calling him at this hour of the morning?* He punched the answer button. "Yes, sir?"

"Rosie, it's T.C."

"Yes, sir."

"Where are you?"

"I'm about to be in the middle of a firefight right now. Where are you?"

"I'm on the roof of the restaurant down the street from Tiny Manchester's place. I've got my M-1. I'm ready to take down the bastard who's holding a gun to my daughter's head."

Rosie smiled. *T.C. Crosby is one tough son of a bitch.* Then he wondered how the hell he got over here and remembered the sound of the powerboat going by the packing house while he sat on the tailgate of his truck with Mac and the others. The odds were improving. He now had himself and T.C. in firing positions and he knew Chuck and Billy were on their way too.

He said, "Okay, T.C. I've got you. Keep your cell phone near your ear. When I give the three-count, you will be cleared to fire on the dude holding Hope. After you take him out, you are cleared for any target of opportunity. You copy?"

"Roger. Copy."

"We have two more friendlies inbound by helicopter."

"Roger. I saw them land."

As Mac walked through the door to the parking lot, Rosie came up on the headset and said, "Gents. We have a friendly sniper on the roof on the restaurant by the drawbridge. He will target the guy holding the hostage with the long dark hair. I will target the guy holding the older woman. When we pull triggers, I need Billy and Chuck to waste the other three guys. Pull triggers at the end of my three-count. Copy?"

Billy came back with a "Copy."

Chuck said, "Copy. We're ready."

Mac listened to the headset as he prepared to confront Bobby Chong and his men. He wondered who in the hell was the other sniper. Then he, too, realized that it had to be Hope's father. He grinned. *Well now, isn't this a hell of a way to meet your girlfriend's father!*

He walked into the parking lot with his hands held high. "Let the women go!"

Bobby's men aimed their weapons at Mac as he approached Bobby and the hostages.

"Hold your fire," Bobby said as Mac walked toward him. He saw the empty shoulder holster and noticed that he appeared to be unarmed. He suspected that was exactly what Callaghan wanted him to think. He figured he had a gun concealed on him somewhere.

He pushed Hope toward one of his men and said, "Hold the girl."

Then he walked toward Mac and pointed his pistol at him. "That's far enough, Callaghan. Where's the girl?"

Mac gestured toward the packing house. "She's in there."

"Bring her out."

Mac shook his head and pointed at Eunice and Hope. "Not until you let these two go."

Bobby sneered menacingly at him. "What makes you think you're in a position to negotiate with me?"

Mac shrugged and pointed toward the drawbridge that was currently in the process of being raised. "I guess that's up to you. But, if you and your men are planning on getting off this island alive, you may want to consider talking with me."

Bobby looked over his shoulder and saw the bridge going up. Then he turned back and looked at Mac. "You may change your mind when I start executing hostages."

Mac nodded. He needed to stall this guy until Rosie started his countdown. "Well, I guess that's up to you."

He gestured to the other men in Bobby's team and continued, "Look. I don't know who you guys are, but if you have any plans to see the sun come up tomorrow, I recommend you let go of those two women. Now."

"I don't think you're in any position to be making demands, Mr. Callaghan."

"And I don't think you understand just what you're up against, Mr. whoever you are."

"My name is Bobby Chong. It's quite obvious that you don't know what you're up against. Maybe this will help you understand."

Bobby lowered his pistol and fired a shot into Mac's right thigh. Bobby's move caught him by surprise. He had no time to react. He collapsed to the ground as he felt the searing pain of the bullet penetrate his thigh.

He instinctively reached down to stanch the flow of blood as it leaked through his fingers. The blood wasn't too heavy and it wasn't too dark. He knew Bobby must have missed the artery. It wasn't a mortal wound but it still hurt like hell.

Mac fought through the pain and looked up at Bobby. "I guess you've made your point."

Bobby stood over Mac and pointed his pistol at his face.

"Where's the girl?"

Just then, Amanda Anderson opened the door of the packing house and walked into the parking lot. She had seen Bobby shoot Mac and decided she couldn't take it anymore. Tiny and Sean couldn't react fast enough to stop her and because she walked out, they decided to follow her. So did Moses.

She walked across the parking lot and screamed, "I'm right here, you bastard!"

Amanda's abrupt entrance caught Mac and Bobby Chong both off guard. They hesitated for a moment to take in the scene behind them. At the same time, Rosie completed his three-count over the headset and T.C. Crosby's cell phone.

The two snipers pulled triggers almost simultaneously. The convergence of their actions unfolded in front of Eunice and Hope like a slow-motion movie. Hope felt something warm spray against her face. It took her a moment to realize that it was the brains of her captor as he experienced the sudden impact of a bullet in the back of his head from T.C. Crosby's M-1 Garand. Rosie's target suffered a similar fate, except Rosie's bullet pierced the center of Eunice's captor's forehead. As the two men's lifeless bodies fell to the ground, the women stood transfixed in shock by the horror that unfolded around them.

Even though Mac was wounded, he instantly reacted to the sound of gunfire. He rolled over on his side and, using his good leg, swept Bobby Chong off his feet. Bobby dropped his pistol but reacted quickly by rolling away from Mac. He pulled a fighting knife from the sheath in his boot and dove on top of Mac. Mac's body armor absorbed the first impact from the slashing blade. The near-miss gave Mac an opportunity to gain control of Bobby's wrist while the men wrestled for an advantage in the crushed oyster shell parking lot.

At the same time Rosie finished his three-count, Chuck McKnight and Billy O'Neill dispatched the rest of Bobby Chong's team. They were sitting ducks in the open parking lot. Before any of them even had a chance to fire their weapons, the veteran operators felled them in their tracks. Although they had eliminated the threat from Bobby's team, there wasn't much any of them could do to help Mac. They knew any shot they took would be as likely to hit Mac as it would be to hit his assailant, so they ran from their firing positions toward the two men as they wrestled on the ground.

Rosie and T.C. Crosby both also tried to get a shot in on Bobby but they were faced with the same problem that kept Billy and Chuck from capping Bobby Chong.

There was only one person in the parking lot who was close enough to help Mac: Amanda Anderson. She did not hesitate to help her friend. She ran to where Mac and Bobby fought and bent over to pick up Bobby's pistol from the dirt. While she bent over to pick up the pistol, she noticed a black blur in her peripheral vision. It was Moses. He had snuck out the door with her when she entered the parking lot. She watched in awe as Moses lunged at Bobby, grabbed his arm and shook him like a rag doll. While Moses kept Bobby preoccupied, Amanda saw her opportunity. As Bobby struggled to plunge his knife into Moses, Amanda Anderson calmly pulled the trigger on Bobby's pistol and shot him in the face.

The impact of the bullet snapped Bobby's head back. As his body sagged to the ground, Amanda grabbed Moses by his collar and said, "Good boy, Moses! Good boy!"

She pulled the dog back, looked down at the now lifeless body of Bobby Chong and added, "That will teach you to screw with us, you son of a bitch!"

She jammed the pistol into the waistband of her shorts, turned on her heel, and moved toward Mac to help tend to his wound.

Chapter Thirty-three

It was a hot summer night on the Chesapeake Bay. The air was heavy with humidity but a gentle southwesterly breeze blew up the bay. After dinner at her parents' house, Hope took Mac and Moses out for a sunset cruise on her father's boat. The *Bamboletta* was a beautiful yacht with a flag blue hull, white topsides, and brightly varnished woodwork.

They slow-cruised past the mouth of the Eastern Bay as the sun set over the western shore of the Bay. The gunshot wound on Mac's thigh was still healing. He was supposed to be using crutches to get around but was too stubborn to bother with them. Hope knew if she took him for a boat ride that she could count on keeping him seated, at least for a little while. After they got underway, she gave him a cold beer and propped his leg up on some cushions as he sat on the aft settee of the big yacht. Moses had discovered a cool spot under the settee. He was lying under Mac. His big brown eyes watched Hope as she conned the boat from her position at the helm.

She set the autopilot on a westerly heading to take them out into the bay. Then she grabbed her glass of wine and headed back aft to join her two men on the aft settee. She sat down beside Mac and curled herself under his arm. She laid her head on his chest and they watched the sun silently slip down below the horizon. The big diesels on the Hinckley idled quietly under the deck as the yacht passed to the south of the Thomas Point Lighthouse.

"Amazing thing, isn't it?" Mac said.

"What? The way the sun is setting behind the lighthouse?"

He looked at her and smiled as he ran his fingers through her hair and softly kissed her forehead. He chuckled. "No. Not that. I mean, that's amazing too but I wasn't talking about that."

She raised her head from his chest and looked into his eyes. "Well, what then?"

"Two months ago, Amanda Anderson was standing on the bow of a big ass yacht plowing through the Strait of Malacca. In the past sixty days, she's been kidnapped, rescued, chased by the paparazzi and shot at, multiple times. Her participation in our sting operation was instrumental in bringing down one of the biggest drug cartels on the West Coast and yesterday, we inducted her into the CIA Training Academy. That's amazing."

"It sure is. She deserved it. And she wanted it." She playfully punched his shoulder and said, "She saved your ass too!"

"Yes. She did. She helped save all of our asses."

"She loves you, Mac. She knows you would have done the same thing for her."

She paused for a moment and looked up over the bow of the boat to check for any oncoming traffic. "You guys are more alike than you may know. I see a lot of the same traits in her that I see in you. She will do well. We'll have to throw a party for her when she graduates. Do you think your house will be rebuilt by then?"

"I don't know. I've asked the builder to replicate the architecture of the old farmhouse. When we did the renovation, we started with the shell of the old house. Now we have to start from scratch. In some ways, that may make it easier but I suspect it will still be a challenge for us to get it finished in less than a year."

"Us?" Hope looked at him. "Why did you say us?"

Mac ran his hand along the side of Hope's neck and gently guided her face to his. He kissed her softly. "Yes. I said us." Then he jokingly looked down at Moses and winked at Hope. "I mean, me and Moses, of course!"

Hope picked up a pillow from the settee and swatted him over the head. Mac recoiled in mock horror as the pillow bounced off his head and thumped to the floor of the teak cockpit. Moses stood up and barked. Hope couldn't tell whether he was perturbed with her or just voicing his support for the impromptu assault on his master.

As Mac covered his head, he said, "I can't believe you just did that! How could you strike a defenseless, wounded man?"

"I'm going to do a lot more than hit you with a pillow, if you don't behave yourself, mister."

He chuckled. "I know, baby. I know. I was just kidding. Yes. I said us. I'd like you to help me rebuild the farmhouse and when it's done, I'd like you to come live with me and Moses. That is, if you think you can stand living with us?"

She looked at him seriously. "Is that a proposal, Mac Callaghan?"

"Yes. It is a proposal, darling. Will you marry me, Hope? I know it might be next to impossible to deal with me and all my baggage, but I can't imagine living my life without you."

She looked at him for a minute and said nothing. Mac saw the shimmer of tears in her eyes and wondered whether he'd pressed her too far, or gone too fast.

Now it was Hope's turn to take her hands and draw Mac's face gently to hers. She kissed him softly. "You know what my dad says about things that people say are next to impossible?"

"No, baby. What does he say?"

"He says you never really know what's impossible until you work to make it possible. He says you have to be willing to push yourself beyond your limits and face your fears. In his mind, when anyone tells him something's next to impossible, it's an invitation for him to explore an opportunity."

Mac nodded. "Well, I'd say your dad's a pretty smart man. I guess you could say we've both lived our lives pretty much that way."

"Yes, I agree. That's just one of many reasons why I love you, Mac."

She kissed him softly again. "I think anything's possible, if I do it with you, Mac Callaghan. I've never met another man like you, and I want to be your wife. I am honored and thrilled to accept your proposal."

She kissed him again and then drew back from his lips for a moment. "But of course we'll need to keep my place in Georgetown."

Mac smiled. "Of course. We definitely need to do that. And, I guess we'll keep the place in the Hamptons, too. Sean and Ben need a place to settle down and raise their kids."

They settled back down on the settee and enjoyed the ride as darkness settled over them. Hope got up for a minute and went to the helm to turn the boat around and head home. The flashing light from the Thomas Point Lighthouse pierced the night sky as their turn was complete. Just as she set the autopilot on an easterly heading toward home, Mac's phone rang. It was a ringtone they both immediately recognized. It was a call from the Agency.

Mac looked at her expectantly. She smiled. "Well, go ahead and pick it up, you knucklehead."

Mac laughed as he hit the answer button. "Yes, T? What's up?"

"Did I catch you at a bad time?"

"No. Actually, it's a terrific time. Hope Crosby just accepted the challenge of becoming my wife!"

"Congratulations, Mac! Oh, that's wonderful. I had a chance to meet her at the hospital while you were in surgery. She is a really neat woman, Mac, and you're a very lucky man."

Mac nodded. "Yes. I am. So what's going on? You know I'm still on the injured reserve list, right?"

"Yes, I do. But we have a situation brewing in the Far East. I need you and your guys to come in and work with Mo Sumner and her folks to figure out some options for us."

"When do you need to see us?"

"Could you be here tomorrow morning? I still need to catch up with Rosie, Billy, and Chuck but I'd like to meet with you guys tomorrow morning, if I can round you all up."

"Hang on a second, T. I am still not supposed to drive with this damn bandage on my leg. Let me check to see if Hope is heading up that way tomorrow."

Mac covered the phone with his hand and looked at Hope. "'T needs to see me and the boys at Langley tomorrow morning. You wanna go up to Georgetown tonight?"

Hope looked at him and batted her eyes. "Sure thing. Besides, it might be fun to kick your ass at pool, again, before I tuck you in for bed, darling."

Mac looked at her and laughed. He uncovered the phone. "I'll be heading to Hope's place later tonight, T. If you can get someone to come over and pick me up in the morning, I can be there for you."

"I can do that, Mac. I'll have a driver pick you up at her house at 0700."

"I'll be there."

Made in the USA
Middletown, DE
15 July 2022